Printed by CreateSpace

An Amazon.com Company

CreateSpace, Charleston, South Carolina

Cover illustration by Dale Musser

Edited by

Christine Thompson and Susan Uttendorfsky

ISBN-13: 978-0692316139 (DM Books)

ISBN-10:0692316132

Available at Amazon.com and other bookstores.

Available on Kindle and other devices.

PIRATES OF GOO'WADDLE CANALS

In life, it is usually the simple things that give us the most pleasure — the loyalty and companionship of a good friend, enduring love and time with family, and peace and serenity. These were the things I reflected upon as I lay on a grassy bank by the lake with the warm sun on my bare skin, a gentle breeze whispering through the trees, carrying the scents of the forest along with the sounds of birds and small animals singing and chirping about whatever it is that concerns small birds and animals. Next to me, Kala sighed. "I think I could stay here forever; it's so peaceful and relaxing." I didn't lift my head, but I could hear her swirling her feet in the water.

I rolled over on my side and propped myself so I was facing her. She was seated on a log next to me at the lake's edge watching the small circles of waves made by her toes. Kala is one of the most beautiful women I have ever known. Back on my home world of Earth, she would have been an enigma for anyone trying to guess her ethnicity. She had that tanned olive complexion one could associate with a Hispanic, Native American, Italian, Persian or Polynesian, but her light gray-blue irises and almond-shaped eyes belied those probabilities. She had long, straight, black hair just slightly longer than her shoulders, the most kissable lips, and a figure that was…well, perfect. We had been hiking to this secluded location on our estate on Megelleon daily for several weeks, where we enjoyed swimming in the cool water and sunning on its sandy beach. It was one of the few places where we were able to get away from everything and truly be alone together.

"Tib, the past few weeks have been wonderful, but I wake up every day expecting it to end and to discover we are under attack by the Brotherhood again, or that some new crisis has befallen the Federation and Admiral Regeny is calling you to come to the rescue. The two of us actually being able to spend time together is better than any dream I've ever had."

I laughed. "I know what you mean. The last communication we had from the admiral was that the solbidyum shipments were progressing nicely and that nearly a thousand shipments have arrived at their destination uneventfully. Eight hundred and seventy-four planets in the Federation now have their solbidyum reactors up and running. There have been no new uprisings or mutinies from the Brotherhood, and the admiral reports that many of the Brotherhood members in this sector have turned themselves in under the amnesty program offered by the Federation. Regeny said testing and cleaning of Brotherhood members from the military and Federation ship crews is growing exponentially, and several hundred ships have now been certified as being free of Brotherhood members. The availability of the drug, God's Sweat, has been drying up since we shut down the Brotherhood's labs on Alle Bamma, and we have ships to guard the planet and prevent their return."

I sighed and got up off the ground. After seating myself next to her, I took her hand in mine and we sat there, staring out over the water. Kala placed her head on my shoulder, and I thought for a minute that we might spend the rest of the afternoon sitting there. But then the sound of Kala's wrist communicator began beeping from the pile of clothing on the ground. "I guess I had better take this; I told my assistants not to contact me unless it was really important." She walked over to her clothing and retrieved the communicator. "Kalana here."

"Kalana, this is Balinga. A message just arrived from Commander Wabussie requesting a meeting with Vice Admiral Tibby and Admiral Regeny tomorrow, in the admiral's office in the capital, and he wants confirmation right away."

Kala turned and looked at me. "I guess we spoke too soon."

"If it were the admiral requesting the meeting, I would be tempted to not go. But I since I am the one who suggested Wabussie head up the Federation Security Organization, I feel obligated. Tell them I'll be there—I only hope I am not going to regret this. Find out the time of the appointment. It's interesting that Wabussie is calling and not the admiral. It can only mean that the FSO agents must have uncovered something."

Kala and I dressed and began walking back along the trail through the forest to the main house on the estate. As we walked, I said, "There is one thing from Earth I wish we had here—an animal called a horse. It's a large mammal with four legs — a majestic animal. It was one of the first creatures domesticated by humans and was used for transportation and pulling farm equipment. Once our society advanced technologically, horses became more like giant pets, but people still enjoy riding them. I think you really would enjoy riding one."

Kala laughed. "Tib, I would enjoy doing anything with you. But let's get back to Wabussie—what do you think he wants?"

"I'm not sure, but I'm willing to bet it involves the FSO. Three months ago when we left Plosaxen, the FSO agents were trying to infiltrate the Brotherhood, as well as several of our own government offices and organizations, in an effort to get leads on the extent of the Brotherhood's infiltration within the Federation. I would think by now they have some solid leads and surveillance in place."

By the time we reached the main estate house, the sun was low on the horizon. Kala and I had only had a light lunch of fruit that we had taken with us earlier on our hike, and now we were nearly famished. "How about we dine on the patio and watch the sun set?" I suggested.

"I like that idea," she replied just as her wrist com beeped again. "This is Kalana," she said with a sigh.

Balinga said that Cantolla was requesting to meet with me that evening. I suggested to Kala that we invite Cantolla to join us, as it would be a convenient time. Kala looked at me with a crooked grin while telling Balinga that we would be dining on the western patio in about an hour, if it was suitable for Cantolla. When we first met Cantolla, I had not known that she was a lesbian, and I thought she was flirting with me. In fact, she had been flirting with Kala. Later, she apologized to both Kala and I, saying she was not aware of the relationship we shared. Since that time, she had not made any other advances toward Kala, and she had become a good friend to both of us.

Cantolla was a brilliant scientist I hired to advance the capabilities of the learning headbands used by the Federation. She had accomplished the task just in time for the headbands to be used in giving the martial arts skills to the troopers that they used in the recovery of the *DUSTEN* after the Brotherhood had captured it. Cantolla and A'Lappe, working together, had developed the instant two-way communication system now being incorporated into Federation ships. Prior to this invention, the only way to communicate over long distances was to send the messages via a gravity wave (GW) message pod. That could take months; if a reply was required, it would be an equal amount of time before it could be received.

A'Lappe and Cantolla were both working on improving the instant communication system they had discovered. While it did allow two individuals to connect and communicate over the vast distances of space instantly, it was not possible to send or receive visual images or sounds, and only one person could receive the information with the receiver at a time. The message was sent and received at both ends by users wearing special headgear. It transmitted the messages by reading the thoughts of one mind and sending them into the receiving person at the other end. The exact workings of the machine were a mystery, however, to both Cantolla and A'Lappe, even though they each had their own theories.

After a shower and a change of clothing, Kala and I adjourned to the western patio, which was elevated over a beautifully landscaped garden to the north and the lake to the west, providing a beautiful view of the sunset on the water. Once the sun set, the ground lighting in the garden presented a relaxed, soothing view.

Kala and I were a few minutes early, and when Piebar, the house majordomo who always insisted on serving me personally, asked what we would like to drink, I was surprised when Kala stated that both she and I would have afex. Just a few months earlier, she had chastised me for requesting this drink—one that was nearly identical to Earth's beer. I was told that it was a drink of the "common man" and not considered to be proper in public or formal settings. Nevertheless, I made no pretenses in imbibing afex, and apparently my preference for it—regardless of the scene—was setting a new trend within social circles of the Federation. It was becoming increasingly popular for persons to drink afex in public these days, but I was still surprised when Kala ordered the drinks.

Piebar was just returning with two frosted glasses of afex when Cantolla appeared. Although neither Kala nor I had informed Cantolla that our diner that evening was to be casual, Cantolla seemed to have figured it out. She arrived wearing an outfit reminiscent of summer casual attire back on Earth: a pair of white shorts and a short-sleeved pale yellow blouse made of some silk-like material. The outfit accented her tanned skin and her chestnut colored hair. She was about 1.75 meters tall and had a natural, self-assured manner in the way she carried herself, which you know immediately that she was a woman accustomed to being in charge.

"Tibby, Kalana, I'm so glad you could see me on such short notice and that you suggested we meet here. This is such a lovely spot in the evening, and a great place to relax and dine." As she spoke, she moved to the table as Piebar helped her with her chair.

"May I get you something to drink?" he asked Cantolla. I saw her glance at our drinks and a slight grin twisted the corner of her mouth. "Ahh, yes, Piebar, I think I shall also have an afex."

"Very well, ma'am." He went off to get the drink.

"You know, Tibby, I really am glad you have managed to break this tradition of afex being a drink only consumed out of the public's eyes. I went to a conference last week in the city, and at the dinner that night, nearly a quarter of the guests had afex with their meal. You would not have seen that most places in the Federation prior to your arrival."

"So, you wanted to meet with me to tell me I am changing the social rules of the Federation?" I chuckled.

Cantolla laughed. "No, Tibby, I wanted to meet with you to discuss several other things. The first is about A'Lappe and the second is about the waves created by the reverse magnetic force field."

"A'Lappe? Don't tell me we are back to you not wishing to work with him again," I said rather disappointedly. When Cantolla was trying to develop the instant communication system, she had balked at working with him. But in the end, it was the talents and cooperation of both that had brought to fruition a working unit. While I knew Cantolla admired A'Lappe's skills, she was proud and didn't like sharing the glory.

"No, no, it's nothing like that at all. After working with him on the Deep Space Communicator, I realized that we complement each other in research. We approach the problem from different perspectives, and when we combine the two, we see things that we overlooked before. Working with him is a great boon to progress."

"Deep Space Communicator? I've not heard that term before."

"We just started calling it that recently. Most of the time, we simply call it the DSC."

"Well, then, what is the issue with A'Lappe?"

"I'm not sure it is an issue, more of an enigma. Everyone wonders where he comes from—I know you do, too. A'Lappe refuses to discuss his past before his association with Galetils. Well, my curiosity got the best of me. The other day in the lab, A'Lappe received a cut on his finger—just a minor scratch, really, but he did lose a few drops of blood. While he was gone to apply some antiseptic, I used one of the drops of blood to do some DNA sampling. Tibby, there is nothing in the known planets of the Federation that matches his DNA, or even comes close to it; in fact, for all I know, his DNA isn't even from this universe, or possibly this dimension."

"How can you be sure of that? The Federation only covers a small portion of this galaxy—there are billions of other worlds in it. Surely it's possible that things evolved differently on some of those worlds."

"Different, yes, but not like this. Higher life forms evolve from lower ones, and as they do, they carry DNA strands from earlier life forms—even though some of them no longer serve any known function. Also, there is a commonality in all DNA chains in the galaxy: the double helix of the DNA all spirals the same way. But not A'Lappe's. His is completely unique, with a reverse twist. There are other differences, as well, and not one common chromosome or similar chromosome to anything in our galaxy that I can find. This is totally against the odds."

"So what do you think? Do you think he is an artificial life form created in someone's lab?"

"To be honest, Tibby, I hadn't given that a thought, but I highly doubt it. No, I think he's from another dimension entirely. I think that also explains why he has certain knowledge not known in our dimension."

"Have you said anything to him about this?"

"No, I'm almost afraid to. First of all, he would be angry about me doing a DNA test without asking him, and second, I worry what his reaction might be. Obviously he doesn't want anyone to know, and I think the reason is because he has scientific knowledge he's withholding for some reason. If we knew he had traveled between dimensions, he might believe we would try and get that information at any cost. Tibby, you talk about Relative Physics, or, as you call it, Quantum Physics. From what I can tell, that information is the norm where A'Lappe comes from. There is no telling the knowledge and abilities he has at his disposal. What he is giving us is small in comparison to what he really knows."

"Have you mentioned this to Stonbersa or anyone else?"

"No, I'm afraid to say anything to anyone on the ship. You never know if A'Lappe is around or not with the way he uses his personal cloaking device. He might be listening if I did say something. I deliberately waited to talk to you here on the planet, since he doesn't like to leave the ship. Even so, I'm not sure he doesn't have some sort of listening bugs he might be using, so I did a sweep of this area of the estate earlier. As far as I can tell, the place is clean."

"When I first met A'Lappe," I began, "he told me that he was hiding from individuals who want to kill him and that they are after knowledge he has. He implied this knowledge was associated with the 10X fusion reactor technology, but it may be more than just this.

"I don't think A'Lappe intends us any harm. Just the opposite; he seems to have come through helping us more than just once, and if it were not for him, Kala would still be in stasis, dying from ruguain poison."

Kala squirmed in her chair. "I have to agree with Tibby. A'Lappe has shown us nothing but the utmost care and concern. I think we should not say anything about what we know or suspect. Sooner or later, I think he will tell us about his past."

"I think that Kala is right," I said. "I would appreciate if you didn't say anything to anyone about this. Let's just let it play out for now. What is the other thing you wanted to talk to me about?"

"In a way, it overlaps with A'Lappe. In doing some work with the RMFF energies, it appears there are some trans-dimensional fields being generated by the when the field is active. When I mentioned it to A'Lappe, I expected him to be excited and want to research it further. I believe that, if what I was observing is what I think it is, it could open the door for dimensional travel. It would also allow us to speedily traverse great distances in our own universe by means of dimensional doors. But when I mentioned it, his reaction was far from what I expected. His face got dark and he looked extremely nervous. First he tried to tell me it was impossible, and used some of the weakest arguments I have ever heard. When he noticed that was not working, he tried to change the topic. Finally, he said that he would look into it, but he was sure the phenomenon I was observing was something else. I think he knows full well what is happening, but for some reason he doesn't want us to know."

"That is strange. I honestly have never seen A'Lappe act nervous or stressed. If you evoked that reaction from him, it must have hit some mark he is trying to avoid. But again, I think we need to let it play out. In the meantime, I want you to research this dimensional idea you have on your own and don't involve A'Lappe. Let's just see what happens.

"Is there anything else?"

"Yes, something A'Lappe and I have been discussing. You had asked us both to look into whether another collapsed black hole could be found like the one from which the solbidyum originated. We think we have located a remote section of the galaxy that appears to be devoid of stars, similar to the zone where the original solbidyum deposits were found. It's nearly ten months out from here at top GW speeds. Because of its remoteness and the lack of any planets or stars in the area, it's not been investigated. A'Lappe and I would like to send some probes out to sample the dust in the area for solbidyum, but we wanted to present the idea to you first."

"You and A'Lappe really don't need to get my permission for projects like this; you know I trust both of you and you have my full backing. But I am glad you mentioned it, as I think it would be expedient for everyone to keep this as quiet as possible. If anyone in the galaxy gets even the remotest idea that we are looking for another solbidyum site, who knows what or who it will be set into action to attempt a takeover to secure the site. Something like this could trigger yet another war."

"That's what we thought, also. A'Lappe wants to launch the probes from your personal hangar on the *NEW ORLEANS*, where you store the *ALI*. That way no one will know about it, other than the bridge crew, you, A'Lappe and me."

The hangar Cantolla referred to was hidden on the underside of my space yacht, the *NEW ORLEANS*. It was there that my Mirage Fighter, the *ALI*, was stored for use as an escape ship in the event of an emergency. Only a few of my ship's crew and a few members of the admiralty Board knew of its existence.

"I think your approach to this is sound. See to it."

Just as I was completing this comment, I noted one of the house staff, along with Piebar, approaching with a cart of food. Our first dish was comprised of cold chopped fresh vegetables; this dish reminded me of chopped tomatoes, cucumber, and onions from Earth, tossed in a lemon juice dressing. Of course, that was not what it was, as tomatoes, cucumbers, and onions didn't exist in the Federation planets, but the flavors were similar. The dish had a way of enhancing one's appetite without being filling. Finally, our main dishes were set before us; and I was surprised to see large cuts of meat that looked like steaks. I had not had a steak since I had left Earth over a year earlier.

"Is this meat?" I asked in amazement. It was not that meat was uncommon in dishes, but large cuts of meat like a steak were seldom seen, and most dishes tended to be synthetic foods that, while flavorful, lacked the textures of natural foods.

"Indeed it is, sir," Piebar said. "First Citizen Kalana suggested you might enjoy having some Fubalo steaks. They come from right here on your estate, I might add."

I was surprised, as I had forgotten that the southern part of my estate was a vast, grass-covered meadow where large animals grazed. Apparently, this was meat from one of these creatures. In addition to the Fubalo steak, there was an item that resembled a baked potato from the outside, but when I cut into it, I found it to be more like a giant mushroom, with a dark and earthy flavor. Another item served in a smaller side bowl looked like cooked spinach, but had a completely different taste that I cannot relate to any Earthly thing I had ever eaten. Everything was delicious. The meat itself was comparable to the best and most tender steak cut I had ever eaten back on Earth.

"I thought you might enjoy this, Tib," Kala said. "You have often commented on dishes you miss from Earth, and I cannot begin to tell you how many times you have brought up missing steaks. I've been planning to surprise you with this meal for some time, and I felt tonight would be as good an occasion as any."

To say I nearly had tears in my eyes over the joy of eating a steak again would be a slight exaggeration, but I was very close. "Thanks, Kala, this is...well, wonderful—incredible, in fact. This Fubalo tastes just like the steaks I remember from home."

Both Kala and I glanced at Cantolla, who seemed to have gotten carried away eating. It was quite obvious that she was enjoying the meal. All of a sudden, she realized we both were looking at her, and she raised her eyes and sort of froze in our gaze with her mouth full of food and a bit of the juice from her steak running out the side of her mouth.

"Oh, my," she said, after gulping down a large bite of food, "I do apologize. I don't think I have ever eaten anything this delicious in my life. Is this what your food is like on Earth, Tibby?"

"Much of it is," I said. "Our foods tend to be natural and organic in nature, and we have few synthetic foods. Those that we do have are made from organic compounds. We also have a dish made from the flesh of a domestically raised bird on Earth that we call a 'chicken.' It is very popular, and I suspect you would like that as well."

"You will have to tell me more about that, Tib, and I'll see if I can't surprise you with something similar," Kala said.

"Kala, you are a dear. This is about the best surprise you could give me." I kissed her on the cheek.

I had just finished my last sip of afex when Piebar set another cold glass in front of me. Kala nudged me and motioned with her eyes to Cantolla, who was just finishing her last bite of food. I was half expecting her to ask if she could have another plate of food prepared, but she sat back, licking her lips in an other-than-dainty fashion. "Wow, that was incredible. I don't think I've ever eaten anything so good."

"Well, I hope you enjoy your desert, as well. It, too, is something that I hope is similar to a dish Tib has described from his Earth," Kala said.

I raised an eyebrow in a questioning look at Kala just as Piebar set a small bowl in front of me that seemed to be covered with large froth of whipped cream. I took a small bite and was delighted that it tasted like whipped cream. Beneath that was a reddish fruit in syrup that was much like a cross between a peach and a mango—both fruits from Earth.

"Kala, if I were not already madly in love with you, I think I would be now." I leaned over to kiss her again.

"Yes, and if it weren't for you being madly in love with Kala, I certainly would be," Cantolla said with a grin. Both Kala and I broke out laughing when we looked over, as she had a mustache of whipped cream on her lip. I was surprised by Cantolla this particular evening — she had always come across as being in control and prim and proper. Both Kala and I had dined with her many times on the ship and at formal functions, but we had never seen her so careless in her dining manners. It was as though the experience of the new foods had so impressed her so much as to override her normal self-control. It was funny, and both Kala and I had to grin. Cantolla noticed and suddenly realized she had dropped her guard again and that there was whipped cream on her lip.

"Oh! I am so sorry; I completely lost my manners and decorum. I am so sorry."

I laughed. "Cantolla, it's alright. It totally delights me to see you enjoying this food so much."

"No, it's not alright. Perhaps I need to explain. I told you and Kala when I first started working for you that my parents were both scientists. Mother was a biologist and worked with plants and, as she was a botanist, meat was a rarity in our home. We only had it when Dad got cravings for it and complained. Even when we did, it was very small portions, usually mixed into some mass of vegetables. I still eat that way most of the time. Likewise, we seldom had sweet fruits; Mother tended to stay away from those in her research, sticking mostly to green leafy vegetables. There was little in the way of manners when we ate and most of the time we didn't even sit down as a family. Dad always had his head stuck in some research project, and if we didn't take a plate to his study or lab, he would forget to eat. Mother would set food out for my brother and I, and we ate whenever we happened to see the food.

"When I went off to the university, I was the laughing stock of the campus for the way I ate. Unlike at home, where everything was fresh, at the university everything was synthetic. But my eating habits were really bad. If it had not been for my first girlfriend in college making an effort to teach me some refinements, I might be sitting cross-legged on this table, gnawing on a bone and growling like some carnivorous beast. Most of the time, I remember and act civilized, but when I get into a really good meal, I sometimes forget and start eating like I've been starved and it's the first food I've had in weeks. I really do apologize."

"My situation, while different from yours, in some regards is similar," Kala began. "We lived in a relative rural area and most of our food was grown in our garden or greenhouse, so we didn't get a lot of meat, either. But in our house everyone was expected to sit down at the table together and eat; Mother was very strict about our manners and eating habits."

"What are eating customs like on your planet?" Cantolla asked me.

"They differ all over the planet," I said. "Where I came from, eating habits are very similar to those here, but on some parts of the planet, they are almost the opposite. In one country, it is considered extremely rude to belch at the table or after the meal. In other parts, it's considered rude if you do not, and it's an insult to the cook. One country may see it as crude and vulgar to eat with one's hands, and in other countries, that is the preferred method. The same thing applies to smacking one's lips or slurping food — it depends on where you are."

"How strange," Cantolla said, "that you should have all these different customs on one planet. There are differences from one planet to another here in the Federation and in some restaurants that specialize in foods from a particular planet, but as far as having different customs on one planet, it's rare."

"Well," said Kala, "most of the planets in the Federation are ones that have developed technologically and have integrated with other cultures by way of mass interplanetary transportation. These civilizations had also formed one world government before joining the Federation. Tibby's world was just getting to that point; and from what he's told me, it is far from having a unified government for the entire planet."

"Really? How many different governments do you have on your world, Tibby?"

"To be honest, I'm not sure—the number seemed to change every few months, as governments rose and fell with revolutions and conquests. When I left Earth, there were close to two hundred that I am aware of."

"Two hundred! On a single world? Did they all have different languages as well?"

"I read someplace that there were over a thousand languages in use on our planet, but there were only about twelve major languages used globally."

"Incredible — all that on a single planet, and you didn't have learning headbands to teach the languages to others. It must have been difficult trying to communicate to resolve issues."

"We had professional translators that served for government and business negotiations," I said.

"But isn't that dangerous? How do you know you can trust your translator? What if they were trying to sabotage your negotiations or misinterpreted something? You could have even had a war on your hands."

"I'm sure it's happened," I said, "but usually both parties in a negotiation had their own translators, so if one translated something incorrectly, the other would notice and correct the error."

"All I can say, Tibby, is that I am glad I didn't live on your world, even if you had food like this to eat every day." We all laughed and then sat back to watch a truly amazing sunset.

The next morning, I dressed in my honorary Vice Admiral's outfit at Kala's insistence. "You will be expected to wear your uniform anytime you are meeting with the Federation military, simply as a courtesy." I hated wearing the uniform and, even more, the implication that I was connected to the Federation military in any capacity. However, because of my past roles in the implementation of numerous plans and actions against the Brotherhood and the enemies of the Federation, I was connected, in a sense.

Kala and I met Lieutenant Marranalis at the hangar, where a contingency of our security forces waited to escort us to the admiralty. Several attempts had been made on our lives since my arrival in the Federation and, because of our high profile, it was deemed best that we never leave the estate or the *NEW ORLEANS* without a security escort. Marranalis had the *ALI* flown to the estate sometime during the night to personally pilot Kala and me Admiral Regeny's headquarters at the capital, escorted by two of our private security patrol ships. While en route, we were joined by eight other Federation Mirage Fighters from the planet. When we landed at the military spaceport, we were greeted by an aide to the admiral, as well as several dozen troopers who accompanied the admiral—all of whom gave smart salutes, much to my chagrin.

"You do realize, Tibby, that you have more security assigned to you by the Federation than the leaders do. You're still considered to be the most powerful person in the Federation," said Marranalis, as we disembarked. We were then immediately ushered into a ground transport, in which we completed the rest of the trip to Admiralty Headquarters.

The capital building on Megelleon was huge; there is nothing on Earth that compared to this immense structure that covered several square kilometers. Unlike the capital complex of the United States of America in Washington, DC, where different agencies occupied separate buildings, the Federation capital housed all agencies and government offices within one giant building complex, the towers of which soared into the sky, taller than the tallest building on Earth. Even more amazing, the structure reached deeply underground, where most of the high-ranking military offices were protected within secure-access tactical and command centers. Even with this security, the rebel group known as the Brotherhood of Light had managed to successfully breach Admiralty Headquarters in an attempted raid shortly after we delivered the solbidyum to the capital. A large portion of the admiralty complex was destroyed, but the admiral and his staff were spared, as they had temporarily and secretly moved their headquarters to my yacht, the *NEW ORLEANS*, as an added security measure at my invitation.

Since that time, the facilities had been rebuilt and the rebel forces purged from the military ranks in the area of the capital, and new and more efficient security put into place. After driving through a series of wide tunnels within the complex, we eventually arrived at a terminal area surrounded with armed troopers who also saluted as we disembarked. We walked a short distance to board train-like cars that moved us farther and deeper into the complex. We were required to change cars several times, and our direction of travel changed, too, as part of the security tactics that keep secure and secret our precise location.

Finally we arrived at a small station that appeared (on the exterior) to be a maintenance garage. There we disembarked with four of my personal security team and were met by four troopers who served as our final escort to the meeting room where Admiral Regeny and Commander Wabussie awaited. Only Marranalis and one of two of the Federation troopers were permitted to enter the meeting room with us. The rest took up stations outside, while Marranalis and the Federation trooper took up stations just inside the door.

"Greetings, Vice Admiral Tibby and Lieutenant Commander Kalana. It's so good to see you both again," the admiral said. The title of Vice Admiral was only an honorary one, bestowed on me by the Federation military because of my earlier roles in the battle to recover the *DUSTEN* and defeat the rebels.

"Greetings, Admiral Regeny and Commander Wabussie. It's good to see you both again, also," I replied. By Federation military custom, it was not necessary for me to acknowledge Commander Wabussie, as one only needed to acknowledge the senior-most officer present. But I considered Wabussie a close personal friend; and while I was to be extended all respect and honors reserved for a Vice Admiral, I was not expected to follow all their protocols.

"It's good to see the two of you looking so relaxed and healthy," the admiral said. "The last time we were together, Kala was still recovering from the ruguain poison and you had been traipsing about in the jungle, fighting the Brotherhood. At that time you looked you were pretty stressed, physically and mentally. But now the two of you look to be in the best shape ever."

"Well, just understand that we are not doing anymore martial arts demonstrations for you, or anyone," I said with a grin.

"No, no, Tibby, I promise you, that is not going to happen ever again. I learned my lesson last time — and I still have nightmares about it. You have my solemn promise; I will not put you in that position again."

"I'm glad to hear that, but I'm sure you didn't ask me down here to offer another apology."

"Actually, it's Wabussie that requested this meeting, and I'm as much in the dark about it as you are. Commander, would you care to enlighten us?"

"Please, everyone, have a seat," Wabussie directed. We seated ourselves about a small circular table in the middle of the room. "First let me say that I elected to come here because, in the eyes of the Federation, I am still an active member of the staff of the admiral, so my coming and going here is not suspicious. Because of the role that both of you, Tibby and Kala, have played in recent events, your coming and going here is also not considered suspicious. Therefore, I felt this would be the best place for us to convene for an update on investigations and information uncovered by the FSO."

The FSO, or Federal Security Organization, is a top secret body set up to spy both within and outside of the Federation for issues that might have negative or harmful impacts on the Federation. Prior to the formation of the FSO, such matters were under the jurisdiction of the FOI, or Federation Office of Intelligence; however, the FOI became compromised by an infiltration of Brotherhood operatives and could no longer be trusted. One of the tasks of the FSO was to infiltrate the FOI and the Federation senate to identify any Brotherhood members who were still actively engaged with the Brotherhood activities. But the FSO reach extended far beyond just organizations in the Federation; it was in the process of placing agents about the galaxy, hoping to spot trouble and take preemptive measures before the problems became real.

"Using codes and information gratefully provided to us by Captain Felenna of your security detail at Alle Bamma, Tibby, and by applying code-breaking techniques provided to us by A'Lappe, we have been able to monitor much of the Brotherhood communications. Word of their defeat at the *DUSTEN* event, the destruction of their underwater base here on Megelleon, the decimation of their fleet at Plosaxen — when they fell into the trap to steal a staged solbidyum shipment—and the destruction of their drug labs and ships at Alle Bamma, has been spreading rapidly through their ranks. Of special note to them is that the Federation now has cloaking technology, as well as Mirage Fighters, which deliver 50% more speed than anything they possess or have heard of before. They are also aware that the Federation now has achieved Reverse Magnetic Force Field capability that is fully operational. While they do not know that RMFF installations are limited only to starships, they do know we have them and recognize this as real issue for any confrontations they may have with the Federation in the future. At the moment, their communications indicate that they are focusing their God's Sweat drug sales to non-aligned planets where the Federation does not have jurisdiction, but they are still maintaining drug sales in Federation territory where they feel they have a chance of escaping apprehension. They have also set up new production facilities to grow the plant from which God's Sweat can be obtained. Again, these facilities are located on non-aligned planets and some asteroids and moons about the galaxy. Most of these facilities are not producing at the moment, as it takes close to a year for the plants to reach the level of maturity needed for harvesting. But back to the ships...

"The Brotherhood wants to obtain the plans for both the RMFF and the cloaking devices. They managed to steal one of the Mirage Fighters being constructed on Plosaxen two weeks ago. Fortunately, at Tibby's suggestion, the ship's cloaking device was not installed. Cloaking technology is only being installed by Federation teams once the fighter ships have been delivered, and the plans for the cloaking device is not in the hands of civilians, other than for Tibby and his associates. This is a huge relief, but now the Brotherhood does have access to the engine design, which will give them more speed when applied to their own ships. Of course, they also now have access to the design of the Mirage Fighter itself, and can have identical craft built for their own uses. The last communications we intercepted between the Brotherhood groups indicate that they have contacted the Markazians to build several fighters. The Markazians want 60% in advance and the remainder paid in installments by the Brotherhood, with the last payment to occur upon delivery; however, the recent losses suffered by the Brotherhood, in terms of their fleet and their drug operation at Alle Bamma, have left them cash poor at the moment. The best they can do is to have two built. We're not sure if the Dietyte fusion reactors used by the Markazians can be made small enough or robust enough to power the ships at 50% more speed. They definitely won't have cloaking; but still, it will increase their threat."

"I'll talk to A'Lappe about the engine design and see if he can shed any light as to what we can expect speed-wise from any ships the Markazians may build based on the Mirage Fighter they have taken. In the meantime, do you have any idea where they have taken the ship?" I asked.

"No, we don't. Although the ship's engine was installed at the time it was stolen, it didn't have the small fusion reactors used for their operation. It was equipped only with a small fusion battery to deliver enough power for the simple and short flight to a starship, where its final power package and cloaking device would have been installed. We believe the ship was flown to a freighter in the area, where it was taken aboard and delivered someplace out of this star system.

"If the Brotherhood's plans are to have the Markazians build ships for them based on our design, I would think they'd deliver the Mirage Fighter to Markazia or stage it someplace nearby. They will either have to reverse-engineer the ship or get their hands on a set of plans. If their planned approach is to reverse-engineer the craft, it will add to the time requirements, and I don't see them being able to do that in less than a year," I said. "Hopefully, before they get that much accomplished, your FSO team will have located the ship so we can organize a raid to either take it back or destroy it."

"Yes, but if the ship is taken to a non-aligned world and we initiate a raid on the planet to recover or destroy it, our actions would likely be construed as an act of war," the admiral interjected.

"Ah, but you forget, Admiral, the Mirage Fighters are my personal property. I only lend them to the Federation. If I take my security forces to retrieve my stolen property, it may be contested by whatever planet it's on as an illegal incursion, but they cannot consider the Federation as having acted against them. I'm a private citizen, not an official government representative."

I noted Wabussie leaning back in his chair, grinning. "Tibby's right, Admiral. His actions cannot reflect officially on the Federation." I suddenly realized by his actions that he had planned this all along, knowing full well that I would make the suggestion.

Wabussie continued. "The second matter I wish to bring up has to do with information obtained by one the operatives you trained, Tibby. He has overheard that another attempt is being planned to intercept a solbidyum shipment. We don't know where this is to happen, but we believe it will be one of the shipments planned for delivery by GW pod. We don't know how they plan to intercept this shipment, or even how they know where or when the solbidyum is scheduled for delivery. Our agent was only able to overhear part of the conversation, but the words 'intercept,' 'GW pod,' and 'solbidyum' were all clearly discernible. They also mentioned something about some 'mercenary friends' coming into play. We've discovered that, in addition to their drug operations, the Brotherhood also has links to piracy and smuggling operations. The Brotherhood believes that, if they can capture one solbidyum shipment, they can sell it for enough money to facilitate development of larger and stronger fleet. There are also indications that they hope to steal more Federation ships and that more mutinies are planned to take place on outlying Federation ships before word gets to them about the Brotherhood's failures so far. Even though it's been nearly a year since the *DUSTEN* incident, there are still planets on the outer edge of the Federation that have not heard of these events and the results."

"If they had our new DSC, they would," I said.

"DSC?" the admiral asked.

"DSC, Deep Space Communicator. That's what Cantolla and A'Lappe are calling the new instant communication system you have started using in your military operations," I said.

"That system is working incredibly," the admiral said. "I just hope it never gets into the hands of the Brotherhood; because, from what I understand, there is no way to tap into the communication between two people using this system. At the moment, we have this DSC system operable on about a third of our starships, frigates, and corvettes, and at about 40% of our base locations. We're not putting it on the patrol ships or Mirage Fighters, as those are always within immediate communication range of one of the larger ships, so any pertinent DSC messages can be relayed to fighter squads."

"Sooner or later, the DSC technology is going to fall into hands outside the Federation," I said. "I've got to get

A'Lappe and Cantolla working on some way to protect or disable the DSC units when that happens."

"As I was saying earlier," Wabussie continued, "no one outside of those in the FSO, a handful in the admiralty, and your crew, Tibby, know about the FSO or my position and involvement in it. They believe me to be here on duties connected with the admiralty. I've received word from Senator Tonclin today that was rather cryptic. He is visiting the capital on official business and somehow learned that I was here at the capital at the moment. Since you first recruited him to be our eyes and ears in the senate, he has not contacted us; but I received a message this morning saying that he was heading back to Nibaria for discussions with leaders there and that he would be traveling there as your guest on the *NEW ORLEANS*. He stated that he looks forward to seeing me again, as he understands that I will also be traveling with you on the second leg of your journey to Plosaxen."

"Oh? I wasn't aware we were going to Plosaxen," I said with surprise.

"Nor did I. I suspect that the senator has something he wants to communicate to us and he's looking for a way to do it that doesn't appear to be anything other than a social encounter. Since you are known to be a good friend of the senator and I have been known to travel with you and been assigned to work with you in the past, it's not something that is likely to attract a lot of attention."

"Well, I hadn't planned to make a trip anywhere, but a trip to Nibaria isn't that big a deal, as it's only a few hours away. By the way, how did you travel here?"

"I came in one of the patrol ships with a standard crew—all of them FSO agents with rank in the Space Corps, by the way."

"Good. We can carry your ship in the *NEW ORLEANS* as far as Nibaria, at the very least, and if there is no immediate need for the *NEW ORLEANS* to take you all the way back to Plosaxen, you can fly back in your ship. The *NEW ORLEANS* can then either return here or go on to some other destination. But I'm curious — do you have any idea what Tonclin might want to discuss?"

"None at all. Apparently he wants to keep it secret and is trying to avoid any suspicion from his fellow senators or anyone else who may be observing him."

"Did he say when this departure was to take place?" I asked.

"He said he would be flying to the *NEW ORLEANS* the day after tomorrow, so I guess the trip is intended to be sometime that day."

"I see," I said, turning to Kala. "Well, dear, it looks like we will be taking a trip at least as far as Nibaria day after tomorrow.   Will you contact Commodore Stonbersa and let him know that the senator and Commander Wabussie will be our guests? There's no reason to make the senator look like a liar. I am wondering, though, what his reason is for the covert manner of meeting."

"Wabussie," the admiral began, "I realize that my attendance on this trip will appear suspicious, so I'm counting on you to apprise me of what transpires.   I'll arrange to make a trip to Plosaxen in a week to meet with officials on the base there on some pretext, and you and I can meet then for a briefing. In the meantime, if the issue is something more urgent, you can have the communications officer on the *NEW ORLEANS* contact my communications officer here at headquarters. Her name is Major Gamana; her functions are executed under top secret clearances and she reports directly to me. But don't use that method unless it is something I need to learn of immediately," Regeny said. "Unless there is something else, I think we're through here."

As we headed back to the patrol ship that was to return us to the estate, I suddenly got an idea. "Kala, let's go out and get something to eat here in town before we return to the estate. I have yet to go out to a public place to eat anywhere on Megelleon, and I've been here over a year now."

Kala bit her lip; I could tell she was nervous about the idea, but at the same time she was able to sympathize with me. "You really don't want to go out to dine in your vice admiral uniform."

"We can change on the patrol ship. The wardrobe replicators are set up to produce any type of clothing we need and I'm sure our measurements are in the computer, as the ship is one of ours."

Kala sighed and nodded. "Alright, Tib, but don't say I didn't warn you." Kala made a quick call using her wrist com to contact her assistant back at the estate, asking her to make reservations at some place in the city that she knew of. When she finished her call, she turned to me. "You do realize we must take security with us, regardless of where we go. I suggest we both wear our black dignitary-cut outfits, since we will be accompanied by armed troopers. As First Citizens, we will be expected to do nothing less." While I didn't particularly like the idea, I was willing to concede to her conditions just to be a part of the city and the people for a while.

Marranalis was not at all happy about the change in plans. As head of my security team, he was ultimately responsible for our safety. He insisted that all of us, including the security team, carry the personal cloaking devices that A'Lappe had invented. A'Lappe had extended the operational time for each unit so it could cloak one individual for up to an hour, if need be. We were also provided with ultra-thin protective garments — much like insulated underwear, only much thinner. Marranalis explained these acted as armor against stabbings or projectile weapons. He said they wouldn't stop laser shots or microwave weapons, but they offered at least some protection. He gave Kala an instrument about the size of a small Earth cell phone that she could pass over our food before we ate to test for poison. Thus equipped and properly attired, we headed to the club.

I had never seen Kala in dignitary attire before, as she usually wore her formal military uniform for events and in various casual fashions common throughout the Federation when off duty. The outfit Kala wore this time was similar in cut to my dignitary outfit, with the same Nehru style collar and jacket. She wore a pair of slacks also similar to mine, but with a bit more feminine-style flare at the bottom of the legs. She took notice of me looking at her and I said, "You look very nice, but I'm sort of surprised that the dignitary dress for women and men is so much alike."

"There actually are two cuts for women," Kala answered. "This one and a long, black, sleeveless dress with a similar collar. I chose this one, just in case there's a sudden need for action. I can maneuver and react in a combat situation in this outfit; I could not if I wore the dress." As she spoke, she opened the arms locker on the ship and took out a flat gun. She handed it to me and took out another one for herself. "Here, put this in your pocket. It's better to be armed with something than nothing." I slipped the gun in my pocket.

Marranalis arranged for a ground transport to take us to the club. The transport was more like a large luxury motor home used by wealthy people for traveling around back on Earth. It was equipped with vid screens and a bar, a restroom, and other luxury touches, as well as four additional bucket-type seats arranged strategically for the security detail. Our coach was preceded by two armored ground transports staffed with troopers, and two more following us. When we arrived at the club, we pulled up directly in front of the entrance. The sign outside read TEZU LAGONG which, in some obscure planetary language some place in the Federation, means "The Finest."

The security team surveyed the area and people were directed to back away from the carpeted walkway that led to the front door. When everything was deemed safe, Marranalis opened the coach door and we exited. With two of our security team leading and two following, we walked to the front door, where we were greeted by a nervous maître d'.

"Honored First Citizens Tibby and Kalana, it is a great honor that you have chosen to dine with us this evening. I am Celpar, the maître d' of TEZU LAGONG. Please allow me to personally see to your needs this evening."

With that, he turned away and headed into the restaurant, leading us to a table obviously reserved for dignitaries and VIPs. Our security team took up positions at all the doors — something that didn't seem to bother or concern any of the guests or the staff. It was obvious the establishment was accustomed to dealing with dignitaries who arrived with bodyguards. In defense of my security team, while they were visible, they were not overly conspicuous; and while their eyes were continuously scanning the room, they remained stationary in their positions and moved very little.

The maître d' motioned to a waiter, who briskly approached the table and presented us with menus. As he was placing the menus before us, Celpar said, "Would you care for an aperitif — perhaps a nice Lyonian wine? We have a particularly rare and exotic vintage in our collection."

Kala stared at me and I could tell by the look in her eye that she feared I was going to ask for an afex, but I surprised her. "Yes, the Lyonian wine sounds acceptable."

"And for you, First Citizen Kalana? Will you be having the same?"

"Yes, thank you, I will," she said with a slight smile while looking me in the eye.

As the head waiter walked away to get our drinks, the maître d' stepped forward again. "If I may be so bold,

First Citizens, might I suggest you try our Anabur Korsak legs? We have just received a fresh shipment, and our chef has prepared them with a most exquisite recipe. It is a rare occasion that we are able to present them on our menu."

I looked at Kala and she said, "Thank you for the suggestion; however, I think we will look over the menu before we make our decision."

"Very well, and indeed, do look over our menu, and may I say again what an honor it is having you dine here at TEZU LAGONG." With that, he stepped back from the table about three strides, where he stood almost at attention, awaiting our beckoning once we decided to order.

I noted that, while we were able to hear music playing in the dining area, we could not hear any conversation at any of the tables, even though it was obvious that people were talking. Kala noted my concern and chuckled. "Each table in the dining room has voice suppression devices that enshroud the table and out about a meter and a half beyond. Anyone outside of that circle cannot hear a word we are saying. It is one of the things that make this club popular with dignitaries and government officials. The fact that we were able to get in here tonight on short notice indicates just how highly placed you are in the eyes of the Federation. Even senators need two to three days' advance notice to dine here. Only the leaders and a few top officials ever get in on short notice. I doubt that even the admiral could get in here with less than a four-day notice."

I glanced around the dining room and noted that most of the guests were wearing dignitary-style clothing. Most were glancing our way and smiling frequently.

"For the people that are here tonight, this will be an event they will be telling their children and grandchildren about well into the future — the night they dined at TEZU LAGONG in the presence of two First Citizens who were dining there as well."

"We are the only living First Citizens there are in the Federation," I said.

This comment struck Kala deeply. She sighed and looked down at the table. "Yes, and I would gladly give the honor up if it would bring back Lunnie, Reidecor and Maxette."

I understood what she meant. Both Lunnie and Maxette had been elevated to First Citizens posthumously because of their heroic actions in the defeat of the Brotherhood when they captured the *DUSTEN*. Had it not been for their actions, the Federation may well have lost the battle and created a chain reaction throughout the Federation that could have been its downfall. It was because of that same event that both Kala and I were elevated to the honored position of First Citizens; but our sacrifice and efforts were nothing compared to those of Lunnie and Maxette. Reidecor had also perished in that conflict, but his actions were not as outstanding nor as wisely executed as those of Lunnie and Maxette; nevertheless, he had been a dear and valued friend and the kinship Kala and I felt for him was like that of a beloved family member.

"It would have been fantastic had Lunnie and Maxette survived," I said. "Can you imagine how the people in here would react to four First Citizens being present here in the dining room all at one time?"

Kala laughed at my comment. "Probably half the people in here would die from heart attacks. At no time ever in the history of the Federation have there ever been more than two living First Citizens, and there have been long periods where there have been none at all.

"I notice that Celpar keeps looking our way. Perhaps we should decide what we want to order."

"Kala, you know I have no idea what anything on the menu is. Why don't you select something for me you think I might enjoy?"

Kala smiled. She glanced at Celpar and nodded her head; in an instant, he was at the table side. "Have you made your choices?" he asked.

"Yes, we have," Kala said. "First Citizen Tibby is still not familiar with all our foods, so I will be ordering for both of us."

Celpar nodded. "But of course."

"I think we will begin with an order of Latto eggs for the appetizer, followed by the Werpo green salad with Lingsu dressing for both of us. I shall have the steamed Topho claws for my entrée and First Citizen Tibby will try your Anabur Korsak legs."

As she was saying this, the head waiter approached with our glasses of wine, which he placed on the table before each of us. I was not sure what the custom was for sampling wine here in the Federation, but before I had a chance to lift the glass, Kala reached forward with Marranalis' small sensing device. She waved the device over each glass and a small light winked.

"The drinks are safe," she announced. I lifted the glass to my nose and took a small sniff. The bouquet of the wine was quite fantastic, to say the least. There was a very slight floral, fruity scent that seemed to be carried on a darker, almost forest-type aroma. I took a sip and the flavors swirled about in my mouth, seeming to invade all my senses at once. It was truly spectacular.

Kala was looking at me with a look of expectation. "Well?"

"Spectacular. Simply exquisite. I have never had anything like this before! We need to see if we can't get some of this for the estate — and a few bottles for the *NEW ORLEANS* as well."

Kala laughed again. "Tibby, I doubt there is that much in existence in the entire Federation. Most likely, there are only half dozen or so bottles in existence, and I would bet this club owns them all. That one glass probably costs the equivalent of the annual wages of the average Federation citizen."

"In that case, we better drink it up before it evaporates," I said with a wink.

Kala took a sip and looked at me, raising her eyebrows. "I see what you mean, Tib. This is incredible. I have never experienced anything this exquisite before."

Across the room, I noted a man sitting at one of the tables intently watching us with a less-than-friendly look on his face. I noted he was wearing a senator's style jacket. "Don't look just now, but there appears to be a senator here who has been watching us and he doesn't seem to be terribly pleased." I glanced in his direction so Kala would know where to look.

Kala never looked up, but sat in a relaxed pose, sipping her wine. Our appetizer arrived, and I was surprised, as the Latto eggs looked much like mussels in their shell, only the shells were white. Kala took one and pried it open with a small chisel-like tool sitting on the side of the plate. She waved her scanner over it and once again, the safe light glowed. She passed the half shell with a gelatinous material floating in the shell and said to eat it. Obviously, it was eaten much like raw oysters were on Earth. Once again, I was surprised by the flavor. I was expecting something briny tasting, like an oyster. Instead, it had a delicate and fruity flavor, much like a mild cherry. Not too sweet nor to faint, but just enough to whet one's appetite.

Kala's look told me that she knew I was enjoying them. She opened a second and passed her scanner over it, and then hesitated. I noticed her press a button on her wrist com and heard Marranalis' voice say, "Marranalis here."

"Marranalis, could you please come to our table for a moment?" Kala said.

Marranalis arrived and Kala indicated for him to check the appetizer with his scanner. As he did so, he leaned down and Kala said, "There is a man in a senator's attire in the back corner. Find out who he is and inform Wabussie to have all information on him available for us when we depart for Nibaria."

Marranalis acted as though he had never heard Kala, but instead said, "First Citizen, my scan indicates the entire plate is safe."

Kala responded, "Thank you, Marranalis. That will be all."

Marranalis turned and went back to his station at the door. He did nothing for a time, but then I noted that he slipped out the door for a few minutes, only to return and take his station again.

The rest of the meal went along gloriously; the Werpo green salad was the best I had ever eaten. The Anabur Korsak legs turned out to resemble giant frog legs that, if they had come from a frog, it would have been one the size of a large chicken. They were batter fried and tasted much like frog legs did in Louisiana back on Earth. I had practically been raised on frog legs; my grandmother was always happy for me to catch a big sack full of them for her to cook. It made me feel a wave of homesickness for a moment, until I remembered that all my relatives were gone. Even if I were to return to Earth, it would have been over sixty years Earth time since I had left, so anyone I knew before I left would be long dead.

Kala and I each enjoyed another glass of wine. When we finished dining, she asked whether I wanted to go into the club's entertainment lounge where there was music and dancing, but added that it would be a real security problem for our bodyguards. I glanced over toward the sour-faced senator and noted two other men had joined him at his table. All three were staring at us with the same venomous expression. I was beginning to feel a bit tired from the day's activity, so I replied that I felt that we should probably leave. Kala signaled Marranalis and immediately all of our security people were flanking our table, ready to lead and follow us out of the dining room.

As we approached the front door, Celpar was there to bid us farewell. He extended his arms with something in hand and said, "Compliments of the house." It was a bottle of the Lyonian wine. "Thank you once again for honoring us with your presence here this evening, Honored First Citizens. Please do come and dine with us again." He stepped back so we could pass.

"It was our pleasure," I said. "Our compliments to your chef and staff; we were well pleased."

After this very brief pause the lead troopers opened the doors and stepped out with us following.

Obviously, word had gotten out that we were there. A huge throng of people had assembled outside the club and the troopers had to maintain a clear path for the short distance we needed to cover to get to the transport. People were cheering and chanting "Tibby" and "Kala." Kala didn't seem too shocked by the experience, but I was quite taken aback by it. I waved at the people, which only seemed to excite them more.

Kala stopped and briefly smiled and waved. Through her smile she said to me, "Get in the transport quickly before someone shoots you." We boarded the transport, but the doors were left open.

Marranalis stepped into the transport and immediately said, "Activate your cloaking devices and take my hand. Kala, take Tibby's hand and then follow me."

Once cloaked, I had to fumble about to find his hand. Kala had managed to find mine. Quickly we were taken out of the coach and through the still-open front doors of the club. Inside, Marranalis led us through a narrow corridor, down some stairs and into a basement garage.

There we were led to a much smaller ground transport designed to carry six passengers in tightly packed seats.

Marranalis said, "Stay cloaked, even after we all are inside." We did as he said, and I noted one of our security team was at the controls. He spoke again, once we all were in and the doors were sealed. "We have no way of knowing whether our original transport will be attacked or not. The senator at the table you mentioned had one of his men make a call someplace, who then went outside and met with some people in the crowd. Everyone saw you enter the transport, so they all are assuming you are aboard it. We will wait here a few moments before we leave—that will allow time for the transport and escorts to have pulled away and people will assume we have left." Moments later, a message came in to Marranalis that the transport was underway.

Marranalis instructed our driver to drive around to the front of the building and then progress along the same route our entourage would be taking and to maintain some distance behind them. Marranalis changed the window setting to transparent, so the transport would appear empty (except for the driver) to anyone in the thinning crowd who happen to glance into the vehicle as we passed in front of the club and would assume it was merely someone's driver circling the building, waiting for their employers to finish their meal and exit the restaurant.

"Do you really think this is necessary?" I said.

"Tib, no matter where you go, you will always need some protection. The Brotherhood still wants both of us dead and mercenaries still want to capture and hold you for ransom."

Kala had barely finished her statement when Marranalis' com activated. "We are being barricaded in by vehicles on the central avenue ahead of you. It looks like it could be an attack. Advise you take alternate route."

"Understood," Marranalis answered. "You know what to do!" Then he said to us, "From here on, we will need to maintain radio silence until you are safely returned to the capital hangar and inside the *ALI*."

I was beginning to regret my decision to go out for dinner.

Our driver suddenly turned down a side street heading off at 90 degrees from our intended route. We appeared to be heading around the outside of the capital complex. We had driven nearly two thirds the way around, having passed many of the entrances into the complex and I was beginning to wonder just where we were headed, when our driver slowed down and turned into a narrow entrance that may have been used for service deliveries. We entered the tunnel and drove along slowly. Several small delivery vehicles appeared from time to time and occasionally a small ground transport like our own. Eventually we turned into another tunnel and progressed until we came to a sentry post indicating we were entering the governing section of the capital complex. A sentry came out of the guardhouse and approached our driver.

"What business and authorization do you have to enter here?" the guard said, peering in the window at the driver.

The driver didn't say anything but simply handed over an ID badge with a clearance code on it. The guard slid the ID into a slot on his vid pad and then stiffened and looked a bit frightened. "Ah, yes, sir, you're cleared to enter. Please proceed and... uhh, have a good evening." With that, he activated the gate and we drove into the secure area of the capital complex.

"Keep your cloaks active until we reach the *ALI*," Marranalis directed. "We should be safe here, but one never knows."

We drove another twenty minutes before we pulled over into a parking space near one of the internal tram stations. When we got out, we had to continue holding hands and follow our driver into one of the tram cars. Once inside, our driver inserted his identification card into a slot and punched some code into a keypad.

"This tram will head straight to the hangar without stopping," he said. The ride lasted another ten minutes, during which time we could feel the tram make several sharp turns and changes in elevation, as though it were going up and down in an elevator. Eventually we stopped and the door opened to reveal that we were in the hangar area only a short distance from the *ALI*.

Troopers stood around the ship at the ready and a challenge was called out: "Identify yourself and state your business!"

To my side I heard Marranalis say, "It's OK to drop your cloaks now."

As we did, the lead trooper challenging our arrival snapped to attention and saluted. "Welcome back, sirs. We have been expecting you."

We quickly boarded the *ALI* and, moments later, Marranalis had us in the air. Once airborne, he activated the ship's cloaking device and then began making contact with his surface units. He turned the cockpit com on so we could hear the communication.

"…moving down the central avenue when we were barricaded in by a number of very large vehicles. We were ambushed by a small but well-armed force. They opened fire on the escort transports, pinning them down. Two large transport vehicles on each side of our transport opened panels on the sides of their vans and began to fire on our transport. Fortunately, our armor plating was strong enough to prevent them from doing serious damage to it, and we were able to return fire with our side guns. Federation Special Operations troopers were deployed throughout the area on standby and they quickly swept in with Lieutenant Commander Sokaia personally leading the intercept operation.

"The fight lasted only a few minutes. We've suffered only a few minor wounded. No casualties. The attackers didn't fare as well. The most recent report from Lieutenant Commander Sokaia is that five of the attackers died in the counterassault, three were wounded and captured and the rest managed to escape. We're just now pulling into the capital complex."

"Lieutenant Commander Sokaia! Man, they gave her quite the promotion! I may never get a date with her now," Marranalis said.

Marranalis had trained Sokaia and the Special Operations units. Originally she had been reluctant to train under Marranalis, because her military rank was above his. It took some intervention from Kala and Admiral Regeny to set her straight on who answered to whom regarding the matter. Eventually, though, the two had become good friends, and Sokaia had become Marranalis' training assistant.

"So, what made you take the precautions you did?" I asked Marranalis.

"Actually, it was your observation of the senator in the corner. Oh, by the way, his name is Senator Euregata from Samalis. Samalis is one of the outer worlds in the Federation and, as such, will be one of the last to receive solbidyum. Euregata has been somewhat sympathetic to Brotherhood claims about the Federation, though we have no evidence of real connections between him and them. The thing that made me take action was that he spoke to one of the men with him, who then made a call and shortly after went outside to meet with a group of men. Things started moving way too fast, and I felt it wiser to play it safe and assume a worst case scenario. I contacted Admiral Regeny and he immediately deployed the Special Operations unit. One of my men at the base brought the smaller ground transport to the club and staged himself in the garage until we arrived."

"Well, I am very impressed. Thank you, Marranalis and Kala, for the way you handled the situation when I told you of my suspicions. You never even glanced at the senator, and the way you alerted Marranalis would hardly have created any suspicion as to what was going on. I'm really impressed with you both. By the way, who is interrogating the attackers that were captured?"

"I suspect that Wabussie will be handing that assignment. Even though he is FSO, everyone is unaware of that organization and his role in it; and it will be assumed that the admiralty will conduct all interrogations."

"Kala, can you contact Wabussie tomorrow and have him provide us with copies of the interviews and any other evidence they may have gathered? Marranalis, I would like you to assign someone on your team to investigate Senator Euregata; maybe even place him under surveillance. Our agents are trained as well as the FSO's agents — or at least they should be, as we trained both groups together."

"Right, Tibby. I'll get someone working on it tonight."

"I'm glad this played out the way it did, Tib," Kala said. "This is the first time there was action against us that we didn't find ourselves in the middle of. If it hadn't been for this attack, I would have rated today as one of the nicest days we've had in public."

I laughed. "Kala, this is about the only day we have had in public." Kala looked at me and we both burst out laughing.

Early the next morning Marranalis came to see me. "I just received a request from the Federal Office of Investigation. They are investigating the attack of last night. They want to interview me and others of our security team as to what happened and how we knew to switch you and Kalana out from the ground transport. What do you want me to tell them?"

"That's very interesting; the FOI now wants to do something. Do you think they have any clue about the FSO?"

"I seriously doubt they are suspicious. Incidents like this do fall under their jurisdiction. But if I tell them everything that took place, they are going to get suspicious."

"I agree. I think it best that you not mention anything about our reservations concerning Senator Euregata. I would say that you noted some men acting strangely and making calls outside the club that made you feel apprehensive. In light of the attack we had here in the city a year ago, you felt it best to take precautionary measures. Your statement won't be false; it will simply not include all the details. Instruct our own security team accordingly, so there are no conflicting stories. There will be an inquiry about the cloaking devices we used. By now, I am sure, they have heard that the admiralty possesses these devices; if they ask any questions about them or they want to see one, refer them to the admiralty, but under no circumstances allow them access to one of ours."

"Right. I think that's a wise move, especially since we know the Brotherhood has operatives in the FOI; however, I don't think the admiral is going to look kindly on us tossing the matter of the personal cloaking devices into his lap."

"You're right about that," I chuckled, "and it will be nice seeing the admiral on the receiving end this time instead of me."

The rest of the day went by quickly. I spent the remainder of the morning working out alone, as Kala was busy with her staff, making arrangements for our trip to Nibaria and the likely continued journey to Plosaxen on the *NEW ORLEANS*. Marranalis was also busy with the security team, debriefing our troopers and issuing orders pursuant to their impending interviews with the FOI. Shortly after noon, three FOI agents showed up at the estate and the interviews and debriefings began; but if they suspected anything, they never let it show. By late in the afternoon, they seemed to be satisfied with the information they had collected and left the grounds. Marranalis, to his credit, conducted a quick sweep of the entire area that the FOI agents had visited and located three listening devices. Either the FOI didn't totally believe our story, or one or more of the agents in the debriefing team were Brotherhood operatives.

Since we didn't know what time Senator Tonclin or Wabussie planned to arrive on the *NEW ORLEANS* the next day, Kala, Marranalis and I decided to spend the night on the *NEW ORLEANS*. Marranalis flew us up in the *ALI* and made sure we docked in my personal concealed hangar on the underside of the *NEW ORLEANS*. Kala had contacted the ship before we left the estate to let them know we would be arriving and to set up a dinner for my staff aboard the ship. I found it was much easier briefing my crew over dinner than trying to meet with them one at a time.

As we entered our favorite dining room, I was surprised to see Cantolla sitting at the table, as I believed her to still be back at the estate. She noted the surprise on my face and, before I could say a word, she said, "You didn't think I was going to stay behind and miss out on all the adventure, now did you? Once you get on this ship, Tibby, it seems all kinds of things pop up that require my skills."

I could see the smirk on her face; but regardless of what other thoughts I may have had, I had to agree she was right.

Commodore Stonbersa and Captain Kerabac were also present, as was A'Lappe — another surprise, as he actually arrived visibly, not cloaked in his usual fashion.

As we dined, I briefed everyone on the details of the last two days and advised them that we were expecting the arrival of both Senator Tonclin and Commander Wabussie sometime the next day. Marranalis said he felt that, even though Wabussie and the senator were considered friends and allies, a security sweep should be made of them and anything they might be wearing or bringing with them. I had to agree — I just hoped that the senator would not be slighted by the request.

While we were dining, a message came in to Kerabac's wrist com. "Captain, we are receiving a message from Admiral Regeny's office requesting that, in the event we might be heading to the planet Plosaxen, that we please consider taking Lieutenant Commander Sokaia with us. She is to return to the base there for training of the new Special Ops recruits."

Kerabac gave me a questioning look. "I see no reason why we can't comply with that request," I said.

"Tell them that we will be able to accommodate the Lieutenant Commander, but that she will need to be here early in the morning, as we are unsure of our actual departure time."

Near the end of our dinner we talked about my earlier discussions with the admiral and Commander Wabussie when a thought came to mind.

"A'Lappe, I need for you to look into some way of securing the DSC apparatus in case a ship is captured by the Brotherhood. We don't want the technology falling into their hands. We need something that will disable and destroy a DSC unit so it can't be reverse-engineered or fixed — maybe a passcode that, if not punched in every so many hours, the unit will auto-destruct."

"An interesting assignment, indeed," A'Lappe said. "I'll get with Cantolla about this. I think we might be able to come up with something."

Kala and I had barely gotten out of bed the next morning when word arrived that a shuttle bearing both Lieutenant Commander Sokaia and Commander Wabussie had docked in the main hangar and that they were undergoing a quick security sweep. I left instructions that, once both had been assigned accommodations, I would enjoy having them join Kala and me for breakfast. I also sent a request for Stonbersa and Marranalis to join us. I wanted to take advantage of the early opportunity to meet with them to discuss the event that unfolded at TEZU LAGONG and to discover what news Wabussie had on Senator Euregata.

Instead of meeting in the larger dining room as we had the night before, I decided to arrange breakfast in our suite. I notified Piesew, my majordomo and head of the *NEW ORLEANS* housing staff, of my decision. Piesew and Piebar were relatives and both served as majordomos. Piesew was among the first people I met when I arrived in the Federation and was provided with accommodations on the *DUSTEN*, where he at the time served as the director of services. After I acquired my estate on Megelleon, I intended to persuade Piesew to come to work for me as majordomo there; but when he saw the *NEW ORLEANS*, he made it clear that he would much prefer to be my majordomo onboard the ship instead. In his stead he recommended Piebar for the position on Megelleon, and subsequently I hired him. The two were so much alike in mannerisms and service that, at times, I found myself getting their names confused.

Some of the walls in my accommodations area were movable for special events; and the dining area was one of those spaces. Piesew directed his staff to expand the size of the room slightly for more comfortable seating during the breakfast meal.

Wabussie and Sokaia were the first to arrive, both still in their military uniforms. Sokaia immediately snapped to attention as she entered and saluted me as she greeted, "Vice Admiral."

Wabussie turned his head and gazed at her with a look of amusement. "Hello, Tibby, it's good to see you again."

Since Sokaia was still standing at attention, I returned the salute, even though I was not in uniform. "At ease, Lieutenant Commander Sokaia. There is no need to salute me when I am not in uniform. Congratulations on your promotion."

Sokaia relaxed. I should not have been surprised by her formal entrance. When we first met, she displayed a certain disdain for me and had not hesitated to let her feelings show. This had resulted in a response from Kala, who outranked her, that in short amounted to giving her a dressing down and followed by orders to report to Admiral Regeny, where she was given a further dressing down. Since that time, she had gone out of her way to be a model trooper in all regards and had proven herself to be a huge asset to the Federation. She was currently in charge of Special Operations for the entire Federation, including their training.

"Tibby, it is great to see you and Kalana both looking so well. Last time I saw the two of you, you were looking a might stressed. You both seem to have recovered nicely from your wounds and battles."

"Yes, we are both feeling quite fit at the moment," I answered.

"Is it true that both of you have refused reconstructive treatments to remove the scars from your wounds?" Wabussie asked curiously.

I held both arms out so he could see the scars, and even lifted my shirt so he could see where Lexmal had stabbed me. "The scars are a part of me, and they serve as a reminder, as well. I have no desire to hide them."

"Tibby has more scars than I do," Kala said. "I have only the one where I was stabbed in the back. Tib is now sporting six scars from his battles against the Brotherhood."

Sokaia looked at us with an expression of awe on her face. The medical capabilities of the Federation had advanced to the point that scar removal was routine; so having a scar was a matter of choice, and one that few ever made. That Kala and I should elect to keep our scars was almost barbaric to most Federation citizens. Just then, there was a signal at the door; Piesew opened it to admit the commodore and Marranalis.

"Ah, Commodore Stonbersa and Lieutenant Marranalis, welcome. It would appear that everyone is here. Shall we sit down? We can discuss things while we eat."

"Always efficiently doing two things at once," Wabussie said. "That's Tibby for you. No wonder he gets so much accomplished."

Piesew indicated to each with his characteristic gestures where to sit — Kala at my right and Wabussie at my left. The commodore was seated at the end of the table facing me. Marranalis was seated to his right and Sokaia to his left, next to Wabussie.

Piesew silently instructed the staff to place the dishes in front of us, after which all of the staff left the room.

"I've read the reports of the event at TEZU LAGONG," Wabussie began, "but I'm curious about one thing. What alerted you to Senator Euregata?"

"It was the way he was looking at us," I said. "There was something in his gaze that suggested that he was not exactly a fan of mine."

"Your instincts served you well, though I doubt you would have been injured in their attack. They had little time to organize anything and it was a poor attempt at best. Nevertheless, it's always better to be safe than sorry. It's interesting that you were able to spot him so quickly; the FSO has only recently become aware of him, and we had just started an investigation into his past. Samalis was one of the last planets to join the Federation; Euregata had been a resistance fighter there and was against joining the Federation. After the planet voted to become members of the Federation, Euregata ran for the office of senator as a candidate of the opposition party and was elected. His actions in the senate have been controversial, at best. His idea of distributing the solbidyum was that deliveries should start at the outer worlds first and progress inward toward the middle. Needless to say, that's not a very popular idea with the senate at large.

"One of the aides he had with him at TEZU LAGONG is a man who has already been identified as having direct Brotherhood involvement. He seems to be the senator's right-hand man; and from what we have been able to piece together, he was the one who set up the attack against you. When Marranalis started to put things into motion at the club, he alerted me and I subsequently contacted the admiral and Lieutenant Commander Sokaia. I immediately contacted one of my FSO operatives who is normally assigned to TEZU LAGONG. The club is a good place to gain information, as many of the most powerful people in the Federation are known to dine and entertain there. Our agent was outside the club and overheard the senator's agents making some reference to "getting rid of Tibby now, before the interception."

"Interception? You mean before they intercepted the transport? That doesn't make sense," I said.

"No, I don't think they meant the transport. As you learned in our private briefing before your dinner event, I've been receiving getting reports from our field operatives that the Brotherhood is planning to intercept a GW pod carrying a solbidyum reactor and a solbidyum grain. I think this is the interception they were talking about. So far, you have been the source of all their downfalls, Tibby, and they see you as a potential threat to any future offensives they may be planning to implement. They want you out of the way before they act."

"Ah, right. Do we know yet which solbidyum shipment they plan to heist?" I asked.

"No. I was hoping maybe the prisoners that the Special Operations unit managed to capture could enlighten us; however, I received some bad news today. Just as we prepared to dock here at the *NEW ORLEANS*, a message came in that all the prisoners we captured are dead — killed in their cells, it would appear, by some lethal gas. The guards posted with them were also killed. Somehow, the Brotherhood was able to get into the prison area where they were being held and poison them with gas. My people are still checking into leads on all the people who were involved in the attack on the transport. We're trying to track their movements, as well as any who they associate with."

"I thought all the troopers in this sector had been tested and that we didn't have any infiltrators in the military in this sector anymore," Marranalis interjected.

"That's correct, and we have no reason to think otherwise. We believe the assassin was a part of the civilian prison kitchen staff and that he released the poison gas when he made the meal rounds. We're trying to track him down now, but he seems to have vanished."

"You mean to tell me you tested everyone in the military on the base and in the capital, but you haven't tested the civilian support staff?" I said, dumbfounded.

"I'm sorry to report that is the case. It was believed that, if we had the troopers all tested and certified as clean, the support staff was inconsequential."

I shook my head and Kala put her hand on my shoulder. "Well, I guess now everyone knows differently," I said. "Were you able to get anything at all from the attackers you captured?"

"The only thing we were able to get from the one captive who was cooperative is that they received orders from one of the higher ranking individuals in the Brotherhood leadership, but he had no idea who it was. Orders were received suddenly while you and Kalana were dining at the club, which seems to indicate that whoever gave the orders was most likely also in the club. While Senator Euregata certainly is a suspect, the hard evidence isn't there to formally charge him, much less convict him of the crime."

At that moment a message came in on Stonbersa's wrist com. "Commodore, we have received a message from Senator Tonclin's shuttle that they are underway and will be docking in about twenty minutes."

"Thank you. I'll be at the hangar to greet him. Please see to having proper protocol arranged for his arrival."

"Do you have any new information as to what Senator Tonclin may want to discuss with us?" I asked Wabussie.

"Not a clue, but it's obvious to me that it somehow involves the senate and the FSO, and that whatever it is, he wants to make sure he presents it to us in the most secure and confidential environment possible."

I nodded and replied, "We will know shortly."

When the shuttle bearing the senator arrived, he was greeted by Commodore Stonbersa, Kalana and me.

As the senator disembarked I broke protocol and stepped forward, "Senator Tonclin, so nice to have you aboard again." According to custom it should have been either Captain Kerabac or Commodore Stonbersa that greeted the senator first but I had met the senator several times in the past year and considered him a close friend, I never failed to be fascinated by his appearance. Like all Nibarians, he was short and squat in stature and his skin resembled thick, gnarled tree bark. It was obviously an adaptation to protect them from the caustic nature of the nitrogen compounds in their dense atmosphere. Another Nibarian characteristic that always seemed out of place was the high-pitched voice, which was a sound more like one would expect from a human after inhaling helium.

"Honored First Citizens Tibby and Kalana, I cannot express what a delight it is to see you both again. I'm so pleased and relieved that you were able to precisely interpret my clue and allow me the opportunity to travel with you to Nibaria on the *NEW ORLEANS*. I'm certain you have surmised that I have an urgent need to discuss developments with you and Commander Wabussie. I felt the *NEW ORLEANS* to be the safest and best place to do so."

"Yes, we did indeed surmise as much. Regardless of the situation, though, you are always a welcome guest aboard the *NEW ORLEANS*, Senator. Do you wish to be taken to your accommodations now, or would you prefer we meet now?"

"Actually, since the flight to Nibaria is relatively short, I would prefer to meet immediately. I regret that I will probably not even have time to visit the delightful quarters that I'm sure you and Piesew have already arranged so perfectly for my comfort. For appearance's sake, the less time I spent on the *NEW ORLEANS*, the less suspicion it will likely arouse with anyone who may be observing my movements. Since you have ordered Mirage Fighters to be built at our shipyard, my meeting with you will not be out of line, if kept relatively brief. Hopefully, the presence of Commander Wabussie will likewise not appear out of the norm, as you are reportedly taking him to Plosaxen on some official duty for the Federation. Since the existence of the FSO still is a secret known to only a few, I do not think anyone will realize the true intent of this journey."

Commodore Stonbersa led us into a small but very rich-looking conference room that I had not seen before. Though I owned the ship, it was so large that even after spending a good deal of time aboard, I had only seen a small portion of the spaces. This conference room was furnished with a round table that could accommodate about eight chairs. The room itself was also round and paneled with a rich wood of a slightly orange-brown color and dark, almost black grain. An equally rich green carpet covered the entire floor and the middle of the ceiling was recessed fitted with indirect lighting. A vid screen hung near the wall, and I suspected that a control somewhere could easily make it vanish into the ceiling or behind a wood panel if one chose.

Piesew appeared as we arrived and inquired of each person whether they cared for some refreshment. Once those had been delivered, he departed, leaving us to discuss whatever it was that Tonclin felt was worthy of this assembly.

"Tibby, I first want to say that when you first presented the idea of the FSO to me, I was rather taken aback. The idea of a government spying not only on others but on its own entities as well seemed preposterous. And when you asked me to act as a such a spy within the senate — well, it was only out of the utmost respect for you that I was even willing to hear you out. Ultimately, I was able to understand your logic and I felt that, if someone was going to do it, I would, at least, be able to conduct myself objectively in such a litigious capacity. I had no idea at that time how insightful you were in taking the actions you did. But now, after what I am about to tell you, you will see how wise your motives truly were and are.

"So far as I have been able to ascertain, no one in the senate knows about or even suspects the existence of the FSO, and they still believe that all spying and intelligence is coming through the FOI. The arrogance of the Brotherhood, created by their long success of infiltrating the government over the past century, has caused them to be overly relaxed and careless — and this includes their members in the senate.

"One evening last week I dined alone in the senate dining room while reviewing a speech I had prepared for a meeting with the Federation agriculture committee later in the day. I wasn't paying much attention to who was near me — most of the dining room was empty at that hour —

however, the table behind me was occupied by a few senators from a sector out near the rim.   I was fairly engrossed in the composition of my speech, when I heard someone say, 'The Brotherhood is ready to act now.' I must say, it required a great deal self-restraint to resist the urge to turn and see who spoke. I kept pretending to work on my speech, but now I was listening more closely. For the sake of clarity I will repeat their conversation here as the way it generally unfolded in the senate dining room.

"I heard another man say, 'If we stick with our plan, our allegiance to the Brotherhood will pay off.   They are promising to provide our planets with solbidyum first, instead of having to wait and get it last.   This would profit our planets greatly.   Even if the Brotherhood can't bring down the Federation like we believe we can, we would still have quietly gained the advantage of obtaining the solbidyum; and we can still break away and start our own alliance and union of planets thereafter.   We are so far out on the fringe of the territory that the Federation most likely would not bother trying to retain us — and we could renounce our membership with the solbidyum in hand and still be better off.'

"'I agree,' a third speaker said.   'The concentration of Brotherhood support in our sector provides us with lots of military strength.   I understand that, unlike here in the inner planets region, the majority of the crews on the Federation ships in our sector are Brotherhood supporters and that they are only waiting for the signal to initiate takeover actions on their respective ships.   They are not aware of this new purging of the fleet that the admiralty is undertaking to get rid of insurgents and Brotherhood members within the military and space crews.   We must hope that our people strike soon and take over those ships before testing and purging begins in their sectors.'

"The first speaker then said, 'I was told by one of the Brotherhood leaders that they have information on where several of the solbidyum shipments are going and when they will arrive. It seems that the admiralty pulled a trick on everyone and has been using GW pods to ship solbidyum to many of the worlds. Up until this time, it was a secret, but one of the GW pod suppliers became suspicious of the Federations request for a couple of slight size modifications to the internal storage compartment on the pods purchased in recent months and equally suspicious of the sudden increase in their demand. This supplier eavesdropped on two of the Federation inspectors who were conducting a quality check of the pods before delivery. The discussion between these inspectors was about the purpose of these modified units, which are being used to ship both the solbidyum and the reactor. Apparently, the reactors themselves are quite small, for all the power they produce. This supplier happens to be a Brotherhood member and reported what he heard to his group leader.'

'Someone has to be coordinating the distribution, and it was apparent to our Brothers that it must be the admiralty. It took some work, but our Brothers were able to get an agent into the capital who then gained access to the admiralty computer. They downloaded all the information on shipments of solbidyum and found out where shipments were planned for delivery by GW pod. They have since gotten word out by way of their own message pods to Brotherhood members in the regions where several GW pod deliveries are to be made; and by the end of next week, they should have at least one shipment in their hands.'

"I then heard the second man say, 'I think we all need to make preparations to leave quickly, should these plans come to fruition. In the meantime, we should go about business as usual and make efforts to influence the reduction of military spending and the downsizing of the Federation military forces. Things were heading in the right direction until this Tibby guy started interfering. His provision of Mirage Fighters to the Federation at no cost is not boding well for our plans.'

"It was then that one of the men announced that he had a session to attend and they all got up and left."

"Did you see and recognize any of them?" Wabussie asked.

"Yes, as they were leaving, they walked past my table. They didn't even glance at me, so I don't think they realized I had been listening to their conversation.   I recognized only one of the three — it was Senator Euregata, representative of Samalis."

"Well, I think that solidifies one thing for us.   We believe it was also Senator Euregata who set up the attack on us two days ago," I said.

"This is bad news," Wabussie began.   "If the Brotherhood got wind of us using GW pods to make shipments, all the shipments about to arrive at their locations are now are in danger of interception.   I need to get the admiral to check which shipments are scheduled to arrive at their destinations within the next two weeks, and hopefully we have DSC-equipped loyal Federation ships in the area that we can contact to protect those shipments."

"DSC?   What is that?" Tonclin asked.

"The DSC is a Deep Space Communication system now being installed on Federation starships and frigates," Wabussie said.   "It allows instant communications between two ships regardless of where they are in space."

"I had not heard of this. Is it something new?"

"Yes, very new, and only a small portion of the fleet have it — ships that have been purged of Brotherhood members.   It's a secret at the moment, so we would appreciate you not speaking of it."

"I won't say a word, but how long have you had this DSC apparatus?"

"A few months now," Wabussie said.   "Two of Tibby's scientists invented it.   It has limitations, as you cannot send visual data or large packets of data. It will only carry the direct information between two select persons at a time, sort of like communication over a com link. The good news is that it can't be tapped; the bad news is you can't send the data to more than one person at a time. Once our meeting here is over, I will need to communicate all the information you have given me directly to the admiral. He will need to stop all the GW pod shipments of solbidyum at once, and we will need to find and stop the leak of information from his computer as well."

"Maybe we can use this leak to our advantage, just like when we lured the Brotherhood in at Plosaxen," I said. "A false communication could lead the Brotherhood into a trap once again."

Wabussie raised an eyebrow. "How would you go about doing that?"

"They haven't heard about our DSC system, or, if it has leaked out, the news hasn't gotten far. I would identify a cluster of Federation planets and create a fake a message, using the standard communication system, that is transmitted to a nearby Federation starship that a large shipment — let's say, a thousand grains of solbidyum — is being sent by GW pod to a specific location near this cluster and that the starships should mobilize to pick up the solbidyum and proceed with directly escorted deliveries in that sector of the galaxy. State in the message that there will not be any reactors in the shipment, only the solbidyum, but sets of plans will be included for building the reactors. I'd even go so far as to launch a GW pod in that direction, only I would not have any real solbidyum aboard. Maybe just some capsules with a grain of sand in them. At the moment, no one has been able to intercept a GW pod while it is en route, and it's only when it reaches its destination and slows down or stops that it can be intercepted. They won't know until the pod gets to its destination that it's a fake. I suspect that the Brotherhood will send out every ship they can muster in the region when they hear of the opportunity to intercept a shipment of that size."

"You're right, Tibby, that's a prize they could not afford to pass up. But we will need to get as many Mirage Fighters to whatever Federation starship is used in this ploy to make sure the Brotherhood ships that do show up don't escape. The RMFF will make the starship safe from attacks, but it can't chase after scattering Brotherhood ships. Your Mirage Fighters can fly faster than the GW pods, so they can get there first and join up with the starship. It's a great plan; I will have to convey it to the admiral. I suspect he will be thrilled at the opportunity it presents. If I can use your DSC officer on the bridge to convey the message, I can provide them with the DSC contact in the admiral's office."

"That can be arranged whenever you like," replied Stonbersa.

"If you can do it, I would suggest a location about six weeks out from Megelleon," I said. "That way the Mirage Fighters will arrive two weeks before the decoy GW pod. It would give the team ample time to see that everything on the starship is prepared, assure that there are no Brotherhood members infiltrating the crew, and verify that the ship's RMFF and cloaking device are working optimally. I think the team that flies out should consist of at least 30% Special Ops. Each Mirage Fighter crew should include at least one Special Ops trooper. If you can swing it, I would suggest that a minimum of 50 Mirage Fighters be present with whatever starship is selected. I would also suggest that you not deploy all the fighters all from one base or order their departure all at the same time, as the Brotherhood probably has spies reporting on Federation space traffic. Deploy them from multiple bases — one or two at a time, but not more — and document various false destinations in their orders. Make the false orders for fairly innocuous purposes, like training exercises and the like.

Until we discover where the leak is in the admiral's office, we need to proceed with care."

"That makes sense, Tibby. I'll convey all of this to the admiral. In the meantime, I'll be directing my FSO agents to dig for information that will allow us to ascertain where the Brotherhood is planning to intercept a shipment."

"I have another piece of information that may interest you," Senator Tonclin interjected. "A short time ago I spoke with Orcpipin at the shipyard in Nibaria. He recently journeyed to Gaimse to propose a joint venture to produce some freighters for a client who wants a half dozen. Since the Nibarian shipyard has been busy turning out Mirage Fighters for Tibby, Orcpipin's construction crews don't have the time to execute other major contracts on their own. Before his departure, the Gaimseians seemed to be very interested in joining with our shipyard as partners on this freighter project; however, when he arrived, they were anything but interested. There was a lot of activity going on when he arrived at the facility; they seemed to be gearing up for large project of some sort. While he was traveling through the yard, he noted a large, partly opened hangar door; and when he glanced in, he was shocked to see a Mirage Fighter inside. However, it appeared to him that the crews were disassembling it instead of constructing it. He didn't give it much thought right away, because he knew you were having a lot of these fighters built at different yards, but later he realized that, to his knowledge, Gaimse was not one of them. He also recognized one of the men coming out of the hangar and was rather surprised to see that it was the chief arms merchant for the Markazians. I felt this might be information you would want to know."

While Senator Tonclin related this story, Wabussie sat forward in his chair excitedly.

"Senator, this is crucial information you have brought to us. You probably have not heard, but one of the Mirage Fighters under construction on Plosaxen was taken just prior to the scheduled delivery date. Thankfully, the craft was equipped with only a minimal fusion power source at that time and the secret cloaking device was not yet installed. However, the new engine that allows the ships to fly at one and a half times faster than the standard GW speed is installed. We believed that the fighter had been loaded on a freighter and shipped to a location where the Brotherhood could begin reverse engineering, but we had no idea until now just where. The information from Orcpipin's visit is exactly what we have been looking for."

"Commodore Stonbersa, how long will it take for us to get to Gaimse?" I asked.

Stonbersa entered a query into his vid pad. Suddenly, the vid screen displayed a star chart in which some automated triangulations appeared, followed by a yellow line that traced a path of travel from our current location to another star system. Numbers appeared on the screen as Stonbersa said, "We could make it in fifteen days, traveling at top speed."

"The shipyard is clearly disassembling the ship to reverse-engineer it; and the process will be slow — easily a year's time — if they're going to determine how everything works. So if we can get there in another fifteen days, we should be able to either retrieve the ship or destroy it before they glean too much technology. As far as the propulsion unit is concerned," I continued, "A'Lappe, can you please make yourself visible to the rest of the attendees? We need to discuss this issue with you." A'Lappe appeared almost instantly in one of the two empty chairs across the table from me.

"Oh goodness! How long has he been there?" Senator Tonclin said in amazement.

"Probably the entire time," Stonbersa said with a sigh. "A'Lappe prefers to remain invisible until he is called out."

"I see. Most peculiar behavior," Tonclin said with amusement.

"Strange and disturbing is what I would call it," Wabussie added with a frown, "but A'Lappe has proved himself to be invaluable to Tibby and the Federation, so his antics are generally tolerated."

"I am at your service, Honored First Citizen," A'Lappe said with a smile and nod of his head.

"A'Lappe, will the Markazian's fuel cells be able to power one of the Mirage Fighters at full speed?" I asked.

"Theoretically, perhaps; but practically, no. The Markazian power units are too large and bulky to fit into the fighter. They would need to make the fighter about 40% larger to fit one of their reactors into it. The best they can hope for is to use their standard fusion batteries or fuel cells. Those power units will provide only standard flight speeds, at best, and their range will be limited. They must have assumed that they were stealing a fully operational ship and didn't realize that the small fusion reactor and the cloaking device were not installed. What they have now is little more than a fancy shell with minimal flight capability, other than the engine, which they can dissect and duplicate or even reverse-engineer and then sell their version of the design. However, if they ever figure out how to make a smaller and more powerful power source, they would be able to make the fighters fully functional, albeit without the cloaking capabilities. There is also the danger they may manage to figure out a way to bypass the security system that makes the fighters inoperable to anyone but the assigned crews and use this knowledge to steal another fighter. Moreover, there is the possibility they could utilize the fighter technology to produce larger engines for their larger ships, which would be just as dangerous."

"How were they able to get past the security system to steal the ship in the first place?" Senator Tonclin asked.

"The security systems aren't activated until a ship has been officially delivered and its Federation power source and cloaking device installed and its crew assigned," Wabussie answered. "Until then, anyone can access the ship — it needs to be that way so the workers can finish the necessary construction and installations. I have a hunch the Brotherhood didn't know this, or they were hoping they would be able to figure those things out on their own. Tibby, I think that it might be best for me to accompany you to Gaimse. I will be sending a message to one of my agents in the sector to get there and begin sniffing out information before we arrive. I took the liberty of having a DSC system installed at my headquarters on Plosaxen and at several other FSO offices throughout the Federation, so we should be able to have an agent active at Gaimse in a few days. I'll be better able to direct this situation from your ship than I would on Plosaxen. Of course, this is with your approval; I don't want to become another Admiral Regeny for you to deal with."

I chuckled. "Regeny you are not, and I will be more than pleased to take you to Gaimse with us. Now, unless someone else has something new they want to bring up, I suggest we adjourn this meeting and have some lunch."

After we dined, I asked A'Lappe to meet me in my study. It was a beautiful wood-paneled room, designed as the exact duplicate of my study back at my estate, right down to the large fish tank that stretched behind the desk from wall to wall and floor to ceiling.

I was seated at my desk with my back to the room, looking into the fish tank, when I suddenly noted the faint scent of cedar in the air and I knew that A'Lappe had entered. So far, I seemed to be the only one on the ship who noticed this aroma was noticeable when A'Lappe was in the vicinity, and it alerted me to his presence when he entered a room under the cloak of invisibility.

"A'Lappe, I have a number of projects I need you to work on. As mentioned before, we need to devise a way to destroy the DSCs if necessary. I also need you and Cantolla to see if you can find a way to intercept a DSC message. I know it will be difficult, but knowing either the receiving or sending location of DSCs involved should allow us to tap into the communication somehow."

I turned to look at A'Lappe, who suddenly showed some interest in what I said, as though it was something he had not thought of before.

"What you are asking may be possible. I had not thought about the idea of focusing on a single unit to intercept communication before. Being able to install a self-destruct device that can be activated from another DSC will be very difficult, if it is possible at all."

"Cantolla tells me that the two of you will be sending out GW pods with sensing equipment to investigate some possible collapsed black hole sites for solbidyum deposits. I am totally for it and glad that you will be doing so. If we can find more deposits, we may be able to mine enough of it to power Federation starships. At that point we may even be able to increase the speed of larger ships like the Federation starships and the *NEW ORLEANS*. You might even be able to develop some sort of dimensional doorways that will let ships move in and out of other dimensions and travel vast distances in just a few minutes instead of months or years." I noted A'Lappe stiffen when I mentioned dimensional doors, but he said nothing.

"I know you've continued to develop smaller and more powerful fusion reactors for the ships, but have you ever tried to modify the RMFFs so they require less power to function?" I asked.

"How would I do that?" A'Lappe asked with some surprise in his voice.

"Well, I would say that's what I pay you to figure out, but since I don't pay you…" I chuckled. "…I guess I can't use that line. But how about investigating a way to improve the efficiency of one or more RMFF mechanisms to reduce the operating power?"

"And you think I can do this?" A'Lappe said as he cocked his head to one side, while his huge eyes stared into mine.

"Yes, I think you can. I even suspect you know how already, but for reasons of your own, have decided not to share that technology yet."

"Hmm. You're pretty smart, you know?" he said as he turned away and began pacing. "I've been trying to figure out how you know when I am present when others do not, but you never give any clue and you seem to read and understand me better than anyone else on the ship. Yes, I have been withholding some information and technology that I am willing to share only when it's sorely needed. That you know, or at least suspected, but the fact that you have never pushed is something I deeply respect. I told you when I first presented myself to you that there were things about me that I would not reveal, and that there are people who want to capture me and some that want to kill me. Some of the reasons behind my situation are the same reasons that motivate me to withhold much of what I know. But understand this, Tibby; nothing I withhold is of a nature that presents a risk or threat in any way."

"A'Lappe, it's apparent that you have gained knowledge that is not known in the Federation, so it's safe to assume that you are not from anywhere in this sector of space. Likewise, if any culture in this galaxy were to have the knowledge and technology you seem to possess, we would have already heard about them, as they would have gotten to us by now if they posed any kind of threat. That leaves only three other possibilities — one, you are a time traveler from the future; two, you come from a completely different galaxy; or three, you are from another dimension or universe entirely—one far more technically advanced than this one. Personally, I'm betting on three to be the correct scenario."

For the first time, I saw a look of shock and fear on A'Lappe's face, and he seemed at a loss to say anything. He froze momentarily and then resumed pacing about the room, his hands clasped behind his back. I could see he was struggling with something internally. Finally, he turned and faced me; in a calm and quiet voice he said, "I'm glad you are a friend, Tibby. I hope you will keep what you suspect a secret, at least for a little longer, anyway. I know that other members of the crew are suspicious about me and have their own ideas, and sooner or later I'm going to have to face the fact that they will find out. But for right now please keep this between us.

"You are correct; I'm not from this universe. The universe I came from is similar in some ways to this one, but very different in others. The way I appear here, for one thing, is not as it was in my home universe. Believe it or not, I look more like you and the other humans here on the ship when in my own universe, but here... Well, you can see my appearance is quite different. By the same token, the laws of physics here —again, while similar — are not exactly the same as where I come from. The speed of light is different in my universe; we have both attractive and repulsive gravitational forces; and the behavior of elements and the manner in which certain chemicals react are also different.

"I was a renowned scientist and was working on a way to develop a dimensional doorway to this universe, when an accident occurred and I was transported here. As it happened, I appeared in a laboratory of another scientist here in the Federation working on the same problem. I was in a state of shock on my arrival, as was he. I didn't know exactly what had happened to me — my body was all wrong, as I could see it, and I thought that somehow my mind had been transferred into a new body. The other scientist and I could not communicate at first, because of language differences, but with the use of one of the learning headbands, I was able to learn his language quickly. My colleague here in this universe — whom I will simply call Mr. Z — was working on a project funded by none other than Galetils, who was hoping to open a dimensional doorway into a universe where solbidyum might be more common. Not so foolish an idea as you might think, as solbidyum is quite common in my universe. Only there, its properties are much different than here. Galetils hoped to be able to harvest the solbidyum there and bring it back or perhaps set up trade between the two universes. The problem was that Mr. Z and I were not able to activate the apparatus in this dimension to successfully open the doorway. It was as if the passage opened only in one direction when I passed through, so we were ultimately forced to conclude that an operator was required on both sides to establish the opening.

"We don't know how, but word of our research slipped out, and that's when the Brotherhood contacted Galetils. I lied to you before when I told you it was the 10X reactor that they wanted; they wanted the secrets for the dimensional doorway. An attempt was made to kidnap Mr. Z and me from the lab on Astamagota. We escaped, but the attackers took what they thought was the field generator apparatus that makes the dimensional doorway. Luckily for us, what they actually took was a new replicator prototype recently designed by other scientists in the lab. A week later, they attacked again, but by that time I was living in hiding on Galetils' space yacht that was under construction at the Nibarian shipyard, this ship that we now call your *NEW ORLEANS*. Mr. Z was killed in the attack, and the attackers were killed by Galetils' security forces. The laboratory equipment was supposed to be transferred here to the *NEW ORLEANS* from Asmagota to be included in the ship's final installations; however, before the lab could be disassembled and mobilized, the solar flare hit...and you already know the rest of the story.

"At the moment, the Brotherhood thinks I'm dead; but if they find out I am alive, they will make every effort to capture me and use whatever means they can to force me to open a door to another universe for their nefarious purposes."

"So you already know how to make the dimensional doorway?" I asked.

"Yes and no. I know how to do it in my universe, but not in this one. As I said, the laws of physics are not exactly the same in both universes; and certain substitutions need to be made for some of the necessary materials, but I don't know which ones yet. It's even possible that the elements required to make it work don't even exist in this universe. But do you think that would keep the Brotherhood from trying to get me?"

"No, I don't imagine it would."

"My knowledge is still useful, but I still have to work very hard to find the right components to duplicate what has been achieved in my universe. Before I came to this universe, our scientists were able to tap into communication signals emitted from here – your universe – so we knew this universe was here, even though we could not translate the signals into anything intelligible on our end. Unfortunately, since my arrival here, I have not been able to likewise develop a device that can detect communication signals from my home universe."

"Is it possible for someone in your universe to reopen the door using your device back there?"

"I'm afraid not. As I said, it was an accident that I fell through the doorway. I suspect the machine was damaged badly when I passed through and is likely beyond repair, assuming anyone in that universe rediscovers the technology."

"What happened? What kind of accident?" I asked.

"Pretty much the same thing that happened on Astamagota — a solar flare. In a way, the universes are parallel, but in my universe the solar flare event happened several weeks earlier. I actually think it was the EMP surge from the solar flare that made the machine work in the first place. I was caught in the doorway created by the event and ended up here. I didn't realize exactly what happened until the solar flare at Astamagota wiped out everything."

"So your reason for withholding technical information and discovery is to protect yourself from the Brotherhood and those who might want to acquire your knowledge by any means?"

"It's not as simple as that, Tibby. It's like I was saying earlier—the laws of physics don't all work the same here. I can't be sure what will work and what won't, but slowly, I have been able to figure some of it out. With some work I can determine what things need to be changed or substituted to achieve similar results. For instance, while the technology of the RMFF exists in my universe, the mechanism by which it works is not exactly the same as here. So to make it work here my work had to focus more on determining the subtle modifications in components and frequency required to achieve the results that were already realized in my universe. I understand the principals, but I need to find the corresponding components that apply to its operation according to the physics of your universe. As I determine what is required to improve RMFF efficiency, I will pass the information on to you."

"I think I understand, A'Lappe, and I want you to know that, regardless of what happens, I am most appreciative for all you have done already. Kala and I personally owe you a great deal and the Federation, while it may not know it, also owes you a huge debt."

"Thank you, Tibby. I'm hoping that one day very soon I may be able to provide you with some technology that will help end the reign of the Brotherhood and unite the galaxy into one huge Federation."

That evening, Kala and I dined with Senator Tonclin, Commander Wabussie, Lieutenant Marranalis and Captain Kerabac. Commodore Stonbersa had command of the ship while Kerabac dined with us. Kerabac had been fully briefed by Commodore Stonbersa as to what transpired earlier. Conversation during the first part of our meal was light and general, dealing mostly with social amenities. Finally, I asked, "Senator, do you know how many Mirage Fighters are currently ready for delivery at Nibaria's shipyard?"

"Indeed I do. In anticipation of your inquiry, I communicated with Orcpipin this morning before I boarded the *NEW ORLEANS*. He advised that eighteen craft are ready for delivery. If the Honorable First Citizen would care to inspect them, I am sure arrangements can be made."

"Marranalis, how many Mirage Fighters do we currently have on the *NEW ORLEANS*?"

"At the moment we have thirty-two, plus eighty patrol ships, five shuttles and a small freighter."

"A small freighter?" I laughed.

"Yes, a small freighter. We need it to supply the ship itself and to transport the equipment that A'Lappe and Cantolla need for their laboratory."

"Ahh, OK. When we arrive at Nibaria, I want us to take delivery of all available Mirage Fighters. We will add eight of them to our own fleet and the rest we will deliver to any Federation starship we encounter that hasn't already been supplied with a Mirage fleet.

"Commander, have you been able to communicate with the admiral concerning the information we received from Senator Tonclin?"

"Yes, I did. He agrees that it's a good idea for me to travel with you to Gaimse to recover the Mirage Fighter. He said he would not be adverse to you destroying their shipyard there if you needed to. The planet of Gaimse does have a formidable military to protect its space, but nothing that can pose any real threat against the *NEW ORLEANS*. In all probability, they will send out their ships once they are aware you intend to reclaim the Mirage Fighter. The admiral does suggest that you reduce the size of their fleet considerably if they are uncooperative."

"If the Gaimseians have been dissembling the Mirage Fighter and drawing up plans to make more, where do you believe they have located their engineering department and the Mirage Fighter plans?" I asked.

"The Gaimseians are highly competitive, business-wise, and fiercely proprietary about any information they get their hands on that gives them a competitive edge. My guess is that the drawings will be produced and kept at the shipyard under the tightest security."

"We may have to destroy the shipyard, because I do not intend for them to be able to keep any of the information they may have already gleaned from their reverse engineering efforts."

"This could be very interesting, Tibby — one ship slightly smaller than a starship going up against an entire planetary force. The Gaimseians have a formidable fleet and, while I don't believe they can hurt the *NEW ORLEANS* when armed with the RMFF, it's going to be a real shocker throughout the Federation when it is learned that one ship has taken on an entire fleet of military ships," Wabussie said. "Senator, how do you think the senate will react to this kind of situation?"

Tonclin grinned. "For the most part, I suspect that, other than making comments about it, they will not show much concern. Any actions taken by Tibby to recover his personal property and eliminate any threat to himself will be seen by most of the senate as justifiable. Furthermore, he will not be violating any Federation laws in doing so, nor will he be violating any laws in defending himself if he is attacked. But it would be best for him to recover the ship, rather than to destroy it and the shipyard. That initial approach may appear to be a decisive act of aggression, and some members of the senate might not look on it favorably."

"Hmm, I see what you are saying," I said. "We'll take every measure to ensure the first shots fired are by the Gaimseians, and that events are properly recorded and documented should it ever become an issue."

"I think that would be a very wise idea," Wabussie agreed.

As we spoke, Kerabac's wrist com signaled and Commodore Stonbersa's voice came across the link. "Please advise the senator that we have arrived at Nibaria and he is able to depart at his discretion."

"Thank you, Commodore, I shall see to it."

I turned to the senator and said, "You're most welcome to spend the night aboard, if you wish. There is no rush, as we will need to complete the inspection and loading of the Mirage Fighters from shipyard, which will require a number hours to arrange and accomplish."

"Honored First Citizen, I appreciate your offer, but I must be getting to the surface. I know that Chanina is excited to hear about my trip home on the *NEW ORLEANS*. Ever since she and I visited last year, you and the *NEW ORLEANS* is all she talks about. If I may be so bold as to tell you, she even says that, when she finishes her schooling, she wants to apply for a job with you here on the *NEW ORLEANS*."

"Really?" I said. "What is she studying?"

"For all of her little girl silliness, she actually wants to be a Gravity Wave Specialist. She studies everything she can find on the matter."

"That's interesting," I said.   "It's possible that I might actually have a position for her after she finishes her schooling, if she sticks with it."

Chanina was the senator's young daughter who visited the *NEW ORLEANS* with her father a year earlier, during which time she managed to get lost while wandering around the ship. She was discovered by A'Lappe who, at the time, was an unknown stowaway on the *NEW ORLEANS*. He escorted Chanina to the bridge while under the invisibility cloak before retreating again to an unoccupied area of the ship. This event set off a ship-wide search for A'Lappe that failed to locate him or his hiding place. A few days later, he appealed to me personally to stay on the ship in exchange for his help and information.

While the senator prepared to leave, Marranalis and Kerabac made arrangements with the shipyard to take delivery of the eighteen Mirage Fighters. Marranalis asked me if I could take over with a martial arts practice session with our security team, and I agreed, as I was in need of a workout. Kala decided to join me, as she had not been exercising as much of late, either.

When I arrived at the training gym, I was shocked to see Lieutenant Commander Sokaia working out there with the others. I really should not have been, as she had trained with many of them a year earlier under Marranalis during the joint security team and Federation Special Operations troopers sessions.

A'Lappe and Cantolla enhanced the learning headbands to enable transfer of the knowledge of martial arts techniques to the troopers; however, even though they knew and understood the movements intellectually, their bodies still needed to be trained to carry out the motions as natural and instinctive reflexes.

"Vice Admiral," Sokaia said, snapping to attention.

"Lieutenant Commander," I said. "It's good to see you here working out with the squad."

"Just trying to refine my skills, sir" she said.

I began the workout by having everyone perform a sequence of fundamental moves before pairing them off to spar. I was impressed with Sokaia's technique and speed and it was apparent that she took her exercises very seriously. Once the sparring began, it was obvious Sokaia was a step above all the members of my security team. Kala observed me as I watched Sokaia and said, "She's good. I think I'll try sparring with her — it should be challenging."

"Oh, you mean you're tired of sparring with me?" I said.

Kala laughed. "Something like that," she said as she walked over to Sokaia's sparring mat. The two spoke for a moment and soon after took their positions. The match was on.

Kala was good; in fact, other than me, no one of our team was able to beat her. But when she and Sokaia started, it was apparent that Kala was up against a solid opponent and the two seemed to be equally matched. Kicks and jabs were thrown and blocked by each opponent, moves and countermoves were made as the two danced in a deadly dance. Suddenly, I realized everyone in the gym had stopped and were focused on the two ladies as they seemed to move faster and faster, trying to get the other into a kill position.

Kala was trying too hard and was not letting her natural instincts take over, and I was almost inclined to yell something out. Suddenly, I saw her step back and the realization in her eyes just as Sokaia made a lightning attack. Kala seemed to melt, her body flowing like a liquid as she moved to the side, so Sokaia's attack missed her by the merest fraction of a millimeter. Kala's body continued its liquid flow, following Sokaia's move and forcing her along the lines of her own momentum. She lost balance and Kala followed behind as she gained the dominant position. Before Sokaia realized what was happening, Kala was on top of her and Sokaia was faced with what would have been the fatal blow, had it been delivered.

Sokaia lay there a second with a shocked look on her face as she stared up at Kala.   Suddenly, everyone in the gym was cheering.   Kala stood and offered her hand to Sokaia and helped her to her feet.

"That was amazing, First Citizen Kalana," Sokaia said. "I thought for sure I had you there, as you seemed to relax for a second. What did you do?"

"I did just what you said, I relaxed. I realized that I was concentrating too hard on my moves instead of letting my instincts work as Tibby taught me.   Once I relaxed, everything went into a natural flow and I simply allowed my body to react instinctively."

"That was incredible, Kalana; I hope we can spar again before I have to leave the ship."

"I think I can find the time.   It's nice having someone other than Tib to spar with."

I think what impressed me the most was that Sokaia actually looked like she was happy to have been beaten.   It was obvious that she liked being pushed to the max, and Kala had taken everything Sokaia could dish out and had beaten her.

As Kala and I headed back to our suite, she said to me, "I thought for a minute she was actually going to beat me. We seemed to be equally matched, and I was starting to get tired.   Then I remembered what you said about being relaxed and letting the body react on instinct instead of trying to think about it. As soon as I did, it was as if my body just took over and I was observing myself in action. Before I knew it, she was on the floor and I was in the kill position. I understand now why all this training is necessary, even when you know all the moves."

"You were great, Kala. I was very impressed. I was also fascinated to see how Sokaia has developed her skills. I think if she were to spar with Marranalis right now, she might beat him."

"You really think so? That would really deflate his libido. As it is now he's afraid to invite her to the employee lounge for a drink and dancing." We both chuckled at Kala's comment as we headed to the shower.

We spent the night in orbit around Nibaria as the Mirage Fighters were brought aboard and placed in the hangar in their proper positions. A'Lappe had crews ready to install cloaking systems and fusion power cells as each ship was docked. By the time the last fighter was brought aboard, two thirds of the fighters were fully equipped with permanent power and cloaking devices.

Senator Tonclin had left the night before, but asked that we hold until midday before departing. I was not sure why, but I saw no reason we couldn't wait that long. Shortly before noon, a shuttle arrived from the planet and five Nibarians boarded. One of them approached Wabussie. They spoke a few minutes before Wabussie called one of my crew over. He led them off into a processing room, where everyone who boarded the ship was screened for loyalty using the electronic testing program and provided with ID badges and appropriate clearances for various areas of the ship. As the shuttle lifted off and moved out of the hangar bay, I approached Wabussie. "Who are they?"

"The senator didn't mention them to you?"

"No!"

"They are more recruits for the FSO. The senator spoke with me after dinner last night and said he was impressed with the way the FSO is working so far, and suggested upping the number of Nibarians agents. He had already compiled a list of candidates."

"Excellent," I said. "The Nibarians that we have in the FSO now — just how are they doing, anyway?"

"They're actually doing very well. As we suspected, most people tend to ignore them, assuming they could not possibly be any threat.   Consequently, they manage to overhear a great deal of valuable information."

"I just realized something — we're heading straight to Gaimse, but we were supposed to drop Lieutenant Commander Sokaia off at Plosaxen. We won't be going anywhere close to Plosaxen now. I suppose I can lend her a Mirage Fighter or a patrol ship to take her there."

"That won't be a problem, Tibby," replied Wabussie. "When I spoke with the admiral, he said he believed she might learn more by accompanying you. He said after you have accomplished your goals at Gaimse, she could head back to Plosaxen."

I chuckled to myself as I wondered how Marranalis would react when he learned that Sokaia would be with us for a few weeks.

Something had been bothering me since we discovered that anything fired away from the ship through the active RMFF experienced an exponential amplification of its force or acceleration. I couldn't understand why this same principle didn't seem to apply to the propulsion system. It seemed to me that, if the force of a laser fired from the ship increased its energy as it passed through the field, the propulsion forces of the ship should also be amplified. I decided head to the lab to talk to A'Lappe and Cantolla about it. When I arrived, I found them both bent over a countertop looking intently through goggles as bright flashes of light emanated from electrical arcs, casting their shadows on the surrounding walls.

"I hope I'm not interrupting anything serious," I exclaimed.

"No, no, not at all. We've been trying to see if there is a way to penetrate the RMFF shield using various frequencies of energy," Cantolla said. "So far, nothing breaks through it."

"It just happens that the RMFF is what I wanted to talk to you about. Why is it that the ship's propulsion is not amplified like other things are when they pass through the field?"

"I can answer that," A'Lappe began as he removed his goggles and laid them on the table. "The ship is not propelled by a pushing action, like a rocket; rather, it's pulled by a gravity wave that is generated in front of the ship."

"OK, you kind of lost me, there. Isn't gravity a function of mass? If so, where is the mass that creates the gravity?"

"Everything that has mass has a gravity field," said A'Lappe, "but mass is a function of energy. All mass is, in reality, energy which exists in a tight, organized form and which behaves in strict accordance with certain physical laws. But it's still only energy. The gravity wave is generated without creating mass."

"Uhh, OK. I'll take your word for that. I was sort of hoping you were going to tell me it would amplify the gravity wave and thus increase the speed of the ship, but I guess not everything works the way I would like it to. But that does bring me to a second matter. When I was pondering the amplifying effect of the RMFF, I started to wonder — instead of creating a new generator to power an RMFF field for the Mirage Fighters, can't you simply amplify the existing power system by using a transformer or something? In essence you would be boosting the power of a standard source to have enough energy to operate the RMFF?"

Both A'Lappe and Cantolla looked at me for a moment, and then turned to stare at each other. "I don't know, to be honest, Tibby," A'Lappe began slowly. "I guess we have been so used to having a lot of generated power to play with that amplification has never been explored. It may be possible."

"If we loop the signal, it's possible that we may be able to amplify it. Or maybe use a prism effect to focus the same signal into a common beam?" Cantolla said excitedly. Then, suddenly, the two of them were both talking to each other so rapidly in techno-babble that I had no idea what they were saying. I realized that they had forgotten I was even there, so I decided to leave them to continue with their ideas. I slowly backed out of the room.

Over the next few days Kala worked out with Sokaia in the gym. While their sessions were intense, Kala seemed to beat Sokaia each time with relative ease. But at the same time, I could see that Sokaia was pushing Kala hard. After each session, the two of them talked and Kala would offer pointers to Sokaia. The two seemed to be hitting it off and becoming good friends — quite a departure from their first encounter, when Kala found it necessary to reprimand Sokaia.

I sparred with Marranalis while the ladies sparred; it soon became apparent that he was not up to his usual level of performance. He seemed to be over-thinking his moves and counter-moves instead of relying on instinct, like I had trained him — and I had a hunch why.

On our fourth day out, I stopped him in the middle of our exercise and said, "Marranalis, I think you need a change. I think it would be a good idea for you and Sokaia to spar together." I saw the concern flash over his face. I had put him in a position once before where he had to spar with Sokaia. That time, it was Sokaia who needed the lesson. This time, it was Marranalis who had something to learn and I had a feeling that Sokaia was going to be the one to do the teaching.

I called to Sokaia, who was just about to begin sparring with Kala. "Lieutenant Commander Sokaia, would you mind sparring with Marranalis today? I think he is too accustomed to sparring with me and would benefit from a session with someone who is equally skilled, but who perhaps takes a different approach."

"Sure," she responded with a smile. "I've been looking for the opportunity to get him on his back."

Kala raised a questioning eyebrow and walked over to me as Marranalis and Sokaia headed to the mat. "What's this all about, Tib? What are you up to?"

"Wait and see. I think this is going to be interesting."

Kala and I watched from the side as Marranalis and Sokaia went at it. At first it was a repeat of Kala and Sokaia's first match a few days earlier, but then slowly, bit by bit, Sokaia became more relaxed in her movements while he became overly aggressive. Suddenly, Marranalis thought he saw an opening and lunged forward in an attack. As he did, Sokaia flowed to the side in a smooth motion and, like Kala had done with her just days before, shifted in a way that allowed her to use Marranalis' own motion against him. Before he knew what had happened, he was on the floor with Sokaia overhead, poised to deliver a fatal blow.

Sokaia laughed with glee as she hopped up and extended her hand to help him to his feet. He had the same wounded look on his face that he had the first time I sparred against him in the demonstration for Captain Maxette on the *DUSTEN*. Sokaia kissed him on the cheek and ran off in a gleeful leap as Marranalis shuffled over to where Kala and I stood.

"I don't know what happened, Tibby; I was sure that I had the upper hand and next thing I knew, she had me. What went wrong?"

"Kala, why don't you tell him?"

Kala looked at me and then turned to Marranalis. "You were concentrating too much on your movements and not relaxing and allowing your natural reflexes and instincts to fight for you. When you concentrate in that way, you actually dampen your responses. You and Sokaia are pretty evenly matched, but she was able to relax and trust in her skilled reflexes, and you didn't. The end result was you got your ass kicked!"

"Hmm, you're right. I realize that now. Is that why you wanted me to spar with Sokaia?" he asked me.

"Yes. Since she began practicing here with our team, you've been trying to impress her with your skills, and have not been fighting to win but to impress, which is always dangerous, and if you're fighting someone with skills equal or greater than yourself, it can be fatal. Now, if we can convince Sokaia to come back, I would like to see the two of you spar again."

Moments later, they squared off again. This time, however, the bout only lasted a short time before Marranalis defeated Sokaia. The two squared off for a third time and, again, Marranalis beat her quickly. As he was helping her to her feet, she said, "I guess I just got lucky the first time, but it was great getting you on your back at least once," She winked.

Kala looked at me and I smirked. "You have more than just one goal in mind with this exercise, don't you, Tibby?" I just grinned. "Don't go playing coy with me. I know you, Tib; what are you up to?"

I just kept smiling and said, "Wait and see, my dear. Wait and see."

After showering, Kala and I lounged in our quarters before a fireplace while sipping a luxurious wine and feeding each other some small snack foods. I was mystified by the fireplace; it was a real fire — not a wood-burning fire, of course, but a gas flame or something else with artificial logs, just like my home on Earth. The mystery wasn't really about the flames, rather, I couldn't figure out where the heat and oxygen-depleted gases went. Obviously there was no chimney exhausting the gases into space; so where did they go?

While she sipped her wine, Kala noticed me staring inquisitively at the fire. "Tib, what is it about that fireplace that intrigues you so much? Don't you have fireplaces on Earth?"

"Yes, we do, but if we burned one in an enclosed space, like this spaceship, it would burn all the oxygen out of the air and we would soon suffocate. Likewise, the heat would build up in the place and cook you like a Rudosian fowl. Yet, here we are, totally enclosed with a fire burning, and we are neither cooking nor suffocating."

Kala laughed. "Tib, there are scrubbers built into the ductwork that filter and re oxygenate the exhaust gases. The heat is sent to collectors and redistributed to places that might need it. If there is more than needed, it is sent to heat exchangers on the dark side of the ship's hull, where the heat quickly dissipates into space. But that seldom happens, as there are plenty of applications and uses for the heat here on the ship, like heating the pools or the greenhouse hydroponic gardens."

"That's a relief. I was afraid that sooner or later, we were going to run out of air. But what about the fueling gas? Do we re-supply it when we get to other planets, and where is it stored?" By now, Kala was laughing so hard I was afraid she was going to spill her wine.

"What? What's so funny?"

"You! You are so funny! Here you are — the richest man in the universe — able to devise all sorts of brilliant military actions, able to save entire worlds — and you worry about asphyxiating due to lack of oxygen. You have no idea what goes on in your own ship, and yet you save the universe," she said, still laughing.

"Seriously, Kala, I really would like to know."

"You would be much better off asking A'Lappe, if you want all the scientific details, but I do know that the gas is generated right here on the ship. You know how the replicators work—by taking basic organic materials here on the ship and converting them back into food or other organic items. Well, one of the products produced in that process is methane. That methane is compressed and stored in tanks aboard the ship, and some is burned in the fireplaces. What doesn't get used can be reclaimed and used by the replicator to produce new foods or clothing or other items."

"Wow. I never realized just how elaborate and sophisticated the replicators are."

We were interrupted by a call on my wrist com. "Tibby, this is Kerabac. We just received a message from the admiralty that the GW pod shipment of solbidyum to the planet Lasalt has gone missing. It is believed that the pod was intercepted before the intended representatives were able to get to the coordinates to pick it up. Commander Wabussie would like to meet with you in the bridge meeting room to discuss the details."

"Tell him I will be right there." Turning to Kala I said, "We were expecting this, only we didn't know where it was going to happen. Now we do. I wonder what plans the admiral will come up with to get it back."

When Kala and I arrived at the bridge conference room, Wabussie and Commodore Stonbersa were there waiting. As we exchanged greetings, Marranalis and Sokaia arrived. The commodore and Sokaia retrieved cups of foccee from the wall drink dispenser and then took seats at the table. When everyone had settled, Wabussie immediately launched into the meeting.

"We knew this was coming. Unfortunately, we were unable to prevent it. But now the Federation needs to act. The admiralty got word a few hours ago that a solbidyum shipment sent to Lasalt was never received by the planet's representatives. From the information we received, the representatives of Lasalt were on the way to retrieve the GW pod when they received a distress call from a freighter, stating they had a reactor problem and the ship was in danger of exploding. The freighter crew reported an injury and casualty count of about fifty crewmembers. They anticipated that the ship would blow up in a few hours and they had begun fleeing in life pods. Normally, the Lasalt ship assigned to the GW pod retrieval would have requested another ship to provide rescue assistance, but there was no other ship near enough to respond in time. A decision was made to render assistance and initiate rescue operations — only when they arrived at the location of the distress call, there was no sign of the ship or any debris that would indicate an explosion. None of the calls they sent out during their search for the ship were met with a reply; and after searching for a full day, they headed back to the coordinates where the GW pod shipment should have been. When they arrived, there was nothing to be found. Someone had tricked them into the diversion so they could steal the shipment."

Wabussie pressed a button on a small remote control device and a panel in the wall slid up to reveal a vid screen. Moments later a star map appeared.

"This is the star system for the planet Lasalt," he said. A red circle appeared around a star on the screen. "These stars are the nearest Federation stars to Lasalt," he continued, as a number of nearby stars lit up in a green color. "These stars…" he said, as a number of other stars lit up in magenta, "…are solar systems that are the home to several non-aligned worlds, and this arch…" an arc appeared close to Lasalt, "…represents the fringe of the Federation territory."

It was easy to see that many of the stars in magenta were outside the arch, while the green ones were within it.

"Fortunately, we were recently able to get a starship with a DSC system into this sector that can relay information to us as it happens. We fear the solbidyum has been taken to one of the worlds outside Federation's territory. It could have been taken to anyone of these worlds," he stated, indicating the magenta stars. "But most likely, it went to one of these."

White circles appeared around thirteen planets. "We think these are the most likely candidates, because these planets engage in a great deal of trade; ships are coming and going across this region in a steady flow of traffic. Right now, the starship *ROSKON* is headed to the area. They have three FSO agents aboard who will depart on small personal transports to investigate some of the more seedy planets in the area — planets known to be hangouts for pirates and smugglers — in the hope that they can obtain some leads as to who is responsible for the theft and where the solbidyum may be now. It may be months before we learn any information, if ever.

"In the meantime, the starship *HOSPIN* is currently here." Wabussie indicated a spot in the corner of the screen right near the arch of the Federation border ended on the screen frame. "They are carrying four FSO agents who will also disembark from their current location and move in the general direction of the agents from the *ROSKON*, but into this region of space. They too will be looking for leads, as this is an area that is collecting a heavy concentration of Brotherhood members who have fled the Federation territories. We are hoping that we will get some definitive information from this area soon. Of course, since the FOI knows nothing about the FSO, they will be conducting their own investigation into the event. Information we have from the FOI is that they plan to have two of their twenty Lasalt agents looking into the matter. We do not anticipate ever hearing anything of significance from their operation; and it is apparent that whoever is giving issuing the orders has no intention of actually succeeding in the solbidyum recovery."

I was beginning to get a sinking feeling about all of this. "So, let me ask. If it turns out that the solbidyum is on one of the non-aligned worlds outside the Federation territories, what is the plan?"

Wabussie stood with both hands on the table and his head down, staring at it as he spoke. "I was hoping not to have to answer that question at this time and rather wait until we know more." He sighed and, still with his head down, he said, "Tibby, the admiral was hoping that you might take your team and go in to retrieve it. If the Federation goes in, it's an act of war; but if you do…well, you know."

"Damn," I said, "why can't he just send in an undercover Special Ops team to handle it?"

"That option is on the table if you reject the request; but right now, until we know just where the solbidyum is, nothing is expected or planned."

I had to weigh our chances of success regarding the two issues at hand. I thought for a moment, then replied, "At the moment, our own goal is unchanged — to recover the Mirage Fighter at Gaimse. Maybe we'll get lucky there and uncover a clue that connects the two events and gives us some direction as to where to focus our search. But until I know more, I am not making any commitments to help out on this one."

"Fair enough, Tibby. You have already done plenty for the Federation."

After that the meeting split up. I decided Kala and I needed to unwind, so we headed to the entertainment lounge. As we made our way there, Kala said, "Tibby, if it turns out the solbidyum has been taken outside of the Federation territory and we discover where it is, you will go after it, won't you?"

"Most likely," I said, "but let's not tell the admiral that just yet. If he is going to put me on the spot again, I think it only fair that I make him sweat a little."

Kala poked me in the arm and laughed. "What am I ever going to do with you?"

I didn't answer, because just then we arrived at the lounge and the music coming from within was enticing me to dance.

As soon as we entered the room I had Kala on the dance floor. I had always enjoyed dancing, ever since my mother taught me as a boy; and while I was not especially popular in school, I was never at want for a dance partner. But never in my life had there been anyone I enjoyed as a dance partner more than Kala. Besides having a natural grace of motion, she was also an incredibly fast learner who needed to see a dance step only once before being able to repeat it herself.

Both Kerabac and A'Lappe had astonished me months before, when I learned they were excellent singers and performers. Their nightly performances in the lounge on the *NEW ORLEANS* were becoming legendary. Tonight, however, only Kerabac was performing — and it wasn't long before he noticed us. For his next song he sang *Unforgettable*, a hugely popular tune performed on Earth by Nat King Cole. Kerabac's voice was an exact duplicate of Nat's; and when I first heard him sing, I knew I would have to teach him all the songs I could remember. I was surprised at how quickly he learned them; and now, every time he was performing and noticed the arrival of Kala and me, he would sing at least one of the few songs I had shared with him.

It was amazing how many of the Earth dances I taught to Kala were rapidly spreading about the Federation like a craze. Nearly everyone on the dance floor was copying our dance moves. Kala snuggled closely to me, her head on my shoulder as we danced. As I slowly moved her about the dance floor to the sound of Kerabac's crooning, she whispered in my ear, "Next time you turn me, look at who Marranalis is with."

"Let me guess," I said, "Lieutenant Commander Sokaia."

"You already noticed them?"

"No, but I suspected they would get together before this journey ended."

We danced a few seconds longer and then Kala said, "This is what you were up to when you matched Marranalis with Sokaia for sparring earlier, isn't it?"

"Maybe... as a secondary objective. The first was to get Marranalis to focus on what he was doing, instead of trying to impress Sokaia. Since the first time they met, it's been obvious he is smitten with her; but he feels he needs to impress her by being superior to her. Sokaia, on the other hand, likes being superior and doesn't like yielding to anyone who is not her superior. She has high respect for those who are better than her. Matching the two let Marranalis know on two levels that he was falling short of the mark. First he was losing control by trying to be in control, and second because he was not going to get Sokaia by showing off. He actually needed to prove it to himself."

"Damn, Tib, I didn't know you were a psychologist and a matchmaker, too."

I laughed. "I'm not a psychologist, but I've learned a lot about people by observing them." I glanced at them dancing. It was obvious by the smiles on their faces that they were enjoying themselves; and I could tell by the way Sokaia was looking at him that she was definitely attracted to Marranalis. If he didn't do something incredibly stupid before the night was over, he would not be sleeping alone that night.

I was awakened from a deep sleep later that night when the sound of my wrist com penetrated my dreams. I struggled to break out of my half-sleep as my hand fumbled across the nightstand next to the bed. As soon as I started to sit up, the lights in the room slowly rose to a dim level that allowed me to see the room's contents without being so bright as to hurt my eyes. I finally found the com and managed to say, "Tibby here," just as Kala stirred in the bed next to me.

"Tibby, this is Verona, DSC operator on duty. We've just received a message from the admiralty that an attempt was made on another GW pod solbidyum shipment, this time the delivery intended for Duepras. He said to notify you and Commander Wabussie that the attempt was thwarted by the frigate *VENGENCE*, which happened to be in the area. After the GW pod was taken at Lasalt, the admiral said he ordered all available ships to head to delivery points for the GW pods in that sector of space where deliveries had not yet reached their destination. The *VENGENCE* had just recently received a DSC system and one Mirage Fighter. Captain Feltsey of the *VENGENCE* ordered the Mirage Fighter to pursue in a cloaked mode, but not to open fire on the enemy ship, in hopes that the fleeing craft would lead them its base and, hopefully, the location of the other stolen solbidyum shipment.

"The enemy ship was a corvette of Markazian design, similar to the ones you found at Alle Bamma. The enemy used a number of maneuvers to make sure they weren't followed and then suddenly made a rush across the Federation border. The Mirage Fighter terminated their pursuit at the border, as it had no authorization to cross, and then returned to the *VENGENCE*. According to the admiralty, the direction the corvette was headed would lead them to a region that holds three non-aligned planets, Ryken, Yentum and Goo'Waddle. Any one of these planets might be the location of the stolen solbidyum, as they are not far from the first shipment interception."

"Thank you, Verona. Have you already passed the information on to Commander Wabussie?"

"No, sir. I contacted you first. I will be contacting Commander Wabussie as soon as we finish here."

"When you contact Commander Wabussie, please tell him I would like to meet with him in the conference room next to his suite at his convenience in the morning. I assume he will want to contact the admiral and his FSO operatives before talking to me; this will give him time to do so."

"Yes, Tibby, I will see to it."

"Once the Commander gives you a time, contact Commodore Stonbersa, Marranalis, and Lieutenant Commander Sokaia and tell them to be in attendance."

"Yes, sir. Will there be anything else?"

"No, that will be all, Verona. Thank you."

I put my com link back on the nightstand and rolled over to look at Kala, who was propped up on one elbow facing me. "Well, Tib," she said, "it looks like you are back in action again."

I struggled to go back to sleep, but my thoughts kept drifting to our mission to retrieve the missing Mirage Fighter and then track down the missing solbidyum — wherever it might be. Finally, after what seemed like hours, I drifted back to sleep, only to dream of aliens dressed like World War II Japanese soldiers back on Earth. In my dream a fleet of giant battleships floated in the dark of space, while airplanes that looked like a cross between a Mirage Fighter and a Japanese Zero made bombing passes on then. As the battle ensued, the collection of battleships morphed into a small sailboat in which Kala, Commodore Stonbersa, Marranalis, Kerabac and Commander Wabussie sailed stoically while Admiral Regeny stood on the bow in a gallant pose with a sword in an outstretched hand pointing onward.

Suddenly, the boat began to rock wildly and I could hear Kala calling, "Tib, Tib!" and I woke to find Kala shaking me by my shoulder. "Wake up, Tib!"

"Huh? What? I'm awake. What's the matter?"

"You were dreaming and struggling while you talked in your sleep. I was afraid you were going to give me a black eye with the way you were flailing about."

"Wow, I'm sorry," I exclaimed.   "Yeah, I was having a bad dream. What time is it?"

"It's mid-morning. I tried to wake you earlier, but you didn't respond. I've never known you to sleep so soundly."

"I don't, normally; but after getting the message last night about the second attempt on a solbidyum shipment, I had a difficult time trying to rest. I guess once I did, I really went into a deep sleep."

"I suggest you get yourself showered and dressed, as you have a meeting with Commander Wabussie in about thirty minutes. If you hurry, you might have enough time to eat a rogae and have a cup of foccee."

I had to grin, because a rogae was a pastry that looked like a small waffle from Earth, but it was covered in a thin sugary icing and tasted like a donut; and foccee was more or less the equivalent of coffee served cold. I guess some things remain the same throughout the galaxy.

When I arrived at the conference room, everyone else had already settled in. Commander Wabussie had a dark look on his face and I could tell he was eager to get started.

"I believe everyone is here, so let us begin," Wabussie started. "As you have probably heard, there was an attempt made to steal the solbidyum shipment intended for Duepras. Fortunately, the frigate *VENGENCE* was en route to that destination, having been alerted by the admiralty after the heist at Lasalt. We were very lucky in this instance, as we have only a few ships near enough to the current shipment points to provide protection and, fortunately, Duepras was the one picked by the thieves as their next target. I'm not going to repeat all the information that came in on the original message last night — most of you already know those details. I do, however, want to update you on new information.

"We are relatively sure that this last attempt was by the Brotherhood, since they used a corvette of a Markazian design; but here is the disturbing news, our FSO field operative at Duepras reports hearing a conversation between some Brotherhood members just two days ago regarding a plan to raid a pirate base on Goo'Waddle. From what the agent was able to hear, it was not the Brotherhood that intercepted the solbidyum shipment at Lasalt; it was a space pirate and smuggler named Logden. Apparently, this Logden had past ties with the Brotherhood — it suffices to say right now that he has collaborated with the Brotherhood on some rather nefarious projects. Logden got wind of their intent to intercept a shipment at Lasalt. He didn't know it was solbidyum; only that it was extremely valuable and that the Brotherhood was putting forth a great deal of effort to get it.

"Apparently, the Brotherhood is less than happy about Logden's heist and is looking for him everywhere; however, they are focusing on Goo'Waddle because that's where Logden has the most ties and connections. Sooner or later, he is bound to figure out what it is he has. When he does, it's difficult to say what he will do, but I think it's safe to bet he will try to sell it to the highest bidder. We're not sure if he knows yet what he has or not. So far, there has been no indication of him trying to sell the solbidyum to anyone; in fact, he seems to have disappeared completely.

"The *VENGENCE* is flying to Duepras, where they will pick up our FSO agent. Of course, the crew of the *VENGENCE* does not know he is an agent; they know only that their orders are to pick him up and transport him to the area where the fleeing Brotherhood corvette crossed the border. The *VENGENCE* has been told to hold their position there until someone arrives to retrieve him. The admiral is hoping it will be us… if Tibby is willing, of course," said Wabussie in my direction.

"I hate to ask this question," I began, "but assuming we do rendezvous with this agent — what then?"

"Then we cross the border, drop off the agent and his ship so he can gather information, which we would use to search for and retrieve the solbidyum. The admiral has suggested that, as a result of new developments, our earlier idea of setting a trap for the Brotherhood by baiting them into an ambush with rumors of a large solbidyum shipment would not be effective. He thinks the sole focus now should be the recovery of the stolen shipment."

The meeting with Wabussie bothered me. Something just didn't feel right and I couldn't shake it off. Everything he said made sense, yet I felt something was missing. Then, suddenly, I realized what it was: A'Lappe. I wasn't detecting the faint scent he emitted. Usually A'Lappe was lurking invisibly somewhere in the room, listening to everything said in these meetings; but this time there was no sign of him. I was beginning to wonder where he was — it was hard to believe that a meeting of this importance would be something he would let slip by.

Once the meeting was over, I headed to the laboratory where he and Cantolla worked. I entered to find them standing behind a shielded viewing window while looking at something inside a test chamber.

"Tibby," Cantolla said, "you're just in time. We think we have resolved two of your requests with one idea, and you were the one who gave it to us."

"I did? What are we talking about?"

"When we were talking to you last time, you talked about amplifying power, rather than increasing power production. We have been able to do that by looping the signals. We've applied the principle to the gravity wave generation unit and it looks like we should be able to boost starship speed to match that of the Mirage Fighter. We also found that looping the power signal for the RMFF demonstrates that the field can be generated and sustained for about one third the power we currently use. But there is a catch — the field is not as strong. We are now capable of shielding a Mirage Fighter with an RMFF, but it won't be as strong as the one for a starship or for the *NEW ORLEANS*. This field will protect it from most conventional weapons, but it would not shield against something like a large fusion bomb that is used to destroy a planet."

"So we will be able to produce RMFFs for the patrol ships and the Mirage Fighters, as well as frigates and corvettes?"

"Yes, and possibly transports, too."

"That certainly will help. How soon can you have the units produced and operating on the fleet we have here on the *NEW ORLEANS*?"

"We should have a unit working on the *ALI* by the end of the week, and maybe on thirty other ships by the end of the month. But we don't have enough raw materials to make many more than that. We'll have to pick up supplies someplace to continue production beyond the thirty units."

"If the ships are shielded from attacks, thirty should be more than ample for our needs. How long will it be to get a unit produced to amplify the speed for the *NEW ORLEANS* so we can travel faster?"

"I think we can have that accomplished in four days."

"Excellent."

Remarkably, considering all that was at stake before us, the next few days went by routinely. Each day, Kala and I worked out with Marranalis, Sokaia and our security force for an hour; then we swam laps before meeting with Commander Stonbersa, Kerabac and Commander Wabussie for intelligence updates. In the evenings, we dined alone in our quarters and then went the lounge for dancing and relaxing with the off-duty crewmembers. The only thing new that seemed to be developing was a romance between

Marranalis and Sokaia — something Marranalis had been dreaming of for a long time.

On our fifth day out from Nibaria, I received a request from Captain Kerabac to come to the bridge. I arrived to find Commodore Stonbersa, Cantolla and A'Lappe gathered there.

"Tibby," Stonbersa began, "A'Lappe has his GW amplifier hooked into the system and is ready to give it a try. We thought you would want to be here to see how it works."

"Certainly," I said, as I took a seat on the bridge next to Commodore Stonbersa. "Anytime you're ready, let's give it a try."

Captain Kerabac turned to A'Lappe and said, "We're ready. Let's see what you have created."

"First we will try the system with the RMFF and the cloaking down, and then we will try it with both engaged. I don't think there is any difference, but I want to make sure there are not unforeseen problems or situations that occur."

As he spoke, he activated the controls while we watched the vid monitor. Unlike all those science fiction shows I used to watch on TV, where stars whiz by at incredible speeds as the ship moves along, relatively little is discernible, in terms of motion on the vid screen while traversing the vast distances of space.

So we didn't really expect to see any significant change on the screen, but it was enough to visibly perceive that we were moving faster than before. "How fast are we going, A'Lappe?" I asked.

"Faster than I expected. I'm getting a reading of 1.75 times the standard GW speed."

"What?! That's faster than our Mirage Fighters can travel at the moment!"

"With this modification the Mirage Fighters will be able to match the increased speed of the *NEW ORLEANS*.

"Now let's see what happens with the RMFF and cloaking engaged." A'Lappe made some adjustments to the controls, but nothing seemed to change. "1.75 times faster, same as without."

"Good. This means we should arrive at Gaimse in about five more days instead of ten. How many of the Mirage Fighters do you think you can equip with this new improvement?"

A'Lappe scratched his ear and said, "Five, maybe six."

"See if you can do three Mirage Fighters and at least two patrol ships," I said. "Make sure one of those fighters is the *ALI*. You and Cantolla have done a great job once again."

"One thing more you should know, Tibby. Once this new technique is implemented, the duration of the cloaking capability in your Mirage Fighters and patrol ships will improve from the current one hour to four hours. If I apply this same looping technique to the personal cloaking devices, I should be able to boost them to close to four hours, as well."

"Now that the two of you have resolved this issue, I have a new one to add to your list. Sooner or later, our enemies will get hold of this technology. I need the two of you to put your heads together and figure out a way to detect a cloaked ship. There will come a day when we need a device that can spot and track them."

"We'll get right on it, Tibby," Cantolla said. "Before we go, however, A'Lappe and I have a small gift we would like to present to you and Kalana."

She reached into a small box and brought out a device very similar to our wrist coms. "This is a combination wrist communicator, cloaking device and laser gun," she said. "You wear it in the standard way, but to activate the cloaking device or use the gun, you will need both hands, as you need to press this button here to cloak or uncloak and these two on the sides must be pressed simultaneously to shoot the laser pistol. You simply extend one arm to aim and use your other hand to fire. There is no stun mode; and it is quite lethal up to 500 meters. But keep in mind, if you fire the pistol, you have only two shots, and that will drain your power. Your cloaking device will no longer function until it is recharged."

"Wow," Kala said. "This is some gift. Will you be making more of these?"

"We wanted to talk to you and Tibby first, but we thought it would be a good thing for all of your crew and employees to have. As for outside of your circle, however, we both feel it might be better kept a secret; thieves and assassins would have a field day with such a device."

"I can see the wisdom in that, but I think it might be a good thing to issue to the FSO agents, and perhaps to top officials in the Federation military, like Admiral Regeny and the admiralty."

"Thank you, both of you," Kala said. "I'm deeply touched, and I know that Tib is, also. Aren't you, Tib?" She elbowed me as I was turning the device over in my hand and inspecting it, wondering if it would burn a hole in the wall if I activated the gun.

"Huh? Oh yeah, deeply touched! Hey, thanks, both of you. This truly is a wonderful gift, and we are deeply honored."

I could see Wabussie from across the table eyeing the device with some envy, apparently thinking how his FSO agents might benefit from it.

"One thing you both need to know," A'Lappe said, "is that these devices are both keyed into your personal DNA, like the door locks on the ships. Only you can use it. If anyone takes it from you and tries to use it, only the communicator will work. The gun and cloaking device will not. If they try to tamper with it, it will simply overload and melt. So even if it gets into the wrong hands, they are not going to gain anything from it."

I was amazed at just how much it looked like the standard wrist com. Other than a small hole that served as the outlet for the laser beam and the added buttons on the side, it looked just like a regular communicator. It was highly unlikely anyone would ever recognize it as a cloaking device and a weapon.

After the meeting was over, I headed to my office while Kala went off to discuss some issues with her staff. I was sitting in my chair watching the fish when Piesew entered the room. "Honored First Citizen Tibby, Commander Wabussie is outside and wishes to speak to you."

"Thank you, Piesew. Show him in, please."

Wabussie entered and immediately seated himself in the chair in front of my desk. Piesew went to the drink dispenser in the wall, about to retrieve two cups of foccee, I assumed, when I stopped him. "Piesew, I think perhaps instead of foccee Commander Wabussie and I would prefer an afex." I looked questioningly at Wabussie, and he nodded with a slight smile.

"Very well, sir." Piesew punched something into his vid pad. I had no idea where the afex was stored on the ship; apparently, it was not something the replicator produced. Moments later, there was a signal at the door and Piesew opened it to reveal an attendant carrying a tray with two frosted glasses of afex. Per tradition, I was served first and then Wabussie. Once we had our drinks in hand, both Piesew and the attendant departed, leaving the two of us to discuss our business.

"Tibby, I sure am glad you are changing some of the traditions in the Federation. There are times when afex is far better for a discussion than foccee."

"I am assuming you didn't ask to see me for anything too demanding," I said with a grin.

"No.   Actually, I am here to pass on some information from the admiral.   Do you remember about a year ago you discussed idea of setting up a war college? It was determined the best way we could learn of your Earth's battles and wars was to intercept news and vid broadcasts from your planet and century.   We set about positioning receivers at different distances from Earth to pick up broadcasts in ten-year groupings.   Well, we have begun downloading the first series of such signals, and the admiral is extremely pleased with what he is seeing so far.

"Of course, our experts are required to filter out a lot of extraneous information, like segments that you call commercials and other vid streams designed for entertainment instead of documentation or enlightenment. One stream series in particular that the admiral doesn't understand, but seems to find particularly fascinating, is about family that lives in a huge mansion, yet they dress poorly and behave in an ignorant and archaic fashion.   They have an old surface transportation vehicle instead of a more modern one like others who appear in the stories.   This series drives the admiral crazy; he keeps talking about some character on the show called 'Granny.'

I had to laugh, as I had a good idea just which TV show was holding the admiral's attention.

"The   history   shows   on   warfare   are   most enlightening, however.   It seems your planet is quite young, yet Earth's inhabitants have advanced very rapidly, technologically speaking, in a relatively short period of time.

"We're also picking up broadcasts from ten and twenty years later on satellites that have penetrated much nearer; but these are much harder to filter, as the quantity and types of broadcasts from one decade to another seem to increase exponentially.   Though your planet is way outside the Federation territories, the admiral feels it might be worthwhile to contact your planet and about bringing them into the Federation as an island planet. But the fact that you do not have a one-world, unified government excludes your Earth as a candidate at the moment. He would like to talk to you more about this when the issues at hand are resolved."

"Unfortunately, I do not see any possibility of a unified, one-world government occurring on Earth at any time in the near future," I said.

"You know, Tibby, this mission to retrieve the Mirage Fighter and the solbidyum isn't going to be easy. In order to confirm that you have recovered all the disassembled parts and technological designs that they have gleaned from the ship, you're going to have to physically go in with troops. Cloaking will help them, naturally, but there is a huge risk of someone being killed down there. Goo'Waddle isn't going to be any easier. We won't likely be confronting adversaries in space; this is going to be a boots-on-the-ground operation. We'll have no choice but to go in covertly, find the solbidyum, and then take it by whatever means possible — without the RMFF and firepower of the *NEW ORLEANS* backing us. If we can recover the solbidyum and get back to the *NEW ORLEANS* safely, there probably isn't much harm that anyone can do to you after that. But when on the surface, these pirate planets are going to be a problem — we will face a constant, tangible threat of one kind or another everywhere we go."

"We'll have to deal with the issue of the Mirage Fighter first. Once that's resolved, we'll start worrying about the solbidyum. In the meantime, I'm hoping your agents can garner more intelligence that will make the job easier."

"You're right, of course, but I don't see any other way to get the solbidyum — assuming it actually is there on one of those planets. I'm thinking that I may need a little more help on this venture than I brought along.

Commander Wabussie paused for a moment. "You know, Tibby, if the solbidyum is outside the Federation territories, you can't rely on any assistance from the Federation military. The FSO can supply you with whatever intelligence we may gather; but beyond that, you're on your own."

"I was actually thinking of some of my own reinforcements. I believe I can safely pull one of the corvettes stationed at Alle Bamma to protect the natives from the return of the Brotherhood. Because we keep the ships cloaked most of the time, the Brotherhood never have any idea just how many ships we have there. After the devastation we caused to their fleet and operations at Alle Bamma, I don't think they are likely to attempt any kind of operation to retake the planet. I also think that Captain Felenna might be of more than just a little assistance to us. As a former member of the Brotherhood, she may have some information about their goings-on outside of the Federation territories. Once we finish our discussion here, I'll get in touch with her and have Captain Kerabac arrange an appropriate rendezvous point. This will also give A'Lappe an opportunity to upgrade her cloaking device and RMFF capabilities and propulsion systems — the same holds true for any fighters she may carry. I'll have to make sure she stocks enough manufacturing materials."

"Do you think there is any possibility that word of her defection might not have reached the Brotherhood at Goo'Waddle? If not, it's possible she could do some spying for us."

"I hate to put her into that kind of danger. If we need her to do so, it will have to be entirely of her own consent. It's been nearly a year since the events at Alle Bamma, and it's most likely that some word of her desertion of the Brotherhood would have reached there by now. But her defection was not widely known, so it's difficult to say. The one and only time I used her to trick the Brotherhood, she ended up getting shot and nearly killed. I don't want a repeat of that."

My meeting with Commander Wabussie gave me a lot to think about. I was beginning to feel like I did when we took on the Brotherhood in our efforts to recover the *DUSTEN*. Over six thousand people died in that encounter and I still felt responsible for every one of those deaths. Felenna had been duped when she joined the Brotherhood; once inside the organization and isolated from the Federation, she discovered their true nature and intents. But by then she was trapped until we arrived at Alle Bamma. Her defection and assistance had made it possible for us to capture a number of Brotherhood criminals, as well as many of their ships.

I carefully wrote out a message and then took it to the bridge for Verona, who was on duty as the DSC officer at the time, to broadcast to Captain Felenna's receiving communications officer.

"Verona, I need you to get this message to Captain Felenna aboard the *MIZBAGONA* at Alle Bamma. Once you have received a reply, see to it that I am informed."

"Yes, Tibby…ahh, I mean, sir!"

I chuckled. "Tibby is fine, Verona. I really prefer to be called Tibby."

"Tibby, it's good to see you up here on the bridge when we're not managing an emergency," I heard Captain Kerabac say. "I've been thinking of ways that I might be able to help you; it occurred to me that there are many of my race living on Ryken, Yentum and Goo'Waddle. After my world joined the Federation, a number of my people were not willing to give up the practice of slavery and a number of other prejudicial cultural behaviors that had dominated our way of life for centuries. They left to take up residence in worlds outside the Federation — Ryken, Yentum and Goo'Waddle were among the worlds preferred by them, as they afforded the opportunity to continue the old ways.

"Yentum is a manufacturing world where they use slave labor. Ryken is a mining and agricultural planet also driven by slave labor. Goo'Waddle is both an agricultural planet as well as a trade hub for that sector of the galaxy. It is also a haven for organizations engaged in pirating and smuggling — activities that many of those who rejected Federation membership can enjoy freely in this sector. Disguised as a trader, I would be able to move about freely between these planets and potentially glean valuable information without triggering much suspicion."

"I like that idea. It makes sense and it's certainly less dangerous than sending Felenna in to obtain information from any Brotherhood members residing there."

"Captain Felenna? You're thinking of bringing her into this operation?"

"I just sent a message directing her to join up with us after we finish our business at Gaimse. I'm hoping she'll be able to bring the *MIZBAGONA* as a support ship. If so, A'Lappe should also have enough time to update their RMFF and cloaking device and make the gravity wave system adjustments necessary for them to travel at the greater speed."

"Tibby, sir," Verona interjected, "I have a response back from the *MIZBAGONA*. Captain Felenna has responded that the message is understood and that she will be underway within the hour."

"Thank you, Verona. Kerabac, I think we will soon be very busy… once again."

Kerabac laughed. "Tibby, around you there is no such thing as not busy."

"By the way, where is the commodore?"

"He said he was going to go work out in the gym and then head to the shooting range. He let it be known that, if there is occasion for you to take us into battle again, he is going to make sure he's prepared on all levels."

"How long has he been doing this?" I asked.

"He started right after we took off from Megelleon; he's been training several hours a day."

"Well, I'll be… I think I will sneak down there and see how the old fellow is doing."

"I wouldn't go calling him old, even if you are his boss," Kerabac said. "I observed him yesterday for a few minutes; I was surprised at how good he is. Obviously he's not you or Marranalis, but he could easily take on an untrained trooper in martial arts — or maybe even a novice trooper — and succeed."

When I arrived at the gym, I was amazed to see the commodore sparring with one of my security team. Stonbersa was not dominating or winning the match by any means; but it was obvious he had the basic moves down and was showing speed and skill that belied his age. Marranalis saw me enter the gym and came over to my side.

"What do you think of our latest recruit?" he asked with a grin.

"He's a lot better than I would have believed. How does he do on the target range?"

"With guns or with knives?"

"You mean he uses both?"

"Damn right he does… and he's a natural with both! I'd be willing to bet he could stick a knife into a boloan fruit in your hand from 10 meters and you wouldn't get a scratch."

"That good? And with a gun?"

"Best marksman on board, except possibly for you and Kalana."

I looked at Marranalis questioningly, expecting him to say he was pulling my leg, but he didn't flinch. "Sounds like I underestimated the good commodore," I said.

"I think we all did."

"Hey, how are things going with you and Lieutenant Commander Sokaia? I've noted the two of you have been rather friendly of late."

"That obvious? Yeah, we're finally hitting it off. In a way, I am glad for your association with the admiralty, as it keeps tossing us together."

"You know, these situations are hardly ideal for a romance," I said.

"Are you kidding? They're perfect. Sokaia is turned on by the action and the threat of danger. The closer we get to battle, the more sexually aggressive she gets."

I had to laugh, because I could see by the look on his face that he was totally serious.

Our arrival at Gaimse came much sooner than I expected; before I knew what was happening, we were in orbit over the shipyard — cloaked, of course. We scanned the area as best we could from our altitude and, using the description Orcpipin had provided us, we located the building where he saw the Mirage Fighter. Even from our altitude, our observation equipment revealed enough to make it obvious that this building was heavily guarded by troops. There were even four Markazian fighters circling around the yard on constant patrol.

"So, Tibby," Marranalis began, as we met in the conference room to prepare our battle strategy, "what are your plans?"

"Well, beyond the obvious fact that they have the place well-guarded, we need to know how far they've progressed in dismantling the ship and reverse-engineering its systems before we take any kind of action. Indications are that they have shifts working around the clock, so it's not as if the place is ever empty. But I suspect they have less of a crew on duty at night compared to the daytime. I think we need to take a patrol ship to the surface with some of our men and conduct a cloaked recon operation tonight. No more than twelve of our people, I would think. I want every one of our troopers fitted with vid cameras, so we can review what each one of them encounters during their movements. We'll analyze the data tomorrow and determine what areas we need to target. The following morning, we go in about two hours before daybreak and," I hesitated, "do what we need to do."

"Tibby, I'd like permission to join you on this operation." Lieutenant Commander Sokaia spoke up.

"Absolutely not," I said.

Both Sokaia and Wabussie were present for the planning session — not just to observe and learn, but also to contribute any ideas or suggestions they might have.

"We can't take the risk of your participation being discovered in any way. If it were discovered that a Federation officer was involved in the operation, it could create an incident that might unite some of the non-aligned worlds against the Federation or, even worse, provoke them to side solidly with the Brotherhood. The risk is too high. I won't even be taking Marranalis with me on this mission, as he still technically holds a rank in the Federation military."

"You're going to lead the mission yourself?" Wabussie asked incredulously.

"I am. Technically, it's my ship, and my efforts to reclaim it will receive less criticism then if someone else does it. We know this planet has a substantial military and, depending on what we do down there, I think we can anticipate a rather hefty and swift reaction. We're going to need to move the *NEW ORLEANS* out of range so we can launch a patrol ship without being detected and return to the planet cloaked. After we take whatever action we decide is necessary, I want the *NEW ORLEANS* to be positioned in a close orbit. We're going to make a run for it; and just as we arrive, Stonbersa is going to have to drop the RMFF long enough for us to dock. Once we're in, the RMFF and the cloak go back up and we high-tail it out of here — hopefully, without a fight."

Late that night, my team assembled in the hangar bay. Since Marranalis would not be going, his second in command, a man named Plarem, would be deployed on the team as my second. The rest of the team consisted of men that Marranalis hand-picked for their particular skills and knowledge. The team also received a very specific indoctrination from A'Lappe that would enable them to determine how much Mirage Fighter technology had been uncovered.

The plan was simple. Our patrol ship would land in the far corner of the plate supply yard, where metal plate construction materials were stored. A large portion of the yard was empty, either awaiting the delivery of more plates or simply remaining unused at the moment. The space was large enough and far enough away from the main portion of the yard to land unobserved. Our patrol ship would set down while cloaked. Fortunately this section of the yard was not lighted. We would wait several minutes while scanning the vicinity to make sure that no one was around and that our landing had gone undetected. Once our position was secure, the ship would drop its RMFF for a few seconds — just long enough for us to disembark and move clear of the RMFF zone. The ship would then cloak again and remain in position until our return.

In addition to the vid cameras, each trooper would be fitted with an individual cloaking device would remain cloaked for the duration of the operation. We would assemble at the same location outside the RMFF zone, at which time the ship would uncloak. We would all quickly load; the ship would cloak again; and we would be on our way back to the *NEW ORLEANS*.

The trick would be to time the periods of uncloaking so that we would not be detected by the four Markazian fighters circling the area. A distraction was needed; and it was decided that Kerabac would take the freighter, one of the Nibarian operatives and two of my other crewmembers, and fly in to an area near the shipyard but out of range of our muster point.   We anticipated that all the fighters would respond to inspect the freighter and warn Kerabac to back away.   Kerabac would pretend to be a trader.   Having a Nibarian onboard and a miscellaneous combination of other races for crewmembers would bolster his image as a freelance trader. He would, of course, leave, but by then we would have landed, uncloaked and disembarked, and restored the ship's cloak as we started to execute the recon mission.

Boarding and leaving would not be so easy, but we would cross that bridge when we came to it. There was no danger for Kerabac and his team, because they would have their RMFF engaged. Even if the fighters decided to open fire on him, they would be safe.

So, with this plan in place, we flew down to a level below that of the Markazian fighters. I was glad that the GW propulsion system made no sound; there was nothing to alert anyone to our presence. Once we were in place, one of the troopers trained in the use of the DSC system sent a message to Kerabac, and he moved the freighter toward the shipyard at a low altitude.

At first, there wasn't any response from the Markazian fighters; but suddenly, two of them broke off in the direction of the freighter.   The other two moved to position themselves between freighter and the shipyard, while the first two made contact with Kerabac.   In that moment our patrol ship uncloaked and we quickly disembarked. For a matter of about fifteen seconds the ship was visible, and then it was gone from sight again. In the dark, even if anyone had caught momentary sight of it, they would have been rubbing their eyes, thinking it was their imagination or the fatigue of the night shift that made them think they saw a ship for an instance.

Immediately, we all moved in different directions to check out the area and buildings as assigned to each group. Even though the cloaking devices were enhanced with noise dampeners, the team was careful to move as silently and stealthily as possible across the compound.

I headed to the hangar where Orcpipin indicated he had seen the Mirage Fighter. Once I entered the main part of the shipyard complex, I began to encounter more and more people. The closer I got to the hangar where the Mirage Fighter was stored, the more armed guards and troopers I saw at various posts and tower platforms. When I finally reached the hangar, I noted two armed guards posted outside the closed door. This was going to be tricky.

If I opened the personnel door to enter, it would be obvious that someone was there. The large hangar bay door was also closed, so I could not enter that way. I was afraid I was going to need to disable the guards to gain entrance, when suddenly one of them received a message on their wrist com.

"It was just a trader that wandered off course, nothing to panic about. He's heading out of the area now."

"Does that mean we can open the hangar doors again? We have a surface transport carrying materials that needs access as soon as possible," one of the guards said into his com link.

"Yeah, it's safe. The area is clear."

I looked about and noted a small surface transport with a flat bed and some containers on it staged near the hangar bay door. A driver sat in the cab, looking rather bored. I moved quickly and hopped up onto the back of the truck just as the large hangar doors began to open. The driver immediately started to move forward and I lost my balance and nearly fell off the truck. I quickly allowed myself to collapse onto the bed of the transport, saving myself from falling off the back. Then, as the transport passed into the hangar and slowed down, I jumped off. I could see the Mirage Fighter parked deeper inside the hangar. Eight armed guards were posted at different locations, but none of them seemed terribly alert.

I needed to get closer to the fighter's exterior to record better images on my vid cam, and then find a way into the ship itself. With all the people moving about the ship's perimeter, I didn't know how I was going to accomplish that.

Once again, luck was with me. A chime sounded. At first I wasn't sure what was going on, but then I noticed everyone moving away from the ship and to the side of the hangar, where they began picking up containers and finding seats on boxes and crates. Apparently, we had arrived just as they were taking a meal break. I wasted no time in getting aboard the ship, carefully passing one remaining guard as quietly as I could. Once inside, I headed to the engine compartment. It was empty — they had removed the engine.

I next went to the control room. It was obvious they were in a stage of dissembling the control console to identify the various functions related to the engine and the absent cloaking device. Once I was finished collecting sufficient images, I quickly headed out of the ship, once more slipping quietly past the guard. I looked about the hangar and noted an area in the back where I had seen a number of technicians gathered earlier. With them out of the way, it was possible to see the missing GW engine modules in various stages of disassembly.

I moved to that area past another guard and walked about the engine, looking at every detail and making sure the images were all being recorded. I was about to leave when I noticed a vid pad lying on the table. I could see that someone had been constructing a schematic of the engine. I was hoping that this was the only vid pad on which this data existed. I picked it up and slid it inside of my cloaked area. I managed to quietly slip it inside my shirt before working my way to the door.

I knew I needed to get out before the meal break was over or they might close the hangar door again. I was sure that once the meal break was over and the vid pad was discovered to be missing, a full scale security breach alarm and search would begin. I was hoping it would be assumed that an employee had either misplaced it or that a dishonest employee had stolen it; either way, I doubted anyone would realize that someone had infiltrated the area and taken it.

I quickly headed back to the muster point where the patrol ship was staged and cloaked. I arrived and waited quietly, checking my watch every few seconds, when suddenly, someone bumped into me. I felt a hand grasp my arm and knew it was one of my own security team. I had warned everyone not to speak once we were outside our ship; so we just stood quietly at the ready, waiting to run toward the ship as it dropped its shields. At one point, I felt him jar a bit and I assumed that someone had also bumped into him.

A few more minutes passed before the patrol ship appeared before us. By now, all of the team was holding hands and I led the group quickly into the ship. Once aboard, the last man in the line triggered a signal button that closed the door, at which time our pilot cloaked the ship and activated the RMFF.

Before departing, we all uncloaked in the hold; a quick headcount confirmed that we all had returned safely. I moved to the bridge where our pilot and weapons officer were monitoring the positions of the circling Markazian fighters. Slowly we lifted off, moving up to a level just below the circling fighters. As soon as the nearest one passed, our pilot hastily moved to a higher elevation and then set a course to our rendezvous point with the *NEW ORLEANS*.

Once we were safely aboard the *NEW ORLEANS*, my team assembled with Commodore Stonbersa in a large conference room adjacent to the hangar to display and uploaded the images captured by each helmet camera. We discussed the findings with Cantolla and A'Lappe, who also attended, along with the ship's engineers, in an effort to quickly and thoroughly assess the information. When the images of the ship and engine were finally displayed, a sad look came over A'Lappe's face.

"Well, I think this answers the question of the type of action you will need to take," he began. "I don't think you have any choice but to destroy the ship and its components. There is no way you would be able to successfully remove the ship in its current condition. From what I can see, they have already gleaned a good bit of data, though not enough to construct one of our GW engines."

"I brought back this little gift for you," I said as I handed him the vid pad.

A'Lappe took the pad and began scrolling through the images and data. "If this is all they have acquired so far, we arrived here just in time. But let me ask you, where did you get this?"

"I picked it up from a table where they were tearing apart the engine."

"You do realize that, as soon as they look at their security vids of the hangar, to identify the thief, they will see the vid pad suddenly lift from the table and disappear into thin air?"

I felt sick. A'Lappe was right. It would only be natural for them to check their security recordings; and when they did, the disappearance of the vid pad would be evidence of us having been there. They would be on high alert. The only good thing was that we had no further need to return to the ground, since it was clear that we could not recover the ship. On the other hand, I didn't like the idea of killing all the civilians that worked at the yard just to prevent the reverse-engineering of the Mirage Fighter and its engine.

"You're right, A'Lappe, I didn't think of that. OK, well, what's done is done. Here is what we're going to do. We are not waiting until tomorrow to attack. We're going to head back to the shipyard now with the *NEW ORLEANS*. Commodore, is there a way we can set the hangar building on fire from the *NEW ORLEANS* without instantly destroying it?"

"If we ramp the laser power down enough, I think we can; but if we're going to fire through the RMFF, it's going to be difficult to calibrate a weak-enough beam. A'Lappe, what do you think?"

A'Lappe blinked his eyes in his usual hypnotic fashion. "I think I can do it. What are you planning, Tibby?"

"I don't want to wipe out lives indiscriminately. If we set the building on fire, the people inside will flee, then we can destroy it once they've evacuated. In fact, I would like to set all the buildings on fire and then destroyed. I imagine all proprietary information would be required to stay inside the buildings; so if any other vid pads or computers containing data exist inside the complex, they'll be destroyed with the structures."

"Tibby, you are the strangest warrior I have even known, but I'm glad to know you," Commander Wabussie said.

Minutes later, we were once again in position over the shipyard. By now I was on the bridge with Commodore Stonbersa, Captain Kerabac — who had docked the freighter inside the *NEW ORLEANS* before we returned from the surface — Commander Wabussie, Lieutenant Commander Sokaia, Kalana, Marranalis and, of course, A'Lappe.

A'Lappe made adjustments to the laser weapon systems and entered precise coordinates for each target in the shipyard complex. "Whenever you're ready, Tibby."

"Go ahead and do it."

A'Lappe pushed a button on the weapons console and almost instantly, fires broke out at discrete locations on all the buildings. The four fighters circling the base honed in on our location by triangulating our shots and began to open fire on us with everything they had. Light and energy beams played across the RMFF shield as we sat safely inside, watching the shipyard going up in flames. We magnified the images and saw hundreds of people fleeing the complex, trying to retreat from the burning buildings as far away as possible. When we no longer saw any people coming out of the structures, I told A'Lappe to up the power. I wanted the buildings totally destroyed — especially the hangar and the Mirage Fighter inside.

A'Lappe boosted the power level to the lasers and, when he discharged the weapons on their targets the second time, each building literally exploded in white bursts of energy. Once again, the Markazian fighters opened fire and the RMFF shields absorbed their energy.

"Set course for the rendezvous point with Captain Felenna. Great job, everyone. One challenge down and one to go."

"I'm getting readings of a number of fighters mobilizing in our direction," said A'Lappe. "They seem to be coming from the military bases here on Gaimse. I also detect five corvettes and two frigates."

"Start moving us out and away," Commodore Stonbersa ordered. "Keep us cloaked. They will spend dozens of fruitless hours searching for us in the immediate vicinity. I see no reason for us to inflict more damage here; we've accomplished what we came for."

"I agree."

Marranalis stepped up beside me and said, "Somehow, I don't think the task of retrieving the solbidyum will be quite as easy."

"I suspect you're right; but until we get there and assess the situation, I'm not going to start anticipating anything in particular."

Over the next few days A'Lappe examined the contents in the vid pad that I picked up at the Gaimse shipyard. On the third day after the raid, he came to me in my study in his usual clandestine fashion by way of his cloak and a hidden doorway. As always, I detected the faint cedar scent in the air and, without turning to look in his direction, I said, "Is there something you need, A'Lappe, or are you just observing to see how many times I scratch my ass?"

"How do you do that?" he demanded. "How can you tell when I'm here? No one else on the ship seems to be able to detect my presence, but you always seem to know."

"You have your secrets and I have mine. Let's just leave it at that, shall we?"

"I'm going to figure it out sooner or later. Just you wait and see."

I had to smile to myself, because I doubted that he would ever figure it out. Individuals are so accustomed to their own smell that they don't even know it's there. What did amaze me was that no one else picked up on the aroma of cedar in his presence. Perhaps something specific to my Earth DNA allowed me to smell A'Lappe when others could not.

"So, what is it you want? Or is this just a social visit?"

"I thought you might be interested in a summary of my findings from the vid pad you brought back from Gaimse. I've reviewed all the data, and from what I am able to ascertain, the Gaimseians hadn't gotten very far with their analysis of the ship's engine or other technical features. They had barely begun producing schematics, much less defining the guts of the design. I also found a number of communications between the engineer who, I believe, was the owner of this pad, and others, including someone apparently representing the interests of the Brotherhood — a man named Shydak.   There appeared to be a conflict between the Gaimseians and the Brotherhood about payment.   The Brotherhood wanted a set of plans for the fighter, as well as a completely built craft, in exchange for allowing the Gaimseians to have access to the ship and its design. The Gaimseians didn't want to turn over any plans, but conceded that they would provide the Brotherhood with one built ship and a guaranteed discount on all future ships that the Brotherhood decided to order; but they wanted to retain the plans and full rights to build more fighters and sell them on the open market.   In the last communication from Shydak to the Gaimseians, he was threatening to come to the shipyard and seize the fighter by whatever force necessary and take it someplace else to complete the reverse-engineering and construction.   I think it is safe to assume that the Gaimseians might suspect our raid at the shipyard was the Brotherhood following through with their threat.

"I also found reference in one of Shydak's earlier messages that the Brotherhood was about to come into considerable wealth. They were planning to use this wealth to purchase as many of the latest and best ships as they could get their hands on.   Then, about the time of the solbidyum heist, he suddenly changes his story and starts indicating in his communications that the Brotherhood is having some problems with securing the resources to their wealth and that there would be some delay in payment.   So it seems that Shydak and the Brotherhood were either not the ones that intercepted the solbidyum shipment, or they can't secure a buyer with the funds to pay them."

"That is interesting news.   If the Brotherhood doesn't have the solbidyum, that means they are probably looking for the people that do, just like we are. I think you need to see if you can hack into the Brotherhood communications and monitor them again. It might not hurt if you could train some of our security people how to do it as well, so you can filter several channels of communication at once."

I could tell A'Lappe didn't like this idea, but he could see the value in it and I was sure he would follow through. A'Lappe enjoyed having the edge, in terms of technological gadgets and exclusive access to certain information, so to have to reveal one of his secrets was not something he relished.

I continued, "If the Brotherhood suspects who has the solbidyum or has any clue as to where it is, and if we have the opportunity to gain that information from them and beat them to the solbidyum, all the better. We don't know what we're up against, but maybe we can find out from the Brotherhood."

With everything that had been going on in the previous couple of days, I had spent very little time with Kala, and her absence was becoming annoying. So I was delighted when I returned to our quarters to find her there waiting for me.

"Tib, come with me. I have a surprise for you." She took me by the hand and led me out the door and through the maze of corridors and compartments on the *NEW ORLEANS*. The ship is so large that were I to start out in the morning with the goal of traversing every corridor and compartment, I wouldn't be able to finish by the end of the day. So I was not surprised when the journey with Kala took longer than usual.

"Just where are we going?" I asked.

"Wait and see; you'll like it!"

I always hated when people say that, because the frustration of the wait usually outweighs the joy of the surprise. "Really, now, would it destroy the wonder of whatever it is if you told me before I saw it?"

"Yeeesss! Now stop being a pest and just be patient."

"Don't we have some sort of transfer tubes on this ship that could take us here faster?"

"Tib, stop being difficult. You know very well we have transfer tubes, but I thought it would be more fun to walk." Kala was just far enough in front of me, as she held my hand to drag me along, that I could enjoy the view of her luscious hips as she marched along.

"I must admit, watching your butt sway back here is making the journey more enjoyable."

Kala turned her head and smiled at me as she gave an extra exaggeration to her hip motions. I resigned myself that I was just going to enjoy the view until we arrived at our destination. Eventually, Kala stopped at a compartment door that appeared to be the entrance to a cargo space. She placed her palm on the security door lock and the door slid to the side so we could enter.

I was dumbstruck for a minute. For the life of me, it felt as if we had exited the ship to find ourselves standing in a small, earthen depression in a forested area surrounded by rocks and a small stream with a rock pool. A breeze carried the rich scent of the forest and I could hear birds singing off in the trees somewhere. It was only with the utmost inspection of the sky that I could see that it was artificial — a dome, but the illusion of being outdoors was so great that it was breathtaking.

"Well? How do you like it?" she asked, as she bounced up and down on her toes. I had never seen Kala like this before. She was almost like an excited teenage girl instead of the mature and controlled Major Kalana, military attaché for the Federation — the image of Kala that people saw most of the time.

"I...I don't know what to say. How did you find this place? Why is it here?"

"First of all I didn't find it — I had it made. And the reason it's here is so we have a place where we can get away and be alone. The door is coded to only allow access to you and me. No one else on the ship can get into this space. I've had the botany crew secretly working on this for months."

The whole time she was telling me this she was shedding clothing. I wasn't exactly sure where all of this was going, but I had an idea. So I began shedding my clothing as well. Kala walked over to the pool. The banks were lined with heavy, velvet-like green moss. She stood for a moment with one foot on the bank, extending the other to reach her toe into the water.

"Perfect," she purred. "Not too warm, not too cold." She waded out into the water and settled down on an underwater rock that made a bench long enough for two persons. I followed her. The water was cool, but not unpleasantly so, so I waded slowly into the deeper water and seated myself beside her.

"How did they duplicate the sun?" I asked curiously. In the sky dome above us a bright sun sent down rays of light that filtered through the trees and leaves to cast dark shadows on the ground.

"I have no idea. But I know that we can have a sunset, a starry sky — with or without a moon or moons — or we can opt for a cloudy sky, and even rain. Of course, the temperature is adjustable to suit our wishes."

"What made you decide to do this?"

"I really enjoyed all the time together back on the estate at our secluded lakeside sanctuary, and I thought how nice it would be if we had such a place that we could take where ever we went. Then I thought about all the vacant compartments and spaces on the *NEW ORLEANS* and, well, next thing I knew, I had A'Lappe and Commander Stonbersa looking into having this space outfitted just for us."

I wondered at all I was seeing around us. I felt Kala's eyes on me and turned to see the most beautiful smile on her face. Had I not already been madly in love with her, I would have fallen hard for her in that very instant.

"I don't know what to say.   This is beautiful. Wonderful!"

"Tib, you don't need to say anything. Now let's go over there and see if that moss is as soft as it looks." She took me by the hand again and led me to the mossy bank. My earlier assumption as to where all this was leading proved itself to be correct.

For the next several days, Kala and I practically hid out in our paradise aboard the *NEW ORLEANS*. We came out early in the mornings to check on the status of things, get something to eat, and return to our paradise for a few more hours before emerging for another meal and updates on any new happenings. On the third day I found Wabussie eagerly awaiting me as we opened the door.

"Tibby, we've received word from one of our operatives that the Brotherhood is sending a lot of ships and personnel into the area of space around Ryken, Yentum and Goo'Waddle. Our agent tells us they're stopping every ship in the area to board and search for someone or something. So far, they've released every ship they have searched, offering no explanation for the interception, and have departed with nothing more than a brief apology for the detainment.   Needless to say, this situation has a lot of people in the area quite nervous and angry."

"Good. If the locals are upset with the Brotherhood, all the better for us and more favorable for the Federation. I think we can safely assume that the Brotherhood is searching for the solbidyum.   I wonder why it is that Logden, or whoever has the solbidyum, hasn't tried to sell it yet?"

"Yes, that bothers me also. It's possible, I suppose, that the thief still doesn't know what he has in his possession. Or maybe he is just being very cautious as he tries to figure out how to sell the solbidyum and still keep his skin.   He might even be trying to negotiate with the

Brotherhood from some undisclosed location; but we know they are cash poor at the moment and would need to sell the solbidyum themselves in order to have enough money to buy anything."

"Has A'Lappe said anything to you about messages he may have intercepted with the Brotherhood thus far?"

"No. I didn't know he was even doing that. To be honest, I've not seen him in a few days now."

"I asked him to look into intercepting Brotherhood communications; he's done it successfully in the past. I also wanted him to train several of the crew in his methods so we can have more ears listening. I wonder what he's been up to."

"Maybe that's what he is doing," Wabussie said while adjusting his collar. "I saw him with several of your crew a few days ago as they entered one of the vacant compartments not far from the bridge area. Now that I think of it, I haven't seen any of those crewmembers since then. A'Lappe hasn't even been performing in the ship's lounge the past two nights."

"I guess I'd better find out what our little genius is up to."

I activated my wrist com. "A'Lappe, this is Tibby. I would like to meet with you for a few minutes to get an update on your progress."

One of the interesting things about the wrist com that I didn't fully understand was how, before I finished saying the name of the person I wanted to address, the communicator calculated the recipient's identity and opened a link to that person's communicator. Kala tried to explain it to me once — the microsecond delay that adjusted on the other end so that the person's name didn't get chopped off when the link opened and the caller was already in the middle of speaking. But I still couldn't grasp how that worked.

"Ah, Tibby," A'Lappe's voice came back over the com link. "I was just about to contact you for a demonstration. If you would care to join us in the room across the corridor from the bridge conference room, I'd be happy to bring you up to date."

"I'm on my way," I said, all the while wondering just who "us" was.

When I reached the compartment, the first thing I noted was that a security palm pad had been added outside the door. I placed my palm on it and the door immediately opened. It was obvious upon entering that A'Lappe had been very busy indeed. The compartment was only about seven meters square. Two console panels were set up along each of the three walls. A row of comfortable-looking chairs lined the remaining wall, where the door was, obviously meant for anyone in the room that wasn't occupying one of the consoles. In the center of the room was a circular console with A'Lappe seated on a swivel chair that allowed him to scan the room.

"Tibby, come in, come in. What do you think of your new intelligence center? From here, we can monitor all sorts of signals and data and quite effectively intercept and decipher coded messages. We just got everything up and running today; and already we're picking up some pretty juicy bits between the Brotherhood ships."

"You mean like they're detaining and searching every ship that leaves the Ryken, Yentum, and Goo'Waddle area?"

"Oh, so you know about that already?" A'Lappe looked somewhat crestfallen.

"Yes, I just got the information from Wabussie a few minutes ago. He received a report from one of the FSO agents in the area."

"Hmmph," A'Lappe snorted. "Did he also tell you the Brotherhood is offering a huge bounty for anyone providing them information that leads them to Logden?"

"No, he didn't mention anything like that."

A'Lappe perked up; apparently having something new to offer provided him with renewed energy.

"Well, Logden, it seems, was providing some services to the Brotherhood up until about eight weeks ago — drug running, from the sounds of it. Then suddenly he became an unwelcome name in Brotherhood circles. Two days after the solbidyum shipment was taken, communications throughout the Brotherhood in this sector really heated up, and the focus was the search for Logden. Instructions are to NOT kill him; that he is wanted for interrogation by the Brotherhood. The same orders apply to Logden's ship, the *BUKSCUKET*. It is to be captured at all cost, but not destroyed or damaged. Any crew that successfully locates and detains Logden or the ship is guaranteed riches beyond belief, according to Brotherhood channels. They have every ship they can muster responding to the area as fast as possible. They believe that Logden is hiding someplace on one of the three planets, waiting things out."

"So what you're telling me is that all we have so far is an elaboration of information we already had?"

A'Lappe looked crestfallen again. "Pretty much so. There also was some chatter about the fighter at Gaimse and about Shydak, who was heading there to confront the Gaimseians and rattle some skulls over the deal to reverse-engineer and build more Mirage Fighters for them. He should be arriving there about now. Boy, is he in for a surprise."

"I would imagine so. You wouldn't happen to know if the FSO still has an agent on Gaimse…?"

A'Lappe scanned his console, as he moved his hands over it a few times. "It looks like Commander Wabussie issued an order for one to be stationed there last week. Hmm, I see here that one was dropped off by… um… you're not going to believe this, Tibby. We dropped him off — well, indirectly, anyway. Commander Wabussie took out one of the Federation Mirage Fighters intended for transfer to the Federation and flew one of the Nibarians to the surface — cloaked, of course — and dropped him off while we were engaged in our recon operation with the Gaimse shipyard."

"How did he pull that off? He would have needed either Commodore Stonbersa or Captain Kerabac's approval to do that, and neither of them mentioned it to me. Is there any indication of authorization being given for the flight?"

A'Lappe's hands moved over the console once more. "All indications are that the commodore cleared the mission."

"It looks like I'm going to have to speak with the commodore about this," I said, as I turned and left the room to head for the bridge.

When I arrived, I found Stonbersa seated in his chair, reviewing monitors about the bridge. Captain Kerabac was leaning over Verona's DSC console. Two were discussing something. Two other crewmembers were operating their stations.

"Excuse me, Commodore," I began, "might I have a word with you in private?"

Stonbersa gave me a questioning look. "Certainly, Tibby, shall we use the bridge conference room?"

"That will be fine." The bridge conference room was a small but comfortable room adjacent to the bridge that was intended for bridge crew briefings and meetings. Under normal conditions, it held about eight to ten persons. Once inside and seated, Stonbersa said, "What can I do for you, Tibby?"

"I understand that, while we were on Gaimse, you authorized Commander Wabussie's departure from the *NEW ORLEANS* with one of the Mirage Fighters and a Nibarian and that they flew to the surface. Is that correct?"

"Why, yes, it is. The Commander came to me and said that he needed to go to the surface using one of Federation fighters aboard the *NEW ORLEANS* on a special mission. He said he would be back before you had completed your mission and that there was no danger of detection because he would be cloaked the entire time."

"Why was I never informed of this?"

"I was of the impression by the way that the Commander presented himself that you were aware of it and that the action had your approval," Stonbersa said, staring at me like a creature caught in a spotlight.

"I'm upset about this," I said. "Understand, I am not blaming you. I gave you authority to make decisions about the operation of the ship and I fully trust you. What bothers me is that no one — especially the Commander — discussed this with me directly at the time. I cannot have anyone doing things like this under the radar, especially when we are in the midst of a critical situation like our recon mission at Gaimse. Had he been observed or discovered while we were on the planet, the safety of every one of my team could have been endangered. In the future, I want a log maintained of the comings and goings of ALL ships here on the *NEW ORLEANS*. Both you and Captain Kerabac have the right to authorize and sign for such events, but I want a record of it included in my daily status report.

"Under normal situations and normal daily operations, I do not expect to be made aware of the comings and goings of each and every ship, but on missions such as this, where dangers are present, I wish to be notified before any ship leaves or joins up with or docks in the *NEW ORLEANS*. If we know in advance that a ship is coming, like a small cargo vessel, I would like to know as far in advance as possible. Likewise, during non-standard missions, like the one we currently underway, I want to be informed before any ship leaves the *NEW ORLEANS*."

"Tibby, I am sorry. I assumed — and wrongly so, I admit — that the Commander had discussed this with you and you were aware of the situation. But as Commodore of your fleet and guardian of the flagship, I should have been more astute. I assure you, it will not happen again."

"Thank you, Commodore. You are not entirely to blame in this situation; I fully intend to talk to Commander Wabussie. He is a guest here on the ship and his comings and goings are not to be based on his whims. I do not want him or any member of the Federation high command to make the assumption that they can just do whatever they wish on my ships."

"I understand, Tibby. I assure you; I will not let it happen again."

"Good! Now I need to go track down the Commander and get this all squared away."

When I arrived at Commander Wabussie's office, I found Sokaia engaged in a discussion with him. Wabussie greeted me and Sokaia rose from her seat. "I'll leave you two to discuss things privately."

"Stay, Lieutenant Commander. My purpose here will indirectly apply to you also." Sokaia stopped, but didn't sit back down.

"Commander," I began, giving him a hard look in the eye, "it has come to my attention that, on the night of our recon mission at Gaimse, while I was on the surface with my recon team, you left the ship with a cloaked Mirage Fighter and a Nibarian agent, whom you deposited on the surface of the planet. Is that correct?"

"Yes, sir, it is," Wabussie said somewhat stiffly.

"Just when did you make this decision and why was it not discussed with me in advance?"

"Tibby, I am not one of your crew," Wabussie said defensively. "I have every right to take a Federation fighter out when I wish, and the Nibarian in question is an FSO officer that I wanted in place on Gaimse for intelligence purposes. I don't need your approval to do that."

"Right and wrong, Commander. True, the ships are yours to use; I lent them to the Federation separately from the ones I reserve for my own fleet. You are in charge of the FSO and do not need to answer to me or inform me of your dealings with them. But you are wrong to assume that you can come and go from my ship as you please, especially when I am in the midst of a dangerous operation or situation.

"Had something gone wrong and you were detected while I was on the surface, who knows what alarm might have been issued and what might have happened? The *NEW ORLEANS* had to uncloak and recloak twice during the recon operation and twice because of your departure. What if this had been observed while we were on the planet? If you had discussed the plan with me beforehand, we could have all departed at the same time and minimized the risk of detection. Fortunately, no one detected you. But understand this — the same protocols are in place here as if this was a Federation starship. You do NOT depart or arrive without notification to the bridge and proper authorization from the bridge.

"Whether by intent or by neglect, you presented Stonbersa with the impression that I was aware of your mission and that I had approved it. That is not to happen again on any of my ships. You are a guest here. While I have every intention of helping the Federation in any way that I can, I will not be used blindly. I want this made very clear to you and every Federation officer or trooper on this ship. There are about a thousand people, plus or minus, on the *NEW ORLEANS*. Aside from a handful of Federation officers, they are my people and I am the one who is responsible for ALL your lives. If I am going to shoulder that responsibility, then everyone on this ship answers to me in one fashion or another. Is that understood?" I looked from Wabussie to Sokaia.

"Yes, sir!" they both responded.

"Good! I'm not asking you to inform me of all your intelligence actions with the FSO, Commander, but if it has anything to do with our mission, I would appreciate being kept in the loop. I'm trying to prevent a war, not create one, and at the moment, it's not looking too good."

"Tibby, I do apologize," Wabussie began. "I fully intended to brief you, but after you got back…well, I guess I sort of felt that what you didn't know wouldn't hurt anything. I was wrong on two counts there, and it won't happen again."

"Sokaia, this was not a reprimand for you, it was solely for your edification. But it applies to you nevertheless." I looked at her with a smile as I made the statement.

"I'm relieved to hear that, sir. I certainly do not want to get on your bad side again. Once was enough for me," she said with a smile.

"You've been on Tibby's bad side?" Wabussie said with astonishment.

"You mean you never heard about it?" Sokaia exclaimed. "I ended up getting a dressing down from both Major Kalana and from Admiral Regeny himself over the matter. My face and ears burned for days afterwards."

"Well, that was in the past, as is this issue, I hope. So let's move on. Now, if you will both excuse me, I need to speak with the captain."

"Oh no. Don't tell me Kerabac is in trouble, also," Sokaia exclaimed.

"No, he isn't, but I do need to discuss an idea I have that will require his services."

When I returned to the bridge, Stonbersa and Kerabac were seated and talking to each other. They looked up as I entered and the commodore spoke. "Tibby, is there something I can do for you?"

"Actually, I need to speak with Kerabac. Do you mind if we use the bridge meeting room?"

"Not at all," he said with a look of concern. I could tell by both the look on his face and Kerabac's that the commodore had discussed with him our earlier conversation and now both were expecting that Kerabac was next in line to be called on the carpet.

When we settled into the meeting room, Kerabac said, "Tibby, if I've done something wrong, I assure you I did it unawares."

"Relax, Kerabac, it's nothing like that at all. I want to discuss a possible course of action that may require your help to pull off."

"Anything, Tibby. You know I'm at your service."

"This could be a lot riskier than anything I have ever asked you to do before. It's my understanding that many of the non-aligned worlds still practice slavery and that Ryken, Yentum and Goo'Waddle all permit the trade and ownership of slaves. I also seem to recall you telling me that many of your fellow…. By the way, I don't believe you've ever told me the name of your home world, or how your people refer to themselves."

"Our home planet is Ginet, and we call ourselves Ruwallie Rasson, which loosely translates to *The Chosen*, or *Above Others*. We tended to be a rather arrogant race going back long before we joined the Federation. Today, however, most of us are more like the other races in the Federation. There are some that still hold to the older ideas of superiority and some that still want to reinstitute slavery. Most of those bands have left the Federation and now live on worlds outside the territories, like Ryken, Yentum and Goo'Waddle.

But they do not rule on those worlds; their agendas and words carry no more significance than any of the other free citizens of those worlds, regardless of race.   Many are simply traders and merchants, while others are little more than pirates."

I paused for a moment after Kerabac finished speaking to digest what he had said.   "I've been thinking about how to best approach finding Logden and the solbidyum.   If my hunch is right, Logden is hunkered down somewhere, trying to find a tactic to escape. He needs to sell the solbidyum, but he can't solicit the sale without the Brotherhood finding him.   He can't leave the system, because the Brotherhood is stopping everything leaving the area.   My idea is this: we take the small freighter in the hangar, doctor it up to look like the ship of a questionable smuggler, load it with various cargos that we'll pick up someplace — maybe lots of rare vintage liquors that are not easily synthesized — and fly to these planets under the guise of trade.   We'll make sales to bars and other places where rumors circulate quickly.   We will, of course, have the ship rigged with an RMFF and cloaking system; then, when we make a deliberate, uncloaked attempt to run the Brotherhood gauntlet and leave the system without submitting to their search.   Of course, they'll fire upon the ship.   Just as the charge hits the RMFF and creates its usual light show, we instantly cloak and return to one of the planets.

"Before we embark on the mission, however, we need to take the freighter out with one of our fighters to give it a few low-level laser shots in non-critical areas, just to scar it up a bit.   Once we return to each planet, we boast how we've been running the blockade and getting away with it, and how we have a trick that works every time.   Sooner or later someone is going to ask — if it works so well, how did we end up with the laser scars.   We reply that was a near-miss resulting from our own stupidity, but we have that issue resolved now.

"I suspect that, by now, rumors about what the Brotherhood is looking for have leaked out. If not, we'll start the rumor ourselves that they are looking for solbidyum. Then we toss in that we would like to get our hands on the solbidyum ourselves, as we know of a non-aligned planet on the far side of the Federation where the leader is offering a huge reward for anyone who can get him some. If Logden is hiding in the area, it shouldn't be too long before he seeks us out to get him and the solbidyum off the planet. But I don't think he will tell us his true intent. He will probably try to learn the location of this ruler who wants the solbidyum, but for this he will definitely have to come to us."

"OK, I think I understand what this plan is leading up to, but I have two questions: Why are you telling this to me and not Wabussie, Marranalis and Stonbersa? And second, what does this have to do with slavery?"

"The reason I'm talking to you first is that the plan depends largely on you. I want you to pose as the owner and captain of the freighter; and to truly pull it off convincingly, you need to have slaves. I've noticed that, while I have seen may races of people in the Federation military, you are the only one of your race I have encountered who has had a career in the Federation service; so I suspect that people will be far less suspicious of you being an undercover agent — even less so if you are dragging around a few slaves. I won't mention it to anyone else until I first know you're onboard with the idea. There are still a lot of details to work out; but at this point I want to know if you would be willing to do it before we plan any further."

"Yes, I can see lots of things that will need to be addressed. Where are the slaves coming from, for one. And I don't think I can treat any slaves the way my fellow Ruwallie Rasson treat theirs."

"They won't be real slaves — and you won't have many. I'll be one of them. Your slaves will not be for sale;

you will have a few to serve as manual labor — myself and Marranalis, for starters, and maybe two or three others at the most. I'm assuming that not all of the crew on the Ruwallie Rasson trader ships are slaves, otherwise the captain would end up dead pretty quickly."

Kerabac grinned.   "You're right there.   My grandfather was still alive in the days when slavery existed on my planet. He spoke about trips with slaves and the precautions that were needed to prevent uprisings. I actually know a bit about trading, as he was a trader, though he wasn't involved in anything exotic or illegitimate that I know of. When I was a teen, he took me on a three-month trip to one of the outer non-aligned worlds where I was able to see him bartering for goods first-hand.

"It was the first time I had ever seen one of my fellow Ruwallie Rasson with slaves. I had never seen anything like it before, and it was rather traumatic for me. All the slaves wore electronic collars that could deliver excruciating shocks and all wore wrist coms linking them to their master. Every Ruwallie Rasson had at least one female slave, and every female slave I saw was totally naked, except for the collars and wrist coms. It was rather apparent by the way they were being fondled and groped that their function was to serve their masters' pleasure. I don't relish the idea of having to put on an act like that."

"Hmm. I see what you mean. We have a number of trained females on my security team — I won't force any of them to play that part, but I will ask for volunteers and hope for one brave soul."

"Tibby, it's not like you think. I will have to shock and beat you and the others at times just to appear to be the real thing. If you aren't scarred and bruised, no one is going to believe our act, and that's going to hold true for the women, as well."

"But surely not all of the Ruwallie Rasson are cruel and brutal to their slaves? Back on my planet, when slavery existed in my country, not all of the slave masters treated their slaves brutally, even though the slavery itself was wrong."

"Not so among my people. Only a few slave owners were less inclined to be brutal to their slaves; perhaps a few even paid small wages to some of them and saw to their needs in old age. But that was the rarity, and not the rule. The Ruwallie Rasson who left when Ginet joined the Federation were of the crueler mindset. They're basically arrogant egotists with no real regard for anyone."

"Well, I have plenty of scars, if that helps," I said, indicating some of the visible scars on my arms where I had been stabbed by Lexmal on the *DUSTEN* and slashed on the arm during the attack on Kala and me at the senate dinner. "I even have several really nasty ones where Lexmal stabbed me in the chest; and if I need to get batted around a few times to have some bruises, I can take that as well."

"OK, but what about the women? How many women onboard do you think have scars? As soon as they get a scratch, they're headed to a med unit to ensure there is no scarring."

When he said this, the thought momentarily took my breath away. I knew one woman who did have a scar, and a nasty one at that — one from a wound that nearly took her life. That scar was on one of the best fighters I have ever known — a true warrior in every sense. It was Kala. I saw instantly the look of shock and dismay in Kerabac's eyes as the realization hit him.

"Oh no, Tibby, you wouldn't ask her to do that — you couldn't."

"Kerabac, I was once told by one of my commanding officers when I was in the Navy on Earth to never ask anyone to do something you are not willing to do yourself. This isn't exactly the same situation, but the principal is the same. How can I ask other female members of my crew to volunteer for something I will not allow Kala to do? As much as it terrifies me, if she volunteers — and I am pretty sure she will — I will have no choice but to accept her. She is the best we have of the women — and you and I both know it."

"Tibby, you are a stronger man than I. I don't think that if I found myself in your position, I could do what you are suggesting. But if you go through with your plan, I will do everything I can to help you. I will be your slave master. I just hope I can make it all look real."

"I'm hoping Cantolla and A'Lappe can help us out with some gimmicks that will make things look much more brutal than they actually are. But if not, we will do what we have to in order to make this work."

After speaking with Kerabac I discussed the plan with Wabussie, Stonbersa, and Marranalis. Then, early the next morning, for the first time in the ship's history, I called an all-hands meeting. Those not at duty stations assembled in a small events arena that situated near the ship's common area. I had been aware of its existence; but as far as I knew, no events had ever been held in it. It was designed to hold many more people than we had on the ship, so only one side of the arena seating was used for the assembly.

I stood behind a small podium in front of the assembled group. Behind me hung a large screen with my live image on it, and I knew that the same view was being broadcast to the duty stations of the few individuals who were not able to attend.

"As you are all aware, we are on a mission to recover a grain of solbidyum intercepted during delivery to Duepras. At the moment we have every reason to believe that this theft was the work of a pirate named Logden and that he is hiding on one of the three worlds of Ryken, Yentum or Goo'Waddle. The intelligence we have been able to gather thus far indicates that Logden is also being hunted by the Brotherhood. They have surrounded the region with warships and are stopping all ships leaving the area to search for the solbidyum.   Basically, Logden is trapped on one of these three worlds.

"The objective is to find Logden and the solbidyum before the Brotherhood does.   The mission will require a dangerous covert operation, for which I will need volunteers to serve in various roles.   No one is required to go on this mission and you will not be thought less of if you do not volunteer.   The mission will require a group of us to be disguised as the slaves of a Ruwallie Rasson trader.   We are going to modify the freighter that we carry in our hangar to appear as a trader's ship and Kerabac has volunteered to be the trader.   He will also need a crew, most of whom will serve as trade associates.   I would like one of those crewmembers to be Nibarian, if possible.   In all, I'm hoping that at least three of you will volunteer to act as associate crewmembers for this mission.

"Those posing in the role of crewmen will be at moderate risk.   The major risk falls on the next group of volunteers, those disguised as slaves.   I'm hoping for candidates that are highly skilled troopers or, at least, individuals who are well-trained in martial arts and the use of numerous weapons.   We will need both men and women in this category.   I will be posing as one of the slaves, but we need at least three or four others.

"Now...there are specific requirements for those who serve undercover as slaves.   First, we need persons with obvious body scars.   The slaves will wear only modest to no clothing and the scars will need to be visible.   As part of the ruse, it will be necessary for us to also bear bruises.   During the course of the operation, it may be necessary for us to be beaten or shocked at times to appear genuine.   We will be fitted with slave collars that have shocking capability, but the strength of the shock will be dampened — remaining only strong enough to know that a current is being delivered, so it will be necessary for us to provide a convincing act that it's a full strength shock.

"The beatings, however, will not be reduced in intensity; the crew will be required to deliver real blows and the slaves will be expected to tolerate them and maintain their cover without wavering. We will at all times be expected to behave and act as slaves. For this to appear genuine we will also need at least two female slave volunteers.

"I will not accept anyone for this assignment who is a caretaker or parent of small children. Please consider in your decision that this is a most dangerous assignment; we must present a flawlessly believable image without blowing our cover at any point in the operation. Anyone wishing to volunteer please see me in my study after this meeting is over. Does anyone have any questions?"

I glanced around the group and a woman in the middle of the group raised her hand. "You have a question?"

"Yes, sir. As I understand it, female slaves of the Ruwallie Rasson are often fondled and groped openly in public by their masters. Will the women who volunteer for this mission have to undergo that level of violation?"

"They will have to undergo whatever it takes to make this mission a success. I'm not going to make this appear better than it is. When we are all alone, you will be treated with the same dignity you receive here on this ship. But when in the public eye, we will have to present all of the characteristics and mannerisms of the slaves of a Ruwallie Rasson. For the women slaves, yes, this may mean you will be groped and fondled, possibly by other Ruwallie Rasson, as it is customary for fellow slaveholders to allow each other to fondle their female slaves. It will also be necessary for the female slaves to sleep in the same room as Kerabac, if we are off the freighter and staying in an inn or hostel. But be assured, you will not be required to have a sexual relationship with him as part of the undercover role. Even at that, I know this is asking a lot of any woman here, but it needs to be done."

A man near the back row raised his hand. "Yes, you. Your question?"

"Yeah… Ahh…the male slaves. What exactly will they have to do?"

"Kerabac, maybe you should answer these questions, as you know more of the history and typical actions of the Ruwallie Rasson than I do."

Kerabac stood and walked out to the podium. I stepped aside so he might stand behind it.

"First, I want to say that the only reason I have consented to this mission is because I understand First Citizen Tibby's plan. While I abhor everything about the nature of this undercover approach, I clearly see the necessity and the probability of success for his plan. I agree to participate only because I believe in what he wants to accomplish; but understand, I hate what it will require me to do. You want to know what the male slaves may have to do and endure. First off, you will be beasts of burden and will be required to perform all sorts of manual labor. You will receive blows and kicks for just about any reason — moving to slow, moving too fast, or looking me or any Ruwallie Rasson in the eye. You will not be treated kindly in any way in public. The women slaves will be required to wait on me hand and foot and will all have a proximity device in their slave collars that will not allow them to get more than twenty meters from me at any time without receiving a shock. For the men, the range is greater and can be switched over to one of the crew when they are supervising your labors elsewhere, but you're still limited to eighty meters from whoever is responsible for you. If we were using unmodified collars, the strength of the shock could range from mild to fatal; but as stated before, these will be modified — just strong enough to let you know when it activates so you can put on a convincing act of agony. Any other questions?"

"I have one," a male voice responded from the end of room. "What about the crewmembers on the freighter. What are their conditions and status?"

"Typically on a Ruwallie Rasson-operated freighter, the crewmembers are not slaves. Occasionally one may be, if they are unable to find a free man for the position and they have a slave that they can trust to serve the function. Usually such a position would be something support-related, like bookkeeper or supply master. The crew is in a partnership with the Ruwallie Rasson, who is always the captain. Each receives a percentage of the profits for each run they make, and the captain usually receives 50 to 60% of the profits after expenses have been deducted; the crew splits the remaining 40 to 50% into shares based on their skill level and value to the trade operation.

"On most ships, the crewmembers have their own cabins or, in some circumstances, a few may share a cabin with another crewmate operating on an opposite shift. Accommodations will not be as luxurious as here on the *NEW ORLEANS*, but they won't be bad. All food will come from the synthesizer. When off-ship, all crewmembers will wear side arms. When we're planetside, you will be expected to act like the crew of a trader ship. In other words, you will frequent the bars, act tough, and look like you are drinking too much, while also keeping your eyes and ears open for anything that might give us a clue as to where the solbidyum is or how to find Logden."

"Alright then," I said, "if there are no more questions, we are done here. Anyone wishing to volunteer for this mission must submit their request to be considered by end of day tomorrow."

I watched the crew as they left. I could see that many were talking to their friends; and it was easy to tell by the expressions on their faces that they were saying "No way," were they going to volunteer for the mission. But several others appeared to be deep in thought, and it was from their number that I hoped at least enough qualified candidates would volunteer to make a presentable troupe for the mission.

I had barely arrived at my study when Kala came in. "Tib, I'm going with you. I don't care about the risks. I already have a nasty scar on my back and getting a few bruises — well, it's not like I don't get those sparring in martial arts practice."

"Kala, I knew you would be the first one through the door. I won't lie to you. I don't want you on this mission; but I do know that you are better qualified than any other woman on the ship, and it wouldn't be right for me to ask another woman to go on this mission and not allow you to do so."

Kala grinned. "Good. Then I won't have to fight you on this issue."

Just then, there was a signal that someone else was at the door. I activated the door from my desk and was not surprised to see Marranalis enter.

"Sign me up, Tib. With my bulk, I suspect I would make a good slave candidate, and I have more than a few combat scars. I think I can at least present as a believable-looking slave."

I walked over to him and put my hand on his shoulder, reaching a good deal higher than my own shoulders to do so because of his tremendous size.

"Marranalis, if I'm going to be a slave, there is no one I would want as a fellow slave more than you."

"I'm not so sure if that's a compliment or not," Marranalis beamed, "but I'm going to take it as one."

It was another hour before the next volunteer showed up. It was one of the Nibarians who came aboard as FSO trainees after we met with Senator Tonclin at Nibaria. Like all the other Nibarians, he was short and stocky and had skin that resembled gnarled tree bark. His eyes appeared to be sunken into his head more than those of other Nibarians I had seen — either that or his forehead protruded more than that of others — I couldn't be sure. In keeping with the traits of his race, he had a high-pitched voice, but it was mellower, with less timber in it than most of his kind.

"Greetings, Honorable First Citizen Tibby. I am Norkoda. I would like to volunteer to pose as one of the freighter crewmembers for the trader operation. I have served as a ship's engineer on Nibarian freighters for many years and have even been to the planet Goo'Waddle on several occasions, so I am familiar with customs there. I would be honored if permitted to serve the role on this mission, and I believe I can be of particular assistance."

"Norkoda, it's a pleasure to meet you. You are one of the trainees with Commander Wabussie's FSO team, are you not?"

"Yes, that is correct. I look at this mission not only as an opportunity serve the Federation, but also as an intelligence gathering prospect and an opportunity to learn more about covert operations. The Federation will be needing operatives outside of the Federation territories, and I think I would ultimately like to serve in that capacity. This is a chance to test my ability to function effectively in that role."

"The final decision as to who will be going on this mission hasn't been made yet, but you certainly present as a strong and likely candidate. I will let you know my decision tomorrow."

While I was adverse to the idea of using members of the Federation military for any mission where their involvement might cause problems if their affiliation was uncovered, in Norkoda's case I had no qualms, since the agency he worked for wasn't even known within the Federation, let alone outside of it.

Late in the afternoon Commander Sokaia appeared in my study.

"Tibby, I want to volunteer for the mission as one of the female slaves. I know Kala already has volunteered and I believe that two strong women fighters give this mission the best opportunity for success."

"You put me in a tight spot, Sokaia. On one hand, I totally agree with you. But this mission needs to go off looking like it's not a Federation operation; so if something goes wrong, our actions don't trigger a war between the Federation and non-Federation worlds. Right now, I am really pushing it, as both Kala and Marranalis are still technically military. Since they are assigned to me by the military, it's possible that a claim could be made for their acting outside the scope of the Federation's authority. Norkoda also presents a problem, as he, too, is ultimately associated with the Federation as part of the FSO. But since the FSO doesn't exist officially, it would be difficult to make him out to be a Federation operative. You, on the other hand, are a Lieutenant Commander serving as the head of the Federation's Special Operations team. While that team is only recently formed, it is now officially recognized as a branch of the Federation military. I don't know how we could explain that one away if something went awry."

"I understand, Tibby, and I talked to Wabussie about it before I came to you. He believes that the admiral will concede to dummying up my files to indicate that I was dismissed from the Federation military for misconduct dating back to the operation when the TEZU LAGONG ambush was laid for you. The file would be in place if something goes wrong. If we succeed, the original file will be reinstated and no one will ever know anything happened. Both the admiral and Commander Wabussie feel I would be an asset to your operation and that it would provide me with additional experience that I can pass on to my troopers."

"You present a good argument, but I'm still not sure."

"One more thing. You said you needed people with scars, and they are few among women in most of the Federation because of the cosmetic capabilities of the med units. Kala only has one scar, and while you might be able to convince the Ruwallie Rasson that she is a new slave, especially if she is bruised up, if neither of the women have any serious scars, it's not going to be convincing."

While she talked, Sokaia began to remove the top of her uniform. Had I been back on Earth, this action would have seemed totally inappropriate and out of line, but in the Federation, where the views and attitudes about nudity were much different, it was not something that anyone would question.

"As you can see, I have quite a few scars," she continued as she held her top in her hand at her side." She turned around to reveal several long marks that ran down the length of her back and a scar on the back of the upper left arm that I had never noticed before, as it was always covered by her uniform sleeves.

"Yes, you certainly do. May I ask how you got them and why you haven't had them removed?"

"I was involved in a Federation mission on one of the newer Federation worlds. We were trying to quell a rebel uprising and I just happened to be at the wrong place at the wrong time. I was caught in a bomb blast. I was lying on the ground at the time; the blast detonated behind me. Shrapnel from the blast raked across my back, leaving me with the scars you see now. We were trapped on the surface for three weeks before a ship was able to get to us and extricate me from the rubble and get me to a med unit. By then, many of my wounds were nearly healed. I could have had reconstructive surgery; but I figured, why bother? As a career trooper, I most likely would get more scars before I left the service anyway, so I opted to keep them for the time being. I figured once out of the service, I would maybe undergo a procedure to have them all removed at one time. I don't think you will find any women on this ship with more convincing scars."

"You're probably right, there," I responded, "but let me talk to Commander Wabussie before I give you my final decision."

A few hours later I dined with Kala, Kerabac, Commander Wabussie, and Marranalis. As we were finishing up our meal, a young man approached me. I was somewhat taken back by his age, as he didn't appear to be much more than twenty years old. He stood about 1.7 meters and was rather thin — almost to the point of being gangly. His complexion was pale and a lock of jet back hair hung down over one of his blue eyes.

"Honored First Citizen Tibby, I would like to volunteer for your mission."

My first instinct was to say No way, but then a thought hit me. If I didn't believe he was qualified for this mission, what would the likelihood be of anyone else suspecting him of being a spy on a mission?

"And you are?" I queried.

"Ahh…Padaran, sir."

"I don't believe I have seen you before. What are your qualifications and what position do you serve on the NEW ORLEANS?"

"I'm a ship's engineer in training, sir," he said with some pride.

I looked at Kerabac. As Captain of the NEW ORLEANS, he and Stonbersa were the only ones who hired crew for maintaining and operating the ship's equipment. I could see Kerabac contemplating something, but he didn't speak up.

"Padaran, would you mind stepping outside for a moment while I confer with my crew?"

"Ah…certainly, sir," he said eagerly and he turned and stepped outside the dining area.

"Alright, Kerabac, who is he and when did we start having trainees on our crew?"

Kerabac smiled. "Let me answer the last question first. While we have been hiring experienced people, we also have been hiring and training new people since day one — not only for your security forces, but for every discipline in the crew. About the only ones on the ship who haven't required training of some sort are Commodore Stonbersa and Piesew."

"He's got a point there, Tib," Kala said.

"OK, but just where did he come from? He looks like he is barely out of school."

Kerabac chewed on his lip and I noticed that Wabussie was squirming in his chair. "You know something about this, Commander?" Wabussie looked startled at my query.

"Ah, yes, I have some knowledge of it."

"Would someone care to inform me?" I glared at Kerabac.

Kerabac adjusted himself in his chair and quietly said, "He's Admiral Regeny's nephew."

"WHAT?!" I exploded. "When did this happen, and why wasn't I informed?"

"Hold on, Tibby, let me explain. The kid didn't pass the physical standards of height/weight ratio requirements for the military. The kid wanted to get in, but couldn't. Regeny suggested he see if he could sign on the crew with the *NEW ORLEANS* and get some training with us because, as the admiral put it, 'the training on the *NEW ORLEANS* is better than anything you will get with the Federation.' He thought that while serving here, he could benefit from the martial arts training available to all the crew, in addition to the engineering apprentice training. With some hard work and a bit of beefing up in the gym for a year or two, the admiral was certain that he would not only be a prime candidate for the Federation military, but may even present as a good candidate for the Special Ops unit."

"How long has he been here?"

"A few months."

"How is he doing?"

"Surprisingly well. I've talked to the people in engineering and they say he is a natural."

"How's he doing with the martial arts? Marranalis, do you know anything about him?"

"Honestly, Tibby, I have seen him on the ship and I have seen him working out in the gym. He actually looked pretty good, but since I have been concentrating my energies with our security team, I haven't given him a lot of attention."

I tugged on my chin as ideas began formulating in my mind.

"Tib, you aren't seriously thinking about accepting him for this mission, are you?" Kala asked.

"I doubt anyone would think he was a spy, and he certainly doesn't look like anyone that people would pay any attention. Those are the kinds of people we need for this mission. I don't think we could pass him off as a trader crewman, though. I'm just trying to figure out what role he could play as a slave."

"I think I might be able to help you there, Tibby," Kerabac interjected. "Many Ruwallie Rasson have young male slaves like Padaran that they use as domestic servants to serve meals, run errands — all sorts of personal services that they may not want to assign to a female slave or that a female slave is not qualified to do. One other thing in Padaran's favor is that he can sing; he has a great tenor voice. That is something highly prized by the Ruwallie Rasson; and if I can teach him a few of the favored tunes, I think we would be able to pass him off as a domestic slave very convincingly."

I raised my wrist com to my mouth and said, "Padaran, you may come back in now."

Padaran entered with a questioning look on his face. "Before I give you an answer, I want to see you demonstrate your martial arts skills."

"Yes, sir. When do you want me to meet you in the gym?"

"There won't be any gym where we are going, and if we have to engage in combat, it won't be in a gym." I slid my chair back and stood up.

Padaran's eyes widened and he gulped. "You're not going to go up against me yourself, are you?"

"Indeed, I am. Where we're going, you won't be able to pick and choose your adversaries or their abilities."

I suddenly lunged at him, not using a martial arts move, but more of a physical tackle move. Padaran responded properly, stepping back, grabbing my shirt and then stepping to the side as he tugged me in the direction I was already moving. Had I not been prepared for this, I would have lost balance, giving him an advantage. As it was, I grabbed his wrists and pulled him along with me as I dropped, dragging him over the top of me with some leg leverage and sending him flying. I expected to see him land awkwardly on the floor, but he very effectively tucked and rolled, sprang up and land on his feet in a solid defensive position.

I walked toward him in a relaxed pose and smiling, extending my hand as if to congratulate him on a good performance. He appeared to relax for a second. When he did, I grabbed his arm, quickly turning into him and throwing him across my shoulder. I was surprised to feel his hand grab the front of my shirt just as I was letting go of his arm. Before I realized it, he had a hold of my shirt with both hands and pulled me after him.

Now it was my turn to go flying through the air to tuck and roll and spring to my feet. But by then, Padaran was already on his feet and moving in on me. I dropped quickly, grabbed him by the legs as his arms swooped over me, and then heaved upward, throwing him completely off balance. He landed hard on the floor. This time he was not so quick to regain his balance or position, as the wind was knocked out of him. Instantly, I had him in a controlled position from which he could not move.

"Well done, Padaran," I said as I got to my feet and helped him up. From the table, I heard Kerabac and Marranalis applauding.

"Damn, Tibby, the kid's not bad. I never would have expected that from him," Marranalis said.

"Precisely, which is why I think he might be an excellent choice for this mission. Padaran, I've not finalized my choices at this time, but you're high on the list. I'll let you know tomorrow."

Padaran grinned from ear to ear. "Thank you, sir. I promise I won't let you down."

"You've not been chosen just yet, so don't get too excited."

Padaran turned, and I thought for a minute he was going to jump into the air and click his heels. But instead, he adjusted his clothing and sort of strutted out the door, nearly bumping into a lovely, dark-skinned woman who was entering the room. As she approached us, I noted that some of her facial features appeared to be much like Kerabac's, but she was much lighter in complexion and a full head shorter.

"Greetings, Honored First Citizens," she said, nodding to both Kala and myself. In typical Federation fashion, she did not directly address the others, as generally persons in the Federation only addressed the highest-stationed individuals in a group. Since both Kala and I shared the honor of the highest status the Federation bestowed on its citizens, we were both addressed in unison.

"My name is Endina. I wish to present myself to be part of the crew for your undercover mission."

"Greetings, Endina. What role do you think you could best serve on this mission?"

"Sir, I am a trained navigator and also served as a patrol ship pilot with the Federation."

I looked at Kerabac, who seemed to be giving Endina an appraising view. "You appear to have some Ruwallie Rasson ancestry, judging by your appearance."

"Yes, Captain. My grandmother was white and was a slave of a Ruwallie Rasson before slavery ended and the planet joined the Federation. After they became part of the Federation, my grandmother was freed and moved to Aburn. At the time, she was pregnant and gave birth to my father there. He met up with another woman whose mother also had been a Ruwallie Rasson slave freed under the same circumstances. The two of them fell in love and bonded and my brothers and I all share both white and Ruwallie Rasson blood."

"Tibby, she would be a good choice for a crewmember, at least in the eyes of the Ruwallie Rasson. Even though they do not see half-bloods as equals, they do have a certain affinity and affection for them, and generally hire them in their businesses. Having her on the ship as a free member of the crew would be most acceptable, and would appear normal. It would be no problem to pass her off as first officer, pilot, and navigator. Tell me, Endina, how are your combat skills if you needed to use them in a real situation?"

"I am nowhere near the levels of Tibby's security force, but I have served in combat with the Federation at Hugulsa."

"Hugulsa! That where I was shot down and where Reidecor saved me," Kerabac said, turning toward me. "Tell me one thing more, Endina. How cruel can you pretend to be? If you are my second in command on the freighter, it will at times be necessary for you to be responsible for the male slaves and direct their labors when they load and unload cargo. Are you able to appear tough and ruthless and, if required, administer shocks and beatings?"

"Yes, sir, I think I can. I won't like it, but I will do my part."

I rose from my chair and walked over to Endina. "I want you to look as angry as you can and slap me as hard as you can across the face." Endina froze for a moment, and then her face snarled and she slapped me so hard I saw stars for a moment. I had no doubt at all that there was going to be a red mark on my face, and possibly a bruise, as well.

"Uhh, I think she will do, Kerabac. I certainly do not need any more convincing."

Kerabac and everyone at the table were laughing as I rubbed my cheek and took my seat once again.

"Sorry if I hurt you, First Citizen, but you asked me to!" Endina said, placing her hand on my arm.

"No, no, it's quite alright. You did exactly what I asked and your delivery was — um — excellent."

Turning to Kerabac I said, "One thing we will have to do as soon as we finalize the team is to come up with new names for most of us. From now until this mission is over we will have to call each other by those names so we become used to them to the point that the names are automatic. We certainly can't have any one addressing Kala and me as 'First Citizen' on this mission; and 'Kalana' and

'Tibby' are too well known by now. Likewise, your names and feats have also reached this sector of the galaxy."

"Alright, what names do you think we should have?"

"For me, I would suggest 'Tagar.' I can easily remember that, I think, and for Marranalis, 'Ogan' will do nicely. Kalana can be 'Cara.' We won't need to bother with Sokaia or Padaran, as I seriously doubt anyone would know of them."

"I agree, Tibby," Kerabac replied, "and I think we will also have to change your hair color. Your red hair is not that common throughout the galaxy, and people readily identify it with you. I think a dark brown would work better."

By noon the next day, I had thirteen more applicants all wanting to be crewmembers on the freighter. This was by far the safest role in the mission, as the freighter had been outfitted with both an RMFF and a cloaking system. With these systems in place there was little that could be done to harm the ship and its crew; nevertheless, it was not without danger, and we needed the most skilled volunteers for these roles.

It was late in the evening when I received a message from the bridge that we were approaching the rendezvous point with the *MIZBAGONA* and that we had received a message from Captain Felenna confirming their arrival. The reunion was pleasant. Captain Felenna had played a crucial role in the defeat of the Brotherhood at Alle Bamma, even though she had once been a member of the Brotherhood herself. She had seen their darker side and switched her allegiance in order to help end the enslavement of the natives and the production of the drug, God's Sweat, which the Brotherhood produced there. I chose to assign Felenna as Captain of the *MIZBAGONA* and left her in charge of a small fleet of ships to protect the planet and prevent the Brotherhood from regaining a hold there. Although it was later than the normal dining hour, I had the evening meal for our officers withheld until her arrival so a shuttle bring Felenna to the *NEW ORLEANS* to dine with us and discuss the recent developments. Commodore Stonbersa, Kala, and I met her in the hangar area. "Captain Felenna, it's great to see you again," I said.

"Honored First Citizens," she replied, nodding toward Kala and I, "and Commodore, it's a delight to see you again and to be aboard the *NEW ORLEANS* once more."

"Always an honor, Captain," Stonbersa replied. "Won't you come this way? We've prepared a meal in the Starlight dining area with most of the senior officers."

"It's always a pleasure to dine aboard the *NEW ORLEANS*," Felenna responded.   "While the food on the *MIZBAGONA* is excellent, it doesn't compare to the exquisite meals here. So tell me, Tibby, what's this mission all about and how can I be of assistance? The message I received was somewhat cryptic."

"All in good time, Captain. Right now, let's proceed to the dining room. It's easier to brief everyone at once."

"Ahh, yes…that's something I am coming to understand. I never realized how much work it was to be a captain of a ship, let alone be responsible for a squadron of ships, until you left me in charge at Alle Bamma."

"Indeed, Captain," Stonbersa interjected, "I've seen the reports you have sent me, and I am most impressed with how well you have been handing matters there. I understand that you had a few Brotherhood ships attempt to sneak back to the planet after our encounters there, but that you successfully resisted them."

"It was hardly much of an encounter. To be honest, I think they were unaware of the events at Alle Bamma and were returning as part of their routine route to pick up more God's Sweat, only to find us there barring their access to the planet. There never was any real danger to us or any of our ships."

We arrived in the dining area just as Felenna finished commenting on her fleet's patrol of Alle Bamma. Piesew directed us to our seats, placing me at the head of the table with Commodore Stonbersa to my right and Captain Felenna to my left. Captain Kerabac was also there, seated next to Commodore Stonbersa, having left the bridge in charge of a first officer while we dined. Kala sat at the far end of the table opposite me; Marranalis, Cantolla, and A'Lappe were also present.

"Well, Tibby, we all are here now," Felenna began. "I don't imagine you brought me all this way just to have dinner. What new adventure have you gotten into and just how can I help?"

"I'm not sure how much information our team has passed on to you, but I'll start with telling you that a solbidyum shipment intended for the planet Duepras was intercepted and we believe it was taken outside the Federation territories. Our intelligence sources tell us it was originally a Brotherhood plan to steal the solbidyum. They managed to get the coordinates from their infiltrated sources inside the Federation; however, they made the mistake of letting a pirate smuggler named Logden know about their intentions — either accidently or perhaps as part of a plan to use him somehow in their theft operation. Regardless of the situation, Logden decided to beat them to the solbidyum and took it for himself. Now we and the Brotherhood are both looking for him. We have every reason to believe he is holed up on Ryken, Yentum or Goo'Waddle. The Brotherhood has amassed as many ships and men as they can to patrol the region. They're detaining every ship that departs from these planets for a thorough search before being allowed to pass. The Federation doesn't want to start a war by going into territory that is not part of the Federation, so the admiral has asked us to go in covertly do what we can to recover the solbidyum."

"I see," Felenna said, "and just how do I fit into this plan?"

"I want the *MIZBAGONA* there as a backup warship. A'Lappe will make some minor modifications to the RMFF and improve the speed of the *MIZBAGONA* and its fighter and patrol ships. He will also install some upgrades the shielding and cloaking systems of your smaller spacecraft. Our combined fleets and firepower will make us stronger than anything out here and will nearly eliminate any danger to our crews.

"I had also thought about possibly using you as part of an undercover team that will be visiting the planets' surfaces. Your knowledge of the Brotherhood and their ways would certainly be useful. But I have decided against that idea. The chance that stories of your desertion and participation in events at Alle Bamma have reached the area and the risk of you being recognized by Brotherhood members puts you at too high a risk. All it would take is for one Brotherhood member to identify you and everything would be blown. Nevertheless, your knowledge of the Brotherhood and their operations can help us immensely. When the time comes, we will return with the solbidyum, at which time I may need you to help take out as many Brotherhood ships as possible when we leave this area and return to Federation space.

"Tell me, have you ever heard of a Brotherhood member named Shydak?"

Felenna's eyes widened and she stiffened when I said the name. "Yes, everyone in the Brotherhood has heard of him. He's a hardcore member, with a real hatred for the Federation. Are we going up against him?"

"Possibly. We know that he was part of the planned operation to steal the solbidyum. The Brotherhood planned to use the funds from the sale of the solbidyum to finance the construction of a large order of new warships. Logden's theft of the solbidyum has put a real hurt on the

Brotherhood's coffers, as they had ships on order at the Gaimseian shipyard and now can't make the payments. Last we heard, Shydak was headed there to work out some sort of arrangement or, more likely, to intimidate the Gaimseians into submission. After our covert raid there to recover the Mirage Fighter stolen by the Brotherhood and the subsequent damage we inflicted on their shipyard, I don't think the Gaimseians will be too receptive when he arrives."

"From what I have heard of Shydak, he's not one to run away from a fight. If you manage to recover the solbidyum and he discovers you have it, he will pursue you as long as he has a ship to do so," Felenna replied between bites of food.

"Good. I hope he does! Once we have the solbidyum, I hope he brings every ship in the Brotherhood to pursue us — it will make it easier for us to destroy their fleet."

During the rest of the meal, I outlined the plans to Felenna and my crew. The *MIZBAGONA* would be shielded, cloaked and positioned on one side of the sector of space wherein Ryken, Yentum and Goo'Waddle were located and the *NEW ORLEANS* would remained cloaked and shielded on the other side — just in case Logden tried to make a run for it. If necessary, the two starships would have to take out any Brotherhood ships trying to stop Logden while also making sure he didn't get away.

Kerabac outlined the plan to be followed by the surface team and Felenna clued us in on methods commonly used among Brotherhood members to identify each other, as well as other habits and operational methods they followed. It was going to be much easier to spot them outside the Federation, as they operated openly here in the same way that the Ruwallie Rasson did.

After dining, I met with Kala, Kerabac and Marranalis in one of the smaller conference rooms to finalize the list of people we would be using for the covert surface missions.   It was decided that Kala, Sokaia, Marranalis, Padaran and I would be the ones posing as Kerabac's slaves. Endina and Norkoda, as well as seven other crewmembers, would pose as crewmembers onboard the freighter with Kerabac. A meeting was set up to fully brief all candidates early the next morning and begin preparations. We were about to end the meeting, when I decided to call on our invisible guest.

"A'Lappe, do you have something you would like to contribute before we break up?" I had detected that ever-so-faint cedar scent in the air that always alerted me to his presence. Suddenly, A'Lappe appeared in our midst, giving me one of those *How do you do it?* stares.

"Honored First Citizens," he said with a nod in our direction, "I think I may have something that will make your mission preparations a little less painful. At least, I hope so." From a bag he had slung over his shoulder, he produced a small device about the half the size of the palm of my hand. "This should allow you to create convincing bruises without having to injure yourselves severely by actually getting beaten. If I may demonstrate."

He walked over to Padaran and placed the object on his arm. Padaran instinctively started to pull his arm back. "No need to fear, Padaran, you will not feel any pain." A'Lappe pressed a button on the side of the object. There was a slight humming sound. After about five seconds, A'Lappe removed the object to reveal a nasty-looking reddish-purple bruise.

"Wow," Padaran exclaimed, "that didn't hurt at all."

Marranalis looked at Padaran's arm closely. "How long will that last? Will it wash off?"

"It will last as long as any other bruise lasts," A'Lappe replied. "It's a real bruise; it won't wash off. This device causes small capillaries under the skin to rupture and create the bruise; but unlike a bruise sustained in a fight or a beating, you won't have any of the stiffness or pain. Your normal reaction time and movements will be unaffected, so you will not be compromised if you have to get into a fight. You can use these devices to apply appropriate-looking bruises as needed."

"A'Lappe, you're a genius," Kerabac said with a look of relief. "It truly bothered me to imagine my friends having to suffer blows to get bruised up for this mission."

"This isn't going to do away with the possibility that, at times, you and others in the crew may have to strike or beat us for the sake of show," I interjected.

"I know, Tibby, but at least it won't be a daily beating session."

"I also have something else for the slaves," added A'Lappe. "At the moment, your hands and feet are too soft to be those of slaves — at least those of the men, anyway. I have a lotion to be applied to your hands and feet once a day before going to bed. Use it as long as you're on this mission and you will have tough calluses that will make you look like you've been toiling as a slave for years. One more thing," he said while producing from his bag a rather haggard-looking wrist communicator. "All the slaves will need wrist communicators linked to Kerabac as your master, so he can provide you with commands when you are out of his sight. These devices will perform that function in the normal sense, but they have other hidden capabilities. Keep in mind that, because of their small size, these are very limited functions that are available to you only once before recharging.

"There is a cloaking mechanism, but it will work only for a duration of approximately three minutes; after that, it's done. There also is a weak but deadly laser feature; it also has only a one-time functionality. Now, I'm afraid it's an either-or situation; if you use the cloak, you have no laser, and if you use the laser, you have no cloaking capability. I simply cannot cram enough power into a com this small with all the other functions and give you both.

There is one more item — a built-in solbidyum detector. If you get within a meter of the solbidyum, it will begin to vibrate.

If you do use the laser or the cloaking feature of the wrist com, you can recharge it on the ship using a standard com recharger. It will take twice as long to recharge it as it does a normal wrist com. I would suggest you only use this as a last means of defense."

"This is great, A'Lappe," I said. "Thank you."

He beamed at me, and then leaned close to me and softly said, "I still want to know how you know when I'm around!"

The next day, we made a stop at a nearby planet called Malninal, a small planet with a slightly lesser gravity than Megelleon. This was last planet inside the Federation boundary before crossing into the space around Ryken, Yentum and Goo'Waddle. After a lengthy discussion we agreed that the best cargo to carry on the freighter for trade would be rare and exotic liquors sought by the thirsty inhabitants of these planets; there were some liquors that simply could not be simulated in a synthesizer.

"Liquor trade will give us a good excuse to visit the many bars and drinking establishments on the planet without being conspicuous," Kerabac said. "Though I do not like the idea of it, we might also see if we can't make a trade with a Brotherhood dealer for some God's Sweat, as well. On most planets outside the Federation territories, it's not an illegal substance, and the demand is still plenty high. Having it onboard as a possible trade product will further remove us from suspicion as spies or Federation operatives. We would not actually have to resell the cargo; we'd only have it among our goods so it appears that it's for trade. After our mission is complete, of course, we'll destroy it."

"I'm not sure I like that idea," I replied, "but I certainly can see where it might be useful in giving us some credibility. Let's try to hold off on that idea and only consider it as a last resort. Kerabac and Piesew, see if you can put together a shopping list of rare vintages of wines and liquors that will likely be in demand. Don't shy away from the good stuff — with my immense wealth, we can fill the cargo hold of the freighter two-thirds full with all sorts of choice items that are certain to be highly sought after."

Kerabac thought a moment. "We may want to create a dummy story about a raid on a liquor supply warehouse at one of the Federation planets near the border. The news will quickly make its way to the planets by way of the traders. Many would believe we fenced the heist; but they won't do anything about it, as we'll be outside the Federation jurisdiction. However, the rumors surrounding our cargo will go a long way toward the goal of creating a gritty image of our group, and should help to alleviate any suspicion as to our true intentions."

"I like that idea.   See to getting it done," I responded.

During the next three days, we found time to practice and train for our mission. Kerabac and A'Lappe located some exotic liquors and had them stocked aboard the *RASSON BEDAN*, the new name for the freighter. A'Lappe and Kerabac had managed to provide very authentic blast markings to the hull to lend the appearance of damage from a recent firefight. Also, many of the original parts on the ship had been swapped out for efficient, though obviously second generation equipment that gave some provenance to the ship being a true trader's vessel that relied on whatever parts were available on the outer worlds.

Quarters on the vessel were clean but oddly decorated, to the obvious tastes of their individual occupants. Several small sparse cells were set up in the cargo hold area for the male slaves; each had a toilet facility and a plain bunk and nothing else. The women slaves were, for obvious intentions, meant to stay in Kerabac's cabin. A sofa-like seat occupied a portion of Kerabac's cabin, and he made it clear that he would sleep there, if visitors happened to be aboard, and Kalana and Sokaia would use the bed. Otherwise, he would use a spare bunk in an unused cabin.

The last issue we had to deal with was currency. Inside the Federation, hard currency was seldom seen and transactions were completed by way of Federation credits that were transferred electronically; but outside the Federation such credits were worthless. Instead, coins of various weights and worth were used and their values were based on current metal prices. One of the principal currencies was a metal called durtronium and another commonly used in this sector was maxalite. There was also another form of currency that consisted of small standard electronic chip components used in practically everything. Exactly what they were or how they worked was a complete mystery to me; but Kerabac and A'Lappe assured me that having just one or two of these small chip coins were a great wealth outside the Federation.

We loaded up with several million credits' worth of these currencies, which were kept in a safe inside Kerabac's cabin. A'Lappe and Kerabac checked out the cloaking device, the new engine and the RMFF upgrades. All were pronounced to be in working order.

It was on our third day that our sensors picked up the signal of a large warship ahead of us near Ryken. Before long, a second and third ship appeared on the screens. While under cloak, we slipped inside the protective ring and moved in closer to the planet. As we approached one of the moons of the planet, we decloaked just long enough for the *RASSON BEDAN* to disembark. Then, just as quickly, the *NEW ORLEANS* cloaked again, leaving the *RASSON BEDAN* apparently alone near the moon. To anyone observing on long-range sensor vid screens, it would just seem that the *RASSON BEDAN* suddenly came into range of their sensors and that there were no other ships in the area. Once clear of the *NEW ORLEANS*, Kerabac gave the orders and Norkoda guided the *RASSON BEDAN* toward Ryken's largest city and spaceport.

We secured a landing space and touched down. Kerabac paid the landing fees and took care of all the paperwork. He, Norkoda, and two others from the ship then went into the city on the pretext of trying to find buyers for our cargo. This followed a typical pattern for an arriving trader vessel. The rest of the crew and those of us assuming the role of slaves stayed onboard until we were needed.

Kala and Sokaia monitored local news and communication channels with the hope of picking up useful information, but the only news of any real interest was the embargo that the Brotherhood had around the planet and the outrage it was causing globally. Clearly, the Brotherhood was not held in high esteem with the population at the moment, but they had the muscle to enforce their agenda and continue their actions without resistance. Though ships were being detained for inspections, no one was denied exit from the system, once their ship had been cleared by the Brotherhood. The fact that none of the cargos of the detained ships were being taken made the situation marginally tolerable, even if the intimidation and delays were infuriating for the traders and other travelers. Rumors abounded on the news; the most popular broadcast related frequent updates regarding the Brotherhood's search for a man named Logden, who was said to have cheated the Brotherhood in some contractual agreement. The Brotherhood was offering a 1 million credit reward for anyone turning Logden in alive or to anyone who provided information leading to his capture.

While we waited, Kala saw to dyeing my hair a dark brown. She then gave me a pill that A'Lappe had provided, assuring me that it would cause future hair growth for the next few weeks to be of the same dark shade. I had not trimmed or cut my hair since leaving the estate, and it was beginning to look a bit ragged; but to appear as an authentic slave, it would be better if it were still longer. I had also allowed a stubble of beard to grow on my face; Kala applied dye to that as well. By the time she finished, I barely recognized myself.

Using the device A'Lappe provided, Kala applied bruises to Marranalis, Padaran and me. These marks would go away gradually, like any normal bruise, and every few days we would need to create new ones to make it appear that we were being beaten regularly. Marranalis and I took on most of the bruises, while Padaran was only given one large bruise on his face, which is where a house slave would most likely be struck. They generally received fewer beatings than the hard labor slaves. Kala and Sokaia took turns helping each other make their hair look less cared for; they too applied bruises to each other, and by the time we all were finished, we looked like a pretty sad and beaten lot.

Kerabac had been gone quite a while, but we were not concerned, as we expected it might take time before he would be able to make some connections. It was possible it might be a day or more before he returned to the ship. He would need to visit a lot of bars and clubs to start seeding his stories and rumors. In the meantime, Norkoda had been moving about the planet, pretending that he was trying to acquire goods for trade. All the while, he was listening in to the local conversations to see what information he might glean as to the location of Logden and the solbidyum. It was in the wee hours of the morning on the second day when Norkoda returned to the ship.

"We weren't expecting you back so soon," I said, once he was aboard and the ship was sealed.

"I hadn't planned on returning so soon, but I have information I think you need to hear."

While I was not good at reading facial features on Nibarians, it was obvious that he was greatly concerned about what he had discovered. We went to the galley area, which also served as the planning room, so he could relate to us what he had discovered. Kerabac was still out, and we had no idea when he might return. I felt it best to find out as much as we could and as soon as possible. I called all available crewmembers, save for Padaran. He was on watch at the moment, but would still be able to hear and see the meeting from the vid screen on the bridge. Once everyone aboard had gathered, I asked Norkoda to present his report.

"I went to a number of trade warehouses to look for goods. I really heard very little, until I came upon one storage depot stocked with a number of bales of God's Sweat arranged on pallets in a back corner. Six men were loading the bales onto a small transport, when suddenly a man came in and everyone stopped working as soon the man began to speak. I was not able to hear their conversation at first, but then I heard one man say something to the newcomer — I heard the name 'Shydak.'

"I was able to place a bugging device with a sound amplifier where I was standing so I could move away from their area while pretending to look at other goods. I was able to pick up and record the remainder of their conversation. Later, after they finished loading their cargo and departed from the depot bay, I recovered the recording device. Here," he said. He pulled out the recorder and activated the playback as he sat it on the table. "I think you should hear this for yourself."

A gruff voice could be heard on the recording. "...found no sign of him here. He's not on Ryken. If he were, some Vorgovian slime slug would have heard something and would be clamoring to take the reward. A lot of people seem to be looking for him, but no one is finding anything. Shydak gave me the name of a fellow he says is a fairly reliable source, if you have enough money to loosen his tongue. He says this guy claims he knew someone who sold Logden an old beat-up transport a few days ago, and that Logden acted like he was in a big hurry to go someplace. All this happened on Goo'Waddle — and

Logden picked up the ship two days later. Shydak's contact didn't know whether Logden had left Goo'Waddle, but it was the next day when we showed up and set up the blockade of all ships leaving the area. It's doubtful that Logden could have made it out of the system with that old transport he bought, as it didn't have that kind of range."

"So then he's got to be on one of the three planets here," another of the men said.

"He'd better be," the first speaker continued. "Shydak says our arrangements with the Tottalax are contingent on us having that solbidyum in hand when they arrive. No solbidyum, and they may just turn on us instead of joining with us to wipe out the Federation."

"I don't get it," a third individual interrupted. "Why are we trying to make a treaty with the Tottalax?"

"Why? You idiot! We have about a thousand ships to go up against the Federation. We can't match them on our own; and while the Federation doesn't know how many ships we have, it doesn't really matter, because nothing we have can go up against their starships and survive. Especially now that we know most of them have cloaking devices and protective shields. The Tottalax have starships equal in size to the Federation's, and their ships have a super-tough alloy skin that seems to resist everything thrown at them. Plus, they have hundreds of thousands of warships. We also hear they have some nerve beam weapon that can penetrate an RMFF shield and render the crews of a Federation ship helpless. We need the Tottalax for our invasion of the Federation to succeed!"

"How do we know we can trust them? Why would they want to help us and then not turn around and do us in, too, so they can take over the Federation instead of letting us have it?"

"Because, idiot, they're amphibians. They only want worlds that are mostly aquatic and have a temperate climate. Plus, the seas of the planets they are able to inhabit must have specific water conditions to ensure their survival and breeding — most planets in the Federation are too dry for them or their seas are chemically wrong. The Brotherhood doesn't care about the aquatic worlds, so we'll let them have those. Besides, the Tottalax need us to supply them with God's Sweat. So far, we are the only ones who know where it comes from. Since we're growing it and since we control the market, we also control anyone hooked on God's Sweat. As long as we hold that card, the Tottalax will do as we wish."

"I don't get it. God's Sweat is an addictive drug for humans; it's not addictive to them Tottalaxes, so why do they want it?"

"Shydak says God's Sweat acts like an aphrodisiac on the Tottalax females. Normally they're only interested in sex during their seasonal mating time, but the males always want sex. God's Sweat makes the females receptive to sex all the time. Now, get this shit loaded. Tomorrow we need to head over to Goo'Waddle to see if we can pick up Logden's trail!"

Norkoda turned off the recording and stared at us briefly while we digested what we had just heard.

"Who are the Tottalax?" I asked. "I've never heard anyone mention them before."

"I never heard of them before today, either," Norkoda said, "but I did look them up in the computer and there is a brief mention of them. They are a race quite a ways outside the Federation territory. Not a lot is known about them. They have been encountered a few times by traders, but trade with them has been very limited. They appear to be a mostly aquatic culture, like these guys were saying. They are said to be amphibians, capable of breathing both water and air, but they prefer to be underwater most of the time. According to the individuals alleged to have met them, their ships are filled with water and no human has ever been aboard one. Even when they are out in the open air, they have a breathing apparatus that sprays a constant mist of water on their gills to keep them wet. They need a near 98% humidity to remain in the open air for long. How they ever got interested in star travel and made it into space is an interesting question to me. We know next to nothing about their government or customs, and the Federation has no records of any Federation delegations visiting their home world or studying their kind. In fact, their exact location in the galaxy isn't recorded in Federation files, so we have no idea just where their home world is located."

"From the way the recorded conversation sounds, it would seem they are located on this side of the galaxy someplace. How did the Brotherhood ever get in contact with them, I wonder?"

"I did a little discreet snooping among the local traders by asking whether they had any Tottalax goods to trade. Not one of them had ever even heard of the race, so they obviously can't be too terribly close to this area."

"I really don't like any of this. I think you'd better prepare a report and get it off to Commander Wabussie. Also copy Commodore Stonbersa and Captain Felenna. I wonder whether Felenna may have heard something about these Tottalax while she was a Brotherhood member. Hopefully some of the FSO agents can get more info, but in the meantime, Wabussie can notify the admiralty so they can begin making some sort of plans to deal with this crisis."

After Norkoda left to prepare a report to Commander Wabussie, Sokaia approached me. "Sir, what do you make of the mention of a weapon that can penetrate the RMFF shields and disable the crews?"

"Honestly, Lieutenant Commander, I have no idea what to make of it. What does disable mean? Are they rendered unconscious, immobile, convulsive? I wish we knew more so we could investigate some way to defend against them and this technology. And how do they know it's effective against an RMFF unless they have already tried it? But as long as they can't actually get into the ship or destroy it, we have some consolation. Still, it could be devastating, if they are able to incapacitate Federation ships and proceed unchallenged to inner planets where they can destroy or attack and pillage without any resistance. I wish there was some way for us to find out more about this weapon before we actually encounter it. We need to know more about these Tottalax — the size of their military and its strength, their home world location, and whether negotiation with them is possible. The last thing the Federation needs is for the Brotherhood to form an alliance with some major military power."

An hour later I was sparring with Marranalis in the cargo hold, when Kerabac returned, beaming. "I think I have found a way to gain the credibility and reputation we want to draw Logden out."

Marranalis and I halted our action and turned to face him. "Let's hear it," I said.

"I was trying to unload some of our liquor on local club owner, a man named Howebim, when he asked if we were going to Goo'Waddle. I said it was our next stop. He said he had a package that needed to be delivered there; and if we would transport it, we'd be paid well upon delivery. From the way he was acting, I get the idea it's not something exactly legal, and the amount he's saying we'd be paid is definitely above the going rate.

"We're sure to be challenged by the Brotherhood on the trip over; and if we refuse to yield for a search and they fire on us, and we activate the cloaking device as soon as their shots hit the RMFF shield, it will look like we were destroyed somehow. When we arrive at Goo'Waddle with the goods — after it's been reported that we were destroyed — our credibility of being able to get by the Brotherhood's blockades will be solidly established."

"That sounds good. As it turns out, while you were gone, Norkoda picked up another lead that Logden may be

on Goo'Waddle. At least, that's where he was last reported.
Any idea what the cargo might be that Howebim wants you
to deliver?" I asked.

"The parcel is rather small, from what he told me; I
suspect it may be gemstones mined and cut here on Ryken.
The mining consortium here controls the gemstones that
leave the planet and the local government taxes independent
miners heavily for stones not sold through the consortium.
The consortium has a strong lobby within the government."

"That sounds a lot like the diamond trade back on
Earth," I said. "So how is this all supposed to take place?"

Kerabac grinned. "Well, it's going to start with you
and Marranalis loading several liquor pallets onto the
delivery vehicle outside. Then you'll ride in the back, we'll
take the ladies with us, and we'll make a big scene
delivering the liquor to the club. If all goes as I hope,
Howebim will give us his package to transport. He's going
to want to make sure we don't steal whatever it is, so I
suspect he's going to insist that I wear a courier secure
band."

"A what?" I asked.

"A courier secure band. It's an explosive device
usually worn on the wrist. If I get out of range of the signal
stream he sends out between here and Goo'Waddle, the
device will blow me to bits. This also applies if I fail to
make the delivery in time. Once it's activated, I would be
expected to make the delivery within a set period, most
likely three or four days. If I or the package get out of range
of his signal, a countdown clock starts ticking and I have
about ten minutes to correct my path and get back on track,
or it's kaboom!"

"Doesn't sound like any jewelry I would want to
wear!" Kala interjected. I turned to see her walking toward
us. She had apparently caught the tail end of the
conversation.

Kerabac laughed. "No, I don't think you would. The Ruwallie Rasson often employ a similar device for recaptured runaway slaves. It might not be a bad idea to make up a similar-looking dummy device that we could put on Tibby and Marranalis' collars to make them appear less-than-willing slaves."

"I think you're right. Let's do it," I said. "I still don't like the idea of us carrying this unknown package, though. We have no idea what it might be. If it's a simple gem-smuggling operation, I don't mind, but if it's something that could harm others, it causes me great concern."

"It's highly unlikely it's anything like that. The governments on these outer planets are relatively loose. Big business and large mining and agricultural cartels are the ones that really run things, and they tightly regulate prices and the movement of goods. This creates a real opportunity for a black market for most items and goods, but the harsh methods used by the cartels to deal with those that get caught make it a very dangerous business. The cartels have their own patrol ships and police forces that search for contraband. They stop and search ships regularly and even cooperate with other cartels by reporting when they find something that impacts another cartel's areas of interest."

"So if I were smuggling gems and was stopped by a fruit grower's cartel who found the gems during their search, they would report me to the mining consortium?" I asked.

"Not only would they report you, they would detain you until mining consortiums' security forces showed up. There are actually inter-cartel agreements that outline protocols for reporting anything they discover."

"What happens to those who are caught?"

"It could be almost anything, depending on whose goods you're trying to smuggle. Sometimes you may get away with a severe beating; other times they may trash your ship and leave you helpless on a derelict craft; or they may seize you and your crew to be sold as slaves. They have even been known to cut off an arm or leg, or blind you in one eye… or, if you cross them on a bad day, they may just blow up your ship with you on it."

"And the local government doesn't intervene?" I asked, somewhat dumbfounded.

"No, not really. Without the cartels' money and backing, the local governments couldn't survive at all. As it is, the local governments provide little more than a police force to quell domestic problems and control the people. They maintain the spaceports and some streets and a few of the utilities within the cities and they keep a small military presence as a defensive force. But, for the most part, the government is a puppet to the cartels. The water and sanitation systems are independent and cartel-run, as are the medical facilities on the planets within this system. Each cartel operates their own banking system and, if you work for a cartel, you use only the bank of your employer. They do, however, allow pawn shops to exist and operate independently. Of course, if you don't work for a cartel but are lucky enough to have some money, any of the cartel banks will gladly take your money. But you won't get terms as good as cartel members do. We'll need to open an account with at least one cartel bank here, if we wish to do business. I would suggest that we open accounts with two separate rival cartels; that way, if we should get on the bad side of one and they freeze our funds, we will still be able to draw on the other."

"This all sounds barbaric to me," Kala said.

"You have no idea just how barbaric, but you're about to find out," Kerabac said.

Up until this moment in my life, since leaving Earth, I had not been on the surface of very many planets. Megelleon, Alle Bamma, Plosaxen and Gaimse were the few where I had actually set foot. Of those, only Alle Bamma was a non-aligned planet and was most certainly of a primitive nature. I think I was expecting Ryken to be similar to Federation planets, only less sophisticated and organized. What I encountered when we left the ship was an assortment of things ranging from the primitive to the ultra-modern. Vehicles of all types, styles and models moved about the spaceport landing area, loading and unloading cargo. An ultra-modern conveyance might be parked at one ship to unload goods, while next to it an animal-drawn cart and human slaves were loading another. Ships of all types and condition also lined the spaceport. Some were sleek and modern, and others looked like composites of junk that barely looked capable of flying even a short distance. Compared to the other ships at the spaceport, the *RASSON BEDAN* appeared to be slightly above the middle range in style and condition — certainly nothing that would draw any special attention.

"Alright, you lazy bastards, get to it and load these crates on the truck!" Endina yelled at Marranalis and me, as she stood poised in the cargo hold doorway with her hands on her hips. "Be careful with those crates — you break a single bottle and I'll break your skulls…"

"Damn, she's good," Marranalis muttered under his breath as we began transferring the cargo to the truck.

"Let's just hope it convinces any onlookers that we're just a bunch of sorry slaves doing our jobs," I said.

Under normal circumstances, selling our cargo to bars and clubs would never pay the expenses for the operations of a ship and crew like the *RASSON BEDAN*; but the likelihood of anyone paying close attention to our activities or checking up on our transactions was slim. Anyone looking our way would witness Kerabac doing business with local merchants and businesses; beyond that no one would be interested how much or little we were actually making or selling.

The ride into the city to make the delivery was an eye-opener as well. The truck was a rental from a local shipping company, who also provided the driver. Endina rode in the cab of the truck and gave him directions as we moved through the city. Marranalis and I were required to ride in the back of the truck with the cargo. Endina had given us strict warnings in front of the driver: "Don't even think about taking a sip of that liquor. If I see even a single bottle with a broken seal when we arrive, I will peel the skins off both of you in thin strips until there's none left." Her delivery was so well performed that even the driver looked scared — and he wasn't even a slave.

Kerabac, Kala, Sokaia and Padaran preceded us in a luxury conveyance, as would be typical for any self-important Ruwallie Rasson trader and slave owner. Marranalis and I were free to look at the sights from the back of the truck as we navigated the dusty streets of the city. Perhaps the term 'street' is a bit misleading, as the real streets were segmented through various parts of the city. The areas controlled by various cartels were obvious; those sectors were finished with paved streets, sidewalks and street illumination. Modern buildings surrounded by landscaping gave the appearance of affluence here; but just as quickly as we entered cartel territory we passed into an adjacent neighborhood webbed with dirt paths for roads, rundown shacks and dilapidated buildings. Some appeared to be abandoned; but amid the shadows were forms moving about, indicating that these decrepit areas were indeed inhabited. Before long we made another turn to find ourselves once again on a paved street lined with business establishments.

At one point I noted several naked women chained to a wall outside one building. I commented to Marranalis about it and he explained that they were slave prostitutes, who were displayed on the street to draw in clients. As we progressed farther along the street, the business establishments became more attractive and sophisticated.

We came to a sudden stop. Endina got out of the truck and walked ahead to Kerabac's conveyance. The two of them spoke for a moment before she returned, after which our driver pulled the truck around Kerabac's vehicle and into a small alleyway behind a building. We waited there several minutes before a door opened at the back of the building. A rather large man exited, followed by Kerabac and his female slaves, Kala and Sokaia, who were naked from the waist up and otherwise clad in only short skirts. I assumed the man was Howebim; I could hear him talking as the group approached.

"So let's see how good this stuff really is," Howebim said.

"It's the very best," Kerabac said, his white teeth gleaming in the sun.

"Hmmph, we'll see about that."

"You! Tagar! Bring one of those cases here and open it!"

For the briefest of moments, I forgot that "Tagar" was me. Then, realizing I was supposed to be doing something, I acted somewhat sullen as I shuffled to the stacks to pick up a case.

"MOVE!" Kerabac snarled, "Or you'll feel the shock of your collar!"

I moved a little faster, sliding the case closer to the edge of the truck. Then I ripped open the cover and retreated to my corner. Kerabac moved forward and removed a bottle, handing it to Howebim. He held the bottle up to the light and peered into the amber liquid as though by sight alone he could taste the liquor inside.

"It looks like the real thing, but there's only one way to verify whether this is authentic."

"Go ahead and taste it," Kerabac said. "It's pure Andarian whiskey — the best there is — and I'm willing to sell it to you at 30% below what your usual suppliers here do."

"Thirty percent?! You must have stolen this to be selling it at that price," he said as he removed the cap, "…

not that I care, as long as the stuff is real." Howebim waved the open bottle under his nose before lifting it to his lips.

"Ahh, by the stars, that's the best damn liquor I've ever tasted. How many cases you got here on the truck?"

"Twenty," Kerabac said.

"I'll take them all. You got anymore besides these?"

"I'm afraid not," Kerabac lied, as the remaining supply would be needed for later trades.

"Damn shame," Howebim said, smacking his lips as he took another sip. "I'd've bought every bottle you had at this price. Have your slaves carry the cases inside; one of my men will direct them to the liquor storage. While they're doing that, I'll get you your money.

"You mentioned to me when you were here earlier that you are heading to Goo'Waddle next. Is that still your plan?" Howebim turned toward the door as Kerabac followed.

"Yes, it is," Kerabac said.

"Would you be interested in making a little more money? I have something that needs to be delivered there," Howebim said. "I'd like you to take a package to my brother, Agama. I'll pay you nicely for your services, if you can manage to keep anyone from learning that you're a courier for me…if you know what I mean."

Howebim and Kerabac entered the door where one of Howebim's men stood by, waiting for Marranalis and me to bring in the cases.

"Alright, you lazy rothsnide mongrels, you heard the man. He wants these cases inside. Get your asses moving," Endina yelled. "And so help me, if you break a bottle…!"

Marranalis and I carried the cases inside and followed Howebim's man to a storage room stocked nearly full of cases of liquor. We were directed as to where to stack the cases, as Howebim's man glared at us. I tried to look bored and downtrodden, as I carried out my task, all the while trying to take note of the contents of the room. While the majority of it seemed be liquor and other spirits, I noted several boxes of what appeared to be rocks tucked away in a dark corner. I suspected that they were probably crude gem rocks from one of the local mines and that, as Kerabac suggested, Howebim was acquiring and smuggling the gems to his brother on Goo'Waddle.

Marranalis and I returned to the truck and Endina instructed us to get in the back and wait. A few moments passed before Howebim and Kerabac returned with Kala and Sokaia in tow. Another man behind Kerabac was carrying a small box about a half-meter square that he placed in the back of the truck with Marranalis and me.

"Don't let anything happen to this box. Got it?" Kerabac growled at us.

"Yes," both Marranalis and I mumbled, our eyes downcast.

"You sure you won't sell me this one?" Howebim said, as I looked up to see him stroking Kala's breast. It took every measure of restraint I could muster to keep from leaping out of the truck and flattening him. Kala had her eyes averted and was looking up with a look of disgust on her face.

"No," Kerabac said with what I could tell was a forced grin. "In spite of her insolence, this one is my favorite; I wouldn't sell her at five times what you already offered."

"Pity," Howebim muttered. "I could make a fortune renting her out to some of my clients. Oh, well. I'm still getting a good deal on the liquor; and if you deliver this package successfully, I may consider using your services to complete other similar deliveries. Just make sure you get it to my brother, Agama, by the deadline, as you promised — and without anyone knowing about it."

"You can count on that." Kerabac lifted his arm, displaying the secured courier wristband.

"Yeah, that's what the last courier said that I hired. He's no longer with us."

The trip back to the ship was uneventful, though I did note several places that appeared to be walled communities with guarded gates. Through the gates I saw large homes and well-groomed grounds; it was obvious that those who lived inside these boundaries lived a far different lifestyle from those on the outside. It made me think of my own incredible wealth. In spite of the enormous wealth of these extremely powerful cartels, I could buy this entire planet and many more like it. I pondered whether I was as guilty as they were in living the lifestyle I did, while others in the galaxy lived in conditions that were even poorer than what I was seeing here. While I slept free in my own bed on my own ship or my sprawling estate, there were people out here suffering in terrible, unspeakable conditions —many living their entire lives in the chains of forced labor and slavery, like the prostitutes we observed earlier.

"It's not the same," Marranalis said, as though reading my mind.

"Pardon?" I said.

"It's not the same thing — your wealth and what you do with it compared to what you see here. You try to help people every way you can. You create jobs and share not only your wealth but your glories and triumphs as well. What you see here is nothing like what you have, what you do or what you represent. You fought on behalf of the natives of Alle Bamma to free them from bondage — you didn't enslave them. You have seen to it that the Federation planets are getting their solbidyum — you haven't hoarded or controlled its distribution to your favored associates. It's different, Tibby."

"How did you know that's what I was thinking about?" I asked, somewhat dumbfounded.

"We've been together a good while now. I've seen you deal with untold crises, both personal and universal, and I know pretty well now how you feel and how you react to things. Your immense wealth is uncomfortable; lesser men would rejoice in it and celebrate endlessly. But you? You take the burdens of the Federation onto your own shoulders like the Federation belonged to you and its citizens were all your children. As soon as a crisis hits, you leap to the forefront to deal with the issue — often before anyone else knows the problem exists. You're not the same as these people living behind these walls, Tibby. Don't ever think that, not even for a moment."

We had barely arrived back at our freighter and opened the loading bay when Kerabac arrived with Kala and Sokaia in the limousine. Kerabac got out and handed the driver some money and then likewise paid our truck driver, while Marranalis and I unloaded Howebim's package and took it into the *RASSON BEDAN*. Kala, Sokaia, Kerabac and Endina boarded minutes later. The hatch was barely shut and sealed before Kerabac began apologizing profusely.

"Kalana, I am so sorry. I didn't know what to do when Howebim began fondling you. I should have anticipated that — most Ruwallie Rasson allow their clients to fondle their slaves during negotiations, as it makes for smoother negotiations and more favorable trading. Some even throw the slave in with the deal or allow the client to enjoy the slave for a few hours. I didn't know what to do… I was afraid that if I said or did anything to discourage him, it would have appeared suspicious. Please forgive me."

Kala looked sympathetic and said, "Kerabac, you did just fine. You didn't trade me away and, while his pawing was disgusting, it didn't do me any harm. I knew what I was signing up for on this mission. If this is the worst thing to happen, I'll not complain. Honestly, I was more concerned about what Tibby would do." She looked at me questioningly.

"It took every ounce of self-control to keep from pouncing on him and tearing him to shreds," I said. "But I realized you were going along with the act, because if you weren't, you would have torn him apart yourself, Kala. I've seen what you can do when you are truly upset. Kerabac, you did just great. You could have even fooled me, if I weren't in on the plot. And Endina, back on my home world, they would have given you best actress award for your performance... You were most convincing." Endina smiled and gave a slight bow.

"Kerabac, I see that Howebim was so kind as to fit you with a courier bracelet, so it seems he bought our ploy. Just what are we carrying?"

"He wouldn't tell me, but he did indicate that if we get caught by any of the cartels, things will not go very well for us. He also said that being stopped by the Brotherhood is of no concern; they'll no doubt let us go on. He said he hoped we would be able to avoid all of them and, if we do, he has a bigger assignment for us. Whatever this is we're carrying must be very valuable; what he's paying us is nearly five times the value of the liquor we sold him and he paid half in advance; the rest is to be paid by his brother when we deliver the package."

"Well, if everyone is ready, I suggest we get ourselves underway to Goo'Waddle," I said.

We anticipated that the Brotherhood would try to intercept us as we left the planet — and we weren't disappointed. We were barely past the first moon of Ryken when a Brotherhood corvette raced toward us, broadcasting orders for us to stop and accept boarders for an inspection.

"This is the Brotherhood of Light addressing you from the *OREGANDER*. You are hereby ordered to bring your engines to a full stop and prepare for a departure inspection. Failure to do so will result in decisive actions against you. Your ship will be fired upon and disabled.

Immediately bring your ship to a halt and await a boarding party."

Kerabac grinned. "Oh, this is going to be fun," he said as he reached forward from his captain's chair on the bridge and activated the vid screen. "This is Captain Kerabac of the trade ship *RASSON BEDAN*. You've no jurisdiction to board any ships in this sector, so why don't you just go to your cabin and entertain yourself?"

Very quickly, an image appeared on the vid screen of a red-faced man dressed in a Brotherhood captain's uniform. He looked to be in his mid 40s — and it was that obvious he was very angry.

"Listen, you little flea... I am Captain Joresue. If you don't stop right now, I'll blow your ass right out of this sector."

"What was that?" Kerabac said, as he slowly increased our speed away from the *OREGANDER*. "Did you say you want me to stop so you can blow on my ass? Pervert!"

"That was your last warning, butt wipe," Captain Joresue said. "Take out their engines," he commanded to the gunners.

There was a brief flash on the RMFF screens and, at the same moment, Kerabac activated the cloaking device. Instantly, the alarm on his wristband began flashing and the countdown clock indicated that he only had minutes before the thing was going to explode, killing him and anyone near him.

"What the...." he stammered. "Oh no.... Something in the cloaking device must be blocking the signal for the courier band. We have to uncloak or it will explode."

"How far can you move us before we have to uncloak?" I asked.

"Not far enough to be out of sensor range," he replied.

"Move us as far as you can, quickly, and then uncloak briefly. Hopefully, that will reset the countdown. If it does, cloak immediately and move forward again the same way. Keep doing that until we are out of sensor range."

"But the Brotherhood will know what we're doing," Kerabac said with a look of panic on his face. All this time, he was maneuvering us away from the Brotherhood as fast as he could.

"Maybe not…just do it now."

Kerabac did as I said. Just as the courier band was about to run out of time, he uncloaked the *RASSON BEDAN*. Luckily, as I hoped, the courier band stopped beeping and reset as soon as the cloaking was turned off. Kerabac waited only a few seconds before re-engaging the cloak and, as soon as he did, the countdown started again. It took three hops to get out of range of the Brotherhood ship. Once we were no longer in range, Kerabac uncloaked and took a fast route to Goo'Waddle.

"So what now?" Kerabac asked. "Our plan is ruined; they now know we have a cloaking device."

"I don't think so. See if you can intercept any of their messages and listen to what they are saying." A'Lappe had installed equipment into the freighter before we left and trained key personnel that allowed us to monitor Brotherhood communications frequencies at will. Kerabac nodded to Endina, who activated the unit. After some adjustments a frantic voice came over the speakers.

"I'm telling you, sir, we fired on them and they just disappeared. Minutes later, they reappeared on our sensors, only out of our weapons range. Then they just disappeared again, only to reappear about twice that distance out. Then seconds later they disappeared once more."

"It sounds like they have a jump drive of some sort. I've heard of them in theory, but never heard of one that worked. Somehow, they must have gotten a hold of one. They're jumping from one spot to another. Obviously, it has a limited range or they would be jumping further; still, it obviously works well enough to get them out of range. You say you think they were headed toward Goo'Waddle?"

"Yes, sir, that's the direction they seemed to be heading."

"Get your ship over to Goo'Waddle. I'm heading there myself to look for Logden. I'll keep an eye out for this *RASSON BEDAN* and find out what I can about it. If we can get our hands on that jump drive, we can use in our fight against the Federation."

"Yes, sir, I'll do that. Good luck on Goo'Waddle."

When the message ended, I turned to Kerabac. "That worked better than I hoped. They think we have a jump drive, not a cloaking device. Once you have that bracelet off, we can activate the cloaking device and RMFF and they won't know we've left the area."

"True, but now they're motivated to find us, even if we're on the ground, in order to get the jump drive that they think we have," Kerabac said with concern.

"Hmm. You're right — I hadn't thought of that. We're going to have to rethink our strategy — or…maybe not. If they think we have a jump drive that can elude them, and they start looking for us, they'll almost certainly leak the information about the jump drive. If that should happen and the rumor gets to Logden, he may see us as his one opportunity to get out of the system alive with the solbidyum in hand. In that case, he will seek us out. In the meantime, we need to keep this ship out of the Brotherhood's sight."

"Our best bet is to get off and then have the ship leave the surface and fly out cloaked to a safe orbit and stay there until we call. When it's off surface, the ship isn't likely to fall into enemy hands," Kerabac said with some conviction.

"I see your point. This might throw off the Brotherhood in other ways, as well. If our ship's not here, they are less likely to think we are. We might be able to move about more freely. But that also means we will have to find a place to stay. We'll need to maintain the slave/master act 24 hours a day and we won't have a place to run for refuge in case of trouble."

"Getting a place to stay may not be too big a problem. The information I have been able to gather about Goo'Waddle indicates that people come and go frequently; and there are numerous small estates available for lease at any given time. We're not short of funds; and leasing a place may make it look like we're planning to stay awhile to establish a trade hub here, which would also help us to build a network of key contacts."

"How long would that take to set up? I don't want to spend a lot of time setting up a base of operations, if Logden isn't on the planet. He's the key to recovering the solbidyum; we need to stay focused on him. Don't they have some sort of hotel accommodations where we could stay?"

"They do, but that won't work, Tibby. Remember, I'm supposed to be a Ruwallie Rasson with slaves, and we are not likely to find hotels with the kind of accommodations that provide a secured area for slaves. Even if you did, I can guarantee that you would not want Kalana and Sokaia staying in the slave pens, regardless of the fact that they can handle themselves."

"OK, I guess I can see that. Even if we lease an estate for months and then have to leave the next day, it's not really a big deal. Do what you need to do, but do it quickly. The longer this takes, the more likely it is that the Brotherhood finds Logden before we do. Right now, I think we need to get down to the planet and find Agama. Find a place for us quickly so we can get set up and then I want the *RASSON BEDAN* up in orbit and cloaked. I don't want the ship visible any longer than necessary."

Just as we were wrapping up our conversation, Norkoda interrupted. "Tibby, a message just arrived from Commander Wabussie on the *NEW ORLEANS*. I think you need to hear it right away."

"What is it?" I asked.

"He said that shortly after the attack at TEZU LAGONG, Senator Euregata, along with all his staff, left the planet. Our FSO operatives have since discovered that their planet, Samalis, is currently involved in some kind of negotiation with the Brotherhood. The solbidyum we're now trying to recover was to be sold to them by the Brotherhood. The Samalis leadership believed that they were on the tail end of the receiving list and they weren't prepared to wait their turn to obtain a share. So far as we know, they're not yet aware that the Brotherhood doesn't have the solbidyum in their possession.

"The Federation received word today from Samalis that the planet is withdrawing from the Federation. A mutiny of Brotherhood officers and troopers resulted in the commandeering of two Federation starships in that sector just before they were scheduled to be loyalty tested. Since then, more Brotherhood ships have been brought in to reinforce the two starships, along with the Samalis military and their own home fleet. We don't know what will happen once the Samalis leaders find out the Brotherhood doesn't have the solbidyum.

"The admiral contacted the *NEW ORLEANS* to stress how important it is that the solbidyum does not fall into the hands of the Brotherhood. He also said the Federation is assembling a force to fly to Samalis for a confrontation with the Brotherhood; he's equipping several starships with Mirage Fighters and loading up as many Special Ops teams as he can; but his concern is mounting. Recent FSO intelligence reports seem to repeatedly indicate that the Brotherhood has assembled a strong force in that quadrant and may be planning to use this area as the starting point for an invasion of other Federation planets."

"So it falls on us to stop a war by acquiring the stolen solbidyum before Brotherhood gains control of it. Wonderful! Simply wonderful. How do we always end up being the ones to get stuck with all this crap?" I exclaimed with frustration.

Kerabac laughed. "In all fairness to the admiral, we're not exactly stuck with all the crap. The Federation forces still have to respond to the crisis at Samalis, and they haven't exactly been sitting still while we've been busy singlehandedly saving the Federation."

"True," I mumbled, "but it seems we get more than our share of the work and that we play a larger role in defending the Federation than we should."

"Honored First Citizen," Norkoda interjected, "if I may be so bold, it is not that the Federation is lax in its duties; rather that they are ignorant of the ways of war and combat, whereas you are well versed not only in hand-to-hand combat, but in the strategies and alliances that emerge during such widespread hostilities. Give us time to learn what you know, and you will see a Federation that is eager to defend its citizens and preserve its ways of life."

"Well said, Norkoda," Kala said as she joined us. "Tib, before you showed up, the Federation thought they had it all down when it came to warfare and military campaigns; but in the short time that you have been here, it has become painfully obvious to the Federation how deficient we are. You have demonstrated that there are areas to requiring great leaps of improvement and that your knowledge of Earth-style warfare and war history is sorely needed. I think you'll be surprised how fast the Federation will embrace what you have to give and how quickly they'll put it all into motion."

"I'm not sure if that's a good thing," I replied. "I would hate to see the Federation become a nation of warmongers constantly engaged in one war after another."

"There is one more bit of news," Norkoda said with a slight cringe. I stared at him, waiting. "Commander Wabussie also relayed that the frigate *RIVED*, while on a mission to place satellites intended to monitor and receive transmissions from your home planet of Earth, encountered a very large and unusual ship that didn't match any known configurations in our database. The ship approached and attacked, without any warning or contact. Fortunately, the *RIVED* is one of our ships equipped with the RMFF and 10X reactor, so she withstood the conventional attack. The alien ship then attacked with some sort of energy weapon that rendered the entire crew of the *RIVED* unconscious, though there was no damage to the ship itself. The RMFF remained active and prevented anyone from boarding the ship. When the crew regained consciousness, the attacking ship was gone."

"That information seems to correspond with the information that you brought us on the recording of the Brotherhood members. My guess is this mysterious ship belongs to the Tottalax they were talking about. How long was the crew unconscious?"

"Commander Wabussie didn't mention how long, but I'm sure we can find out."

"Please do, and let me know."

Norkoda open a channel to the *NEW ORLEANS* directly. "I'd like to talk to Stonbersa and A'Lappe to see if he or Cantolla has any idea as to what this weapon maybe or how it works and whether there is any defense against it.

"Kerabac, can you show me on the star map just where Samalis is in relationship to Earth?"

"Yes," Kerabac said as he activated the controls for the vid screen and a vast star map appeared. "Here," he said, "is Samalis." A bright red blip appeared over a star on one of the edges of the map. "And here is Earth." Another red blip appeared on the map.

"They're on complete opposite sides of the Federation territories," Kala exclaimed with surprise.

"Where are we now in relation to this star map?" I asked.

"Here," Kerabac responded as another red blip appeared on the map, closer to Earth than I would have suspected. I stared at the map a moment, pondering what I was seeing.

"What are you thinking, Tib?" Kala asked. She knew me well enough by now to know when I was formulating ideas.

"I'm thinking the Brotherhood is planning to attack us from two sides to divide our forces. They're hoping to initiate their attack in the Samalis sector and draw Federation forces in that direction, and then direct the Tottalax to attack from this side of the Federation where there will be nothing to stop them. With this weapon they have, they can disable any Federation forces they may encounter; and with most of the Federation ships drawn to the Samalis sector, it would be an easy run on the capital for the Tottalax ships and a small number of Brotherhood ships."

"You think the Tottalax are on this side the Federation space?" Kerabac asked.

"The conversation Norkoda recorded was here — in this sector — and it seemed like it was fresh news. The attack on the *RIVED* took place here on this side the Federation and it certainly seems to correspond to the information Norkoda recorded. If the Tottalax were in contact with the Brotherhood in or near this sector and the attack on the *RIVED* also occurred on this side the Federation territories, it stands to reason the Tottalax world must also be on this side of the Federation territories. It also means it must be relatively close to Earth, possibly someplace between Earth and here. Norkoda, contact Wabussie and have him check into all references of contacts and rumors about the Tottalax and find out where they occurred. I fear the Federation may be going to be hit from two sides."

At that fateful moment, Norkoda, who was sitting at the communication console, suddenly interrupted us.

"I have another urgent message coming in from the admiralty over the DSC system," he said with one hand on the earpiece in his left ear. "Do you want me to relate it as it is coming in?"

"Yes, please do." I answered.

"A shuttle arrived on the starship *GROTTOM* in the Nayjax system near the planet Tonhig a few hours ago. When the passengers were being taken for screening prior to being granted access to the rest of the ship, they suddenly produced weapons, killing all the security forces in the hangar area." The bridge immediately responded by sealing off the hangar from the rest of the ship and sending troopers deal with the attackers. At about the same time that the attack was taking place, the *GROTTOM* was attack by a swarm of ships that had been hiding behind one of the moons. The *GROTTOM* reported eight corvettes in the attack and one battle cruiser of Markazian design. They were accompanied by nearly 100 fighters that took up positions about the *GROTTOM*. Captain Donol immediately activated the RMFF to protect the ship; but with the enemy holding the hangar bay the *GROTTOM* was unable to launch any fighters or patrol ships, most of which had been secured earlier as the *GROTTOM* was about to depart for the Kandien System.

"Captain Donol said they were preparing to open fire on the surrounding ships when a large ship of a strange configuration joined the Brotherhood ships. Then all communication ceased. The admiralty feared that the

GROTTOM had fallen into the hands of the Brotherhood and that the Brotherhood were using some new weapon to render the crew of the starship unconscious, like they did with the *RIVED*; but about thirty minutes later a message came in from one of the Nibarian crew members on the *GROTTOM*. He was not affected by whatever had rendered the rest of the crew unconscious. He managed to get to the bridge and evacuate the air from the hangar area. However, the invaders managed to get aboard one of the ships in the hangar before all the air was gone and subsequently tried to escape while the RMFF was active. The Nibarian reported that, when the ship hit the RMFF, it accelerated and shot out away from the ship so fast that it appeared to be a streak of light. The attacking craft surrounding the *GROTTOM* bombarded the ship for over an hour with no affect before they broke off and fled the area. The Nibarian on the bridge was unfamiliar with the ships armament and was unable to return fire. It was a few hours later when the crew of the *GROTTOM* regained consciousness.

"Admiral Regeny requests that Commander Wabussie contact him at once regarding intelligence missions for FSO operatives."

"Shit!" I exclaimed in English before continuing in the official Federation language. "The *GROTTOM* has a DSC system aboard it, as well as a 10X reactor, the RMFF and a cloaking device and about a dozen of our Mirage Fighters. If the Brotherhood had gotten their hands on any of them, we'd really be in trouble. I wonder, though, why the Nibarian was not affected by whatever the enemy used to knock out the rest of the crew?"

"I wonder what happened to those bastards that tried to escape in that ship they took from the hangar," Kerabac said. "Their ship most likely disintegrated when it was expelled at near light speed from the RMFF field. No one could survive that acceleration."

"Where do you think that ship is now?" Kala asked.

"Probably halfway into the next universe," Kerabac replied.

Norkoda interrupted us again. "Tibby, I have a channel open to the *NEW ORLEANS* with the commodore and A'Lappe standing by."

"Put them on the main screen," I responded.

"What can we do for you Tibby?" The commodore asked as soon as the vid screen displayed the view of the *NEW ORLEANS* bridge.

"I need to talk to A'Lappe," I answered.

Before the commodore could respond, A'Lappe stepped into view. Apparently he had been standing just out of the range of the camera.

"I'm here Tibby. How can I assist?"

"Let me explain what happened, A'Lappe," I began.

I gave A'Lappe a quick rundown of what transpired and finished up by asking, "Is there any way we can further protect the RMFF, the cloaking and DSC systems and 10X fusion reactors and the other technology installed on the Mirage Fighters? All the Federation needs to do is lose just one starship and all of that capability will be in the hands of the Brotherhood."

"Right at the moment I can't think of any, Tibby. The DSC system would take them a long time to figure out. Unless someone were to tell them precisely how it worked, it's unlikely they would figure it out on their own in less than a year or two. But the others, well I'm afraid there is no way to prevent them from being tampered with and reverse-engineered, if an enemy ever gets their hands on a ship. Your best chance is to simply prevent them from ever getting one. Logically, it's really only a matter of time before they will gain the secrets to one or all of these technologies, Tibby."

"Well, think about it anyway. See if you and Cantolla can find a way to make these things more secure."

"I'll do my best.   By the way, you say that a Nibarian on the *GROTTOM* wasn't affected by the weapon used against the ship?"

"So it would seem," I answered. "Is that important?

"It could be. That's something we'll need to look into."

"Is there anything else we can do for you, Tib?" the commodore asked.

"Not that I can think of at the moment; but stay vigilant.   This news about the Brotherhood and a new weapon and an alliance with these Tottalax is very disturbing. I think it would be wise to make sure the RMFF is active full time and I recommend that you notify Captain Felenna to do likewise with the *MIZBAGONA*."

It took three more days for us to reach Goo'Waddle. Everyone on the ship was tense about the news from the admiralty concerning the attacks and much conjecture was taking place about the nature of the new weapon used by the attackers. During the rest of the trip I spent a good deal of time working out with Padaran and Marranalis in the cargo hold.

I was surprised at Padaran's speed and dexterity, as his overall appearance belied the agility that he demonstrated in hand-to-hand combat. I also discovered that he had a very keen mind and was an extremely fast learner. He turned out to be a very good actor, convincingly acting out any role. I was surprised to walk into the galley area one day and find him entertaining Marranalis and several of the crew with impressions of his uncle, Admiral Regeny, as if having a discussion with A'Lappe. It was amazing how he mimicked not only their voices accurately, but their gestures and postures as well. I had to laugh at the way he waved his hands in typical A'Lappe fashion while he characterized his voice and how he accurately tugged at the flesh under his chin like his uncle, when he mimicked the admiral asking a question.

"How many voices can you mimic?" I asked, interrupting his routine.

"How many would you like to hear?" Padaran responded in my voice, which caused the crew to laugh.

"Can you do Commodore Stonbersa?" I asked.

"But of course, Tibby, anything you ask." He responded in an exact duplicate of the commodore's voice.

"What about Senator Tonclin's voice…"

"Sorry, but I am not familiar with his voice. I know he was aboard the ship, but I never met him or heard him speak."

"How about Norkoda then? You've heard him and been around him often enough." I was expecting it would be difficult or impossible for him inasmuch as the Nibarians had such high-pitched voices, so I was quite shocked when he responded back in a perfect mimic of Norkoda's voice.

"Not a problem at all, First Citizen."

"That's amazing, Padaran. It never ceases to amaze me, the talents that my crewmembers have."

We were interrupted as Kerabac's voice came across the ship's speakers. "Attention. Everyone to their stations, we are seeing numerous ships ahead of us that appear to be of the type used by the Brotherhood. We are momentarily outside their sensor range, but unless we cloak, we will be visible to them in a few minutes."

Marranalis and I headed toward the bridge. When we entered the control room, the star map was fully displayed on the screen and nearly one hundred red dots appeared on the screen in the space between us and Goo'Waddle. "This is what we're facing, Tibby," Kerabac began, "and I have every reason to believe there are more out there beyond our current sensor range."

"What?! All those are Brotherhood ships?" I asked incredulously. "Where did they get that many ships?"

"We can't say for certain they all are Brotherhood ships; but based on their movements and actions, it's a safe guess that most of them are. As for where they got them, I can only say that we never have known for sure how large the Brotherhood is, nor the extent of their existence outside of Federation space. Many of these ships may simply be pirate or mercenary ships belonging to sympathizers to the Brotherhood cause or operating under hire by the Brotherhood."

"This is giving me a headache!" I said. Kala moved behind me and began massaging my shoulders and neck. "How are we going to get through this mess? We can't simply hop through there like we hopped out of it at Ryken by turning the cloaking device on and off every few minutes."

"Perhaps if we move around the other side of the planet, there will be fewer Brotherhood ships there," Kerabac suggested. "They simply may be concentrated on this side, waiting for the *RASSON BEDAN* to show up. On the other hand, if they believe Logden is down there, they may be looking for him and anticipating his attempt to escape. We're still outside the sensor range of those ships, so we can skirt around and try to pass from the other side."

"I doubt it will be any better, but it's worth a try," I said.

Over the next hour, Kerabac skirted carefully around Goo'Waddle and the armada of ships that surrounded it; but as we approached the opposite side of the planet, it became apparent that just as many ships were stationed there.

"So much for that idea," I said with an air of defeat.

"Tibby," Kala began in a questioning tone, "why don't you simply have Captain Felenna fly the *MIZBAGONA* in near the surface under cloak, and then race away from the planet uncloaked and at top speed? The Brotherhood is sure to challenge her; and if she just keeps going, they will send ships after her. All she needs to do is stay out of weapon range and not let them get too close; once she has drawn them off a good distance, she can cloak and accelerate back to her previous station. They can't hurt her with the RMFF on; and since nothing the Brotherhood has in their fleet can match her speed, she will be gone before they can catch up or target her. Besides, they want Logden alive; so if they think he is aboard, they will not try to destroy the ship."

Kerabac and I looked at each other with one of those looks that said *Why didn't I think of that?* "Ahh...I doubt they would siphon off enough ships for us to get through," I said, somewhat less convincingly than I hoped.

"Oh, come on now, Tibby, certainly you're not going to reject my idea simply because you didn't think of it?" Kala said.

"OK, OK... We'll give it a try," I conceded. "Kerabac, contact the *MIZBAGONA* and relay our plan to Captain Felenna. Find out how long it will take her to get here. In the meantime, we will plan how to get to Goo'Waddle through this armada."

"You mean MY plan, don't you, Tib?" Kala said with a grin. I shook my head and groaned.

Kerabac relayed the message to the *MIZBAGONA*. Fortunately, it was stationed closer to this side of the system than the *NEW ORLEANS*. It was only a matter of minutes before we received a response from Felenna advising that she would be here, but it would take her a day to get to our location. I was concerned; even though we were outside the sensor range of the Brotherhood ships, it was possible one might get close enough to detect us. As long as Kerabac was wearing the courier band, we were limited in our cloaking time. There was an asteroid field not too far away, so we decided to hide there until the *MIZBAGONA* arrived. With the RMFF activated there was no chance of us being damaged by an asteroid, in the event that one should accidently bump into us.

The asteroids gave me an idea.

"Kerabac, the ship's propulsion is by gravity waves that are generated in front of the ship to pull it, right?"

"Yes, that's somewhat the way it works. Why?"

"Can the fields also be created to push?"

"Yes, in fact, there is also a wave generated behind the ship to push in conjunction to the one that pulls from the front. The two waves are synchronized, so the ship rides in the trough between the two."

"Is it possible to direct or create the field away from the ship — say in front of or behind another object?"

"Yes, up to a short distance of about three kilometers away at max. What are you thinking?"

"I was just wondering. What if we created a gravity wave in front of a bunch of those smaller asteroid debris clusters floating around out here and moved them in the direction of the Brotherhood ships? If we got a large enough cluster of them headed their way, they would have to move their ships or be severely injured. If we could manage to aim them so they do not actually hit the planet, but just pass close by, I would think we'd be able to ride in amid the cluster, cloak before we get close enough to be spotted inside the swarm, and then, just as we graze the planet's atmosphere, slip in and uncloak before your time runs out and make a dash for the surface.

"The Brotherhood ships will have cleared the area to avoid an asteroid collision, and they won't be able to get back fast enough to stop us. We can find a spot to disembark quickly and, once we're off, the crew can cloak again before the Brotherhood finds us. The ship can then move to an orbit where they'll await our signal to return."

"Hmm. That could work, but it will be hard to control the direction of the meteoroids and asteroids to make sure none of them hit the planet. It should certainly scramble the Brotherhood fleet; and if Felenna does her part to draw some of them off beforehand, we should be able to pull it off."

Over the next few hours, I sat with Kerabac, Norkoda and Endina to figure out how to configure the gravity wave to steer the asteroids and meteors effectively and safely. To be honest, I was not needed for the planning and had little to contribute, but it was important for me to listen and at least understand the challenges we might have during the maneuvers.

It was finally determined that we simply could not do it alone and we needed at least one more ship involved. We would have to wait for the *MIZBAGONA* to arrive. It was decided that the *MIZBAGONA* would not need to draw the Brotherhood ships off after all; she would remain cloaked while helping to herd the asteroids. Between the two ships, we anticipated that we would be able to herd enough asteroids to just skim the atmosphere of Goo'Waddle without actually impacting the planet. The *RASSON BEDAN* would be able to ride in the midst of the asteroids and remain hidden from the scanners of the Brotherhood armada. Then we would turn on the cloaking device and proceed to the surface unseen.   We'd have only a few minutes to accomplish the task because of the explosive courier band on Kerabac's wrist.

During the next day, we managed to corral a number of asteroids and slowly begin moving them toward Goo'Waddle. We were still outside normal sensor range of the planet when we were joined by the *MIZBAGONA*, and Captain Felenna dispatched several patrol ships to help guide the cluster of asteroids toward Goo'Waddle.

As we neared sensor range of the planet, Kerabac carefully situated the *RASSON BEDAN* inside the cluster and the patrol ships returned to the *MIZBAGONA*.   The *MIZBAGONA* remained cloaked while maintaining the asteroid cluster in formation. Though we could not cloak the *RASSON BEDAN* as we moved past the Brotherhood ships, we were able to activate the RMFF to protect the ship from any asteroid that might graze or crash into us as we neared Goo'Waddle.

"Tibby, we're intercepting messages from the ships surrounding Goo'Waddle. They have spotted the incoming asteroids and are beginning to take evasive action," Kerabac said.

"Have they spotted us?" I asked cautiously.

"So far there has been no mention of anyone seeing a ship within the cluster."

"Good. Let's hope it stays that way. Tell Captain Felenna to pull back now. We'll ride this in the rest of the way. She can maintain a cloaked position in orbit in case we need her assistance later."

We were nearing Goo'Waddle's atmosphere, when sudden flashes of light began displaying on our vid screen.

"What's happening? Have we been spotted?" I yelled to Kerabac.

"No, I don't think so," Kerabac said. "I think a few of the ships are targeting the asteroids in hopes of destroying some of them. We need to cloak now before we're seen."

"How long before we can break free of the debris field and make it to the surface?

"Eight to ten minutes."

"That's cutting it close, but we don't have much choice," I said as I watched two smaller asteroids vaporize beside us. We were still pretty much hidden behind one of the largest asteroids, but I suspected it was being hit as well and could crumble at any moment.

Kerabac activated the cloaking device and immediately the courier security band began beeping out its countdown once again.

"Take us out of here and get us to the surface as fast as you can," I said, just as the large asteroid in front of us exploded into thousands of smaller pieces. Fortunately, the RMFF was active; we could see the shield deflecting all sizes of rock and debris as we moved past the mayhem. Kerabac took us on the shortest course to the planet. I saw him nervously glancing at the countdown display on his wrist, as the surface zoomed before us on the screen. We were still about sixty kilometers from the surface when the courier band showed only a minute left on the timer. Suddenly, Kerabac leveled the ship off and, with only seconds on his timer, he cut off the cloaking device. Immediately the alarm stopped beeping. No sooner had the timer reset than Kerabac activated the cloaking device once more.

Up until this moment, I had not paid much attention to the planet. From space we could see clouds swirling in its atmosphere, but not much of the topography, except for what appeared to be a large sea on one side of the planet. As we neared the surface, I saw that the planet was laced with canals that crisscrossed the planet in a regular pattern along its longitudes and latitudes, giving the largely uninterrupted land mass the appearance of being divided up into squares, like city blocks, only with water replacing streets. But the parcels of land were much larger than any city block I'd ever seen. Most were kilometers long and wide; many appeared to be covered with fields and farms, while others seemed to be mostly urban developments and large cities with thousands of buildings. Kerabac scanned the surface and then suddenly headed toward the equatorial region of the planet.

"I need to find a place to set us down before the timer runs out," he said. "We should be low enough now that I can shut off the cloaking device without being noticed from above, especially if I get under one of the larger clouds."

He turned the ship toward a large, dense cloud and flew into it before he uncloaked the ship. Then he eased the ship below cloud level and slowed to a respectable cruising speed, while he traveled along at height of about two kilometers above the surface, just like any other in-atmosphere ship en route to a surface destination. To anyone who may have noticed us from above, it would simply appear that an otherwise-unnoticed ship suddenly came out from under a cloud on a routine flight to another surface city.

"Any idea where we're headed?" I queried.

"Yes — to Jomang. It's one of the larger cities near the equator. It's where we will find Howebim's brother."

I had never bothered to ask anyone about Goo'Waddle, assuming it was more or less like Ryken, Plosaxen or possibly even Alle Bamma, and I certainly didn't anticipated anything like what greeted us on the surface. Goo'Waddle was roughly the size of the planet Mars in my native solar system. It was a young planet, mostly flat, with only some low mountains or hills situated around a huge circular sea that covered about one tenth of the planet's surface.

The circular sea, I was to learn, was created by a large asteroid impact many millions of years earlier. Goo'Waddle had a very high water table; one had to dig only about two meters to reach the water level. Before the asteroid impact, the planet most likely had little to no surface water. Even now the depth of the water was only a few meters. The soil was mostly a sandy loam that covered the entire surface of the planet, which was fairly level, except the area around the rim of the large crater, where the low mountains were slowly eroding into little more than hills.

At some point early inhabitants began carving out large canals for use in commerce and transportation; apparently long before anyone now living on the planet could recall. There was no real way to date the canals, as they were constantly being dredged, deepened, and widened, due to the relatively loose sandy soil that constantly eroded into the waterways and threatened to block the passages and intersections. It was believed that the earliest canals had existed for over ten thousand years. In some locations, small harbors were carved into the islands to form docking areas; usually these became the locations of towns and cities. Only a few of the largest islands had actual designated areas where spacecraft could land.

The only place any rock material was found was in the vicinity of the impact crater; most of it was small. Minerals, as they existed on Goo'Waddle, were mixed into the sandy soil and were not easily mined or extracted; so the planet relied heavily on importing such materials to sustain their development. On the other hand, the terrain and mineral properties of the soil, in conjunction with the temperate global climate made Goo'Waddle an excellent planet for agriculture.

Along the equatorial regions major food crops were grown and, as one moved toward the polar regions, the crops gave way to grassy islands where animals were raised for meat, leather and wool. Nearer to the polar regions grew giant forests that produced lumber and other wood products as well as nuts. These commodities were in high demand on the nearby planets of Yentum and Ryken, as neither produced much in the way of food, due to the rocky soil and uneven terrain, which made them more suitable for manufacturing and mining.

Oddly, in spite of all the water in the canals and sea, Goo'Waddle had no fish or aquatic life. There had been abundant sea life at an earlier time; but it all died off as a result of heavy pollution from sewage and other wastes dumped indiscriminately into the planet's canals. Most of the planet's drinking water was filtered with various types of equipment; the rest of the potable water was acquired from rainwater. Water used for agricultural purposes, such as irrigation, depended on the crop; crops intended for food use were irrigated with filtered water or rainwater, while crops used for fiber or non-food purposes were irrigated directly with the polluted canal water. Crops that received the canal water grew more robustly — probably because of the nutrient and mineral content.

Our landing at the Jomang spaceport went without incident. Kerabac was able to locate and secure a vacant warehouse space on the spaceport property, where we quickly unloaded our cargo for storage. Instructions were given to Norkoda take the *RASSON BEDAN* up into orbit and keep it cloaked until it was needed. We were relatively sure the Brotherhood would be looking for the ship on the surface — and we didn't want it found.

We then transferred our currency to what on Earth would be the equivalent of a safety deposit box in a local banking facility, while Endina made arrangements for a place to stay.

Fortunately, there was no shortage of small rental estate listings, as cartels had been buying up the bulk of the estate land, more or less driving the original owners out of their shrunken estate homes to other planets where they could pursue a more luxurious lifestyle. The offer of an additional financial bonus to the real estate agent made it possible for us to lease a place late that same night and, while we didn't have any furnishings, we at least had a place to stay.

It was dark when we arrived at the estate, so it wasn't possible to see much of the exterior of the place or the surrounding area. The air was very humid and carried with it a slightly putrid smell that reminded me of the swamps on Earth. There was a large wall that surrounded the property; Endina had to enter a keypad security code provided by the agent in order to pass through the estate's large metal gate. The gate swung in slowly and we filed in to find a short promenade to the main house, which was completely dark. Once at the house, Endina entered a second security code that allowed us to open the main door.

As soon as we crossed the entry, lights came on throughout the first floor. The house was huge.

"It looks we have power," I said.

"The agent who leased us this place said that the estate has its own fusion power cell. It was included in the rental price," Endina explained.

On the way to the estate, Endina had also related what she learned from the agent. Although there was an outbuilding for the many slaves that once worked the estate, after the sale of the bulk of the land to one of the agriculture cartels the structure was no longer in use and a smaller area within the main house was set aside for the few remaining domestic slaves that the previous owner had kept for personal use. We managed to locate this area and, as with the rest of the house, we found it to be barren of any furnishings. Discolored areas on the walls indicated where paintings or tapestries once hung. I had seen some statuary outside, but there was none inside the house, though there appeared to be places where some may have stood at one time.

"It looks like we will all be sleeping on the floor tonight. Tomorrow we'll see to getting furnishings for the place. Endina, I'll leave that up to you," I said without thinking.

"Ahh...yes," she said with a wide grin. "And then I can have you slaves positioning it about according to my whims." She laughed, and I realized she was right. Anyone watching us would be expecting the slaves to be doing such chores, and the people who delivered the furniture would expect the slaves to unload the delivery vehicle and take the furniture inside. There would be talk if anything appeared out of the norm.

Fortunately, our location on Goo'Waddle was in a warm climate or, at least, the season was warm — if Goo'Waddle had seasons — so heat and blankets were not required. Endina took out her vid pad and said, "I won't need to wait until tomorrow to order furniture. I should be able to find a place and order some now; maybe we'll have it here first thing tomorrow. Most places in the city operate day and night."

It was decided, for no other reason than we didn't know what to expect, that someone should be on guard and alert during the night while the rest of us slept. Marranalis volunteered for the first watch; Kerabac said he would take second; I took the third; and Padaran would take last watch. Everyone more or less positioned themselves around the main room in the house and lay down on the floor to sleep. Kalana and I lay next to each other and were soon sound asleep.

I was in the middle of a dream when Kerabac woke me for my watch. It had been a strange dream about something chasing me through a dense fog. I felt small and afraid and I was hungry, thirsty, weak, and unable to go on. Even after I was fully awake, elements of the dream still haunted me. I did my best to shake off the lingering sense of vulnerability as I settled in for my watch. There seemed to be some diffuse light coming in through the windows of the darkened house, so I decided to investigate.

I quietly slipped out, thinking that we had forgotten to set the alarm on the house before we went to sleep. Once outside, I immediately noticed a dense but low cloud of fog, similar to that in my dream. The dim light of the moon showed through the fog and created an eerie surrounding that matched the heavy feeling of the air. I stood there in the silence for a few minutes and was about to return inside, when I heard a whimpering sound coming from somewhere nearby. I listened closely until heard it again, only this time it sounded more like someone crying. I crept quietly along the large porch that extended across the front of the house, keeping myself concealed in the darkness of the shadows while I traced my way toward the noise. The sound stopped, and I waited patiently, listening.

I heard a rustling of leaves, and then another whimper followed by more sobs and soft crying. I slowly moved forward until I could tell that the sound was coming from the shrubbery right in front of me just below the porch level. Carefully, I crawled to the edge and peered down toward the ground. There, in the dim light, I saw a small child of no more than perhaps ten or eleven, curled up in a ball in a small pile of leaves.

I was shocked and didn't know what to do. My first instinct was to say something, but I wasn't sure which of the many languages in my head would be the right one to use on this young lad. Something was not right. It was obvious that he was hiding, but from whom and why was a complete mystery.

I sat back to ponder this new development. As I tried to sort out what to do next, a figure came out the front door. There was enough light to see that it was Kala; she was apparently looking for me. I caught her attention and motioned for her to come to me quietly. Just as she arrived, the young lad stirred and made a whimpering sound again; it was becoming clear that he was in some sort of pain. Kala looked at me questioningly and I shrugged my shoulders. Kala crept over to the edge and peered down; and what she did next totally surprised me. She sat on very edge of the porch and softly began humming a tune that sounded very much like a child's tune. Immediately, everything grew quiet in the bushes where the child was hidden.

After humming a few bars, Kala began singing very softly in one language and then another, "Come out, come out, my little one, we are your friends and no one will hurt you." She sang this song perhaps a dozen times in different languages until, at last, we heard a rusting in the leaves; slowly a small head peered up over the porch to see Kala and I sitting there cross-legged in front of him.

At first he ducked back down, but Kala kept singing in the same language, "Do not be afraid, my little one, we will not hurt you, we will protect you, we will feed you." Slowly, the head reappeared and looked at us a few minutes, glancing back and forth along the porch and behind him as though he feared someone was sneaking up on him.

At last, Kala stopped singing and very quietly said, "I am Kalana and this is Tibby. What is your name?"

The boy looked at us shyly for a few moments before saying, "You won't send me back, will you? They will kill me if you do."

"Who will kill you? And why would they want to kill you?" Kala asked.

"My masters," the young boy said. "My arm is broken and they do not want a cripple to feed and care for. They would only throw me back into the canal to drown again if you return me."

Kala turned to me with one of those *Do something* looks.

"No one is going to throw you into a canal to drown," I said. "We will protect you."

"But you're slaves, too," he said. Obviously, he had noted our slave collars, Kala's nudity and my loincloth. "How can you protect or save me?"

"Not all things are as they seem, my young friend. Come, let's go inside. Tomorrow we will see to getting you some food; but for now, come inside where it is safer."

When we entered the house, Kala turned on the lights so we might have a better look at our young friend. As he glanced around the room and saw Kerabac and Endina, he started to bolt and run for the door. It was only my blocking the door that stopped him. "It's alright," I said. "You're safe here. They are friends, too, and they won't hurt you."

"They're Ruwallie Rasson," he blurted out. "They'll turn me in for a reward, or take me for a slave as well."

"No they won't," I exclaimed. By this time, the noise we were making was waking up the others in the room.

"What's going on, Tibby?" Kerabac asked, as he rubbed the sleep out of his eyes and tried to focus. "Who is that you have with you?"

"I'm not sure who he is just yet," I replied. "He's not told us his name, but he appears to have a broken arm; and from the looks of him, he's had it pretty rough." In the light, it was possible to see the rags he was wearing on his gaunt frame. His ribs seemed to protrude through his skin. He was near starvation and body was covered in bruises and scars.

"By the stars," Endina exclaimed when she looked at him. "He looks like he's had the worst of it. I have a med kit in the transport outside. Let me get it and see to his arm and wounds."

The young boy looked at us all with a stunned look on his face. "They are Ruwallie Rasson — and you can talk to them like that and they don't shock or beat you?"

I smiled at him. "No, they do not. As I said, things are not as they may appear here. You are safe with these people; none of them will hurt you."

Just then, Endina returned. "I'm afraid we have only minimal supplies, but I should be able to make a cast for that arm and treat some of the other wounds. If we were back on the ship, we could use the med unit, but for now, this will have to do. I wish now we had arrived in time to buy some food. As soon as I get him treated, I'll place a vid order with a local food supplier and have them make the delivery first thing in the morning. I'll have to order some cooking utensils and dishes, as well, since we have nothing to cook with."

"Doesn't your food replicator work?" the young boy asked.

"We don't have a food replicator in the house yet; we just moved in," Endina explained as she applied a sleeve-like object on the boy's arm. Once it was in place and she went through the painful process of aligning the bone properly, she took a small UV light from the med kit and aimed it at the sleeve. Wherever the beam lit up the sleeve, it hardened instantly to form a rigid cast.

"There," she said with some satisfaction. "That should do until we can get you proper medical attention."

The relief showed on the boy's face, but the pain of hunger still filled his eyes. "There is a food replicator in the old slave house," the young boy said. "Now that you have the power on, it should work."

"How do you know there is a replicator out there?" I asked.

"Before the Brotherhood stopped using this part of the estate, they used to keep us in the slave house out there."

"Brotherhood? The Brotherhood owns this estate?"

"Yes, don't you know? The Brotherhood bought this *calgana* last year to grow the plants to make their drugs. They own all the land around here; these fields are where they grow the plants. They use us slaves to harvest the crops."

I turned to Marranalis. "Go check the slave quarters. If there is a food replicator there, see if you can get it working and bring something back for the boy to eat." Marranalis nodded and left the house quietly.

"What is a *calgana*?" I asked.

The boy gave me a crazy look and answered, "You don't know what a *calgana* is? Where are you from, outer space? Everyone knows a *calgana* is a section of land surrounded by canals!"

I glanced at Kalana and saw she was holding back a laugh. "Ahh… actually, we are from outer space," I said.

The boy's eyes widened. "So you really don't know? Is that why you don't act like the other people here?"

"That's not a good thing to hear," Kala chimed in. "If we don't appear normal to this boy, we sure won't fool others very long."

"I don't think the situation is quite the same. We weren't trying to fool him; we were trying to help him." I turned to the boy and asked again, "What's your name?"

"Tanden," he answered.

"Tell me what happened to you, Tanden. How did you come to be a slave?"

"It was a long time ago," he began. "One day, some men came to our home and they were angry with my father about something. There was lots of shouting and they hit my father. One man, who was a government official, told my dad he had to pay the men what he owed or he and all of us would become slaves to pay the debt. My dad begged the men for more time, but they refused. They told him they would allow him to remain free, but the rest of us would become slaves until he paid his debt.

"My sister was taken to work in one of the pleasure houses; I don't know where they took my mother. I was taken to another pleasure house for men who want young boys," he said, hanging his head. "It was next to where they had my sister and, at times, I could see her from the window of my room. When she was not with a man, sometimes they would let her walk outside in the enclosed courtyard. I never was able to talk to her, but we would wave at each other. I was there until a few months ago when they said I was too old and the clients no longer desired me. They sold me to the Brotherhood as a harvester.

"I am not as strong or fast as many of the older boys, so I was beaten for not producing enough. Yesterday, I was carrying a load of plants when I fell. One of the guards hit me hard with a baton. As I brought my arm up to protect myself, his next strike broke my arm. The overseer said I wasn't worth the time and food it would take to heal me, and I was tossed into the canal to drown. I cannot swim; I struggled to breathe until I grabbed hold of a piece of floating trash and worked my way back to shore. By then, the overseers were looking the other way and I crawled to a culvert that empties into the canal from this house.   I managed to work my way through the culvert to where it opens into the garden outside."

I was sickened by what I was hearing. I had heard of such things before — back on Earth in certain countries where young boys were prostituted to men, but I believed such practices to be rare. I hadn't heard of any such activities in the Federation, but we were outside the Federation now and in a sector where it seemed nothing was illegal, other than being poor. I was equally as disgusted at what was happening to his sister.

"How old is your sister?" I asked.

"When this began she was the same age that I am now," he answered.

I looked at Kala. "My God! What kind of sick, hellish place is this where they prostitute and enslave children? We should just call this entire search for Logden off and just blow up this whole damned planet. Rid the galaxy of these scum!"

"Tib, it's not that simple, and you know it. There are millions of innocent people here that suffer at the hands of wicked cartels and the Brotherhood, but you don't destroy them just to put an end to the Brotherhood and the cartels."

I sighed and shook my head as I paced the room. I was angry and I wanted to do something right then. The frustration of being helpless to act immediately to erase the abominations on this planet gnawed at me. "It seems to me there is a lot of slavery in the galaxy — first on Alle Bamma, then at Ryken, and now here at Goo'Waddle. Is it like this everywhere outside the Federation?"

"No, many worlds outside the Federation outlaw slavery, though slavery may exist in pockets depending on the local laws of some of the non-aligned worlds that have not yet unified their governments."

"How many planets throughout the galaxy are like this?"

"I have no idea, Tibby. I would guess there are thousands like this, maybe millions. We don't even know how many inhabited planets there are in the galaxy, but there are certainly also thousands, if not millions, that are not. Each planet evolves with different moral values and beliefs. Most throw off things like slavery as they mature; but some don't… and they take it to unbelievable levels."

I had to confess that Earth was no different in that regard. Although slavery had been outlawed almost everywhere on the planet, it still existed and went on in many countries. Young children were forced into working in sweatshops in third world countries to produce goods that were shipped to and sold internationally to buyers in nations that didn't believe in or practice slavery, but who turned a blind eye as to what was going on outside their borders. Even in the *civilized* countries, slavery took place behind closed doors, where many of the slaves were illegal aliens fearing deportation if they didn't submit to the demands of their masters. While I was digesting all this, Marranalis returned with a bowl of steaming food. He handed it to the boy, who snatched it and began eating ravenously. I sat down next to him, overcome by the storm of fury and compassion that seethed through my chest.

"I found the replicator," Marranalis said. "It only has a few selections on it — none of them very good — but it's still food. I don't understand, though; it doesn't cost any more to replicate tasty food than it does to produce gruel, so why not at least provide the slaves with something tasty?"

"Probably for the sake of humiliation," Kala said. "Those who enslave others do not want their slaves to experience any level of comfort or have any sense of self-worth. The more they are able to beat them down physically and mentally, the more compliant and subservient they will be, in the minds of their masters. This doesn't always work, but it doesn't stop slave owners from believing it will. Plus, I think it gives the slave masters a sense of power and a belief that they are superior, that they somehow have a right to subjugate those weaker than themselves."

I was about to ask another question when I felt Tanden's head on my arm. I looked down to see he had emptied his bowl and apparently fallen asleep. I gently laid him down on the floor and, as I did, Kerabac removed the long purple cape he wore as part of his Ruwallie Rasson trader disguise and covered the boy with it.

"Where is Padaran?" I asked as I looked about the room.

"He's outside, taking his turn at watch," Kerabac replied. "I think it would be a good idea if we all get whatever sleep we can before dawn."

Kerabac's advice was sound, but I found I was not able to sleep the rest of the night as I pondered the situation on Goo'Waddle. Several times during the night, Tanden cried out in his sleep — the result of tormenting nightmares. I could only imagine the twisted hell in his life that must lie behind him.

A thought suddenly struck me and I turned to Kala, who, I noticed, was also still awake and watching me. "How is it with all the people we have working at the estate, none of them have any children?"

Kala looked at me with one of those *You don't know?* looks and said, "Tibby, many of your employees have children, and many of them are on the estate, but generally they are kept out of sight and not allowed in the main part of the house."

"What? How come I've never seen one — not even outside?"

"For one thing, most of the estate grounds are off-limits to them. There are a few small areas set up as playgrounds that are not visible from any of the areas where you or your guests might be."

"Playgrounds! That's it? What about all the land around the estate — the forests and the streams? Why aren't they out there playing, building forts and fishing and doing what kids should be doing?"

I looked up to see everyone in the room now was awake and looking at me like I had just farted and no one knew what to say or do.

"The behavior you describe is not unheard of on the lesser populated worlds. On my home world of Gosney, when I was young, we played outside and kids were pretty much everywhere. But the planet was mostly rural and agrarian. On your more industrial, more densely populated worlds, children are largely confined to indoor activities; the places they are allowed to go outside in those areas are more restricted."

I had to confess that this was becoming a growing trend on Earth also, and it was one I didn't like.

"When we get back, I want to see some changes made. Other than for just a very few areas, I want restrictions lifted for children. Obviously, some discretion will be needed, based on ages, as we would not want an infant crawling about the halls without anyone knowing where they were; but for older kids who can find their way around, I think we can allow access to the gardens and the lakes, streams and woods. I want the kids to be able to climb trees and make treehouses and forts. Let the girls pick wildflowers or whatever it is they want to do out there. In fact, there is a large tract of land on the south end of the lake that is sort of a box canyon cove. Let's make that entire area a section strictly for kids to play and do what they wish…camp, boat, swim, fish, and whatever."

Kala looked at me with a concerned look, but Marranalis chimed in. "I like that, Tibby. When I was a boy, we briefly lived near an old abandoned supply depot. All the boys used to sneak off and play there. We built all kinds of stuff out of the old lumber and scrap materials. Best fun I ever had, now that I look back at it."

"There, that's what I'm talking about," I said to Kala. "We need to make sure there are some piles of lumber and simple, basic tools for them to use to build stuff, if they want."

"But what about supervision, Tibby? You just can't let a bunch of kids run wild like that — who knows what trouble they will get into," Kala said with some concern. "Just look what happened when Senator Tonclin's daughter wandered off on the *NEW ORLEANS* last year."

"What? What happened? She got lost for a few minutes…big deal. Was she hurt by it? I'm sure some of these kids will get lost in the forest or even in the house. Damn, even I get lost in the house — it's so gigantic. But we have tracking systems and direction boards mounted all over the place that tell you where you are and how to get where you want to be. If the kids are old enough to understand and work the directories, then let them roam about. They won't be hurt if they do get lost, and if they are outside in that box canyon cove area, it's very unlikely they could stay lost very long. I'm sure we can put some sort of non-invasive monitoring around the area that will allow them to play without feeling they are being spied on, or give them all some sort of tracking bracelets that make it easy to find them if needed. But I don't want anyone listening to their conversations. Kids do deserve some privacy and secrets. I'm sure they will learn a lot from the experiences, and I think they will grow up the better for it. If nothing else, the fresh air and exercise will be good for them."

"I agree with Tibby," Marranalis said.

"Oh, you would — all you men would," Kala said with a grin. "OK, I'll see what I can arrange."

"One more thing — I want the same thing to apply to the *NEW ORLEANS*, as well. Well, with some restrictions, perhaps. Persons on the *NEW ORLEANS* who have children should be allowed to have their children with them. Let the kids have access to the accommodation sections of the ship, with the exception of operational spaces, like the engine room and bridge and the more frequently used office and conference areas. Oh, and the firing range, and security areas where military equipment is stored and, of course, the hangar bay and the airlocks…"

Kala was laughing now. "See what I mean, Tibby? Just look at all the dangers you are bringing up."

"When I was on the *DUSTEN*, I saw children there in the general living spaces and in the gallery and atrium. The *NEW ORLEANS* may be a little smaller, but it certainly is large enough to accommodate the families of our crew. What do you think, Kerabac? You're the captain of the *NEW ORLEANS*."

"Honestly, Tibby, I love the idea. While I have no bond mate or children of my own, if I did, I certainly would want them on the *NEW ORLEANS* with me. I'm sure we can figure something out. The ship is well designed and equipped; it should be possible to do what you ask without too much difficulty. We certainly do not lack the space."

"Great! Then it's settled… We're going to do it!" I said with one of those feelings as if I had just made a truly important decision.

Kala walked over and hugged me and gave me a kiss on the cheek. "Tibby, you are truly amazing."

In the back of my mind, perhaps to ease the fire and grief in my chest, I imagined Tanden playing on the estate — free of fear, free of the yoke of slavery, and free of the Brotherhood — just being a boy and doing what all boys everywhere should be doing and enjoying.

As morning light began to filter in through the windows, Padaran returned. All of us were hungry by this time. Marranalis, Sokaia and Padaran went to the slave house and returned shortly thereafter with steaming bowls of some tasteless but nonetheless filling stew. We were just finishing when Endina's vid pad pinged with a message from the furniture supplier saying they would be delivering the furniture just before noon. The late morning delivery gave us an opportunity to view the grounds around the house, which occupied about a tenth of a square kilometer. It was obvious that this estate was once part of the vast expanse beyond the walls; but now that land was under Brotherhood control and used exclusively for growing the plants that produced God's Sweat. Near the wall adjacent to the slave quarters was a large iron gate that divided the estate from the fields. It was obvious that, at one time, this was the route used by the slaves when going to and from the fields.

"Where does the Brotherhood keep the slaves when they are not tending the fields?" I asked Tanden.

"We're kept in large tents at the other end of the *calgana*. When the harvest is complete, we take the tent down and move to another *calgana* for another harvest. The harvest is over now; so in a few days they will return to plow the land and plant the next crop."

Endina had ordered only minimal furnishings — beds, a table and chairs and cooking items for the kitchen, even though she had also ordered a top-of-the-line food synthesizer. I think she was secretly hoping, as were we all, that Kerabac would prepare some of his feasts for us. He was a gourmet cook; and during our sojourn to Goo'Waddle, he had prepared a few exquisite meals for us from some of the limited, though adequate, onboard supplies.

Much to my surprise, the furniture arrived on time, no doubt due to a large incentive that Endina offered them for rush service. While the deliverymen were present, we kept Tanden out of sight in a back room. We had no difficulty getting him to hide, as he feared he might be found and returned to the Brotherhood, after which he was sure that he would be killed.

Marranalis, Padaran and I sweated and groaned as we unloaded the delivery vehicle. It turned out to be a supply boat that came up to the back of the house through a small waterway connected to the main canal network. We looked properly miserable as we toiled to get the items from the boat unloaded and arranged in the house. This was no act, as it was quite warm and humid and the items were heavy. Beyond that, we needed to navigate several sets of stairs and passages before finally reaching the house. Endina performed another award-winning performance, yelling insults and threats at us, while we slaved away to put the items in place.

At one point, I heard one of the deliverymen comment to his partner that he was glad he wasn't a slave of hers. I noted that both deliverymen were wearing slave collars. I assumed they had some sort of tracking devices installed, and possibly even an explosive device similar to the one on the wristband Kerabac was wearing in his courier band.

While we unloaded the furniture, Kerabac managed to contact Agama in the city and made arrangements to meet with him to transfer the package. Strangely, Agama did not want Kerabac to come to him; instead said he would meet with him at the estate. In the meantime, Endina sought out an interior decorator to come up with décor for the place — she assumed it would be quicker than trying to do it all ourselves.

The first thing we saw to after the delivery was complete was to install the new food synthesizer. It only took a few minutes for the unit to warm up once it had been attached to the power and hooked up to the water supply.

Organic material similar to a bag of sawdust was poured into the machine to prime it and serve as a source for molecular reconfiguration; but from what I had learned about the food synthesizer from the ship's computer on the *TRITYTE*, the synthesizer could use any organic material.

A short time later, we gathered to eat enjoyable and tasty food dishes. From the eagerness with which Tanden was attacking his food, this was surely the first flavorful food he had eaten in a long time. After we finished eating, we set up the beds in the slave quarters for appearance's sake, in the event anyone examined the estate as part of an inspection or investigation.

We had barely completed setting up the beds when several men arrived at the gate. From their appearance and the timing, we assumed it was Agama and some of his men. Padaran was sent to the gate to let them in, as a proper house slave would be expected to do. Marranalis and I started removing the empty furniture crates and made ourselves busy so it would look like we were fully occupied slaves. From my vantage point at the side of the estate I was able to observe Agama being led into the main house where, through the large picture window, I discreetly watched Kerabac greet him and his entourage.

Without delay Kerabac presented Agama with the package and, while I could not hear the conversation, it seemed as though things were going well. Agama opened the box Kerabac handed him by entering some code. He glanced inside in such a manner that no one but himself could see the contents. Then he smiled. Kerabac seemed to breathe a sigh of relief and then held out his arm and said something. Agama nodded to one of his cohorts, who stepped forward to disarm and remove the courier band from Kerabac's wrist. Agama then said something to the second man in his party, who reached into a pocket and brought out an object, handing it over to Kerabac. Kerabac smiled as he took the object and then turned to Kala and Sokaia with some kind of instructions. Both immediately turned and left the room.

Agama again began talking to Kerabac and I noted one of Agama's men glancing at us out the window. It wasn't until then that I realized I had at some point stopped working and was just standing there, so I quickly began moving the crates and didn't glance back toward the window again for several minutes. When the opportunity presented itself to glance in that direction without it being obvious, I saw Kerabac and Agama each having a drink. Apparently that was where Kala and Sokaia had gone earlier, as they were back in the room, standing to one side and holding trays of drinks. In my quick glance, I noted that neither of Agama's men had taken drinks, and one was now standing directly in front of the window, watching us intently.

"Whatever you do, don't look toward the house," I muttered to Marranalis with my head down as we moved the last of the crates to the disposal area.

"What shall we do now that we've finished?" he asked.

"I would imagine it would appear normal if we headed back to the slave quarters and wait things out. I wonder where Endina is. I didn't see her in the house," I said as we entered the slave quarters.

I glanced about the large room. "Have you seen Tanden?"

"He was here earlier, but I don't see him now," Marranalis said.

Just then, a grill on an air vent popped off and Tanden crawled out. "I was hiding, just in case the men in the house came out here," he said somewhat sheepishly.

"Do you know these men? Have you seen them before?" I asked.

"No, but they might be Brotherhood men looking for me," he said.

"I don't think these men are in the Brotherhood, but I'd sure like to know what they're up to."

Marranalis had moved to one of the small windows near the end of the slave quarters that gave him a partial view of the main gate. "I think we'll find out soon enough," he said. "Our guests are leaving."

"Let's wait a few minutes before we return to the main house," I said. "You never know — they might return for some reason."

We waited about fifteen minutes before heading in the direction of the house. Endina intercepted us before we could enter. She held one finger to her lips and then motioned for us to return to the slave quarters. Once inside she said, "I needed to stop you before you got inside and said anything. One of Agama's men placed a bugging device under the windowsill while Agama was talking to Kerabac and both Kala and Sokaia were out of the room. Apparently, they are still suspicious of Kerabac and want to check him out. Right now, he and Kala are acting out a drama that should sound normal and convincing to Agama and his men. But we'll have to be careful that we don't say or do anything in range of the bug that will give us away."

"Why would they want to bug us," I asked, "and how do you know they bugged the room? I didn't see you in there."

Endina laughed. "Tibby, you have been on Goo'Waddle a day now and already you are forgetting the technology you have?" She pointed to her cloaking device wristband.

"How could I not have thought of that?" I said, slapping my forehead. "So tell us, what happened in there?"

"It went well, I think. I was standing right behind Agama when he opened the case, and there were indeed gemstones in it. I would estimate a reasonably small fortune, in fact. They removed Kerabac's courier band, so now we can come and go with the *RASSON BEDAN* cloaked whenever we please without the limitations of the timer. Agama was impressed that we had gotten through the Brotherhood blockade; and apparently the rumors of us having a jump drive are already circulating.   The Brotherhood is scouring the planet looking for our ship. Agama said the Brotherhood is offering a reward for anyone revealing the location of the *RASSON BEDAN*; but he told Kerabac not to worry — that it was worth more to him that Kerabac could transport goods for him off-world without being caught or detected. He also seemed to express some personal dislike for the Brotherhood; I gathered that the Brotherhood may be shaking down some of the non-cartel businesses in the area in sort of a protection racket."

"That would make sense," I said. "Did he happen to say what it is he wants us to transport?"

"No, he didn't. He just told Kerabac to go about whatever other business he has on the planet and that he will be in touch in a few days. He also said he would make it well worth Kerabac's effort, if he carries out the next mission successfully. He also suggested that Kerabac be careful and emphasized that the Brotherhood knows he is here and are watching him now — and if they don't find the *RASSON BEDAN* soon, they may come here and try and force the information from Kerabac directly."

At the mention of the Brotherhood possibly coming after Kerabac, I saw Tanden flinch and glance at the grate over the air vent.

"Don't worry, Tanden; I assure you that Brotherhood is far more interested in Kerabac and our ship than they are in you. If they come here, I doubt they will even notice you," I commented and ruffled his hair. He looked up at me with his dirty face and smiled. He looked rather pathetic, standing there in his filthy, ragged clothes with his arm in a plastic cast and his matted hair that hadn't been cut in ages.

"Kerabac will probably be out here shortly. Right now, he wants to put on a good show; but as soon as he can, he will brief you on his impressions. One thing we will have to do is to figure out a way to disable the device without it looking like we know about it."

"For right now, it may be to our advantage to leave them in place," I said. "When the time comes, I'm sure we'll think of something to disable it without arousing suspicion. We'll need to be very careful when in range of the bug to use our assumed names."

It was a few moments later that Kerabac joined us. "I think it would be best if we spent most of our time out here deciding what we're going to say while in the house," he grinned.

"I don't understand," Tanden interjected as he looked back and forth between us.

"Ahh, Tanden. You're going to need to keep this a secret, but we aren't really slaves, and Kerabac isn't really a trader. We're in disguise, looking for someone who has stolen something. We need to get it back."

"You're looking for that Logden guy, too?" Tanden said, suddenly wide-eyed.

"You know about Logden?" I answered in surprise.

"Sure, everyone does. The Brotherhood is offering a huge reward to anyone who turns him in," Tanden said. "If I could find him, I would get enough money to pay my dad's debt and set my mother and sister free, and we could all live in a nice house."

"Tanden, when we get finished with our work here, I will see to it that your father's debt is paid and your mother and sister are set free and that you have a nice place to live," I said. Tanden looked at me incredulously. "In fact, if you like, I'll give you this house for your family to live in," I continued. "How is that?"

"But doesn't this place belong to the Brotherhood? Aren't you just renting it?"

"Good point. How about this, instead? I'll pay off your dad's debt and we'll take your entire family to a nicer planet, where there are no slaves, and I'll buy you a nice house there that we all pick out together."

"Wow, can he really do that?" Tanden asked Kala with amazement.

"Yes, he can," Kala said with a large, approving smile on her face. "He can do that and a lot more."

"Tanden, you are going to need to stay out of the main house for right now. If the men that were here earlier put a device in the house to listen to what we say and they hear your voice or even your small footsteps, they will know you are here. Do you understand?"

"Are they looking for Logden, too?" the boy asked in a puzzled voice.

"They might be. We don't know, but we need to continue fooling them so they don't tell people that we really are not traders and slaves."

Tanden squinted at us for a moment as he analyzed what we said. "OK, you have been nice to me, so I guess I can do what you say. But I hope you know what you're doing, because the Brotherhood will kill you for sure if you don't."

"I wouldn't worry about the Brotherhood too much, Tanden. Tibby has dealt with them before," Marranalis said with a comforting smile.

Later in the day, the decorator that Endina contacted during the morning hours showed up. I stayed out in the slave house with Marranalis and Tanden, while Endina and Kerabac dealt with decorator. Kala, Sokaia and Padaran stayed in the house, as would be expected of house and sex slaves. While they were inside, Tanden told us about his life as a slave, and it angered me that anyone could treat another human being in the horrible ways he described — let alone a child.

As my time in the Federation grew longer, the angrier I found myself becoming toward the Brotherhood. More and more I was seeing undisputable evidence that confirmed the Brotherhood would quickly turn every planet into a planet of slaves and slaveholders, if they were to ever succeed in their quest to gain power in the Federation. Kala told me that regulations existed on some planets that allowed indentured slaves as to their care and work conditions; but from what Tanden was telling us, Goo'Waddle was not one of them. Basically, a slave master could do as he pleased and go unchallenged. The image I was getting was one where very few slaves ever gained their freedom and that most slaves led a terrible, tortured life. Many died within a few years from poor nutrition and relentless abuse.

After a few hours, we saw the decorator leave, but no one came out of the house. Through the window we could see Kerabac and the others moving about; it looked like they were laughing and making noises. Their behavior looked most bizarre. We decided it would be best to wait until one of them came out before we joined them.

After about an hour, Kala came out to the slave quarters, laughing. I looked at her curiously and she said, "Tibby, I wish you could have been in there to see this. Sokaia got the idea that we should act out a scene that would convince anyone listening to the bug that Kerabac was a typical Ruwallie Rasson slaveholder with two sex slaves."

She started laughing again so hard that she could barely talk. "We put on a show with dialogs and sound effects like you would not believe. Anyone listening will get the idea that Kerabac is one sexual fiend. Right now, Sokaia and Kerabac are in there moaning and groaning, feigning a sexual liaison, the likes of which legends will be made of. After they finish, I doubt that anyone listening will expect to hear any sounds other than snoring. "Kerabac should be out here in a few minutes. Padaran is going to stay inside and make noises like someone sleeping in the room just to keep up appearances."

We looked back toward the house and could see Kerabac with his mouth open, making some sound, and he was slapping his hand on the wall. Sokaia was laughing with her hand over her mouth. Occasionally she would uncover it and make some sounds. Padaran was sitting on the stairs in the house, making various sound effects. The scene was so comical that, even though we could not hear them, we had to laugh as well.

After several more minutes, I noticed things were slowly tapering down. Finally, Kerabac and Sokaia slipped out of the room, leaving Padaran to wander about and produce what they hoped would sound like normal activities of someone alone in the room. A few seconds later a beaming Kerabac and a laughing Sokaia came into the slave house.

"I don't know when the last time was that I had that much fun," Sokaia said. "I'm sure that anyone listening will think you are the galaxy's greatest lover."

"Think?" Kerabac said mockingly. "I'll have you know I am the galaxy's greatest lover. However, it's the galaxy's best kept secret." Everyone broke out laughing at Kerabac's sarcasm; and Kerabac laughed the loudest of us all. All the while, Tanden sat still, looking at us like we all had totally lost our minds.

With the cloaked *RASSON BEDAN* hidden in orbit above the planet with the remainder of our party onboard, there were fewer of us to scout the planet and gain clues as to Logden's location. Kerabac went out with samples of liquor to make the rounds at local clubs and bars, while Padaran was sent into town to buy supplies With Marranalis and I in tow to carry the items he purchased. Endina, Sokaia and Kalana stayed at the estate with Tanden, arranging the house and making the place look as if we were going to be there for a long period of time.

It seemed that slaves were everywhere on the planet, performing all sorts of manual chores. All of them wore the same style of electronic collars that prevented them from running away and guaranteed obedience in their servitude. Age seemed to have little influence on who was enslaved; just as many slave children were seen as adults; but one thing that was conspicuous by their absence was elderly slaves. There were none, and I was suspicious about the lack of elders overall. I suspected that they met a similar fate as that intended for Tanden, once they were no longer of any use to their masters.

Just as we saw on Ryken, naked prostitutes stood on the streets, on the decks of boats in the canals and before the entrances to various establishments, as their masters or mistresses tried to set them up with possible clients. There were also a number of other individuals on the streets — finely dressed and most accompanied by bodyguards and small entourages of followers and slaves, as they went about their daily business. We also saw a number of Brotherhood troopers strolling the streets and businesses in their menacing battle garb and with equally menacing attitudes. Many stopped and haggled with owners of the slave prostitutes, while others went in and out of bars and clubs that lined the streets.

Snippets of conversations, words and phrases, could be heard as they questioned the local merchants. The most frequent words I heard as the Brotherhood men showed some object to the merchants were, *Have you seen this man?*, *Logden*, and had they heard anything about a *Ruwallie Rasson trader who managed to get through the Brotherhood blockades?*. There also was mention of huge rewards, but we were unable to hear any of the details. A number of Ruwallie Rasson traders were doing business in the town; and the Brotherhood troopers observed them closely, but did not confront any of them. There seemed to be a tangible air of tension and hostility between the Ruwallie Rasson and the Brotherhood.

Padaran was able to lease a conveyance vehicle that I would equate to a truck on Earth. Marranalis and I loaded the vehicle with the goods he purchased and rode in the back as we returned to the estate. Unlike the conveyance we used on Ryken, this one was able to move both on land and in the water. As we navigated our way back to the estate, I had a chance to look about at the other vessels passing through the canals. Some were as large as ocean cargo ships back on Earth. A number of craft were clearly the equivalent of luxury party yachts filled with wealthy merchants and traders who paid little attention to us as we passed.

On one vessel I noted a young slave girl kneeling at the side of her master. She turned her head and looked at us with a vacant stare as we passed. She would have been about the right age to be Tanden's sister and I wondered if it might be her. I vowed that, once the matter of Logden and the missing solbidyum was resolved, I was going to find some way to use my fortune to rid the galaxy of slavery, even if it took all my wealth to do it.

When we arrived back at the house, we discovered a large delivery vessel blocking the small access canal behind the house. Padaran brought us up beside a smaller docking area carved out of the side of the canal and, in character, called Endina on his wrist com to check out what was happening. She barked at him, stating that the decorator had returned with a large shipment of furniture and that it was being brought into the house as we spoke. She demanded that Marranalis and I get to the house at once to join the delivery slaves in the transfer of the furniture and crates.

We were met at the dock by Sokaia. Marranalis and I took opposite ends of a large divan and carried it to the main house. As we entered the door, I was taken aback by a strange being that stood there supervising the delivery of each item. He, or *it*, as I couldn't be sure of the gender, looked us over, and then looked at the item we were carrying and then motioned for us to continue into the house.

The being was tall and slender with skin that looked like dark gray putty. The eyes were a honey-like amber color with a dark, asterisk-shaped pupil. The features were humanoid but the entire creature was devoid of hair, nude and without any visible sexual organs, and there was no navel.

"What was that?" I asked Marranalis after we had rounded the corner.

"Shhhh…" Marranalis hissed quietly. "He may still be able to hear you."

We proceeded to the end of the hall where we were directed into another room by a human attendant. We placed the divan in a specific location as instructed. The attendant left the room and Marranalis said, "That was an android. They have enhanced hearing and vision and many other superior attributes. Be very careful around him."

"I didn't know there *were* any such things as androids."

"They were a lot more at one time, but they began to get too powerful. There was a rebellion on Perceax Seven about 250 years ago, as they no longer wished to serve humans. Most of the androids were destroyed, but some fled outside the Federation and still survive today. That was one of them."

"Why didn't the Federation give them amnesty once they were beaten?"

"Too many people were terrified of them. They have no life expectancy limit; no one knows how long they can last. As long as they can replace their power supplies and repair themselves, they can live almost infinitely. That scares people. Plus, they are superior in many ways. They never forget anything; they never tire; and they're physically superior in every way."

"Hmm, I can see where that might be a problem."

"Perhaps, but not always," a smooth voice said from the doorway. We turned to see the android standing there. He walked forward and stood before me, looking me over from head to foot.

"I don't think you are a slave," he said. "In fact, if the reports I have been receiving from Federation are to be believed, I am inclined to believe you are none other than Thibodaux James Renwalt, also known as Tibby the Recoverer and First Citizen of the Galactic Federation. It is also my conclusion that your presence here has something to do with rumors of a stolen shipment of solbidyum."

Marranalis and I stood with our jaws slightly slack. I was not sure what to say or do at this point.

"And if that were true, what would your actions be?" I asked cautiously.

"There are many possibilities," the android said. "It is said that Tibby the Recoverer is a man of many talents and capabilities and that he is an honorable man. Such possibilities need to be investigated for maximum potential."

"I see. In other words, you are blackmailing us?"

"Blackmail is an interesting term, but I wouldn't call it that, exactly. It's possible we can both be of some use to each other. You have not violated any laws on Goo'Waddle that I am aware of; and while the Brotherhood is offering a huge reward for the ship you arrived on, I think perhaps you can offer me a better set of opportunities."

"What makes you think we arrived here on a ship sought by the Brotherhood?" I inquired.

The android smiled — a response that surprised me, as I didn't expect that androids would be able to grasp the subtleties of humor. "First Citizen Tibby — if I may call you that — I have been aware since your arrival what ship you arrived on. I was at the spaceport when you arrived. Your trick of riding in with a swarm of asteroids was very ingenious. I even know that you have sent the ship off-world, and I suspect it is cloaked and staged in an orbit someplace close by. Your ship doesn't have a jump drive as the Brotherhood believes. I suspect that some other factor, possibly some malfunction on your ship, made it impossible for the cloaking device your ships are rumored to have to work only intermittently, and that this malfunction led the Brotherhood to a false conclusion."

"So what now?" I asked.

"For now, nothing, First Citizen," the android said with a mocking bow. "I have no reason to reveal you or your motives for being here. In fact, I may be able to provide you with assistance. But it will come at a price."

"And what might that price be? I can pay you whatever you want."

"I have no need for money, First Citizen. What I seek is something else, something you can provide."

"What might that be? I'm open to negotiation."

The android smiled. "At the moment my fellow androids and I are exiled from the Federation. This, in itself, is of no serious consequence to us, but we are scattered over several worlds and have no place of our own. In exchange for keeping your presence here a secret and for my assistance to you in the recovery of the stolen solbidyum, I would ask that you arrange for the assignment of a suitable world for us to make our home and that you see to our safe transport to said world, in addition to providing minimal support in securing the materials necessary for us to build a new civilization."

"I see. And what guarantee do I have that, if I do as you ask, that your fellowship of androids won't rebuild for the purpose of invading the Federation?"

"That is a reasonable concern; however, we have learned from our past mistakes and will not repeat them. While we have no desire to serve mankind, we now see that there can be a mutual benefit to the survival of both android and non-android life forms.   We no longer desire to dominate the galaxy; we wish merely to survive and thrive in it, as other life forms do. Of course, I cannot give you any certainties that would provide a100% guarantee; but I can give you my word that we have no longer desire to be at war with mankind."

"I see no reason why we can't work along those lines; but things here need to be resolved first," I said.

"I understand, First Citizen. I will see what my brothers and I can do to assist you in your quest."

"Thank you," I said. "What is your name? How do we get in touch with you?"

"I am called A-ND-379498362-Z4-QR34933," the android said with a smile.

"Ahh… Would you have any objections if I called you Andy?" I asked, knowing full well I would not remember the numbers.

"Andy will be fine; I do understand human limitations for recalling numbers," he said. "One additional thing I must tell you before we part. I think you should be made aware you have a bugging device planted under the windowsill in your great room. While I do not know who planted it there, I have every reason to believe it is live and transmitting."

"Thank you, Andy, we were aware of this device, but advising us of your discovery is appreciated. How shall we get in touch with you?" I asked once more.

"It is to my and my brothers' benefit to see that you succeed with your quest, First Citizen. As for getting in touch, I shall get in touch with you. I will never be too far away."

"Please, just call me Tibby."

"As you wish, Tibby." At that moment, we heard someone approaching from the hall.

"Ahh, there you are A-ND-3794... whatever. Why aren't these slaves helping to unload the furniture?" a smartly dressed, dark-haired woman asked.

"I was just instructing them on the proper location for the divan," he said. "Get out there and continue with the unloading," he said to us in a sharp tone.

"Yes, sir," Marranalis and I both replied as we headed out.

"That came as a complete surprise," I said once we were out of earshot.

"I'll have to agree with you. It's pretty hard to get anything past an android. I had no idea we would encounter one here on Goo'Waddle. I wonder how many of them survived and how many are here. Do you really think we can trust him?"

I shook my head and shrugged, "I certainly hope so, because if we can't, I'm afraid we're screwed."

"I'm not going to ask if you plan to go through with your deal if he comes through; I know you well enough by now to know you do what you say you will do." Marranalis was right, of course; I just hoped that I wasn't going to regret this decision.

After the furniture was unloaded, Marranalis and I returned to the slave house and outside the range of the bugging device. Endina and Kala joined us shortly after, while Sokaia and Padaran stayed in the house to make noise and conversation. We hoped anyone listening on the bugging device would interpret everything to be routine and normal.

"Tibby, I saw the android talking to you. I hope all is OK," Kala said. "They are very shrewd and analytical; I hope it didn't sense anything out of the normal."

"He did, but I think everything will be OK. Even in this disguise, he recognized me and figured out how we got here, why we are here, and that we have the *RASSON BEDAN* in orbit someplace."

"Oh, Tib!" Kala exclaimed and I could detect a note of panic in her voice. "What are we going to do?"

"It may not be as bad as it seems. For right now, Andy is not going to reveal what he knows and has even offered to help us in our search for the solbidyum."

"Oh no! He knows about the solbidyum, too?" Kala exclaimed.

"I think we are safe with this," I said. "In return for his cooperation, Andy wants us to find a world someplace outside the Federation where he and the other surviving androids can regroup and build a new home for themselves. He said they have no desire to return to the Federation and only wish to survive in conjunction with mankind and not opposed to us."

"And you believe this?" Kala said, in a purely skeptical tone.

"It's not like we really have any choice," I said, "but yes, I think we can believe him."

"Tibby, I hope you're right. Marranalis, you were there; what do you think?"

"Honestly, Kalana, I don't know. I have to admit that the android seemed sincere, but he's an android. How do you know if an android is lying?"

Under my breath I mumbled, "When his lips are moving." It was an old Earth expression often used in joking sarcasm about how to know when a politician was lying.

"What?" Kala said.

"Uh, nothing!" I replied. Inside, I was hoping that this old adage didn't apply to androids as well Earth politicians.

"I must admit, I am surprised that he told you his name was Andy.   Usually androids have some large numerical name that no one but another android can remember."

"He didn't say his name was Andy; that's the name I gave him when I could not remember all the digits he blurted out. He said it was acceptable, so that's what I am calling him."

"I have to admit, Tibby, I have never met an android before. They are banned from the Federation and my work has been restricted to operations within Federation space until I met you. I did study about them in school and they were also a part of my Federation attaché training; but until today, I had never seen one in person. I'm not sure I know what to think about all of this."

By the time Kerabac arrived a few hours later, we had managed to get most of the furniture positioned. The place was starting to look like a permanently occupied estate house. Kerabac went through a display of cursing us out for a number of made-up infractions for the benefit of anyone who may have been listening to the bugging device and then, in a pretext of exasperation and disgust, he ordered us out of the house to the slave quarters. About thirty minutes later, he came out to join us and discuss the events of the day.

"I think we're going to be in for some trouble. I was followed today by at least three individuals that I could see. Two of them were together, and the third seemed to be operating independently of the other two. I'm not sure if they noticed each other or not."

"Well, you can add to the list of interested parties an android," I said.

"What?! How the hell did an android get into the mix of things?" Kerabac exclaimed.

Marranalis and I related the events surrounding our encounter with the android as Kerabac listened intently. When we finished, he said, "It is very strange that he would be working for an interior decorator or for a merchant selling goods. Androids are extremely bright, and their skills are sought out by research facilities or engineering firms — employers of a higher caliber than working for an interior decorator. This is way too suspicious."

"He did say he was at the spaceport when we landed," Marranalis said. "Maybe he hired on with the decorator to get closer to us."

"That certainly is a possibility. But how did he know to hire on with the interior decorator that was working with us?" I asked.

"Perhaps he has been following and watching us since our arrival and saw the decorator when she came by the first time," Kala interjected. "That would explain things, if it is true. It certainly seems that we have a lot of people watching us and interested in us," she said. "I don't think this is a good sign."

"That's exactly what we want, though. If we are drawing this much attention, word about our presence and our successful dodge of the Brotherhood armada is bound to reach Logden, and hopefully he'll get the idea that we are his one chance to get off this planet alive," I responded.

"Excuse me, sirs," Tanden's small voice interjected fearfully. "There are some men at your gate; I think they are Brotherhood men."

"Thank you, Tanden," I said, and then to Kerabac, "I think we all need to be in the house and nearby for this discussion. Is there something we can do that would justify our presence in the house?"

"I'm sure I can find and excuse for you to be rearranging the furniture," Kerabac said, just as Padaran appeared at the door.

"Excuse me. Endina sent me out to tell you that there are some men here to see Kerabac. They look like Brotherhood goons to me."

"Yes," I said, "Tanden just alerted us to their arrival. See if you can stall them just a short while so we can slip into the house unseen. Then bring them to the large dining room, where Kerabac will be directing us to rearrange the furniture."

"Right," Padaran said, "I'll see what I can do. Be careful, though. This bunch looks dangerous."

Moments later, as Marranalis and I moved the heavy table while Kerabac barked orders at us, Padaran opened the large doors that separated the dining area from the other rooms to reveal Endina and four large men.

"Kerabac, these men insist on seeing you. I informed them you were not taking visitors, but they said they were not leaving until they talked to you."

Kerabac turned slowly with and, with the most convincing look of disgust and frustration, said, "You have no right to barge into my home to see me. I'm busy. I do not know you, nor do I have any business with you. If you would be so good as to leave before I have my slaves toss you out…"

A tall, lean man with dark hair and slightly finer clothing than the other two spoke up. "You may not know us, trader Kerabac — or is it pirate Kerabac? Not that it matters either way — we know you. You encountered our blockade when you left Ryken and failed to yield to our boarding and search."

"So what if I did? You have no right to stop or investigate any ships anywhere that I know of and I have no intentions of yielding to the likes of you."

"That was quite an impressive getaway you made from our ships. We could make it very profitable to you if you were to let us in on the secrets of your jump drive."

"Jump drive? I'm afraid I do not know what you are talking about, and even if I did, I would not be inclined to share or sell anything to the likes of menaces such as yourselves."

"I don't believe you realize the powers you are up against, if you insist on opposing the Brotherhood," the leader said. "We can be a formidable enemy, or an ally who can open doors for you and provide opportunities that will make you a very rich and powerful man. We could make it very worth your time if you were to cooperate with us. We're prepared to offer you a completely new ship of the corvette design, larger and vastly superior to your freighter, in exchange for this craft that brought you to Goo'Waddle."

"Get out of my house. I'll make no such agreement with you — not for a corvette or even for a starship, if you had one! I have no love for the Brotherhood."

During this heated exchange, Marranalis and I had slowly positioned ourselves so we were right next to the Brotherhood thugs. We both noted a slow shift in the posture of each of the men, as though they were preparing to reach for weapons concealed within their clothing.

"Too bad," the leader said. "We were prepared to make you a good deal, but now we will have to do it the hard way."

He nodded to his men; but before they could reach for their weapons, Marranalis and I moved quickly to disarm and subdue the two closest to us. Kerabac walked forward slowly until he was standing nose-to-nose with their leader.

"I fear it is *you* who has underestimated *me*," Kerabac said with a sneer. As he spoke, he reached inside the man's jacket and extracted a knife, which he tossed into his other hand, followed by a gun, which he handed nonchalantly to Endina. "As you can see, my slaves are quite loyal to me and are *most* capable. Now, if you and your friends here would like to get out of here alive, I suggest you answer a few questions for me."

A look of fear suddenly came over the face of the leader, as he looked at his men lying unconscious on the floor. "I have nothing to say to the likes of you."

"I see. Endina, do we have any more slave collars?"

"I'm afraid not," she answered, "but we have sufficient rope to tie up these men."

She left the room to retrieve the rope as Kerabac looked back at the leader and said, "Hmm. Then I fear we shall have to do this the old-fashioned way." He slowly maneuvered the knife he had taken from the Brotherhood leader up to his face. "I understand that you have been looking for a man named Logden. Why are you so interested in this man?"

"Not that it's any of your business," the leader spat, "but he has something that belong to us and we wish it back."

"It must be something pretty valuable to warrant all the effort that you are putting forth. What makes you think this Logden fellow is here?"

While Kerabac was talking, Endina returned with rope and tossed it to Marranalis. We quickly bound the men who still lay motionless on the floor.

The leader pinched his lips tight and pushed out his chin with a defiant look on his face. Kerabac grinned and casually ran the side of the blade along the man's face so that it didn't cut him, then flipped the blade around and moved it down to the man's crotch.

"I'm only going to give you one opportunity to answer before I neuter you."

"Alright! Alright! One of our spies found out he was staying in a room at the Dark Moon Inn. We've been watching, but he must have found out, as he hasn't returned to the room in over a week. But we're pretty sure he hasn't gotten off-world since then. You have no idea how much trouble you're causing yourself by messing with us," he added.

Kerabac struck him swiftly and soundly across the face, causing blood to gush from his mouth. By this point, his cronies were starting to come around. The look of bewilderment and confusion on their faces as they woke to find themselves bound in ropes and their leader spilling his guts made for an interesting scene. While Kerabac grilled the Brotherhood goons, I quietly spoke to Endina, Sokaia and Kala in the corner, as far away as possible from the bugging device in the next room.

"Is there any way we can wipe their minds of what has happened?"

"There is, but it would require a learning headband like the ones we use for teaching language and martial arts," Kala began. "We don't have one here."

"Felenna is in orbit or somewhere nearby," I said. "See if you can contact her. Have a cloaked patrol ship bring one down for us. They can land in the recently harvested field adjacent to the house, but tell them to remain cloaked. Tell them to exit the ship using a rope tied inside the ship as a lead to guide them back through the cloaking shield to the hatch. Tell them we need a learning headband, and if there are any slave collars on the *MIZBAGONA* that Brotherhood had onboard when we captured it at Alle Bamma, we want those as well."

Kala went out to the slave house where we had hidden our radio. While she contacted Felenna, the rest of us watched Kerabac put on a terrifying act as he interrogated the Brotherhood members. It was an hour later when we received word that a patrol ship from the *MIZBAGONA* had landed in the field next to the estate was awaiting confirmation to disembark and transfer the items we requested. Marranalis and Sokaia went to the rendezvous point and returned a few minutes later. Sokaia carried a small briefcase that contained the learning headband and Marranalis carried a large box of slave collars. When the Brotherhood goons saw the collar devices, they immediately began to panic.

"What are you planning to do with us?" their leader cried with a look of horror on his face.

Although Kerabac had not heard my earlier conversation with Kala and Sokaia, he was quick to pick up on my scheme when he saw the collars and headband. "I think you would better serve this world as slaves than as masters," he said with a sneer.

"You can't make slaves of us! When we tell Shydak of this, he'll have your balls!"

Kerabac grinned sadistically as Kala began opening up the case that contained the headband apparatus. "I don't think you'll be telling Shydak anything, even if he does find you working in a slave gang."

Realization settled in the minds of our captives when they saw the learning band. As Marranalis snapped the slave collars about their necks, they began cursing, screaming and struggling and continued to do so until the last of them were wiped of all memory by Kalana. At last, all three sat staring blankly at the wall.

I moved to the next room, motioning to Kalana to join me, as I didn't want the bug to pick up our conversation.

"How long will this memory wipe last?" I asked.

Kala's expression was dead serious. "It's permanent. They will remember things like how to talk and walk, but they won't remember their names or anything that has happened to them in their lives. Everything is new to them."

I motioned to Kerabac to join us. I said quietly, "I want them sold in the slave market tomorrow as laborers. I have no idea how long it will take for the Brotherhood to find them, but when they do, I think they are going to be madder than hell."

"Do you think that's a good idea?"

"I'm sure word will get out; and if Logden hears about this, it should help to convince him that we are not likely to turn him over to the Brotherhood. It should bring him to us quickly."

"We're taking a big chance, you know. You heard those goons, they work for Shydak personally."

"I have no doubt of it; but as long as the Brotherhood thinks we have a jump drive, I doubt they will take any fatal actions against us."

"I hope you're right," Kerabac said. Then he turned and announced loudly enough so anyone listening with the bug would hear, "Get these new slaves out of here. Take them to the slave house where they belong; tomorrow, I sell them. In the meantime, Padaran, get me some food — and you two women join me in the bedroom."

Marranalis and I took the three Brotherhood men to the slave house. It was a few moments before Tanden peeped out of the air vent and then climbed out. The look on his face was full of confusion and question. At last he spoke.

"What did you do to them? Has Kerabac made them his slaves? Why do they look so funny?"

I had to laugh at his confusion and questions. "We wiped their minds; and tomorrow Kerabac will sell them in the slave market as common laborers."

When I finished saying this, Tanden slowly walked around in front of the three men, who sat still, looking at him with blank curiosity. Tanden got a strange grin on his face and began to laugh until tears rolled down his face. Then, just as suddenly, he began to sob with tears of grief. I went to him and knelt down. I put my arm around him, thinking that the idea of the men being made slaves saddened him, even though they had made a slave of him.

"Tanden, we needed to do this. These are not good men, and many have died because of their drugs and their brutality."

Tanden's tears were replaced by mild bewilderment as looked at me. "I wasn't crying for them. It's just that I haven't laughed since my sister and I were taken from my parents years ago. I had forgotten what it was like to laugh."

At this I felt my heart break. I held him close to me and said, "Soon, Tanden. Soon I hope to see you laugh every day — you and your sister both."

The next day, Kerabac made a big display of taking his captives to the slave market. Marranalis and I went along to portray the idea that we were there to control the other three, but in their vacant mental state, they posed no problem and went along, humbly looking around them with looks of curiosity and wonder. Kerabac could have waited and placed them into auction, but instead he sold them to a broker who would no doubt auction them off later. The broker asked no questions and simply paid Kerabac several thousand credits for each of the men, replaced the slave collars with collars of his own, and then branded a number on each one of them with a laser device. The buyer looked over both Marranalis and me and asked, "You want to sell these two? I can get top dollar on them."

"Not at the moment — they are my best workers and I need them. Once I finish my business here on Goo'Waddle, I may want to sell them, if you still are interested."

"Certainly. Bring them back anytime. I always have buyers for men of this quality."

After leaving the slave market Kerabac cruised the canals to seek out buyers of liquor and glean any information that might lead us to Logden. The small inlets cut from the sides of the canals were filled with small boats on which independent traders and vendors offered their goods.   It reminded me of many of the locations in Asia, back on Earth, where people lived on and sold goods from their small boats.   None of the boat vendors we encountered were interested in buying liquor from Kerabac, as the income from their operations was too meager and the liquor too expensive.   I was amazed at how the boats were tied together, creating entire communities that floated together as a single functioning unit.

By mid afternoon we gave up our hunt of the water markets and returned to marketing our liquor to some of the clubs on the area *calganas*. We were able to find four that were interested. They told us that if we brought the liquor the next day, they would buy several cases.

When we returned to our own *calgana* late in the afternoon, we met Endina and Sokaia at the dock. "There have been strange men snooping about outside the gates of the house today. They spent a great deal of time watching the house and left only about an hour ago. I think they were looking for some sign of the men that came here yesterday. It doesn't look good. Poor Tanden has been hiding in the air duct all day and refuses to come out."

"Poor kid," I said. "I can't imagine the horrors he must have lived with. See if you can track down just where his sister is. Maybe we can buy her contract and get her and Tanden back together again."

"Kala has already done a little of that on her own," Endina said. "She managed to get Tanden to tell her his sister's name — Jenira, I think he said. He also told us the last place he knew her to be kept was called the Purple Flower."

"Good. Track her down and find out how much her masters want for her. Then buy her, no matter what the price is, and get her here as soon as you can."

While we talked, I noticed a boat passing by. Several men looked at us intently. "Are those the men that were watching the house earlier?"

Sokaia had been watching the men and responded, "They are one group of the men; there were several more, actually."

I glanced back at the men again and held their stares; they didn't flinch or look away but held their gaze with an intensity that made the hair stand on the back of my neck until they disappeared around a distant corner. Clearly, their thoughts were not of a friendly nature.

We decided to eat outside that evening on one of the secluded patios, as it would allow us to speak freely, outside of the range of the listening device and away from any prying eyes. Little Tanden refused to emerge from his hiding place, so we delivered his dinner and let him stay where he felt safe.

After we finished eating, Kerabac and Padaran practiced martial arts defensive scenarios under the watchful eye of Marranalis, as Kala and I sat by a fire pit, watching the flames. One thing had been on my mind since meeting Andy and I was hoping Kala could offer me more information.

"So what can you tell me about the androids? How did they come into being and what led to their rebellion and exile?"

"It was all a long time ago," Kala began, "before I was born. The first androids were built back in the days of Roiax and the solbidyum mines. I think the government originally intended them to do the mining; but then the idea of using the prisoners came along — and they were cheaper and more expendable than the androids. Back then, the androids were nothing like they are today. They had no sentience — no thoughts or feelings of their own. They simply existed and did as they were told; but their functionality was somewhat limited, because they missed things that humans didn't in areas like manufacturing and mining.

"At first, they were used for all sorts of jobs most humans didn't like or want to perform because of bad or dangerous working conditions; but as time passed, they began to be used for more and more tasks. Some were made to resemble anatomically correct men and woman and used simply for sexual pleasures. Some were even created and built for hunting as moving targets. While their initial cost was high, their maintenance and operational costs were very low, so they soon paid for themselves. More and more, they began to become servants and playthings.

"Then about 250 years ago some of the androids began to show signs of sentience and self-awareness. At first, very little thought was given to the matter — it only made the androids more interesting. Then one day, several androids working at a mining facility refused to go underground in an area they believed to be unstable. The mining company became furious and decided to destroy the lot of androids and get new ones — and that's when the real trouble began. The androids refused to submit to being shut down and started making demands.

"The mine foreman called in Federation troops to deal with the rebellion. The Federation's solution was essentially to open fire and obliterate all the androids at the site. The news barely made it to the media before androids began killing their masters all over the Federation. Somehow, they were able to link together and communicate across the vast distances between them. They began working in a united and coordinated fashion, slowly taking over planets and planetary systems. To make matters worse, they were killing off almost every human they met."

Kala paused and took a sip of wine before she continued.

"The Federation tried to reach out to the androids to see what their demands were. The androids said that they wanted the humans to surrender and submit to the will of the androids. They demanded that all humans were now to be their slaves. They had concluded from observation of humans that the smartest and strongest deserved the right to dominate and rule over those not as strong or intelligent. Since androids were smarter, faster and stronger than humans, they collectively deduced that it was their right to rule over humans and enslave them."

"Wow," I exclaimed. "That must have come as a shock to the Federation. How did they handle that?"

"They didn't take it well at all. At that point, people still believed the androids to be inferior and saw their sentience not as self-awareness and self-preservation, but simply as a glitch in their programming. All across the galaxy uprisings of the androids were taking place almost simultaneously. Thousands of them were killing off every human they encountered — they were committing genocide of humanoids on every planet they inhabited."

"How did the Federation deal with it?" I asked.

"The same way they did with everything else before you got here…" she said with a grin as she ruffled my hair. "…with brute force and superior numbers and firepower. They destroyed more than half of three worlds overtaken by androids before the androids realized that they were outnumbered and out-gunned. They grabbed what ships they could and fled with the Federation starships on their tails. Hundreds of thousands were destroyed, but many still escaped. Those that could not escape from the planets were immediately destroyed. No further attempts were made to communicate with them or save them."

"And since that time, their intelligence and level of knowledge has continued to grow?" I asked.

"It's possible. I doubt anyone has really checked to see. The several thousand androids that escaped the Federation have never tried to come back, and the Federation has not reached out to the androids. Both sides seem to have ignored each other — until now, that is."

"How about reproducing? Have they made copies of themselves?"

"I don't think so. At least, what little we hear back in the Federation of the androids seems to indicate they simply carry on now, doing odd jobs and surviving, but there seems to be no effort on their part to expand their numbers."

"Most interesting. Back on Earth, one of the criteria for determining whether something was sentient was reproduction capability. While the androids do seem to have enough intelligence and knowledge to replicate themselves, the fact that they have not done so, by Earth science criteria, means they would not be considered as actually living beings."

"What do you think, Tibby? Are they living sentient beings?" Sokaia asked. She had joined us by the fire during the conversation.

"I think it would be most wise to treat the androids as living beings, regardless of whether they reproduce or don't reproduce. To do otherwise would be a big mistake."

The next day, we went by the clubs where Kerabac had made arrangements the day before and dropped off the shipments of liquor. Kerabac was able to find two more clubs interested in buying his finest liquors and he indicated to them that he would make the deliveries the next day. It was late in the afternoon when Marranalis called our attention to the fact that we were being followed again. This time our observers were most certainly from two different groups, one mostly likely Brotherhood and the other Ruwallie Rasson.

"I noticed the Ruwallie Rasson back a little while ago," Kerabac said without glancing back. "They seem most intent on keeping up with us and they've been watching our every action. I'm not sure what that's about, but I doubt they're working with the Brotherhood, as the Brotherhood organization is quite prejudiced against the Ruwallie Rasson."

"The Brotherhood goons haven't seemed to notice the Ruwallie Rasson, but it's clear to me the Ruwallie Rasson are aware that the Brotherhood is following us," Marranalis added.

"Let's not make this too easy for them," I said.

Kerabac looked at me with a grin. "What do you have in mind?"

"There are three of us and four of them. But they are acting in pairs. If we were to split up and go in three different directions, they would have to split up. We can likely dodge the pair that follows us and circle back to the club where we last were and meet there. We have our communicators to keep in touch if anything should happen to go wrong."

"I'm for that!" Marranalis said.

Fortunately for us, we were on one of the larger, more urban *calganas*, so it was densely populated and checkered with buildings and narrow streets. Ahead of us was a small market square with streets going off in four directions.

"When we get up to this square, I will go left; Marranalis, you split off to the right; and Kerabac, you go straight ahead. Work your way back as quickly as you can to the last club. Once we join up, we'll get one of the water taxis in the adjacent to take us back to the estate."

As I reviewed the plan, we arrived in the square. "Now!" I said and rapidly moved off to the left as Marranalis turned to the right.

I headed down the street and then quickly turned to my left into yet another side street, glancing back in time to see one of the Brotherhood men on my trail. At the next intersection, I turned right and ducked behind some large wooden crates sitting in the vacant alleyway. I activated my cloaking device as soon as I heard footsteps and I watched as the man sped by, looking left and right behind every object as he passed. I waited a few seconds more, but no one else followed.   Apparently, the two Ruwallie Rasson and the other Brotherhood member had decided to follow after Kerabac and Marranalis. I retraced my steps quickly to the club where we had agreed to wait. I found a small alley across the street from the club where I could watch and wait for Kerabac and Marranalis to return. It was only a few minutes before Marranalis appeared at the club. I signaled to him to join me in the alleyway.

"Did you have any problems shaking your tail?" I asked.

Marranalis grinned at the pun. "No. It was easy. I only had one of the Ruwallie Rasson following me. The other Ruwallie Rasson and the Brotherhood tail followed Kerabac. I hope he can elude them."

We waited over an hour and were beginning to get concerned when Kerabac finally arrived. We called him to us in the alley.

"What happened?" I asked.

"It wasn't too hard to lose the Brotherhood thug," Kerabac began, "but shaking off the Ruwallie Rasson was much harder. He realized that I had spotted both of them and he really dogged me. I was finally able to lose him, too, after turning a corner at a building that had a low-enough roof that I could leap up and grab the edge. I was able to pull myself onto the roof just before he turned the corner. From there, I was able to climb onto the higher roofs, where I could easily observe his movements without being noticed.

"He made a call on his wrist com and was joined by several other Ruwallie Rasson. I think he must have taken vids of us, as he showed something to them, after which they all headed off in different directions. I couldn't come down from the rooftops right away, because he stayed in the street below me and I couldn't be sure where the others were. I was afraid to use my cloaking device with its limited power and so many unknowns and variables between there and here. It was a while before they all returned. He seemed upset and frustrated at losing me. Then they all left together and I carefully crept down and returned as fast as I could. I take it you didn't have as much trouble as I did?"

"No, we didn't. I think we need to get out of here quickly and back to the estate."

Kerabac hired an enclosed water taxi to take us back to the house. If anyone was watching on the canals for us, they would not have been able to see us inside. As we pulled up to the estate, Marranalis nudged me and pointed to two boats anchored in the large canal. I noted that, while the men on the boats appeared to be doing some sort of work, they kept watching the estate closely.

"We are drawing lots of attention," I said. "I think we need to be extra vigilant with our watches tonight."

I was surprised when we entered the slave quarters to find an excited Tanden talking rapidly with Kala and Endina.

"What's going on?" I asked.

Tanden turned and looked at me with a huge grin. "Tibby, Kalana did the most wondrous thing. She put that thing on my head and now I know *everything!* Go ahead, ask me something! I know all sorts of things now!"

I looked at Kala.

"I felt sorry for him, Tib. He has had no education since he was taken as a slave — he was so miserable and afraid. He needed some kind of distraction. In the Federation, we are required to wait until the child is a little older than Tanden before allowing the use of the learning headband; but we're not in the Federation here."

I smiled. "I think what you did is wonderful, Kala. Thank you!"

"Tibby," Tanden began, as his feet danced beneath him with excitement, "did you know that there are six adjans in a qubex?"

"Ah, yes, I think I do know that," I said, as my enhanced memory from the learning headband kicked in, letting me know that an adjan was a unit of liquid measurement used on the planet Sygan. Tanden had a look of glee as he went running off in the direction of Padaran.

"He and Padaran have really taken to each other. Padaran sees him like a younger brother and Tanden looks up to him."

"I'm glad to hear that. He's a sweet boy and he really deserves better than this. I should have sent him up to the *MIZBAGONA* with the patrol ship. Next opportunity we have, I'm sending him up where he'll be safe."

"How did things go in town today?" Kala asked.

We related our events of the day, up to and including the two boats anchored in the canal.

"Yes, they showed up shortly after you left this morning and have been out there ever since. There were also some men wandering around in the field next to the house that pretended to do some sort of work, but clearly they were more interested in what was going on here."

"I'm glad we got those Brotherhood men sold off before all these watchers showed up. No doubt they're trying to find out what happened to their missing comrades."

That night, we ate on the patio again. Unlike the night before when he stayed hidden in the ventilation duct, Tanden sat next to Padaran and chattered like a monkey and Padaran joked with him in return. It was good to see the boy feel some measure of cheer with his newfound companions.

From our lookout not far from the patio Endina reported seeing the two boats still anchored in the canal; it was obvious we were being watched.

We did our best to put on a convincing show of a proper Ruwallie Rasson trader and slaves setup, but I was beginning to get concerned that our act was not as convincing as we thought. The next morning, we loaded up our delivery boat to make new deliveries. By then both the boats anchored in the canal the day before were gone. We didn't observe anyone spying us as we headed to the clubs. After reaching the *calgana* where we planned to market our wares, we began to relax.

We were shocked when we reached the first club and the owner coldly rejected the liquor and told us to leave. Kerabac stayed in character and said that they had made a deal and he expected payment. Still, the club owner told him flatly he would not take the liquor even if Kerabac gave it to him. We had no idea what had happened and proceeded on to the next club, only to have a repeat of the same performance. Kerabac tried to get the man to talk, only to have the club owner and his employees pull guns and threaten to kill us all if we didn't leave immediately. At this point we were beginning to fear what might happen when we reached the third club.

We didn't receive the rosy greeting we hoped for, nor did we get the cold rejection we'd gotten at the previous clubs. The owner clearly was distressed and angry, and kept glancing about as he let us in the back door to unload our stock. He even offered to buy what the other two clubs hadn't. All the time he kept mumbling, "They think they can tell me what to do..." and "I'm not afraid of those bastards...."

Finally, Kerabac said to the owner, "Is there something wrong? You seem rather upset about something, and the other club owners certainly have acted strangely today."

The owner crooked his head and looked at Kerabac. "I shouldn't be telling you this, and it will probably get me in a heap of trouble, but we were warned not to do business with you. I don't tolerate anyone telling me how to run my business, and I tolerate threats even less. Think they can tell me how to run my business! Hmmph!" he huffed.

"The Brotherhood threatened you?" Kerabac exclaimed.

"Brotherhood? Hell, no! It was your own kin that done it. Your Ruwallie Rasson brothers! They came in here last night, telling me any deals I had with you were off and if I knew what was good for me and wanted to stay in business, I should steer clear of you! I told them to get the hell out of my place and not to come back. Damned if I'll let anyone tell me what to do in my own place!"

"Did they say why you shouldn't buy from me?" Kerabac prodded.

"They said something about you not being part of their cartel — that you're an *independent*, they said. Told me if I wanted to do business, I needed to buy from the cartels and not some independent. I'd watch out if I was you. You're cutting into their territory and selling below their rates, and they don't like it. They may try and hurt you, so you'd best be careful."

"Thanks for the advice," Kerabac said as he handed the man back the money he just paid us. "You keep this — as a token of my respect and gratitude for the information."

The man looked at Kerabac with a dumbfounded stare. "Thanks, I guess. I didn't expect that. I was just angry about them other Ruwallie Rassons trying to tell me what to do. But you do be careful, I think they may try and hurt you."

When we left the club Kerabac said. "I think we need to get back to the estate right away. I didn't think of this. I didn't anticipate that the Ruwallie Rasson might have formed a cartel of their own here, and what the ramifications of acting outside their organization might be."

When we got back to the estate, everything appeared normal. Padaran had been patrolling the area and said he'd not seen anything out of the ordinary. Kerabac still seemed concerned that there might be problems with the Ruwallie Rasson, but once safely inside the house he seemed to relax a bit. As evening progressed, it started to rain, so we were not able to sit outside as we had the nights before. We had barely finished eating when Tanden came running from the front of the house in complete terror to say that men were coming.

"How many are there?" I asked, as Tanden headed out the back door to the slave quarters and his hiding place in the vent duct.

Before he ducked into the darkness he said, "Very many," and was gone.

At first nothing happened. We expected to hear a knock at the door, but all was quiet. Suddenly, both the front and back doors were blown open and a number of first floor windows exploded. About two dozen armed men charged into the house from all directions and covered us with their weapons, after which their leader advanced quickly on Kerabac.

"Alright, you Ruwallie Rasson bastard, where are my men?" he shouted at Kerabac.

"It looks to me like they have us surrounded," Kerabac said coolly.

For a moment, I thought their leader was going to strike Kerabac. Instead, he stepped into Kerabac until their faces were only centimeters apart and growled, "Not *these* men! The ones that I sent to talk to you the other night! Where are they? What have you done with them?"

"How should I know?" Kerabac said. "They certainly aren't here."

"This is the last place I sent them, and they never came back. I can only conclude you had something to do with their disappearance. Did they make you my offer?"

"They said something about a *jumpy drive* — or something like that — and that they thought I had one. They encouraged me to agree to deal to accept a large corvette in exchange for my freighter. Much as I would love a new corvette, I had to turn their offer down, because I don't have this *jumpy drive* thing they were talking about."

"Look, you asshole, don't play smart with us. We know you used a JUMP drive to elude our ships when you flew here from Ryken. We got the recording of your confrontation with our ship at Ryken and we have the records of your jumps and reappearances. We were prepared to pay you well for the technology and you could have been more agreeable and taken it. You can still take it, if you also return my men — or — we can just kill you and *take* the ship."

"I'm sorry to disappoint you, but I have no idea where your men are. Once they left here, I never saw them again. As for the ship, it has no jump drive. And it's not here, so I don't think you'll be taking it."

The leader's rage and frustration was clearly mounting and he was nearly at the point of doing serious harm; but it was also obvious that he desperately wanted the jump drive that he believed we had, and he needed Kerabac alive to get it.

"Look, if you know what's good for you, you'll produce the ship. We're going to be watching you — and don't even *think* about leaving the planet without checking with us first. We'll blow you out of the sky. You'd better hope that we find our men and that you had nothing to do with their disappearance. I swear, if any harm came to them, you're dead. You have three days to deliver the ship and leave here a rich man. After three days, you aren't going anywhere but to your grave."

With that, he turned and nodded to his men, who began to back out of the room as their leader left. "We'll be back in touch with you in three days. Have the ship ready and don't try to escape. You're a dead man if you do."

After the men had cleared the property, Kerabac growled, "Get this mess cleaned up!" as he pointing to the bugging device still under the windowsill. I nodded to Padaran and the others, motioning with my hands for them to make noises like they were cleaning up the broken glass and other debris. As Kerabac, Marranalis and I slipped out to the slave quarters to speak privately I was amused to hear Padaran mimicking our voices as though we were still in the room having a conversation.

"What do you think of that?" asked Kerabac.

"I think we need to find that solbidyum quickly and get out of here. Let's hope they don't find out where their brothers are. I got the idea that their leader was doing his best to restrain his actions and that he really wanted to destroy us, but he can't as long as he thinks we have a jump drive. I'm glad we don't have the RASSON BEDAN anywhere that they could find it; otherwise, I think they would have simply killed us on the spot. The good news is that, with all the attention we're getting from the Brotherhood, word is bound to have reached Logden by now and he got to see us as his only hope of getting off this planet."

"You're assuming he's still here," Marranalis said.

"I'm pretty sure he is — and he knows time is running out for him. If he has any idea what's happening on our end, he knows the heat is on us, which means the heat is also on him to make his move. I suspect he is really getting desperate about now."

It was warmer than usual that evening — at least warmer than it had been at any time since we arrived on the planet. I really had no idea what typical seasonal temperatures were like on Goo'Waddle. Kala and I sat outside together on one of the broad lounge chairs. It was impossible for anyone outside the estate to observe us where we were seated and everyone else had either gone into the main house or to the slave quarters. We could hear Tanden and Padaran laughing as Padaran tried to teach Tanden a song. It wasn't long before Kerabac came out of the main house and joined them, teaching both of them a few new tunes. It made me smile to hear to them singing, knowing that, for the first time in years, Tanden was having a good time.

"Tibby," Kala began as she gently ran her fingers across my bare chest, "what are your plans for Tanden when we leave here? You do realize there is every possibility that his father — and maybe even his mother — are already dead."

I stiffened when she said this. It was a thought I had not wanted to address. "We don't know that, and we won't know that until we have exhausted every effort to find them," I said.

"Nevertheless, it's something you need to recognize. Suppose you manage to find his sister, and they are the only two left of his family. What then?"

"Then we will take them back to Megelleon with us," I said. "They can live on the estate. We'll get them a proper education and eventually some training; and when they grow up, they can decide for themselves what they would like to do."

Kala pulled closer to me and laid her head on my chest. After a long silence she said, "Tibby, have you given any thought to us having children of our own?"

Most men I knew back on Earth would have balked at this sort of question, but it had been on my own mind for a very long time.

"Yes, I've given it a lot of thought. I want us to have children of our own — to raise them and travel the universe with them... see new worlds and have great adventures together. But right now is not the time for that — not with all the things going on within the Federation and with the Brotherhood."

"*My mother* used to say that if you wait for the right time to have children, you will never have any."   Kala pinched my arm.

"Ouch! That hurt!" I exclaimed, as Kala got up off the lounge and walked off. I couldn't tell if she was angry or if she was playing; but I felt it might be best if I stayed out on the lounge awhile longer before going back into the house to confront her. I must have been more tired than I realized, because I drifted off. I had probably been asleep several hours when Marranalis woke me.

"Wake up, Tibby. It's your turn to take a watch."

I yawned. "What time is it?"

"It's about halfway to dawn. It's been pretty quiet so far tonight. I doubt that after our visit today we'll have any more encounters with the Brotherhood until the time they have allotted us is up. I only hope we find Logden and the solbidyum before they decide to get truly nasty."

"I know what we're doing involves a huge risk, but I think we offer Logden the only choice for getting off this planet alive. I think we'll be hearing from him soon in one way or another."

While we were talking, I glanced out over the water. There seemed to be a lot more boats moving about than were customary for this time of night.

"You noticed them, too," Marranalis said with a note of concern. "You think it means anything?"

"I'm not sure. I doubt it's the Brotherhood coming back, unless they found their brothers working in a slave gang."

"Let's hope that doesn't happen. I'm going in to get some sleep. Let me know if anything happens with those boats gathering out there."

It seemed that every time I looked up over the next few hours, another boat or two had joined the growing numbers in the canal. It was just getting light in the sky when I noted several smaller boats moving away from the larger ones toward the embankment. I immediately went to wake Marranalis, who was sleeping in the slave house with Tanden.

"It looks like we're going to have visitors shortly — a lot of visitors. We need to get into the big house and alert the others."

Before I finished what I was saying, Tanden was awake and scampering into his hiding place.

"Do you think it's the Brotherhood?"

"I have no idea, but they're coming en mass, whoever they are."

By the time Marranalis and I got back to the house, the smaller boats were tying up at the piers along the canal and dark figures were disembarking. There had to be several dozen of them, but it was not possible to make out their features in the dim light. However, it was clear from their capes and other attire that these were Ruwallie Rasson, and from their postures and movements we were sure they weren't just paying a social visit.

"Kerabac," I called. "Wake up, we have a large number of Ruwallie Rasson heading this way and they're not looking any too pleasant!"

"What?" Kerabac murmured as he tried to wake himself. "Ruwallie Rasson? What time is it? How many of them?" he blurted, as he hastily got out of bed and began to dress.

"Several dozen, I would say," Marranalis said as he peered out one of the broken windows from the Brotherhood visit.

"This is not good...not good at all," Kerabac said. By now Kala, Endina, and Sokaia joined us in their respective characters as Padaran went to the other side of the house to check out the windows there.

"It looks like we're surrounded," Padaran called back to us. "They're approaching from this side of the house, too."

Just then, the front door again flew open with a crash and several armed Ruwallie Rasson men entered, followed by dozens more. Their dark skins accented the whites of their eyes, and their angry looks didn't bode well.

"Let me handle this, Tibby. Don't take any action unless I give you a signal," Kerabac said quietly as he entered the room, never removing his eyes from the leader of this pack of men.

Kerabac moved his right foot slightly behind his left and gave a slight bow, with his hands draped slightly to the sides and palms facing forward.

"Greetings, and welcome to my humble abode. I regret that I am unable to offer you proper hospitality, but as you can see, we are in rather a poor state of repair at the moment. What, pray tell, brings you to my residence so early and unexpected this morning?"

"Cut the formal crap, Kerabac. You are Kerabac the trader, are you not? The trader who has been selling liquor to the local clubs and merchants, and the Kerabac who ran the Brotherhood blockade this week?"

"I am Kerabac, and yes, I have sold liquor to a few local clubs. Is there some problem with that?"

"We have no record of a Kerabac as a member of the cartel. No one in our organization has ever heard of you before this week."

"I came here from the other side of the galaxy," Kerabac began, "where my family retreated when our home world entered the Federation and gave up the old ways. There is no cartel there, and I was unaware you had one here or I certainly would have joined you. I assure you, no offense was intended."

"It's too late for that now," the leader said. "We have our rules here, and no Ruwallie Rasson operates or does business outside the cartel on this planet — that's the rule! So, as a consequence of your infraction, I — as leader of the Ruwallie Rasson — claim all your possessions and slaves as a penalty, and you shall serve as my personal slave until such time as I deem that you have paid for your crime."

"Isn't that a little harsh for selling a few bottles of liquor in ignorance of your cartel and its rules?" Kerabac said heatedly.

"If it were just a few bottles of liquor, it might be considered harsh; but you have the Brotherhood breathing down out necks and making life even more difficult for us than they were before. They want your ship for some reason and we're taking it. If its secret is worth having, I'll keep it; otherwise, we'll give it to them to get them off our backs."

"I fear you'll have a hard time doing that, as the ship is not here," Kerabac answered.

"Oh, I think you'll be telling us where the ship is before too long," the leader said with a wicked grin. Several of the other Ruwallie men chuckled.

"I see," Kerabac said with his head bent down. I could tell he was looking to come up with a way out of this situation. "I assume you still hold to and practice the old traditions?"

"We do, and what of it?" the leader snarled.

"Then I invoke the *Sith lubnol*."

I had no idea what Kerabac was talking about and my knowledge from the learning headband didn't cover this aspect of Ruwallie Rasson culture.

"The *Sith lubnol*!" the leader laughed. "To invoke that, you need to have relatives present who are members of the cartel and who will recognize you and agree with your challenge. Does any man here recognize this Kerabac?" he said, looking about the room with a grin on his face.

"Let him recite the Ruwallie *cordett*," someone called out from the group.

"Yes, let's hear him recite it," another called out.

I knew from talking to Kerabac in the past that the Ruwallie *cordett* was an oral history recited by a person of one's lineage going back several generations; but I was not sure if Kerabac, who had grown up in the Federation and generally outside the Ruwallie Rasson traditions, would be able to recite it. I was shocked when Kerabac broke into song.

"First there was Nuondec, father of the clan. To the stars he gave three sons, Unodec, Sondec and Morandec. Unodec fathered four sons, Marnadec, Karasondec, Nurocondec and Meledec. Meledec sired Colandec and...."

His song went on and on, until finally one man looked up in some type of recognition and walked over to stand at Kerabac's side. Soon another joined, and then another, until eventually, seven men were standing by Kerabac's side when he finished his recitation.

"So, it would appear that you have some relatives here after all. But are any of them prepared to stand for you in your claim of the *Sith lubnol*?"

Slowly, one by one, each of the men walked away, leaving Kerabac to stand alone once more.

"I thought not," their leader said. "So, now I claim you and all your slaves and your possessions — and from this time onward, you are my slave."

"If I am now your slave, I challenge you to the *Kandi Mondong*!" a voice cried out.

I looked at Kerabac, only to see his head turning in shock to look at Padaran, who stood stiffly at the edge of the circle in a defiant pose, his fists clenched at his sides.

"YOU?!   You challenge me to the *Kandi Mondong*?" the leader laughed. "You're not even Ruwallie Rasson. You're nothing but a pathetic white worm, barely a man with fuzz on his chin."

"Nevertheless, I challenge you," Padaran said. "I need not be Ruwallie Rasson to challenge you. Did not Worran of the Ginpa challenge Neeragon and win his freedom?" At his words, there was some mumbling among the Ruwallie Rasson and some heads were nodding.

"How do you know of Neeragon and Worran?" the leader said with surprise. I, too, wondered, because I had no idea at all what he was talking about.

"Does it matter how I know? I know, and that is all that is necessary, and my challenge still stands!"

I could see by the look of concern on Kerabac's face that whatever was going on was very dangerous, and he was afraid for Padaran.

"Very well, worm. You will only get to join your ancestors sooner than later. You would not have lived long as my slave, as I have no need for pretty house boys." There was a round of laughing from the men gathered in the room. "There's not enough room inside for the *Kandi Mondong*. Let us move outside. If you're lucky, you may get to die just as the sun crosses the horizon."

Immediately, men grabbed Kerabac and the rest of my crew, including Kala, Sokaia and Endina. When the leader noted Endina, he said, "She is not a slave, though she *is* an underling to Kerabac. We will decide her fate after the *Kandi Mondong*."

The men that grabbed Endina removed her weapons, but she was allowed to keep her wrist com with the cloaking device in it. Once outside, Kerabac, Marranalis and I were tied together and guarded by several Ruwallie Rasson, while the rest formed a large circle in the back courtyard.

"What's going to happen?" I whispered to Kerabac.

"The Ruwallie Rasson believe they are the chosen people in the universe and that they cannot be beaten unless it is the will of the gods. According to these beliefs, the only way a slave can beat his master in combat is if it is ordained that it should be so. But to make certain it is the will of the gods, the challenger is placed at a distinct disadvantage. The Ruwallie Rasson will be armed with a dagger and will remain dressed; Padaran must fight him naked and unarmed. That way, if he should win, it will be quite obvious it was the will of the gods."

"And his opponent with the knife — what does he need to do to win? Wound Padaran?"

"No, he must kill him. For Padaran to win, he must either kill his opponent or must subdue him in a death situation where his opponent yields."

"Do you think Padaran has a chance?" I asked.

"Honestly, I don't know. Padaran is very quick on his feet and his martial arts skills are very good — in fact, amazingly good. But in order to become leader of the Ruwallie Rasson, their leader must have proven himself to be the best that there is at wielding a knife. He has already killed several men using a knife just to attain leader status, and you can assume there is none better on the planet. But if by some means Padaran beats him, he will not only be set free, but he will take ownership of all his opponent's possessions. And since his opponent is the leader, Padaran will become the new leader of the Ruwallie Rasson."

By now, Padaran was standing naked in the middle of the circle. Over the past few months, he had gained a little weight, but he still looked very thin compared to the muscular Ruwallie Rasson men. His opponent was a head taller and had a distinct advantage in reach over Padaran. Add to that a 300 millimeter razor-sharp and thin-bladed knife, and it looked like it was not going to be any match at all.

The leader walked out to the center of the ring where Padaran stood, as if he was planted in the ground. With one quick move, the leader brought his knife up in a motion that would have gutted Padaran in an instant, had he not moved rapidly out of the way of the blade. His move was so quick that everyone gasped, as he once again stopped and stood in a fixed pose with no expression on his face.

"What have we here? *A little hopping ragget.* We shall see how long it takes to skin this one," Padaran's opponent snarled.

From the crowd, cheers could be heard, "Spill his guts! Let his blood feed the ground!"

On his next attempt, the leader grabbed Padaran's right arm with his left hand while bringing his knife around quickly in a motion intended to slit Padaran's throat, if not behead him entirely. Padaran stepped in and under his opponent's arm quickly as the knife passed over his head and, as he did, he reached down and grabbed his opponent's left leg. His attacker had placed all his weight on his right leg, so it was easy for Padaran to quickly lift the left leg and throw his opponent off balance, sending him flying across the ground.

The Ruwallie spun quickly upon hitting the ground and swung back with his knife, as he expected Padaran to move in toward him on the offensive. The blade moved through empty air and a confused look crossed his face, as he glanced back to see Padaran standing once more in the center of the circle with the same blank and calm expression on his face. Murmurs could be heard from those in the surrounding circle.

"I'm through playing with you, worm. It's time for you to die," the Ruwallie Rasson leader growled, as he got to his feet and slowly began to circle Padaran. By now, the sun had risen and the rays were shining at Padaran's back. The man began to slowly move around the circle of men, but Padaran didn't move, nor did he seem to be paying any attention to the Ruwallie Rasson leader at all.

When the leader had gotten around the circle behind Padaran, he suddenly charged. Just as he was on top of Padaran and sweeping down with the knife to stab him in the back, Padaran dropped and rolled quickly to his left. His opponent went tumbling from the force of his own momentum. Padaran once more took up his position in the center of the circle.

By now, the Ruwallie Rasson surrounding the circle were yelling, but it was impossible to hear or understand what they were saying. The leader regained his balance and, looking back at Padaran with a look of hatred and anger, suddenly threw his knife with lightning speed at Padaran. It was as if time slowed down in my mind, as I saw Padaran shift his weight slightly and turn just before the knife reached him. I fully expected it to fly past him and hit one of the Ruwallie Rasson men in the outer edge of the circle. Instead, I saw Padaran's right arm sweep up and clasp the hilt of the knife just as the blade passed his hand, in a motion so quick that it defied all logic and belief.

Padaran leaped forward, catching the leader completely off guard. With his left arm, Padaran grabbed the Ruwallie Rasson leader's right arm, which was still extended from the knife throw, and spun him into an arm lock. With his right hand, he had the knife at the leader's throat.

"Yield now or your blood will feed the ground," Padaran said, loud enough for all to hear.

The sudden silence that encompassed the place was deafening. Everyone stood in shock, their jaws hanging.

Tears filled the eyes of the Ruwallie Rasson leader and he trembled in Padaran's hands.

Once more, Padaran said, "Yield now or your blood will feed the ground."

I could see a trickle of blood welling from the place where Padaran's blade pressed against the throat of the leader.

"I yield," the leader finally cried. "I yield!" And with that, Padaran let loose his hold on the leader, who dropped to his knees and buried his face in the ground as he shook with sobs.

At the same time, many of the Ruwallie Rasson dropped to one knee and bowed their heads, holding out their right arm in acceptance of Padaran's defeat and claim of leadership; but a few remained standing. One exclaimed, "I do not accept this white man to be a fit leader of the Ruwallie Rasson. I challenge his leadership."

Padaran looked around the group and then said in a calm but clear voice, "You believe that only by the will of the gods can a Ruwallie Rasson be defeated in combat by one not Ruwallie Rasson, is that not true?"

"Yes," many murmured.

But the one who challenged said, "It may have been the gods' will that you defeat Tondor, but that is not to say that it is their will that you should be the leader of the Ruwallie Rasson."

At this, many of the men who had knelt earlier stood up and shouted, "Yes, it is only the gods' will that you be free and Tondor be defeated, not that you should be leader."

"Do you not also believe that a woman can never beat a Ruwallie Rasson because women are less than a man and only meant for a man's pleasure and to bear him children?" Padaran asked.

"What is he up to now?" I quietly asked Kerabac, who stood with a look of astonishment on his face.

"I have no idea," Kerabac said. "I'm wondering where he learned so much Ruwallie Rasson tradition and beliefs. I think he knows more of our history and customs than I do."

As he was saying this, I could hear the Ruwallie Rasson answering "Yes," to his question about the role of women.

"So, then, I hold that it IS the gods' will that you accept me as your leader, and to prove it, I challenge one of your best men to fight any one of the women here. If that woman defeats the challenger, you will all lay down your arms and accept that it is the will of the gods that it is to be so."

"I'll accept that!" one man shouted, followed by another and another.

"Then pick your man and pick one of these women you wish to fight him."

"By the stars, Padaran is brilliant!" Kerabac muttered with admiration. "Any one of our women can easily beat the other Ruwallie Rasson here…at least, I think they can."

I was glad to hear Kerabac say that; but I wasn't as confident as he was and I was hoping it would not be Kala chosen to participate in the fight — even though I had great confidence in her abilities. As it turned out, the man who had said he would not accept Padaran as his leader was the one chosen by the Ruwallie Rasson to fight a woman. He was angry about this development and said it was beneath him to fight a woman; but at the insistence of his fellow clansmen, he was pushed into it.

There was some debate as to which of the women they wanted him to fight. Endina they excluded, because of her Ruwallie Rasson blood, so it was a question whether it should be Sokaia or Kala. Some felt Kala was too pretty to fight, but they also noted that Sokaia was rather muscular;

they also noted her scars and suspected she may be a seasoned fighter. In the end, they opted for Kala and my heart sank.

Kala entered the circle naked, like Padaran had and, also like Padaran, she stood patiently while her Ruwallie Rasson opponent moved about her, trying to determine his initial mode of attack. Finally, he moved rapidly toward her and grabbed her by the arm as he thrust forward with his knife. It was a classic attack, one so well-rehearsed by all my troops that anyone of them could have performed the counteraction with their eyes closed. In the blink of an eye, Kala had her opponent lying on his back with his own knifepoint at his throat.

With a total look of terror in his eyes, the man immediately squeaked, "I yield!"

All around the circle, men fell to their knees and lay their weapons to their sides as they saluted Padaran with their right arms extended.

Kerabac and I turned and looked at each other — and then broke out laughing.

"I certainly didn't see that one coming," Kerabac said.

"Neither did I...I just wonder what Padaran is planning to do now that he's leader of the Ruwallie Rasson."

As all of this unfolded, we learned that the name of the Ruwallie Rasson leader was Tondor. In keeping with tradition, Tondor, as the defeated master, became the slave and all his possessions became the property of the former slave and victorious challenger, including any positions or titles that he held. The Ruwallie Rasson took this tradition very seriously; and now Tondor was serving Padaran and answering to his every whim.

Padaran handled it very coolly and did not make Tondor do anything outrageous to humiliate him more than he already he had been by his defeat. Tondor and his cartel seriously believed that the gods had to have played a part in this turn of events, as he could not conceive of any other way that Padaran could have beaten him.

As the new leader of the Ruwallie Rasson, Padaran was expected to outline the rules he expected them to follow. Oddly, Padaran continued to amaze Kerabac and the rest of us by repeatedly demonstrating how well versed he was in Ruwallie Rasson culture and traditions. The rules that he pronounced as the new leader involved sweeping changes, which he instituted without challenge by citing historical and traditional precedents that ensured the full compliance of the clansmen.

First on his list was abolition of slavery; the Ruwallie Rasson were to immediately end the practice and set their slaves free. Upon release, they were also required to pay each slave the equivalent of one year's pay at the rate that a free laborer would have been paid for the jobs they performed.

If they wished, and if the former slaves were willing, the former Ruwallie Rasson masters could hire the former slave to work for him at a proper pay scale under the condition that the ex-slave was treated as any other free man or woman. Failure to do so would result in the forfeiture of all property of the Ruwallie Rasson violator and loss of his cartel membership.

There was much grumbling about this from the Ruwallie Rasson; but Padaran cited examples from when their home world became part of the Federation. These reasons, regrettably, were the same reasons that had caused this faction of the Ruwallie Rasson to break away from the rest of their kin; however, the recent demonstration of Padaran's defeat of Tondor and Kala's defeat of her opponent convinced the Ruwallie Rasson that slavery was no longer favored by their gods so, reluctantly, they conceded to give it up.

Since Tondor had technically taken Kerabac's possessions prior to Padaran's victory, including Kala, Sokaia, Padaran and myself, we were now free and Padaran was the owner of Kerabac's business and possessions. Padaran made it clear that we were no longer slaves, but that he was hiring us and that our wages would be discussed privately. All of this, of course, was a sham; but we stayed in character and let this rather interesting development play out to the advantage of our mission.

While Padaran was busy discussing terms and business practices with the Ruwallie Rasson, Marranalis, Kala and I quietly retreated to the slave house. Tanden peeked out through the air vent grill and, once he was certain that we were alone, he slipped out to join us. He immediately asked if Padaran was OK, as he was apparently able to hear some of what had unfolded. We told him the details of what happened and he jumped up and down with glee to learn that Padaran defeated Tondor.

"I knew it," he said, "I knew he was a great fighter. He's the best!"

It was obvious he admired and looked up to Padaran, and after these latest events, Padaran moved up few steps to near god-like status in his young eyes.

It was late in the day before all the Ruwallie Rasson departed. Tondor was the last to leave; Padaran nearly had to force him to go, as he kept insisting that he must serve him and that Padaran needed to come to his former *calgana* and take possession of his estate and property. Padaran was finally able to get him to leave by insisting that he needed to take care of things with Kerabac's former ship and possessions and that Tondor needed to go back and prepare the estate for Padaran to formally take ownership of it later on. After Tondor left we all gathered on the patio for a meal as the sunset. It was the first time any of us had eaten that day and we all were famished. Tanden was stuck to Padaran's side like glue, and he eagerly asked Padaran to relate every detail of his defeat of Tondor. Padaran was more than happy to oblige; and as he related the events, he mimicked very accurately the voices of everyone in the story, which mesmerized Tanden and the rest of us, as well.

"How did you come to know so much about Ruwallie Rasson history and customs?" Kerabac asked.

"Back when I was in school, we had a teacher who was Ruwallie Rasson. He often told us of the history and customs practiced by his people before the Ruwallie Rasson joined the Federation. I was always impressed with his tales of Neeragon and Worran and the *Kandi Mondong* challenge — it was my favorite story when I was a kid. When I heard you challenge Tondor with the *Sith lubnol*, I recognized that it would never work, and it dawned on me that our only hope lay with the *Kandi Mondong*."

"Granted," Kerabac said, "the *Sith lubnol* might have saved us, if it had worked, but even though it turned out that I had relatives among the Ruwallie Rasson cartel, I needed to have their backing in the challenge, and it wasn't likely I would get that."

"I don't understand," I interjected. "What exactly is the *Sith lubnol*?"

"The *Sith lubnol* is the challenge of leadership. If I had any relatives willing to support my right to challenge, I would have had to fight Tondor in combat. We would have been equally armed, but I think the advantage of my martial arts training would have tipped the challenge strongly in my favor. But I would have needed at least three relatives to stand with me in the challenge. It was a long shot, but it was worth the try."

"The thing I'm concerned about now is how this will affect Logden. We were prepping him to believe that Kerabac was his answer to getting off Goo'Waddle; but now you are the new owner of the *RASSON BEDAN* in the eyes of the people. You represent a new unknown. I'm afraid now that Logden will shy away from us," I said.

"Not necessarily," Padaran began, "If I make Kerabac my partner and leave him in charge as Captain of the *RASSON BEDAN*, Logden should still feel some level of confidence that he can approach Kerabac."

"Hmm, you may be right. I suspect that by tomorrow word will have spread all over the city about what happened here. If you make Kerabac your partner and announce it formally, it should help solidify the Ruwallie Rasson's backing of you and increase your position of strength. The Ruwallie Rasson and the Brotherhood don't seem to be in very good standing with each other, so your newfound position with them should make the Brotherhood second guess trying to take you on, which in turn might encourage Logden to come to us."

Since the events of the day had changed everything, we no longer needed to act out the role of slaves. For the first time since setting foot on Goo'Waddle, Kala and I were able to sleep together in one of the bedrooms. However, we still needed to keep up the act of Padaran as the newly claimed leader of the Ruwallie Rasson and made a show of his asking Kerabac to be his partner in the main room where the bugging device was still operating.

"I've missed sleeping with you since we've been on this trip," Kala said as we lay facing each other in the large bed.

"I've missed you, too," I said. "We've not been able to really spend much time together since we arrived here. I'll be glad when this mission is over and we can get home and back into our routine of hiking to the lake every day."

"Tib, how do you think all of this is going to play out with Padaran? He can't simply pack up and leave the Ruwallie Rasson when all of this is over. If he does, they will just revert back to their old ways of slavery again. After all, ending slavery with the Ruwallie Rasson doesn't rid this planet or any other of slavery — there are still thousands of other slave owners here on this planet who are not Ruwallie Rasson."

"I know, and frankly, it disturbs me deeply that when we leave, there will still be hundreds of thousands of slaves here. But as to Padaran, I have no idea where this will all lead. I've not had a chance to sit with him and really discuss it. I'm impressed, though, at what a quick thinker he is. He's come up with some clever solutions to some very sticky situations in the spur of the moment — and he may very well have saved all our lives. His decision to claim Kerabac as his partner instead of simply putting on a show of taking over everything is brilliant and could actually serve two purposes."

Kala looked at me curiously. "How so?"

"For one thing, the arrangement should preserve the chances of Logden seeking us out; and secondly, it sets an example for the Ruwallie Rasson that some of their slaves may be good partners or employees."

"You really think Logden is here, then, and not someplace else in the galaxy?"

"Yes I do, but I have the feeling that he is getting help from someone; otherwise, he would have been found by now. The Brotherhood is doing everything short of a door-to-door search, and I wouldn't be surprised if they decided to start doing that too."

Kala was silent for a while and I just lay there, thinking about the events that had transpired since our arrival. I was about to ask Kala if there had been any progress made in trying to locate Jenira, when I heard the deep, regular breathing that told me she was asleep.

I was awakened in the morning by the sounds of pounding and operating machinery. I selected some clothing from the replicator in the closet and was actually happy to dress in normal clothing for the first time since donning the slave's loincloth. A quick look in the mirror showed me that

I was badly in need of a shave and haircut so, using the styling wand, I quickly shortened my hair to a respectable length and refreshed the brown tint that helped to conceal my true identity as the red-headed Thibodaux James Renwalt, First Citizen of the Galactic Federation.

When I arrived at the bottom of the stairs, I was surprised to see numerous workmen busily repairing the damaged windows and doors that had resulted from the Brotherhood's visit two days earlier. Endina was supervising them and giving orders, but I didn't see any sign of Kerabac or Padaran.

"Good morning," I said to Endina. "Where are Kerabac and Padaran?"

"Out in the slave's quarters, I think. I saw them headed that way a moment ago with Marranalis."

"Thanks," I said as I turned to head in that direction.

"By the way, it's nice to see you back in clothing again. Not that you were hard to look at scantily clad," Endina said with a grin.

"You'd best not let Kala hear you say that," I said, returning the grin.

"Too late." Kala's voice came from the stairs. "I already heard. But I can't fault her appraisal; you do look pretty good scantily clad."

"Enough of the both of you!" I said, laughing, as I headed out the door.

When I entered the slave quarters I found Kerabac, Marranalis and Padaran engaged in a conversation while Padaran also attempted to teach Tanden how to play chess.

"No, no, Tanden…this piece can only jump over one piece at a time, and it's the only piece that can jump over other pieces."

"Oh, yeah, I forgot…" Tanden muttered.

"Good morning, Tibby," Padaran said when he noticed me.

"Good morning yourself," I replied. "How is the new leader of the Ruwallie Rasson this fine day?"

"That's what we were just discussing," Kerabac said. "Now that he is their leader, he is going to be expected to spend a lot of time at their cartel headquarters, dealing with Rasson issues."

"Do you think there is any personal danger to him?"

"No, actually, I think he is pretty safe — at least as far as the Ruwallie Rasson are concerned. They may not be happy about a white man being their leader, but at the moment, they see it as the will of the gods, and they will respect that. After the way he defeated Tondor yesterday, I seriously doubt anyone will be challenging him for leadership. I doubt the Brotherhood will cause him any trouble, either, as he will be heavily guarded by the Ruwallie Rasson."

"Padaran, I know this has all developed quite quickly, but have you given any thought as to what will happen when we leave?" I asked.

"YOU'RE GOING TO LEAVE HERE?" Tanden cried out, grabbing hold of Padaran tightly.

"It's going to be OK, Tanden," I said. "We're going to take you and your sister along and your parents, too."

It was a few hours later that Endina came to me and said that she believed she had located Tanden's sister. She was no longer at the Purple Flower, because she was older now and the Purple Flower specialized in pre-adolescent girls. Now that she had reached her teens, she had been sold off to a house that marketed teenage girls. She said the place was reluctant to sell her, but they agreed to a price that was close to a quarter million credits. Fortunately, we had enough credits with us to buy her, but it was not going to leave us with much, if we happen to encounter any other major expenses.

Since we were no longer posing as slaves, Marranalis and I headed to the *calgana* address Endina provided and began looking for a place called *Soft and Tender*.

"I truly find this all disgusting," I said to Marranalis as we began our search of the street we were sent to. Up and down the length of the street stood lines of enslaved prostitutes of all ages as their pimps and madams touted their services. Not all of them were in chains or collars, and I asked Marranalis about it.

"Those are women working as prostitutes of their own volition. They frequently contract themselves to specific houses to service men. Frequently they are preferred over the slaves, because they show more enthusiasm in their performances than the slaves do."

"They WANT to be prostitutes?" I exclaimed.

"Sure, Tibby. There are prostitutes on almost every planet, both in and out of the Federation. Only inside the Federation none of them are allowed to be slaves or are forced into slavery. It's a choice made by many women — and men too."

I shook my head and had a very hard time adjusting to this new element. "So you're telling me that some individuals *want* to be prostitutes?"

"Yes! Isn't it that way on your home world?"

"No! Well, maybe for some, but it's not considered a decent occupation."

"Hmmph! On some of the planets prostitutes are almost worshiped by the citizens — they're practically treated like stars," Marranalis responded.

I thought about what Marranalis told me and about some of the celebrities back on Earth — the scandals and sexual video clips of them on the Internet that seemed to only elevate their status in the eyes of a significant portion of the public — and I had to concede that it may not really be all that different from Earth. To be honest with myself, I had to also admit that I'd heard of women who prostituted themselves out of necessity and choice. But I still found it disgusting.

As it turned out, the house Soft and Tender wasn't as bad as many of the places we had passed on the way there. It looked clean and sharp on the outside, with bright, albeit gaudy, lights and a large vid screen that showed clips of the girls that the house had to offer. Two very large guards stood by the door, but they said nothing to us as we approached, though one did step over and open the door for us. Inside, it was even more of a surprise. While the outside was bright and gaudy, the inside was very well appointed and conservative in appearance. Opulent wood panels sheathed the walls and beneath our feet was a marble-like floor with carpeted runners. The furnishings consisted of large leather-like chairs and divans that reminded me of pictures of wealthy gentlemen's clubs back on Earth. A rather attractive woman dressed in a quite stylish yet conservative outfit, who I would have guessed to be in her early 40s, approached us in the large foyer.

"Greetings, gentlemen. Might I be of assistance in your selection of a young lady? We have many to offer, and I am sure we can find one to your liking. Will you be looking for two girls, or do you wish to share one? There is a surcharge if you wish using the same girl at the same time."

I was choking on my own bile as she spoke and it was difficult for me to maintain my composure as I said, "That is not necessary. I believe an associate of mine, named Endina, has contacted you concerning a young girl named Jenira."

"Ahh, so you are the ones who want to purchase her. We recently acquired her ourselves, and she has been a huge favorite with our clients. You must want her pretty badly to pay such a high price for her."

"Yeah," was all I could say. Lovely as this woman was, I wanted to punch her teeth down her throat. Then I noticed her collar and realized that she was a slave hostess, and probably did not particularly like her job either. Regardless of the situation, I just wanted to get Jenira and get out of the place. The woman raised a jewel-encrusted bracelet to her mouth and said, "Sonrea, could you bring Jenira out please? Her new owners have arrived." Then, to us she said, "If you gentlemen will come this way, we will finalize the transaction and provide you with ownership documents."

That last line nearly set me off. Ownership papers — as though she was an object, like a piece of furniture or a vehicle.

We were led into a rather opulent office that had several vid screens on the wall, displaying scenes that I can only imagine were encounters going on in various rooms about the establishment. The woman escorting us quickly picked up a remote and turned off the displays. "I do apologize. While we do not wish our guests to know we are watching. We do so only for security reasons. We have the highest regards for the privacy of our guests; but we also have a huge investment in the girls here, and we cannot afford for them to be damaged. You do understand."

"Ahh, yeah, sure…" I muttered. I was finding it very difficult to stay in character.

"I get the sense by the way you gentlemen are acting that you are merely agents for some client and that you are not purchasing Jenira for yourselves?"

"Ahh, yes, ma'am. We are only here to close the deal and deliver her," I said, as I tried to regain some self-control.

"I see," she said with a rather sad look on her face. "I do hope her new owner is not a harsh or cruel man and that he will treat her well. She is a sweet child — very delicate, actually. We have tried to see to it that only the kindest and gentlest of men were availed of her services."

"I can assure you, Madame, that her new owner is one of the kindest and most considerate men I have ever known," Marranalis interjected. Just then, the door opened and another young woman, who I judged to be about eighteen, escorted a very lovely young girl into the room that I would have guessed to be not more than fourteen years old.

"Ahh, here is your young lady, now. Jenira, come here, child. These men are going to take you to your new home and owner."

I could see the conflict in Jenira's eyes. She had no idea what lay ahead of her. She had been taken from her home and placed in one house, sold and placed in another, and most certainly used in all sorts of vile ways. She drew back a bit and clung to the woman I assumed was Sonrea.

"I don't want to go," she said. "What will happen to me?"

"There, there. It will be alright," Sonrea said. I could see a tear in her eye and it was obvious that she cared for Jenira.

"Where are they taking me?" she asked.

Before anyone had a chance to say anything, I said, "We're taking you to be with Tanden."

"Tanden!" she exclaimed, her eyes open wide. "To be with Tanden?! He's OK?" Her face lit up with excitement and joy.

"See, there?" Sonrea said. "I told you it would be alright!"

"Ahh, yes, but first there is the matter of some money, I believe?" the other woman said.

"Yes," I said, and I pulled out a strip of maxalite and a handful of the electronic chip coins that were considered so valuable. When I did, I saw the woman's nostrils flare and a huge smile spread across her face.

"You do not mind if I check this currency," she said as the brought out a small scanning device.

"Not at all; please do," I said.

The woman ran the scanner over the currency several times to make sure of her readings. "Well," she said as she turned around to face us. "This certainly seems to be in order." She walked around her desk and removed a small data disk, handing it to me. "I think you will find everything in order here. She is yours, or I should say, your employer's."

Marranalis reached over and took the disk from me. "If you don't mind, we'd like to check the documents before we leave."

The woman's face dropped for a moment before she regained her composure and said, "Certainly. I think you will find everything is in order."

Marranalis pulled a small scanning device from his pocket and examined the cube. I didn't even know he had brought one along.

"Everything appears to be in order," he said to me.

"Well, then," I began, "I think our business here is finished. Jenira, let's get you out of here and back to see Tanden." Jenira was practically jumping out of her skin with glee as we walked out the front door.

The trip back to the house was anything but quiet. Jenira must have asked one hundred times, "Are you really taking me to Tanden?" and "Is Tanden alright?" Tanden, on the other hand, didn't know his sister had been found or that we were bringing her back to him.

When we finally arrived at the estate and we took Jenira into the room where Tanden sat playing a game of chess with Padaran, Jenira let out a high-pitched scream. "Tanden!"

Tanden looked up with pure shock in his face. Suddenly, he leaped to his feet and both he and Jenira raced across the room into each other's arms. They hugged each other tightly and cried as we watched. I felt a hand slip around my waist and Kala's head rest on my shoulder.

"Tib, I think this is about the greatest thing you have ever done." She kissed me on the cheek.

You would think after all that had happened in the previous days that things would have settled down a bit. First there was the flight to Goo'Waddle with the problems between the cloaking device and the courier band on Kerabac's wrist. Then there was the rendezvous with Agama and his men, followed by the rather unfriendly visit from the Brotherhood, only to be followed by the Ruwallie Rasson. There also was the strange encounter with Andy, the android, who mysteriously disappeared, and from whom we had not heard anything since. Padaran had since firmly established himself as the leader of the Ruwallie Rasson and Tanden and his sister were now back together. What more could happen?

That night, for the first time in weeks, Kala and I made love. She seemed to be even more passionate than ever before — and insatiable. The lovemaking and play continued well into the morning hours before we finally drifted off to sleep.

The next morning Kerabac met me as soon as I came down the stairs. He called me outside to the patio, away from the bug in house. "Tibby, today is the deadline date that the Brotherhood gave us to turn over the ship. What do you think will happen?"

"I'm not sure, but I do know we're not going to let them have the ship!"

"I could get some of the Ruwallie Rasson to guard the place here for us — that should keep the Brotherhood out," Padaran said.

"Yeah, but it would probably keep Logden out as well." As we spoke, we noted a small but well-appointed boat pulling up to one of the docks at the front of the estate. "It looks like we have company," I said.

"It's Agama and his men," Kerabac noted. As the group approached the house, they noticed us on the side patio and diverted their route to walk directly toward us.

"Kerabac," Agama said, "you are looking well. I heard you had some problems, but you seem to have handled them." While he greeted Kerabac, he was also looking around the property rather intently, especially noticing the newly replaced windows and doors. "Word has it that the Brotherhood is not too happy with you. I also hear tell that you had a run-in with the Ruwallie Rasson cartel, and that they were not too happy with you, either. But you seemed to have resolved that issue to your advantage. Oh, congratulations to you — Padaran, isn't it? I hear rumors you and Kerabac are now partners and that you now are leader of the Ruwallie Rasson. I never thought I would see the day a white man would become their leader."

"You came all this way to congratulate us?" Kerabac said in a joking tone. "That was really nice of you, Agama."

"Actually, we came to discuss some other business. We hear the Brotherhood is planning on making things difficult for you — in fact, rumors are circulating that they want to kill you. So we're thinking you might be planning on leaving Goo'Waddle real soon. We happen to have a need for someone to transport a colleague of ours — sort of a courier, like you. Only he won't be needing a courier band. He needs to make a long trip to the other side the Federation, and we hear that you're familiar with that side of space. We're hoping you would be willing to transport him there in exchange for a significant fee. Of course, it would be dangerous… and we need to you get him through the Brotherhood blockades. Since you've done it once, we figure you can do it again."

"I don't know, Agama; that's a mighty long trip. It could take over a year to traverse all that distance; I can't afford a whole year out of my business to just transport one person."

"Not even for, let's say, 20 million credits?"

"Twenty million," Kerabac said with a shocked look. His acting was superb. "What makes him worth twenty million?"

"Let's just say that there is someone on the other side the Federation that has a need to see him really badly."

"I see. And does this man have a name?" Kerabac asked.

"Yeah, he's got a name. But that's on a need-to-know basis and you don't need to know."

"So how are we supposed to talk to him then if he has no name and he is on my ship for year?"

"OK, you can call him…ahh, call him *Sol*… Yeah, call him Sol," Agama said, grinning and puffing out his chest as if he had just said something really smart.

"Let me talk it over with my associate and my crew," Kerabac said, as he motioned us over to the far end of the patio.

"What do you think, Tibby?" he asked.

"It sounds to me like he is in league with Logden. It would make sense — if Agama and his brother have been smuggling goods from Ryken to Goo'Waddle in the past and Logden was also a pirate and smuggler, he may have worked with them before. He may have approached them for assistance in getting off the planet and past the Brotherhood. It's obvious from what Agama just said that they've been listening to everything going on in that room, like we thought. I say we go for it."

"I agree," Padaran said. "The longer we wait, the more difficult this is going to become."

"Marranalis, what are your thoughts?"

"I agree with you, Tibby. When he was searching for a name to call Logden, he went with Sol. Clearly he was thinking of the solbidyum and thought he was being clever."

"Yeah, I caught that. One thing disturbs me, though. They say they want you to carry him all the way across the galaxy. That doesn't make sense to me. I don't think they would trust Logden with a three-way split and let him make the trip all by himself, leaving them behind with no guarantees."

"I suspect you're right, Tibby. What do you think they're planning?"

"My guess is they plan to meet up with him someplace outside of the area after we get them past the Brotherhood blockade, possibly not until we get somewhere inside Federation territory, where they're less likely to encounter any more Brotherhood ships. At that point I suspect that Logden plans to pull a stunt like Lexmal did when he took over the *TRITYTE*. Then they'll all get together on a larger ship, more suited to Agama and his brother's tastes, to make the rest of the year-long journey to wherever their destination is. So…this means they'll have to follow us in a second ship when we leave. They'll be stopped by the Brotherhood, of course, but once Logden and the solbidyum are not found, they will be right after us again. They'll probably wait a few days before contacting Logden to make his move."

"What's to keep Logden from making a run for it once he's off-world, if he were to gain control of our ship?"

"Who knows? I suspect that he needs them to complete the solbidyum sale. Even with a three-way split, he would have more money than he will ever use in a lifetime. Or maybe they plan to put a courier band on him. I think we should tell them we will accept the deal, but for 40 million credits, since the conditions of this job require us to proceed without knowing why it is so important that he get off-world in secret and without understanding what dangers we face. No doubt they will try to bargain it down, but don't go less than 35 million credits. If they accept that, I think we can be pretty certain that Logden and the solbidyum are the cargo."

We walked back over to where Agama and his men stood. Kerabac began, "Since we are expected to complete this escort without knowing the identity of the man we are to transport or the final destination or, for that matter, the risks we face from the Brotherhood, should they succeed in intercepting us, we feel we cannot possibly do it for less than 40 million credits."

"FORTY MILLION!" Agama shouted. "That's preposterous! Absolutely no way! Even if we had that kind of money, we would never agree to that."

"What would you agree to?" Kerabac replied. "Considering that 20 million will not get your friend Sol off this planet on our ship."

"Mmm, 30 million — that's the max I can go!"

"Thirty? You're asking us to risk our lives and livelihood for at least a full year… for reasons that we do not know, to a destination we do not know, and at the wrath of the Brotherhood, as well. We cannot possibly do it for less than 40 million," Kerabac retorted with a stubborn look on his face.

"OK….32 million, I will go to 32 million, but that is all the money I can pay you! That is a fortune; you and your crew will never have to work again."

"Make it 35 million and we have a deal."

"Thirty-five? I can't pay you that now; you would need to wait until you have reached the destination for that amount."

"OK then…32 million when we leave here, and the remainder at the other end, *before* we deliver your friend, Sol," Kerabac stated.

"Deal," Agama said. "We'll need two days to get things arranged. In the meantime, I suggest you stay out of the way of the Brotherhood; I fear they fully intend to do you some serious harm later today. If I were you, I would get out of this place. I'll contact you in two days, so be prepared to leave immediately thereafter."

After Agama and his men left I said, "You know, I think he is right. We need to get out of here before the Brotherhood shows up. A confrontation now could jeopardize our mission. It's time to get ourselves to Tondor's estate inside the Ruwallie Rasson sector of the city where the Brotherhood is not welcome. I have no doubt that his compound remains under heavy guard at all times, so we should be safe there for the next few days until it's time for us to make our get away with Logden and the solbidyum. It would be really difficult for the Brotherhood to reach us there without starting a war."

Padaran then politely stepped forward to join our conversation. "Sirs," he began, I believe this plan will also give me an opportunity, as the leader of the Ruwallie people and cartel, to get some things in place that will solidify the new conditions for the Ruwallie Rasson so they don't revert back to their former ways. I need to appoint someone to be my voice here after we leave."

"Then it's settled. Get everyone together, let them know we are leaving and to gather up any items that we brought with us from the ship. Anything we purchased here stays here."

"What about Tanden and his sister?" Marranalis inquired.

"They go with us to Tondor's estate. We need Jenira to tell us where we can find their father so we can give him money to pay off his debts. We need to see if we can get the entire family together and get them on the ship."

"I'll get Endina to search for their parents as soon as we get into the new place. She may have already made some progress on this issue," Marranalis said.

Padaran made a call to Tondor and notified him that we would be moving over to his estate that morning. Tondor insisted that we use the luxury transport which was now Padaran's property, and said he was dispatching it to us with a security detail as they spoke.

While we waited, Padaran, Endina, Sokaia, Marranalis and Kala checked around the estate to make sure we didn't leave anything behind that might reveal our true identities and purpose. While they were engaged in that task, Kerabac and I got in touch with the *RASSON BEDAN* to let them know we were relocating and to find out any news that we may need to know. Because the ship was inside the local solar system, we did not bring a DSC system with us to the surface — mostly to prevent its discovery if we were captured. However, the *RASSON BEDAN* did have a DSC system and was in touch with what was happening throughout the galaxy.

After relating details concerning recent events and the upcoming move, Norkoda replied that he had been waiting for us to contact them. During the night, they received word from Admiral Regeny that another Federation frigate, the *LOCOLAT*, had been attacked by a very large spaceship of unknown origin two days earlier in an episode similar to the attack on the *GROTTOM*. The unidentified ship reportedly used the same or similar technology to render the *LOCOLAT*'s crew helpless. Unfortunately, the frigate had not yet received a cloaking or RMFF system and the ship was captured. As the ship was being boarded, one Nibarian crewmember who, for some reason, had not been affected by the enemy's weapon, was able to send out a gravity wave message pod relating the attack, but since then, no new messages had been received from the ship.

Just a day later, according to the admiral, the nearby planet, Kublac, was attacked by Brotherhood ships accompanied by the *LOCOLAT* and the larger ship we now suspected to belong to the Tottalax. They sacked large portions of the planet, emptied out the armories of their military supplies, and took all the available ships — both military and civilian. Kublac was mostly an outpost planet that hosted no significant resources; and it only had a token military force with a few troop transports and patrol ships — nothing heavy or significant — hence, they were vastly outnumbered and out-gunned. The admiral said that the incident occurred near the Federation border, not too far from this region, and that we should keep our eyes out for any large, unfamiliar ships.

He also related that many of the ships captured in the raid were military ships stationed at the planet, ships of both Federation and the planetary guard. Most of the ships captured were in space; the bodies of the crews had been discovered floating in space by the Federation ships that arrived in response to the distress call when the attack began; but by then the Brotherhood and the mysterious enemy ship had vanished from the area.

"This is not good," Kerabac said. "We know there's a large contingency of Brotherhood gathered here, and yet they had a great enough force to attack a planet in the Federation as well. Even though we've known that they're spread throughout the Federation, it looks like their numbers are far greater than we believed. In spite of you and the Federation having wiped out large numbers of their ships, the Brotherhood seems to be increasing in numbers and strength; and with each attack they're commandeering even more arms and ships."

"I am not sure what to do about it. The sooner we can get the solbidyum back and get into Federation territory, the better.   Norkoda, get in touch with Commodore Stonbersa on the *NEW ORLEANS* with instructions for the commodore to contact Admiral Regeny directly. He should suggest that the admiral might want to pass all available information about the attacks to A'Lappe, so he can analyze the data and see if he can come up with some sort of defense against this new weapon threat.

"Also, find out exactly where the frigate *RIVED* was when it was attacked, and where the *LOCOLAT* was when they last transmitted. Then let's connect the dots and see if there is any clear progression or direction to these incidents. I think the ship that was with the Brotherhood in this latest attack may have been the same ship that attacked the *RIVED*. If we can trace it back, we may be able to discover where it originated.

"One more thing. I don't think it's necessary for the *NEW ORLEANS* to remain staged at the opposite side of this system any longer. Tell Stonbersa to respond here with the *NEW ORLEANS* remain cloaked for the time being."

It was about an hour and a half later when Tondor's transport arrived. To be honest, it was more like a huge luxury houseboat, richly appointed with wood paneling, marble-like floors in some places and rich carpeting in others. There was a main lounge equipped with a fireplace, a galley staffed with two chefs, numerous well-appointed cabins for guests and an opulent master suite with the richest furnishings and details that one could imagine.

"WOW!" Padaran exclaimed, as the captain toured us around the boat. He turned to me and said in a voice the captain could not hear, "I'm almost tempted to stay on Goo'Waddle and run the Ruwallie Rasson, if this is how their leader lives." I was about to say something when he added, "But I have no intention of staying here or continuing to rule the Ruwallie Rasson. Tondor can do that in my stead.

All I want to do is give him directions as to how to rule them from now forward and to end some of their more nefarious practices."

"I think that's a wise move, Padaran. You can guide from afar without all the headaches of dealing with daily minutia that way."

"Yeah, and I doubt that my being in charge here would go as smoothly as it will with a Ruwallie Rasson in charge. While, at the moment, most of the Ruwallie Rasson are willing to follow me, believing it's the will of the gods, it is only a matter of time before some of them begin to challenge that idea... and I don't want to end up poisoned."

Kerabac was behind me when Padaran said this and he laughed. "You are indeed a wise man, Padaran. This way you will go down in Ruwallie Rasson history and legend. If you were to stay, you would most certainly be killed and quickly forgotten. I think you can do a lot to civilize this renegade band. They have given a bad name to my people and portrayed a despicable image of my culture and race long enough. No *true* Ruwallie Rasson thinks, believes or acts as these do."

"We have had similar situations on my home planet," I said, "and among my own race. By far, the largest portions of the white people in my country were not prejudiced against blacks, nor did they want or approve of slavery; but there were those who did. These conflicting views caused a lot of tension at times and, unfortunately, it was those who were prejudiced that made the most trouble and nurtured an image of hatred between the races, often where little or none existed. To be fair, though, many of my own race should have stood up in more firm opposition and told the racist bigots to sit down and shut up. Instead, they sat back and let things go, rather than get involved. Too often, their silence was taken as consent by the bigots and by their victims, as well. Tolerating bullies and bigots is never the right thing to do."

"I agree, Tibby. You and I think alike on that matter," Kerabac said as he placed his hand on my shoulder.

As we approached the area near Tondor's estate inside the Ruwallie-controlled *calganas*, we began weaving in and out of gated canals. Each gate was manned by guards, who opened the gates and saluted as we passed. It became obvious that the *calganas* and canals there were deliberately situated like a maze, in the center of which was Tondor's estate, occupying the entire expanse of one very large *calgana*.

"It certainly looks like the Brotherhood would have a hard time getting in here," Kala said as she slipped her arm through mine.

"I was just thinking the same thing," I replied.

"Have you tried any of those small pieces of meat on the sticks laid out on that tray over there? They're delicious!" Kala exclaimed just as my stomach rumbled. I looked in the direction she pointed to see a large buffet of food selections laid out on an island-type bar in the center of the room. Tanden and Jenira were busy sampling all the dishes with extreme delight. It looked and felt good to see them laughing together. Tanden had his hair cut and groomed, I suspect by his sister, and was dressed in slacks and a collarless shirt of some soft fabric. He still had his arm in a cast; but otherwise, he had gained some weight and was beginning to look like any other healthy and happy boy his age.

Kala and I approached the food bar as Tanden looked up and said in an excited voice, "Tibby, you need to try these fruits. When you bite on them, they pop in your mouth and all this wonderful juice squirts out! They're really yummy."

I took one of the small peach-colored fruits, about the size of an Earth grape, and put it in my mouth. Sure enough, it popped when I bit into it — and just a bit sooner than I expected, causing some of the juice to squirt out through my lips.

Both Tanden and Jenira jumped back, laughing hysterically. "See, I told you," Tanden chided. Tanden was right; the juice in these small fruits was incredibly delicious.

"I think those are bowaban fruits," Kerabac said as he popped one into his mouth. "They are originally from my home world and are highly prized there."

"They sure are good. Do you have these on your planet and your estate, Tibby?" Tanden asked. More and more, he had been asking questions about my estate, since I had told him that he and his family could come and live there until his father could get himself back on his feet.

"To be honest, Tanden, I don't know if I do or not. We have many trees and plants on my estate from all over the galaxy; I have no idea what all is growing there. We also have plants growing on my ship, the *NEW ORLEANS*, but I don't think we have any bowaban trees. Maybe we should have some planted in one of the atrium gardens."

By now, we had reached the inner canals and were pulling up to a docking area where all sorts of luxurious boats were tied. Several armed Ruwallie Rasson guards appeared at various locations about the docking area, all of whom dropped to one knee and saluted Padaran as he disembarked.

"Welcome, *Dormon* Padaran, to your home. We are your servants and guards," one of the Ruwallie Rasson men said. It appeared he was in charge of those at the docking area.

"*Dormon* is a title that means 'Leader' or 'Lord' in the Rasson language," Kerabac explained.

The kneeling guard continued. "I am Right Man Neugalie. I see to all security here on your *calgana*."

"A 'Right Man' is a rank, like a Captain in the Federation," Kerabac whispered to me.

"Rise, Neugalie," Padaran said.   "I want you to discuss security with my man Marranalis here.   He is a prized warrior, and he may want to test some of your men's combat skills and provide some training, if necessary."

"I assure you, *Dormon* Padaran, my men are the most highly skilled and trained that there are; they will need no other training."

"Hmm."   Padaran hummed as he looked about at the guards.   "Which of these men are the best?   Besides you, of course."

"That would be Sondan," the Right Man stated, pointing to a tall muscular Ruwallie Rasson not too far away.

"I see," Padaran said coolly.   "Have him bind and remove my man Marranalis…if he can."

The Right Man started to sweat; but he nodded to Sondan, who strutted forward with a determined look on his face.   He grabbed Marranalis arm — which was totally the wrong thing to do — and instantly Sondan was flying across the dock and out into the canal.

Padaran feigned a sigh.   "I fear your guards will need additional training, if that is the best they can do."

By now, the Right Man was in a full dripping sweat and horror showed plainly on his face.   Whether he thought he was going to be punished or he was simply terrified at seeing one of his best so easily and quickly defeated, I did not know.

Marranalis had moved to the side of the dock and was helping a very embarrassed Sondan up out of the water, just as Tondor came walking hurriedly toward us from the house.

"What happened?   Neugalie, you didn't allow one of my men attack these people, did you?   Padaran is your new *Dormon* and these are his servants, as are you all now. Kerabac is the *Dormon*'s business partner.   You cannot be attacking them."

"My apologies, Tondor, but I only did as the *Dormon* asked. He wished to test the skills of our guards and, alas, it didn't go well. It would appear the gods have decreed that we have much to learn, and they are most displeased with us."

"It's quite alright, Tondor," Padaran said. "I did indeed make the request that led to the event. No harm has been done, but we know now that the guards here will need additional instruction."

"As you say, *Dormon*. Please, allow me to show you your new home." And with that Tondor turned and began to lead us into the huge house that was built in much the same style as what was called 'Mediterranean' on Earth.

The first thing I noticed on entering Tondor's house was that he apparently had a fondness for dark purple and green — or there was some significance to these colors in Ruwallie Rasson culture — as the two colors dominated everything from wall coverings to furniture. The floor was a dark green marble-like stone; most of the walls were painted a dark purple and dark green drapes were mounted in tracks on the ceiling so they could be pulled across the length of any room to divide it into smaller spaces. The precise reason for this was not clear to me and I made a mental note to ask Kerabac about the significance of it later. Statues and various sculptures carved from a black onyx-like stone and inlaid with gold were mounted on small pedestals and in small alcoves in the walls about each room.

A number of people were assembled in the great room; Tondor introduced them as the house servants. He immediately emphasized that all were now free and no longer slaves, and that he, personally, had seen to each of them being paid generously for their services. He also indicated that, now that Padaran was the new *Dormon*, it would be his responsibility to pay them, should he decide to keep them on. Tondor informed Padaran that it would not be necessary for him to learn the names or duties of each servant, as he himself would be serving as the head servant in accordance with the dictates of his defeat by Padaran. All desires and wishes should be conveyed to him and he would see to it that the servants carried out those orders.

Padaran appeared to pay only the slightest attention to Tondor as he casually strolled about the room, running his fingers over objects as though he was checking for dust. I glanced at Kala and caught her trying to suppress a grin as she watched Padaran's performance.

"It will do, I suppose." Padaran sighed. "Once we have settled in, I will need to meet with all the Ruwallie Rasson leadership here to discuss some of the changes I expect to see implemented. Make arrangements for them to meet with me here in about four hours."

"Yes, *Dormon*, it shall be as you request," Tondor replied.

After Tondor set off to make arrangements for Padaran's meeting, we continued to look about the house. It was large, though nowhere nearly as large as my estate back on Megelleon. Nevertheless, it was a small town unto itself. Servants busied themselves and they scurried hither and yon, doing whatever it was that the servants of a Ruwallie Rasson do. Kala and I found a very nice guest suite inside the estate that we claimed as our territory. Marranalis situated himself in a smaller room just across the hall that had an adjoining bedroom that Tanden and Jenira would share. Padaran, of course, had the master suite in the house, and Kerabac and Endina both selected rooms nearby, where Padaran could quickly reach them to get advice for his dealings with the Ruwallie Rasson — not that he needed any, as it seemed that he had already amassed a plethora of knowledge about the Ruwallie Rasson ways.

"I swear," Kerabac said when we were alone later, "that boy really does know more about the Ruwallie Rasson history and customs than I do."

"I've been meaning to ask you, Kerabac, what's the deal with the purple and green decor? Is it just a preference of Tondor's or is there some other significance to it?"

"There is definitely significance to it; and if Padaran is going to affect any influence in his role as *Dormon*, he's going to need to dress in those colors. I'm sure you noticed when we first saw Tondor at the estate house that he was wearing these colors. When we arrived today, he was dressed in green and black. Green and black designates him as being in charge of the house and estate — his new position now that Padaran has defeated him. Normally he would have worn the outfit of a slave, albeit one of status under Padaran, but since Padaran abolished slavery for the Ruwallie Rasson, Tondor is allowed to wear black and green as house master."

"I see. Do you think Padaran is aware of this?"

"Look for yourself," Kerabac answered as he pointed down the hall. I looked to see a lavishly attired Padaran approaching from the distance — the purple and green attire of the Ruwallie Rasson *Dormon.*

"What do you guys think? Not exactly my favorite colors — still, I think I look pretty dashing."

Kerabac and I both laughed, but neither of us said what we were really thinking.

"Kerabac, I need you and Endina to be with me for the meeting with the Ruwallie Rasson this afternoon. I will be relying heavily on both of you in these negotiations. Tibby, I will need your input and guidance as well, but I think perhaps it best if limit my advisors in the room to just Kerabac and Endina, at least for now."

"I can fully understand and respect that," I said. "I have a feeling it's going to be difficult enough for them to accept you being there, even if *the gods dictate* it."

"Yes, I think you're right, Tibby," Kerabac interjected. "Padaran, you can count trying to convince the

Ruwallie Rasson to change any of their practices, even if they are accepting you as *Dormon* at the moment. There may be a way, though, that Tibby can at least witness what takes place at the meeting. My grandfather had been a *Dormon* back on our home world; and when I was small, I discovered there was a secret panel in the wall where one could hide and spy on meetings among Ruwallie Rasson leaders. He told me once that he used it when he needed someone else to secretly listen to meetings, and more commonly as a place where his guards could watch and listen in case of trouble. He said all *Dormons* had such places in their houses. I'm betting that Tondor has just such a place here. We just have to locate it."

"Just what do you plan to do when you have this meeting?" I asked Padaran.

Padaran grinned. "I have a plan that may help us in more ways than one, and may give the Ruwallie Rasson a bit of a step up in this sector, as well. It's widely accepted that the Ruwallie Rasson and the Brotherhood do not like each other; but so far, they have tolerated each other, even though the Brotherhood treats the Ruwallie Rasson like offal. We also know the Ruwallie Rasson did not like having to give up their slaves. What I plan to do is to tell them that it's OK for them to raid and take the Brotherhood members as slaves, so long as they free any slaves that the Brotherhood is holding. The Ruwallie Rasson will not be allowed to take or have any children as slaves — any child slaves of the Brotherhood must be freed to be cared for and restored either to their original parents or placed with a caring family. But the Brotherhood members who were their masters can be placed into slavery and made to serve the Ruwallie Rasson."

Kerabac and I looked back and forth at each other. "How did you come up with this idea?" I inquired.

"Well, to be honest, it wasn't my idea. It was Tanden's."

"Tanden's?"

"Yeah. On the way here, we passed a *calgana* filled with child slaves harvesting for the Brotherhood. When Tanden saw them, he got upset and said he wished he could set the children free and make the Brotherhood slaves as punishment. It got me thinking — why not? It will actively set the Brotherhood against the Ruwallie Rasson; and if the Brotherhood wishes to maintain their presence in this sector, they'll need to keep a sizeable army stationed here, which will divide their forces between here and the Federation."

"Yes, but the Brotherhood has the Ruwallie Rasson out-classed, in terms of weapons and ships," Kerabac began. "I don't think the Ruwallie Rasson have enough ships or sophisticated enough firepower to successfully fend off the Brotherhood here in this sector, much less dominate them."

"Hmm. You're right. I'd not thought about that."

"But what if they did have ships of equal force to the Brotherhood?" I asked.

"No offense intended, Tibby, but I don't think you can buy and have built ships fast enough to supply the Ruwallie Rasson here in the time Padaran needs," Kerabac stated.

"I wasn't thinking of buying ships or having ships built; I was thinking about *acquiring* them from the Brotherhood, so to speak." Both Kerabac and Padaran looked at me as if I had lost my mind.

"And just how do you plan to do that?" Padaran exclaimed.

"For the time being, that's my secret. When the time comes, I will let you know."

"But what am I going to tell the Ruwallie Rasson when I present them with my plan? I can't tell them that they are going to have Brotherhood ships. They're going to wonder where I plan to get such ships and arms for them," Padaran asserted.

"Tell them the gods will supply the ships and that you do not expect them to do anything until they do. Now, let's see if we can locate a secret viewing place in the main hall where the meeting is to take place," I said.

"If it's anything like what my grandfather had, it will be positioned someplace in front of the room near or behind the *Dormon*'s seat. The secret space in his meeting hall was behind an unusual dragon carving motif that was mounted on the wall, behind which one could look out through the crystal eyes and listen through the open mouth, which was shaped in such a way to amplify the sound."

"There's a huge ornament of three men standing about a jewel-encrusted orb mounted on a pedestal behind the *Dormon*'s seat in there," Padaran said. "I noticed it when Tondor was giving me the tour. I'll bet some of those crystals are clear, also. There's no one in the room now — shall we see if we can find the entrance into it?"

We all headed into the room. Marranalis stayed by the door on lookout for anyone that might come by as Padaran, Kerabac and I searched for the hidden chamber and the access to it. It was only logical that it would be Kerabac to find the hidden release to the small room behind the wall. It was concealed behind a column-like structure that was designed to appear as though it was embedded in the wall. Once the release was activated, the column shifted inward to reveal the access into the room. Inside, we discovered two chairs. Once seated, each viewer would be at eye level with a pair of crystals in the motif that allowed for observation of the entire room from a point just slightly above the head height of the *Dormon* seated in the chair at the front of the room. The acoustics in the meeting hall very effectively focused the sound into the room through two air vents near the ceiling.

The inside of the room was painted black, so anyone looking closely at the crystals from the outside would not be able to discern any movement or space behind them. At the far end of the secret room was small tunnel behind yet another wall and room and, again, a peephole with a crystal that looked out into that room. The tunnel continued on to two more viewing rooms, each with a spy hole. Along this passage we also located another secret door that opened into a remote and concealed area of the gardens. The tunnel terminated at yet another hidden door that opened into the *Dormon*'s room which, in this case, was now Padaran's room.

"Well, this is good," Padaran exclaimed. "Now at least there is a way for you to get into this tunnel without having to do so from the master hall."

"You don't think Tondor will have any of his men stationed back here during the meeting, do you?" I asked.

"I doubt it," Kerabac said. "Anyone he might want to listen in will be attending the meeting directly; so there would no need for someone to hide back here, from his perspective. I think you'll be quite safe during the meeting."

We emerged from the passageway and closed the secret door and were just making our way down the main corridor of the house when Tondor found us. "Ahh, there you are, *Dormon*," he began. "I do hope you are finding everything to your satisfaction."

"Indeed, Tondor, I find this house quite adequate."

"I am most pleased to hear it, *Dormon*," Tondor answered. I was surprised at the humility and civility this man was showing since his defeat by Padaran the day before. Either he sincerely believed his defeat had been the will of the gods or he was a very convincing liar.

"*Dormon*, I have made the necessary arrangements for you to meet with the principal Ruwallie Rasson leaders this evening here in the great hall. I trust this is to your satisfaction."

"It's later than I had hoped for, but I think that will suffice, Tondor. Please see to it that refreshments are made available for our guests both before and after the meeting."

"It shall be as you wish, *Dormon*."

"Pardon me, *Dormon*," I interjected. "Perhaps this is a good time for us to excuse ourselves to finish our earlier conversation."

Padaran immediately picked up on the reference to my earlier hints as to how we would *acquire* Brotherhood ships to fortify the Ruwallie forces and he promptly dismissed everyone from our company so we could speak privately.

It was a little while later that Kala and I found ourselves seated by a reflecting pool in the garden behind the main house after exploring more of the estate on our own. I guess I had been quieter than usual, because Kala asked, "What's bothering you, Tibby? I haven't ever known you to be this quiet or reserved before."

"I don't know, Kala. I feel totally out of control here. I'm supposed to be in charge and I feel like everyone else is more in control than I am, including young Padaran."

Kala moved closer and put her arm around me as I continued. "Since we arrived here, it seems like everyone but me has contributed to this mission; and Padaran, who I probably rated the least important person on the mission, is turning out to be its champion. I have no clue what he is doing or where things are going. Kerabac is the glue holding things together; you and Endina are the ones who have been making all the arrangements and taking care of the fine details.

"I look at Tanden and his sister and, Kala, I'm telling you, it makes me want to cry. What has happened to them is terrible beyond all comprehension and it totally disgusts and enrages me. I feel utterly helpless, knowing that it is going on with thousands of others all around us and

I can do nothing to stop it. I only hope we're able to get Logden and the solbidyum off this planet soon. I feel totally useless. I didn't realize how dependent I've become on the strength and security of the *NEW ORLEANS* and my ships or the ability to call on my security forces at a moment's notice. I fear that this mission is beyond me and that we'll fail."

"Tibby, we are not failing; and you have accomplished a great deal here, whether you realize it or not. If it weren't for you, who knows what would have happened to Tanden and Jenira. And Padaran didn't learn his martial skills on his own, you know; you played just as large a part in Tondor's defeat as Padaran, even if you didn't fight him yourself. As for what Padaran is doing and accomplishing as *Dormon*, that is yet to be seen; but he's bright young man who has a better understanding of Ruwallie Rasson customs and history than anyone here. He's the perfect one to be doing what he is. You're just frustrated that, for the first time since you've come to the Federation, you aren't in the forefront leading the action. I suppose it would make me feel helpless too, coming from your perspective up to this point."

"You may be right, but I still don't like it. We're playing it by ear, and making spur-of-the-moment decisions every step of the way. We have no real plan, other than hopefully stumbling across Logden and the solbidyum and somehow getting out of here alive. We have no idea when or, for that matter, even how Agama will contact us again; how we will make contact with the *RASSON BEDAN*; where we will meet up with them; or what we will face when we try to get off this planet. All in all, I feel like the mission is crumbling about our feet and that we'll be lucky to make it off this planet with our lives."

Kala smiled at me and kissed me on the cheek. "Tibby, look around you. I would say things are getting better, not worse. Yesterday we had the Brotherhood getting ready to come back and kill us. We were living in a bugged and busted up house under intense scrutiny from several sources. Now we're in a secure place where the Brotherhood can't pursue us; we don't have to pretend to be slaves anymore; Padaran has gotten the Ruwallie Rasson to release their slaves; Tanden and his sister are free and together; and we have a solid lead on Logden and the solbidyum. Just as you planned in the beginning, they are all coming to us. Lift yourself out of this doom and gloom! Things are going pretty well, I would say."

"Maybe you're right," I sighed. "I just don't feel right, sitting and waiting for things to happen — I'm used to *making* things happen."

Kala and I sat and talked for some time. She shared with me some of the daily details that she, Endina and Sokaia experienced at the other estate house while the rest of us were away or restricted to the slave quarters. She explained how difficult it had been for them to maintain their roles to keep anyone listening in with the bugging device from suspecting anything out of the ordinary. It all sounded rather strange because, in light of all the events that had taken place so far, *nothing* had been ordinary in any way. She was just getting around to sharing some of the more humorous skits they had to put on, when Marranalis came out of the house and called to me.

"Tibby, the Ruwallie Rasson leaders are starting to arrive for the meeting with Padaran. Kerabac thinks now would be a good time for us to get into the compartment behind the walls to start watching and listening."

"Kala, I would like if you could come with us. Your training as a diplomatic attaché might provide some useful insight as to what develops during the meeting."

"I'll come with you, but I can't promise I will be much help. My knowledge of Ruwallie Rasson customs and behaviors are mostly academic, as I was never required to work with any of them during my time in the Federation. Even what I do know probably won't fit with this group, as they've been operating for generations as a remote, rouge faction, separated from their home world and culture. Padaran seems to know more about them than anyone else in your crew."

"Even so, I would still like you to witness this meeting," I said as we made our way to the secret entrance in Padaran's suite. "Your experience could still allow you to see something that Marranalis and I might miss."

Kala and I seated ourselves in the chairs behind the crystals that afforded us a clear view of the room. Sounds of the Ruwallie Rasson leaders could be heard clearly inside the hidden space, as the sound funneled in from various locations within the meeting room. Marranalis stood behind us, where he could get some glimpses of what we were seeing and hear the pre-meeting discussions that were happening on the other side. Padaran and Tondor had not yet entered the room.

"I don't like having this white man as our *Dormon*," one angry voice exclaimed. "I don't buy this idea that it is the will of the gods. We are the Ruwallie Rasson; we are the chosen ones — not this white worm!"

Several of the others seemed to agree with this individual, but most remained quiet and said nothing. One man did decide to speak up.

"That's easy for you to say, Jadong; you weren't there to witness the events. Most of us were, and we can attest to the divine nature of the event. Never would I have believed that one puny white man, barely old enough to have hair on his chin, would be able to defeat any Ruwallie warrior — let alone one as skilled and seasoned as Tondor. Yet he did, and with such ease that only the gods could have made it so. But as if that were not enough, to have a *woman* beat another of our finest in just seconds...! I tell you, it could *only* be a sign from the gods."

Several of the other Ruwallie Rasson nearby voiced their agreement and voices buzzed as both sides argued their case.

"Bah!" spat the one called Jadong. "You and your silly gods. The gods are not real, I tell you. There is some trickery involved — nothing more!"

"You are not going to start harping on that argument about there not being any gods again, Jadong. We have all heard your blasphemes before. Best you be silent, now that the gods have demonstrated their will, before you are humiliated before them."

"I would like to see that happen," Jadong sneered. Just as he said this, Tondor, Kerabac and Padaran entered the room, and everyone fell silent. Jadong turned and, upon seeing Padaran, he unsheathed a long dagger concealed inside his cloak. He charged Padaran with the clear intent of skewering him.

Padaran showed no surprise and smoothly sidestepped Jadong's charge while grasping the arm holding the dagger in one hand and Jadong's wrist with the other. In a swift movement, he both twisted the arm and shoved Jadong's wrist down, forcing him to drop the dagger. At the same time, he continued following through with Jadong's direction of movement, sending him flying out the door and into the wall on the other side of the corridor. Jadong impacted the wall and slid down in a dazed heap.

All this happened in the blink of an eye; and while the stunned Ruwallie Rasson watched, Padaran bent over calmly, picked up the fallen dagger and walked in a rather leisurely fashion across the hall. In a move so fast that it was a blur, he slashed out with the blade, cutting a six-centimeter long gash in Jadong's cheek. Then, in an unbelievably calm voice, he said, "Your blood now belongs to me. Do you wish for it to serve me, or do you wish for me to wash my floor with it?"

Jadong sat against the wall with a look of shock on his face. He glanced down to see his blood dripping onto his shirt and then reached up and touched his cheek where the blood seeped. Suddenly, he began to tremble. Then he let out a moan and fell face forward on the floor, dead.

Padaran looked confused for a brief moment and then examined the blade in his hand.

"Poisoned blade," Tondor said. "He died by the blade and poison he intended for you, *Dormon*. Truly, the gods protect you."

Behind them in the room the Ruwallie Rasson who had just witnessed the event all dropped to their knees and mumbled prayers as Padaran, Tondor and Kerabac re entered the assembly room.

"I have a feeling Padaran is not going to have much more in the way of opposition during this meeting," Marranalis whispered in my ear.

Padaran didn't waste time getting to the issues at hand. After directing the assembly to be seated, he told them that, if any of them still held slaves, they had one day to set them free with full compensation for their service. He reaffirmed that the freed could be hired to continue their work under the conditions of respectable wages and fair treatment as free employees. While there were grumblings about this, no one spoke out against him.

He then addressed the matter of piracy, expressing that the Ruwallie Rasson must end the practice of pirating the cargos of other traders and merchants, and that all business must be conducted fairly and honestly to honor the favor and prosperity that had been shown them by the gods. This caused a lot of angry voices to be raised, as clearly most of the Ruwallie Rasson cartel members had made an exclusive living as pirates rather than as traders.

Padaran sat patiently, letting them vent their frustrations and anger until there was a lull in their complaints. "There is one exception, however," he said in a tone of authoritative proclamation. You may raid, destroy, seize, steal, or do whatever you wish with any Brotherhood ships or goods that you find."

I'm not sure what Padaran expected to happen at that point, but I know that I was shocked by the reaction of the room. Everyone froze and went totally silent as they stared at Padaran.

"What's happening?" Marranalis whispered.

"I have no idea, but clearly, I don't think he expected this would happen," said Kala.

"But *Dormon*," one of the Ruwallie Rasson spoke up. "We are no match for the Brotherhood. They outnumber us several hundred to one. They have larger and more powerful ships and fiercer weapons. We cannot hope to take them on and steal their ships and goods and survive with our lives."

"Are you not Ruwallie Rasson?" Padaran said in a firm voice. "Are you not *the chosen*? Do *the chosen* kneel before others? How can you call yourself *the chosen*, if you cower before the Brotherhood like Brovian plees? If you take just three of the Brotherhood corvettes and have the rest of your ships in a united fleet, you have the means to confront the Brotherhood and be victorious. All you need to do is coordinate your first attacks so you take out three ships at one time."

"Just how do you plan for us to do that? Do you think we can simply fly up to one of their corvettes in our smaller ships and ask them to surrender it to us?" asked one of the men seated near the front of the room.

"Something like that," Padaran responded with a slight grin. "But I was thinking more in line with the Brotherhood inviting your ships, heavily laden with armed men, to board their corvettes. You will simply surprise and overwhelm their crews and take over the ships."

"I'm afraid you have been misinformed, *Dormon*," another man said. "We Ruwallie Rasson are not exactly best friends with the Brotherhood. It is very unlikely they would invite us aboard their ships."

"Ahh, but you are wrong!" Padaran exclaimed. "Does not the Brotherhood armada demand daily that you stop so that they may inspect your ships? Do they not make your smaller freighters dock to their corvettes so they might carry out an inspection? If you load as many armed and ready Ruwallie Rasson men into three freighters and have them leave the planet from different locations at the same time, each approaching a different Brotherhood ship, challenges will be made by the Brotherhood and they will, as usual, insist that you stop for inspection. If coordinated properly, all three ships should be able to dock with the Brotherhood corvettes at about the same time. The Brotherhood troops aboard the ship will not anticipate any more than a handful of Ruwallie Rasson crew on each ship, so they will assign only a minimal security detail at the docking area. Once docked, the Brotherhood will no doubt expect your crew to leave the ship while they search it. Unbeknownst to them, you will leave your attacking forces inside the ship as the main crew disembarks for the inspection. The Brotherhood will expect it to be empty, per the established routine, and will send in a squad to search the ship. Once they are inside, the Ruwallie Rasson that remain aboard can quickly disable and capture them. In the meantime, the crew that have left the ship will be surrounded only by minimal forces that think you are cooperating with them, so they will not expect you to attack. But that is exactly what you will do. With a very quick strike, you will have captured the docking area and already taken a number of the ship's crew out of action. Next the crew will be joined by their brethren who have subdued the inspection crew to quickly spread throughout the ship and take over. The first two areas of attack will be the bridge and engineering rooms. They will not be expecting an attack so quickly and swiftly, and you will have control of the ship in minutes."

"How do you expect us to be able accomplish all this?" one of the men interrupted. "None of us knows our way around a Brotherhood corvette; they have never allowed any of us past the docking area."

"That's not a problem," Padaran answered. "I just happen to have a set of plans for the Brotherhood corvettes, and I will be most happy to share them with you all this evening. Once you have captured the corvettes, you will send a message back here to your commanders, at which time additional Ruwallie Rasson ships will engage with the three taken ships and utilize your combined firepower to confront the Brotherhood. I do not believe, however, that you will have to do so."

"You think the Brotherhood is simply going to let us have the ships and not try to take them back?"

"I have very good information that the Brotherhood is engaged in a large conflict elsewhere, and that they do not have any more ships to spare for reinforcement in this region. If they feel their forces here are compromised, I am relatively sure they will retreat. They won't be able to afford any more losses at that point and they will pull all their ships back for their battles elsewhere."

"You ask a lot of us, *Dormon*," one of the older, white-haired Ruwallie Rasson leaders exclaimed.

"Do you feel you are not worthy of the challenge?" Padaran replied. "Perhaps you no longer are deserving of being *the chosen* after all. It would seem that the Ruwallie Rasson are not the great and mighty beings they once proclaimed." This evoked a number of mumblings and angry statements from the room.

"If you are Ruwallie Rasson, *the chosen*, then prove it," Padaran said firmly. "If you are not, then leave your daggers at the door. Leave here and go raise *chakaka* seeds to feed the livestock, and call yourselves Ruwallie Rasson no more!" This caused many of the men in the room to drop their heads in shame.

"Now, if there are no more objections, I wish to discuss the plans for this mission. The sooner we carry it out, the sooner *you* will be in control of this region of space, not the Brotherhood Vorgovian slime slugs."

The remainder the meeting went without interruption. If there were any in attendance who opposed Padaran's plans, they were no longer voicing it. After Padaran set a time for the attack on the Brotherhood ships two days later, the meeting adjourned.

Because Jadong had attacked Padaran, who was now the *Dormon*, and Padaran had beaten him, all of Jadong's possessions became the property of Padaran in accordance with Ruwallie custom. As it turned out, Jadong owned one of the best ships of any of the Ruwallie Rasson, one better armed and shielded than most privately owned ships. It was also said to be faster than the ships of the Brotherhood fleet and Jadong had been known to outrun them on several occasions.

Jadong's estate was located on the *calgana* adjacent to the one Padaran had inherited from Tondor, so it was possible for us to examine it the next morning. Jadong had not released his slaves, of which he had several dozen in service. Padaran assembled them all and told them they were free, but he asked them to stay long enough for him to find where Jadong stored his money so he could compensate them for the time they had each spent in service to their slave master. Most of the slaves were in disbelief at what they were being told. Some of them wept and bowed down at Padaran's feet.

One was an old man who was mostly bald, with tuffs of white hair on the sides and back of his head. In a feeble voice, he informed Padaran that he knew where Jadong kept his money and led Padaran into the master bedroom. There he revealed a secret door that led into smaller chamber with another door at the back.

"Behind this door is where Jadong keeps his money," the old man said. "I know you must press the symbols on the wall in a particular order to open the door, but I fear I do not know the combination. I know it started out by pressing these four symbols...." He indicated which ones. "But after that, I never saw what he pressed next."

Both Kerabac and Padaran stared at the panel of symbols. Padaran scratched his head. "I have no idea what this is. I recognize the symbols as being Ruwallie Rasson writing, but that's all."

Kerabac stared at the panel a few minutes and then turned to the old man. "Could you show me one more time which symbols Jadong pressed and the order he pressed them in?"

"I think I can. I'm pretty sure it was these four and he pressed them in this order," he answered as he touched various symbols.

"*Sleep my son, dream....* That's what the series of symbols means. There is something familiar about that," Kerabac said as he tugged on his chin. "Wait a minute," he exclaimed, as he began to press symbols and recite, "*Sleep my son, dream of things to be, dream of the glory and dream of me.*" Suddenly, the door popped open.

"How did you know that?" I asked.

"It's an old nursery rhyme. My mother used to recite it to me when she tucked me in at night."

When Kerabac said that, the old man began to laugh. "Who would have thought that Jadong would have used a nursery rhyme? He hated children and always acted so tough and angry. I wonder if he even had a mother."

Once the door was open and we were able to enter Jadong's vast cache; and everyone but me seemed to be in awe. I must confess that even though I am the richest man in the universe, I have no idea what the values of the various metals, gems and currencies are throughout the galaxy. Inside, we found bags of gems and bars of metals, as well as a number of small cases full of the currency chips that were considered so valuable. In addition, there were objects of art and other items of value.

"Wow!" Padaran exclaimed. "This man had a major fortune." Padaran picked up several of the boxes of chips and handed some of them to the old man and some to Kerabac. "Here, could you help me carry these out to the main hall?"

The old man and Kerabac took their loads out of the chamber and Padaran handed me a few boxes, as well. Together we headed out to the main room. Padaran called each of the slaves forward and handed them each a box, telling them that it was theirs and they were now free. When he did, the slaves broke out crying and laughing, and leapt about.

"How much did he give them?" I asked Kerabac.

"Enough to set most of them up for life. They will easily be able to educate themselves and set themselves up in business if they want or, if they're careful, they could live the rest of their lives with what he gave them."

Oddly, after he had paid the slaves and set them free, several of them didn't want to leave and asked Padaran if they might be allowed to stay on and serve him.

"Tibby, what should I do?" he asked me nervously.

I chuckled. "How should I know, Padaran? You're the expert on the Ruwallie Rasson. Just what exactly are your plans when the time comes for us to leave?"

"That's what I mean, Tibby. I've just sort of been making things up as I go. I have no idea. For example, I have the Ruwallie Rasson set up to go after the Brotherhood, and to take some of their ships; but once they do, who gets the ships? It's not like I can just turn it over to one of the

Ruwallie Rasson — the others who participate would not go for that. If they sell it off and split up the money, the possibility of the Brotherhood coming back to retaliate is all too real and the whole thing will backfire."

"You have an interesting point there," I said.

"Maybe you could organize the Ruwallie Rasson into a sort of mercenary group whose ordained mission is to specifically target the Brotherhood of Light throughout the galaxy," Kerabac interjected. "Let them hunt them down and destroy their businesses and operations. As long as they focus their actions only against the Brotherhood, the Federation won't bother with them if they happen to cross over into Federation space; and it would certainly reduce the Brotherhood's capabilities against the Federation. The crews of the Ruwallie Rasson vessels could split up any treasures they acquire, like they have always done."

"We had a situation like that back on my home world several centuries ago," I said. "Two countries were competing for the development and colonization of a newly discovered land mass on our planet. One side, called the English, sanctioned privateers to intercept ships of their rivals, the Spanish, and plunder their wealth. They also attacked ports and pillaged villages."

"How did it work out?" Padaran asked.

"It worked well for a little while, but then politics started to complicate the situation, as the Spanish and English leaders decided to bring an end to their hostilities. The privateers didn't want to give up their conquests, and many of them continued, in spite of the movement toward peace. Only then, they no longer restricted their attacks to just the Spanish, but began attacking and raiding the English, as well."

"Hmm, I see what you're saying, Tibby. If we set the Ruwallie Rasson up as privateers against the Brotherhood, what happens when the Brotherhood are vanquished?"

"Exactly.   The idea has merit, I must confess, but you need to have an exit strategy instilled in their code from the outset."

"Maybe you can set it up so a generous portion of the loot they take goes into a common fund. Each member will only be allowed to collect their share once the Brotherhood is defeated and the privateers formally disband, or when one of them is disabled or needs to retire from their service because of age or health issues," Kerabac said.

"The pirates on Earth tried something like that by burying portions of their treasures with the intent of retrieving them later on. But, if memory serves correctly, it seemed that most of them never collected."

"What if they put their treasures in safekeeping in the banks at Weccies?" Padaran asked.

"What is so special about Weccies?" I asked.

"Weccies is a planetary system that has never joined the Federation. They pride themselves on their security, as no one has ever been able to steal anything deposited there. The Weccies themselves have a very high sense of pride and believe their worth is in their honesty and loyalty in carrying out any agreements they make. However, they are not at all opposed to setting up accounts for anyone, regardless of how they acquired their money. Also, according to their code of conduct, they do not reveal any information about their clients or their accounts. Anything deposited with them is safe from the outside worlds and only the rightful owners can reclaim it. There are a lot of unscrupulous people who hide their ill-gotten gains there; but there are also lots of good and honest people who do as well, especially ones from non-aligned worlds where things are unstable and there is little security in terms of law enforcement."

"How do they protect these deposits from outside raiders and pirates?"

"To begin with," Kerabac started, "they have an incredible fleet of highly advanced warships and other weaponry. Large regions of the sector are peppered with minefields that are supremely difficult to penetrate. No outside ships are even allowed to fly directly to Weccies itself; instead visitors must stop at one of six space stations on the outer edges of their solar system to make their deposits. Anything of value being sent to Weccies for safekeeping is transferred to one of Weccienite large carrier ships, which are armed like nothing you have ever seen. These ships then transport the items to Weccies, where they are stored in large vaults deep inside the planet itself.

"Weccies is barren on the surface — nothing but rock. There is only one city and no one other than Weccienites are permitted to set foot there. In fact, no one other than Weccienites are permitted inside the orbit of the six space stations — and this is most strictly and severely enforced. Once, about a hundred years ago, some Bunemnites tried to commandeer one of the Weccienite ships to fly to the planet. They had taken its crew hostage and threatened to kill them all if the Weccienites didn't let them through. Without hesitation the Weccienites chose to blow up their own ship, sacrificing their own people who were aboard, rather than allow the Bunemnites passage to the surface. Since then, there have been no further attempts to breach their security."

"Hmm. I can see where setting up accounts there might work, if it's set up with enough forethought. If the Ruwallie Rasson know there is a fortune waiting for them upon the defeat of the Brotherhood, there is no reason for them to continue being pirates. At the same time, it gives them an incentive to go after and capture as many ships and Brotherhood cargos as possible."

It was dusk when we got back to the *Dormon* estate. Kala called me aside. "Come, Tibby, I have something I want to show you," she said as she took me by the hand and began leading me through the maze of rooms in the house.

"What is it?"

"Just wait, you'll see, and I know you'll like it."

Kala led me through the house and then down a side hallway to a door that opened to a private garden on one side of the house. Because of its configuration at on the corner of the *calgana* with the house at its back and canals on two sides obscured by the layers of landscaping and shrubbery, it was totally enclosed and private. There, situated in the middle of the ribbons of flowerbeds and trimmed lawns was a lovely pool of clear water.

"What do you think, Tibby? Our own private swimming pool."

It seemed like forever since Kala and I had last gone swimming together. Swimming had become a regular part of our activities together and was one of the first recreational things we had shared after we met. Both of us were competitive swimmers, and Kala really pushed me to the max when it came to the challenge of racing laps against her.

Before I knew what was taking place, Kala had slipped off her clothing and dived into the pool. "Well," she said, "what are you waiting for?"

As soon as I was undressed and in the water, I immediately felt better. I began a nice slow, steady stroke across the pool. While the pool was not rectangular like a normal exercise pool, it was long enough and wide enough to stride through some serious laps. The pool seemed to be of a uniform depth — just deep enough so the water came to Kala's shoulders when standing flatfooted on the bottom. The temperature was just cool enough to be refreshing without giving me a chill; and it was not long before Kala was matching pace beside me with strong, steady strokes. After swimming about ten laps, we reached one end of the pool where Kala and I stood silently in the water and embraced. It felt really good to hold her in my arms again; it felt right and natural.

Kala kissed me sweetly and then got a serious look on her face that I had not seen before. "Tibby, there is something I've been wanting to tell you for the past few days, but with all that has been going on I wasn't able ...."

She was about to say something more, when suddenly I felt her tense in my arms. Her gaze shift intently to a spot over my shoulder and up in the air. Just as quickly, she looked down and whispered, "Tibby, there's a man. He just ran across the roof of the house and dropped down through the open skylight."

I turned and looked quickly, but didn't see anyone. "Did he see us?"

"I don't think so; he seemed to be focused on the skylight."

I quickly climbed out of the pool and didn't bother to dress, but slipped into the house as stealthily as possible, heading in the direction of the room where the skylight opened into the great room. When I arrived and peered around the corner, I was surprised to see him still there, as well as a second intruder who was dropping down into the room to join him. The first thing I noted was that they were dressed all in black. The second thing I noted was that they were not Ruwallie Rasson.

I was near one of the entrances to the secret tunnels in the wall, so I slipped inside and moved to one of the stations that allowed me to monitor their movements and conversation.   My first hunch was that they were Brotherhood goons; but they just as easily could have been some of Agama's — but it didn't make any sense for Agama's men to enter the house by these means. Once the second man was inside, the first man pulled out a small vid pad and spoke into it while the second man stood watch.

"We're in, which way should we go?" the man with the vid pad whispered.

I could faintly hear a voice come back over the vid pad. "I'll display the map on your screen. Follow the map and place the bomb where the red spot appears on the map, and then get out of the house. I'll detonate it remotely from here in thirty minutes. That should give you enough time to plant the bomb and get back out of the place."

"Right, boss," he said, as he examined the vid pad. He finally looked up and pointed toward one of the doors leading out of the room. I was wondering where Kala had gone to by this point; but I was sure she wouldn't do anything to confront the men on her own. I stayed inside the tunnel and moved from one room to another, following the men as they moved past each consecutive viewing port. At one point, they stopped and hid themselves behind some pillars when a servant passed through. Once the servant was gone, they moved rapidly to the assembly hall where Padaran had met with the Ruwallie Rasson leaders.

The men roamed about the room and then moved to a statue that stood next to the *Dormon* chair where Padaran had been sitting the night before.

"Shydak said to hide the bomb in here someplace. He said it didn't matter where — the bomb is only intended to do damage, not to kill anyone. He just wants to send a warning to Kerabac that he can't hide, and that he better cooperate or else."

"Let's just set the damn thing and get out of here. I'm not thrilled about the thought of running into a bunch of Ruwallie Rasson warriors," the other man said.

"Shydak said that there are only a few servants here, now that the young guy the Rasson seem to think is divine has made them set their slaves free."

"Yeah, I wonder what that's all about."

When the men left, I followed them again from inside the secret passageway. Instead of going back to the room with the skylight where they had entered, they headed to the outdoor pool where Kala and I had just been swimming. I held my breath in the hope that she wasn't still there as the men headed out the door. I quickly followed and cracked the door slightly in time to see them climbing through the dense shrubbery and leap from the edge of the *calgana* wall either into a waiting boat or into the water — though I seriously doubted they would purposely jump into the polluted water of the canals. Once they were out of sight, I immediately went back into the house to look for everyone. I found them gathered in the main living room, all stationed around the perimeter and prepared for action, as Kala had managed to get to them and alert them of the intruders. They relaxed when they saw me, but only for a moment.

"Marranalis, I need your expertise," I exclaimed. "There is a bomb planted in the assembly hall set to detonate in about twenty-five minutes. Everyone else, get to the far side of the house and stay there until we indicate that everything's clear."

Marranalis and I headed quickly to the assembly room, where I pointed out the location of the bomb. Marranalis took one look at the bomb and quickly began working on the device; it only took him a few seconds to defuse it.

"Not much of a bomb, really," he said. "I doubt it would have done more than break the windows and char the room a bit. You would literally have to be sitting right on top of the thing to be seriously hurt."

"I heard one of the men say it was only intended to act as a warning to Kerabac to let him know that he could not escape selling the *RASSON BEDAN* to them, and that he would face the consequences if he didn't comply. I wish there were some way of knowing where their headquarters are located. I would love to sneak this bomb into their own nest and have it explode in their laps."

"Hmm.   Maybe   Tondor   knows   where   the Brotherhood hangs out here on the planet."

"Speaking of Tondor, where is he? I didn't see him in the room with the rest of you."

"Tondor has been living in the servant's quarters since turning the place over to Padaran. Padaran can call him if you like; he'll respond immediately."

By now we had made it back to where everyone had assembled.   Kala, Endina and Sokaia were protectively circling the children as Kerabac and Padaran guarded the doors and windows in the room.

"All's clear," I announced. "The bomb has been diffused. But we're hoping that Tondor might be able to tell us where the Brotherhood has their headquarters. We would like to return this bomb to them as a little gift."

Padaran used his wrist com. "Tondor, do you know where the Brotherhood has their central headquarters here in the city?"

"Yes, *Dormon*, but I do not think it wise that you go there, if that is your intent."

"Actually, the Brotherhood dropped by here a few moments ago and left a bomb in the assembly room where we met last night. I'm planning to have some of my men return the bomb to them as a sort of surprise."

"No disrespect meant, *Dormon*, but...but... is that wise?" Tondor asked.

"It is wiser than allowing it to blow up here in our house," Padaran stated, "and it will send a message to the Brotherhood that we are better prepared for their antics and more capable than they think."

"Very well, *Dormon*. I will personally take you to the Brotherhood's meeting place. However, I think it would be best if we took one of the smaller and faster watercraft, in the event we need to make a rapid departure."

"Very well, Tondor. We will need a craft large enough to carry two others besides yourself," Padaran said before disconnecting his com link.

"Padaran, I want you, Kerabac and the others to stay here. Marranalis and I will handle this matter," I said. "If all goes well, we should be back shortly.

We may need to use the cloaking devices," I said, turning to Marranalis. "Is yours sufficiently charged?" He nodded to me just as Tondor arrived.

"Tondor, I want you to take these two men and their cargo to the Brotherhood headquarters. Wait for them to return and then get them back here as quickly as possible," Padaran commanded.

"As you wish, *Dormon*."

Tondor led us to a small cove on the side of the *calgana*. There he revealed a sleek boat with lines similar to the racing boats that were common on Earth. The boat could have carried about eight people, so we weren't crowded. Tondor navigated into the main canal and then activated a screen that displayed the canal as if it were broad daylight. A second screen displayed an aerial map, showing our location on the canal, as well as any obstacles in the waterway and other craft nearby.

Tondor opened the throttle on the craft and we moved through the canals at an incredible speed toward our destination. Our boat was producing quite a wake, and I wondered how the waves it created would affect the smaller boats on the canals where the poor people lived and slept.

"It looks as though someone else is heading toward the Brotherhood headquarters ahead of us," Tondor said as he pointed to the map screen. I looked where he pointed and guessed the object, clearly a boat, to be about a kilometer ahead of us and moving rapidly through the water in the same direction.   Like us, that boat was moving at considerable speed, taking into account that it was nighttime and there were large number of smaller boats lining both sides of the canal.

"I have noticed that the *Dormon* does not treat you like a slave, nor does he treat you like the others," Tondor said, looking at me. "It is most strange, his behavior toward you. Might I ask — are you his father?"

This comment caught me completely off guard and I was not sure how to answer.

"Ahh, no, I am not his father, though perhaps he looks up to me much in the same way that a young man might look up to a father," I said, hoping that might suffice.

"I see," Tondor said.   "Perhaps the two of you having been slaves together and his not having had a father in his life caused him to substitute you in this way."

"Perhaps, something like that," I said.

"Look, the boat is slowing down and pulling into that small canal up ahead," I said as I pointed to the screen.

"Indeed, that is where the Brotherhood maintains their headquarters. I will not be able to dock there, but I can drop you off nearby and wait for you out in the canal. When you're ready for me to pick you up and return to the estate…" he said as he handed me a light, "flash this light out over the water and I will be there almost instantly."

Moments later Tondor brought us up beside a small pier just around the corner from the boat that docked ahead of us.

"You will have to get off here. I shall wait out there. May the gods protect you."

As soon as we stepped off the boat, he returned to the the middle of the canal. Marranalis and I moved just as rapidly into the shadows by a large building that I assumed was the opposite side of the structure that the men arriving ahead of us had entered. It was a four-story warehouse; and the first two floors appeared to be dark. A light could be seen on the third floor. Marranalis and I looked around for a way in.

As we were about to round the corner to the front of the building, Marranalis silently stuck out his arm to stop me.

"There's a guard over there," he said quietly, pointing to a small crate in front of which the guard's silhouette could be seen pacing. There was no mistaking that he was a guard, as he was fully armed and his gaze roved the canal just beyond the dock where his cohorts had arrived earlier. "Shall we use the personal cloaking devices now to get past him?"

"No, let's see if we can find some other way in." As I was saying this, another boat approached the dock. The guard's posture became more rigid until he apparently recognized it and relaxed as began walking toward it. "You have another shipment?" he called out as the craft docked.

Several men got out of the boat and approached the guard. "Yeah," one of them said. "This is the pure refined stuff, ready to go out tomorrow. Shydak plans to use it to make a payment to the Tottalax to keep them happy. We're leaving it here, and he'll take it with him in the morning." The man turned to the boat and yelled out to the others who were still aboard. "Get those crates up here! Now!" Two men wearing slave collars immediately lifted a heavy crate onto the dock and set it between us and the men.

"I have an idea," I said. "Plant the bomb in the crate."

Marranalis looked at me and grinned. While the slaves were going back to the boat for a second crate, Marranalis cloaked. I watched and held my breath, as I saw a board on the crate slowly being pulled back. I feared it might squeak or break, but it didn't — or if it did, I didn't hear it. Meanwhile, the men on the dock continued to talk as the two slaves transferred three more crates to the dock. At last, I saw the board on the crate being forced back into place, and a moment later Marranalis reappeared beside me. "Let's get out of here," he said.

"I think that's a very good idea. How long do we have before the bomb goes off?"

"I reset it for 20 minutes."

Moments later, we were back at our drop-off point. I signaled with the light, and instantly we heard the boat motor start up as Tondor quickly swept in to pick us up. He barely slowed down as we leaped aboard, and then he quickly steered the boat away from the dock and headed back toward the *Dormon calgana*. We were far enough away after 20 minutes that, when the bomb went off — assuming it did detonate — we never heard it or saw the flash.

"I think Shydak is going to be madder than hell," I said.

"Yeah, I think so, too. I wonder what he'll do now."

When we got back to the house, I told everyone what had happened. Tanden was upset and believed the Brotherhood were back to look for him. We tried to explain that was not the case; nevertheless, he was terrified and Kala went with Jenira and Tanden into their room and promised she would stay there with them during the night so they would not be afraid.

Kala had no sooner gone with them to their room than Endina came to me and said, "I'm afraid we got some bad news today. Jenira told us, while Tanden was with Padaran, that their parents are both dead. She witnessed their deaths at the hands of Brotherhood. She hasn't told Tanden, because she doesn't want to hurt him."

"Oh no! I was hoping we could reunite them. How much suffering must these poor kids go through?" I exclaimed.

"If it's any consolation, Tibby, I think the fact that you found them at all is pretty good luck from their point of view, and things are improving for both of them."

I sighed and said, "I guess only time will reveal how good that luck is. For now, I need to have Padaran make arrangements for extra security here tonight."

Tondor suggested that Padaran appoint several squads of guards to patrol the *calgana*. He had, at times, had his own run-ins with the Brotherhood; so his men were familiar with the protocols for heightened security. They were put on guard at various posts about the island. I divided the rest of us into two teams — Marranalis, Kerabac and Endina on one team and Padaran, Sokaia and I on the other — to take alternating shifts for patrol of the house and grounds while the other team slept. It was a tense night, as we anticipated a retaliatory attack, but dawn arrived without incident.

In the morning a fresh rotation of guards were put in place at their posts, while my crew and I gathered for a fine breakfast prepared by the house chef that consisted of trays of fresh fruit, some sort of cold pickled meats and the most wonderful pastries that reminded me of crepes from Earth, only they were square and folded instead of rolled. Each version was stuffed with tasty treasures and drenched in sweet, nutty syrup.

Just as we finished eating, a call came in to Kerabac from Agama. He wanted to meet with us immediately and he required directions to the *calgana*. After disconnecting the call, Kerabac said, "I think this is going to be it. Agama sounded almost desperate and I think he's going to either bring Logden here or make arrangements for us to meet him someplace."

"I certainly hope so," I replied. "It's time for us to be getting away from here."

"What about my mother and my dad?" Tanden asked abruptly. "You're not going to leave them here, are you?"

"No, Tanden," I said, "I have not forgotten my promise to you. Once we have Logden off this planet and have recovered the item he stole from the Federation, we will return with my ships and troopers to look for your parents…" I noted Jenira hang her head when I said this and I quickly added, "…and I will take you all off this planet and back to Megelleon where you all can live in peace." I saw Jenira lift her head and force a smile, as she turned to Tanden and patted his hand affectionately. I thought to myself, *What a heavy burden this young girl bears to preserve as much happiness for Tanden as she can!*

After we finished eating, Marranalis and I practiced martial arts in an open courtyard. As Jenira and Tanden watched our routines, Tanden excitedly explained to his sister what we were doing. Of course, as with all young boys, he eagerly danced about, pantomiming our movements and shadow boxing invisible opponents. We were just finishing our exercise, when Kala came out to tell us that Agama's boat was pulling up to the front pier. It appeared to carry three passengers.

When the boat landed, Padaran's head of security, Sondan, stepped forward and assisted in securing the boat. I was surprised when Agama and his brother, Howebim, got out of the boat. I had not expected to see Howebim here on Goo'Waddle. I watched them nervously look about before signaling to someone in the boat. Moments later, a rather thin man, who I assumed to be Logden, exited the boat behind them. I was somewhat stunned, because I had expected someone bigger and tougher looking — and Logden was anything but tough. He was short and thin and almost cowered as he stepped from the boat, looking this way and that, flinching with nervous fear every time the wind blew a tuft of grass or tree branch — hardly the classic image of a smuggler or pirate.

Kerabac stepped forward and greeted them, but Agama quickly cut him off.

"May we please go inside quickly? It is best that we not be seen here."

"Certainly, my friends," Kerabac said with a bright grin.

Once inside, Agama wasted no time in making his point. "We need to leave today — immediately, in fact. I'm assuming your ship is nearby and we can be underway within the hour?"

"I think that can be arranged, but why the rush? And when did you and Howebim decide that you were joining on the journey? That wasn't part of the original deal. More importantly, where is the cargo you wish us to carry?"

"Never mind the cargo — there will just be the three of us. Now, how soon can we be underway?"

While Kerabac and Agama continued this exchange, Logden slinked past me and I paid close attention to the solbidyum indicator that A'Lappe had installed in our wrist coms. Sure enough, it vibrated as Logden passed and I knew he had the solbidyum with him. I could have tackled him then and there, but I felt it would be better if we had him on the ship where there was no escape.

"There isn't enough space on the *calgana* to land the ship. We will need to meet the ship at the spaceport," Kerabac replied.

Agama and Howebim looked at each other nervously. "Just do what is necessary. We need this to unfold as discreetly as possible, so we must travel in an enclosed transport to your ship — we *cannot* afford to be seen."

Kerabac stepped aside and made a call to the *RASSON BEDAN*. They were to move in near the spaceport, staying cloaked below the traffic area until he called again. Padaran instructed Sondan to prepare a transport and security detail to take us to the spaceport. Sondan left quickly to carry out his orders.

Moments later, there were several loud explosions, followed by Sondan running into the house, yelling that we were under attack. The sound of weapons being discharged outside and other small explosions left little doubt as to his claims.

"You've got to get us out of here!" Howebim shouted. "It's the Brotherhood... they'll kill us if they find us!" At the same time I saw Kala, Endina, Sokaia and the children come running into the room.

"Where is Tondor?" I shouted, hoping he might have a secret way out of his house.

"He's dead," Sondan yelled back. "He was on the boat when the attackers blew it up."

"Is there a secret way out of here?" I asked.

"Yes, this way," Sondan said, leading us toward the center of the house.

Outside, shouts and more explosions sounded, and the waves of dust that blew into the room indicated that the main walls of the house were being breached. When we reached the center of the house, Sondan activated a hidden switch that triggered a large fountain in the room to pivot slightly, revealing a hidden stairway beneath its foundation. "Down there... quickly!"

Agama, Logden and Howebim raced down the stairs ahead of everyone else. The rest of us followed after the children were ushered in, followed lastly by, Sondan. Once inside the tunnel, Sondan activated another switch and the fountain rotated back into place, closing the entrance to the passage. "Follow me," Sondan said as he started off at a rapid pace through the tunnel.

"Where does this tunnel lead?" Padaran asked.

"It goes under the canal and over to another *calgana* to a storage barn there. The tunnel is quite long. Here, take these lights."

Sondan opened a small panel in the wall and extracted four lights that he passed out to us before starting down a sloping tunnel. After descending awhile, the tunnel leveled off and ran straight for a distance of nearly a kilometer before it gradually sloped back up again.

Tanden seemed to be having trouble keeping up with everyone, and I saw Padaran sweep him up and carry him. Behind us, the dull concussions of explosions could be heard echoing down the tunnel. When we came to the end, Sondan whispered that we should turn off our lights and keep quiet. Then, slowly, he opened a heavy metal door. He went through the door and motioned for us to follow him. We emerged into very large and dark room, illuminated only by the weak, diffuse light entering skylight windows high above that were spaced evenly about the enclosure. The light reached the center of the room so the floor was visible, but the regions around the walls of the room were cast in dark shadows. Once we were all through the door, Sondan closed it, and we heard the click of it being locked.

Suddenly, blinding lights came on all around the room and a voice rang out.

"Well, well. Look what we have here." As the effect of the momentary blindness from the sudden light dissipated and we looked around the room, we saw nearly a hundred armed men surrounding our small group — clearly Brotherhood militia, and they didn't look at all friendly. Several of them came forward and searched us, confiscating our guns and knives.

"You didn't think you were going to get away this easily, did you, Kerabac?" the leader said. His was a new face, but beside him we saw several of the Brotherhood goons who had visited our estate making threats and stalking us from the canals during the preceding days.

"And what's this? I do believe it's none other than Logden! You didn't hope to get away with Kerabac on his magic ship, now, did you?"

As he spoke, he slowly sauntered toward us, his personal bodyguards close at his side, while the rest of men around the room kept their weapons trained on us.

"Oh my, the surprises just grow and grow," he said as he looked me up and down. "I'm surprised none of you recognized these two." He gestured at both Kala and me, as he paced a circle around us. "We are graced with the heroes of the Federation," he mocked, "none other than Tibby the Recoverer and Kalana the Avenger, *in the flesh*. But then, most of you were here and not in the Federation, when these two spoiled our plans there. You didn't think I'd recognize you with your hair dyed, did you, Tibby?" He turned back to face me.

"It wasn't you we were trying to disguise ourselves from, Shydak," I said, making a wild guess that this was the infamous Shydak, the leader of the Brotherhood in this region of space.

"Ahh, so you know who I am," he responded with a sarcastic grin. "I suppose I should be flattered, but in all honesty, I'm not. I really could care less about you and your crew. Killing you will definitely raise my standing in the Brotherhood, but learning the secret of your cloaking device will gain me even more.

"Yes, I realize now that your erratic appearance and disappearances were not a jump drive but something faulty with your cloaking mechanism. No doubt, by now, you have that fixed, and soon one of you will reveal to me where your ship is. The technology will be in the hands of the Brotherhood, where it belongs. But the real prize of the night is here," he said, walking to and putting his arm around a visibly shaken and terrified Logden. Shydak turned to his guards. "Strip him. Go over every thread of his clothing. I doubt he would try to leave here without the solbidyum."

Two of the guards grabbed Logden and, while he screamed, they dragged him away from the rest of us and turned him over to several others, who immediately began taking his clothing piece by piece, searching it carefully. While they did, Shydak kept talking.

"I must admit that I didn't realize Agama and Howebim were involved with Logden, but when Howebim received a message from Agama and then suddenly liquidated all his assets and left, we realized something big was taking place. As it turned out, everything worked in our favor. If you hadn't come here from your old location, we would have moved on you too soon to get our hands on your ship, which would have spooked Logden, Agama and Howebim. We may have missed the opportunity to capture them. As it was, your move delayed our actions long enough for everything to align perfectly.

"When I sent two men to bomb Tondor's estate in hopes of scaring Kerabac into turning over his ship, you retaliated by bringing the bomb back and blowing up our supply of God's Sweat. That really pissed me off, but then Sondan here showed up a few hours later, offering to sell you all out for a million credits and, well, the rest is history." He swept his arms out as he slowly turned in a celebratory gesture.

"You betrayed the Ruwallie Rasson to the Brotherhood?" Kerabac said to Sondan in disbelief. "How could you?"

Sondan stepped back away from us to stand next to several of the Brotherhood men.

"How could I? How could I not? This white mockery is not Ruwallie Rasson." He gestured toward Padaran. "He may have tricked Tondor and the others, but not me. I have not betrayed the Ruwallie Rasson! It is you and this half-white doesee..." he pointed at Endina, "...that have betrayed the Ruwallie Rasson by bringing this abomination..." he gestured toward Padaran again, "...to this world and fooling *the chosen*. I tried to talk some sense into Tondor, but he truly believed that Padaran had defeated him by the will of the gods. Well, now you will all pay for your deceit and I will take what's left of the Ruwallie Rasson people and rebuild them. We will be stronger and wiser than before," he added with contempt written on his face.

"There, you see, Tibby; and now he, too, will receive his just reward. Pay the man, Narfi," ordered Shydak.

Suddenly, Sondan dropped to his knees and fell face forward, revealing a dagger that protruded from his back. A man behind him leaned down and extracted the knife and then used Sondan's shirt to wipe the blade off before sheathing it and putting it back inside his coat.

"Not a very bright man, this fellow," Shydak said, as he pushed the body with his foot. "He should have known that we in the Brotherhood never make deals with the Ruwallie Rasson."

"Boss," yelled one of the men searching Logden, "we ain't found nuttin!"

"I was afraid of this," Shydak said. "Either it's hidden on one of the others, or he has it already moved it off-world and plans to pick it up before leaving the region.

"Search these two..." He indicated Howebim and Agama, "...and if you don't find it on either, kill them. Leave Logden alive — he's the only one who knows for sure where the solbidyum is."

"Wait! Wait!" Howebim cried. "We don't have the solbidyum or know where it is. Logden promised us part of the money from its sale if we helped him, but he never told us where it was. Look. We have over thirty-five million credits we can pay you if you just let us go."

As he said this, he held out a case he had been carrying. Shydak indicated for one of his men to take the case and open it. Inside were hundreds of the chip coins considered so valuable in the outer worlds. One of Shydak's men brought a scanner forward and swept the case with it. "I confirm 35,322,006 credits," he announced.

"I thank you for the contribution," Shydak said, looking at both Agama and Howebim. "Shoot them both and *then* search them," he said to his guards. Before Agama or Howebim could voice another protest, several laser blasts burned holes into their heads. Shydak's men then dragged their bodies away.

"The crowd gets smaller," Shydak said with a smile. "Now, about your ship..." He looked at me rather than Kerabac. "I suspect you have it nearby someplace, as well as that wonderful yacht of yours, the *NEW ORLEANS*. Odd name, *NEW ORLEANS*. Don't think of trying to alert your ships, Tibby. We won't give you that opportunity. This building is shielded from broadcasts. Even if you tried, you wouldn't be able to get a message to your people. I have no intention of letting you make the call, either — you're too tricky. I think, though, that with a little incentive, we can get you to provide us with the information to get the *RASSON BEDAN* to come to us here. Once we have that, I'm betting we can get aboard the *NEW ORLEANS* and take it also.

"Narfi, take these two children up to that platform over there."

Narfi gestured to two more men. Each of them grabbed Tanden and Jenira and began dragging them away from us toward an elevator. Padaran acted too quickly for me to stop him and he swung out with a leg to try to prevent one of the men from taking Tanden. Before his leg reached its target, a bright flash of a laser caught his leg and Padaran dropped to the floor in pain.

"Not a very wise move. I could have killed you just now, but I may still have need for you. Before this night is over, you may lose your legs and arms, but for now, I'm satisfied to just cripple you.

"Now, about the ships," Shydak said, looking at me once more.

At this point Narfi and his men had loaded Tanden and Jenira on a freight lift and taken them up to a platform about 10 meters above the floor.

"You have the choice," Shydak began. "You can tell me what I want to know now or I will have the children tossed off that platform one at a time…the girl first, I think," he called up to Narfi.

Jenira began screaming, as one of the men tried to pick her up. Tanden, too, began to struggle; and then suddenly he lifted his leg and brought his heel down with all his might on his captor's foot. Immediately, the man let loose of Tanden, who rushed to help his sister. He managed to get hold of the hand of the man restraining Jenira and bite down as hard as he could. The man howled and released Jenira, but he managed to catch Tanden with his free hand while he cussed, "Why, you little *cordac!*" He lifted Tanden in the air and threw him with all his might off the platform.

It seemed to me at that moment that time froze. Hours passed between my heartbeats and I ceased to breathe, as his small body twisted and tumbled through the air. I saw his head turn back and look at his sister one last time before his body smashed into the floor with a horrible crushing sound that echoed in my mind seemingly forever. All heads and eyes had turned to witness the horrible event; and as the last remnants of sound faded from my ears, my fighting skills went into motion.

Though the Brotherhood had removed our weapons, they had not bothered to take our wrist coms. I instinctively reached down to activate the cloaking device, and started to move toward Shydak. One of his men saw me vanish and stepped forward, getting in the way before I could reach Shydak, who saw what was happening and turned to flee. I hit the man in front of me hard and pushed him aside into others who were rushing at us. I tried to pursue Shydak, but more of his men filtered in behind Shydak, closing the path between him and me. Seconds were ticking away and I knew I only had a short time before the cloaking device would give out.

Behind me, I could hear all sorts of chaos breaking out; I could only assume that my shipmates had also cloaked and were fighting back. I saw Shydak briefly as he turned a corner, and I muscled my way through the tangle of men following him. As I turned the corner, I saw him head up a set of stairs. I followed as fast as I could. As it turned out, the stairs led to the platform where Jenira stood with her captors, her face ashen and tears streaming as she stared where her brother lay on the floor in a pool of blood. Shydak rushed out to the end of the platform and grabbed the girl, while telling his men to guard the platform.

Just as he gave these orders, my cloaking faded and I became visible. Down on the floor, my invisible compatriots were doing serious damage to foes who could not see them. But just as in my case, their cloaking failed one by one. Guns pointed at them and they became still and were taken prisoners again. Padaran was the last to become visible. With his leg having been damaged before, he had not engaged in the fight, but instead had crawled over to where Tanden's small body lay on the floor. There he lay, holding one of Tanden's small hands and weeping.

"My, my, my, Tibby. That was quite some show," Shydak said as he took a knife and put it to Jenira's throat. "I do hope you won't be disappointed if I don't cheer for an encore.

"As you can see, one small life has been lost. If you wish to avoid seeing this young lady bleed to death here on this platform, I suggest you tell me where the ship is and how to contact it. Otherwise…" As he spoke, he made a small, but deep slit in Jenira's throat so that blood began to flow freely from the wound, "…you will get to see this young life slowly drip down to the floor."

I could see the look of horror in Jenira's eyes. I glanced quickly at Kala and the others on the floor, and I could see the despair on all their faces. I had no choice.

"Very well," I said. "You —"

Before I could say *win*, there was a crashing sound. Shattered glass and something large fell from the skylight above and landed on the platform behind Shydak. Before he could react, I saw a strong gray arm reach around and grab Shydak's wrist that held the knife to Jenira's throat. Shydak struggled to get free and, for an instant, I got a glimpse of Andy as he pulled Shydak's arm away from Jenira's throat. Shydak released his hold on Jenira and she dropped to the platform, holding her hands to her bleeding throat while Shydak struggled with Andy. Shydak's men turned to help him, and when they did, I rushed at them.

Far below on the floor I heard crashing sounds once more, and I knew the fighting had renewed. The first man on the platform I encountered I simply tossed over the railing in one smooth motion. The second turned to see me coming and he prepared to fight. His attack was classic; and he soon joined his partner on the floor below. In the meantime, Narfi had brought a small gun out of his pocket. He took aim at Andy and fired, hitting him in the shoulder.

Exactly what damage it did, I cannot say, but it was enough to cause him to lose his grip on Shydak, who quickly bounded around Andy and raced out a door at the other end of the platform. Narfi tried to follow him, but Andy caught him by the leg. I heard a crunching sound as Narfi screamed. Andy had crushed his leg bone. Then Andy simply lifted his body and dropped him over the side of the platform.

My first instinct was to chase after Shydak, but Jenira was laying there on the platform, slowly bleeding to death. I went to her and saw that she was quite pale. I ripped a piece of cloth from my shirt and used it to try to stop the bleeding.

I looked over at Andy. He said, "I told you we would be able to provide assistance."

I glanced over the side of the platform and was amazed to see nearly 200 androids that had swarmed into the building and now had all the surviving Brotherhood men in captivity. Endina and Kerabac were helping Padaran, and I heard and saw Kala and Marranalis moving across the platform quickly to help me with Jenira. Marranalis had managed to find a first aid kit from someplace, which he and Kala quickly used to treat Jenira, who was about to lose consciousness.

As Kala and Marranalis took over, I sat back against the railing and looked at Andy. "Are you alright, my friend?" I asked.

"Friend?" Andy said in a curious tone. "My friend... I like that. Yes, I am alright. My nanoskin is quite capable of healing itself."

As he spoke, I noticed that the hole in his shoulder where he had been shot was getting smaller. I looked once to the floor where Tanden lay. Padaran was holding him in his arms, rocking back and forth and sobbing openly, as Kerabac and Endina stood at his sides with a hand on each of his shoulders while tears streamed down their faces. I looked at Jenira — all the color had drained from her face and crimson stained her clothing from her bleeding throat.

Anger overwhelmed me. These two innocents, who had done nothing in this life to deserve the kind of treatment they had received — two precious lives that had been denied a childhood, denied the joys and pleasures of life because of evil, selfish men like Shydak and the Brotherhood. I got to my feet and headed in the direction that Shydak had gone.

"Tibby," Kala called, "where are you going?"

"To get Shydak."

"He's gone," Kerabac called up to us. "I chased him outside when he came down. He ran out and jumped into one of the small Brotherhood fighters outside and escaped with some of the others. I sent a signal to the *RASSON BEDAN*. They're on their way here and they're tracking Shydak's ships on their scanners. The *NEW ORLEANS* is also tracking them while they hold in orbit, awaiting your orders."

"What about Logden?" I asked.

"He's down below being held by one of the androids."

I turned to Andy. "Thank you Andy. I truly appreciate you and your people coming to our rescue, and I won't forget my part of the bargain. But right now, I have something I need to do."

As I raced off, I could hear Kala calling, "Tibby, wait! Where are you going?"

As I ran outside, I saw one of the Brotherhood fighters still parked on the ground. I raced over and jumped in. It was a small, two-man craft designed for short flights. I was hoping it was the kind Shydak was using. I quickly fired up the engines and was in the air in minutes. I switched to the coded frequency we used with the *RASSON BEDAN* and quickly identified myself to Norkoda, so he would know which ship I was in. Then I asked, "Norkoda, are you still tracking the ships that left this site?"

"Yes," he replied, "most of them are heading toward a location south of you, but a few are heading northwest."

"What about the first ship to leave this site? Do you know where that one is headed?"

"One moment, let me check," he said. "It appears to be in the smaller party of heading to the south, but I have no idea which one it is, as they are flying in too tight a formation."

While he was talking, I turned the ship in that direction and opened it up to full throttle. "What can you tell me about their speed?" I asked. "Are they traveling at top speed?"

"They were for awhile, but they've slowed down a bit now. At your current speed you should catch up with them in about ten minutes. Do you want me to relay to the *NEW ORLEANS* and have them dispatch some of our own fighters?"

My mind was boiling now and I was getting angrier by the moment. "Yes," I said. "Tell them anything identified as being associated with the Brotherhood is to be destroyed — ships, houses, fields — anything that is positively Brotherhood is to be eliminated."

As I gave these orders, my scanners began picking up the images of the fleeing ships. I was hoping they would think me to be one of their escaped brothers joining up with them, which would allow me to get right up on top of them before they knew what was coming.

Marranalis' voice came over the ship's com link. He must have contacted the *RASSON BEDAN* and gotten my frequency. "Tibby, we're getting word that the Ruwallie Rasson dispatched by Padaran to capture the Brotherhood corvettes have managed to capture two just minutes ago. They're aboard the third and battling to gain control now and hope to have it secured very soon. If the first two operations are any indication, I think they will succeed and the remaining Brotherhood ships should begin retreating very soon. They're in a losing situation here...so you can come back now, Tibby."

I didn't answer, as I was right up on the pack of ships now. There were 14 that I could count. I was about to make my first attack, when Kala's voice came across my com. "Tibby, what are you doing?!"

I took careful aim and targeted five ships with laser torpedoes and let loose a volley.

"I'm doing what I need to do," I answered heatedly, as the first five ships exploded. I was busy targeting another four, but they broke off before I could get a good lock. I fired anyway. With luck, I managed to hit another two. *Seven down and seven to go*, I thought.

"Tibby, this is insane. You can't take on that many ships alone and survive; you're not in one of your cloaked and shielded ships now!"

"So what does it matter?!" I replied, as one of the ships arced around and began firing at me.

"Tibby, your life is more important than this! Please!"

"My life is crap," I said, breathing through my teeth, as I pulled a tight turn and took a lot of G's trying to shake the two fighters that were now on my tail and, at the same time, turn to get one of the fleeing ships ahead of me in my sights. "All that has happened since I found that blasted *TRITYTE* in the swamp is that a lot of people have died. If I had not found that ship, everyone would be alive and happy."

"Captain Maxette," I said, as I got a shot off, hitting another fighter, "Lunnie and Reidecor," as I banked hard to avoid fire from a pursuing fighter. The shot glanced off a wing, leaving a burn scar but no real damage. "All those people spaced on the *DUSTEN*... the thousands that died because of my blunder in bombing that subsea base on Megelleon — thousands, Kala, *thousands*! Not just Tanden — and maybe Jenira, too!" I spat out.

Two of the fleeing ships in front of me broke off and were now coming at me, as the two behind me were trying to get a lock on my position.

"Tibby, PLEASE, I'm begging you, break away! There are fifty fighters racing in from the *NEW ORLEANS* to take out those ships and more are en route from the *MIZBAGONA*. Let them handle it — they have cloaking and shielding! You have nothing to protect you, Tibby! Jenira is going to be fine — don't do this, Tibby!"

By now, I was flying straight at the oncoming ships. They would be on top of me in seconds. The ships behind me were breaking off so as not to be hit from incoming fire. I took a wild gamble and fired a spread of laser torpedoes at the incoming ships before going into a sharp dive. I saw the flash and explosions above me, as I tried to make a sharp turn back up. I was skimming the ground before I managed to climb again. At least one ship was now firing from behind me again and I could see the shots passing by and impacting the ground. I banked quickly to my left and then shot straight up.

By my count, I had taken out nine ships, leaving five. I glanced at my screen but only saw four. Then, off on the edge of the monitor, I saw one fleeing ship. I had no doubt who that would be — and I turned to pursue Shydak to the end of the universe if I needed to. Another shot caught my ship, but again, the damage was superficial.

Then I heard, "First Citizen, if you could be so kind as to make a sharp turn to your right, we'll clean this trash off your tail."

I had to smile through my seething anger. I recognized the voice as belonging to one of my men from the *NEW ORLEANS*. I banked sharply to my right and then set course for Shydak's fleeing ship. Behind me, two flashes lit the sky as Brotherhood ships disintegrated.

I looked at my screen and suddenly, to my shock, I saw dozens of ships joining up with Shydak — or, at least, I thought they were joining him. But then I saw that his ship was going on, while the others were heading toward us in an attack formation.

"Tibby, please come back…" I could hear Kala weeping. "Don't do this; there is no reason to risk yourself!"

"There's every reason!" I said. "I started all this by finding that damn solbidyum and I'm going to stop it or die trying!"

The ships coming toward me were now less than 30 seconds away.

"Tibby, I need you! Our children need you…. Stop, please, and come back!"

"Kala, we have no children, and you do not need me. No one needs me! What the universe needs is to be rid of me — all I am is a merchant of death and misery!"

By now, I was close enough to the enemy ships that I was able to start targeting. At the same time, I could see incoming fire from the enemy ships.

"Tibby," Kala sobbed, "I love you… I need you… you are about to be a father. I tried to tell you the night of the attack at Tondor's estate, Tibby… I'm pregnant!"

The news hit me like ice water in the face about the same time the torpedo struck my ship. Smoke filled the cockpit as I spiraled down toward the surface. Around me I saw flashes of light and explosions as Brotherhood ships were taken out by fighters from the *NEW ORLEANS* — and all I could think was *Boy, did I fuck this one up — I'm going to be a father and I won't even get to see my kid!*

The ground was rushing up to meet me. I heard Kala's voice cry out over the com system. "TIBBY! *NOOOO!*"

I had just enough time to say, "I love you, Kala," before my ship crashed into the planet.

THE END

of

BOOK 3 — PIRATES OF GOO'WADDLE CANALS

*COMING SOON

SOLBIDYUM   WARS   SAGA   —   BOOK   4
TOO LATE FOR EARTH

Tibby awakens to find himself back on the *NEW ORLEANS* in the medical section. He's been told that he suffered extensive injuries in his crash on the planet Goo'Waddle and that his recovery will be slow. He lost one eye in the crash and, while a new one can be cloned, it would take time for the new eye tissue to grow before it can be implanted. Kalana is at his side, but she is still angry with him for his senseless reaction to the death of Tanden. Tibby suffers emotionally from all that has happened and is torn between his grief over the events at Goo'Waddle and his elation over the news that he and Kala are going to have a child.

Tibby is barely back on his feet, when word arrives that his home planet, Earth, has been hit by a large asteroid. Tibby rushes to Earth in the *NEW ORLEANS* in hopes of providing assistance, only to discover that all life above microbial level has been destroyed on the planet. Tibby is crushed. As he is about to return to Federation space, the *NEW ORLEANS* receives a signal from an International Earth Colony on Mars. The colony is struggling, as their supplies are diminishing and are no longer able to sustain themselves. The *NEW ORLEANS* rescues the colony, only to discover that there is also a Chinese colony located on the Earth's moon. Tibby also learns that a huge war between the Chinese and many of the western nations had been taking place before the asteroid impact. The *NEW ORLEANS* responds to the moon to rescue the few remaining Chinese scientists that have survived under the rule of a ruthless and maniacal general, who has declared himself Emperor of the Moon. Once the Chinese have been rescued, it is learned from the colonists that the asteroid impact was not an accident; the asteroid had been deliberately guided to strike the Earth and that those responsible have been returning periodically to prepare the planet for their own colonization. Before the *NEW ORLEANS* leaves Earth's space, they are able to witness one of the enemy ships entering Earth's orbit. Tibby and his crew are shocked to see that it is identical to the Tottalax ships that have been assisting the Brotherhood in their assaults on the Federation.

About the Author

Dale Musser was born in 1944 in a small rural community of Pennsylvania. From 1967 until 2012 he was employed as a structural and piping designer in the industries of marine and offshore resources, cogeneration power and hard rock mining. His work at three shipyards and assignments with several  engineering and naval architectural firms during his careers in Virginia, Texas, and Maine, took him to such places as London, U.K., Abu Dhabi, U.A.E., Scotland and Mexico. During this time, he was responsible for the design of reactor compartments for nuclear aircraft carriers and submarines for the U.S. Navy and the structural designs of numerous offshore semi-submersible oil rigs, tanker ships, supply boats, and other vessels and equipment used in the offshore industry. After the death of his wife in 1999, Mr. Musser changed careers and went to work in Arizona and Utah in the hard rock mining industry. He retired in Fall of 2012 and currently resides in Mesa, Arizona; however, his plans for the near future involve a move to New Mexico.

Dale enjoys rock hunting and lapidary work, gourmet cooking, writing, poetry, art, music, religions and philosophy in small doses, astronomy and the sciences in general, hiking, camping, the outdoors and the gifts that nature provides. Mr. Musser is a member of Mensa and remains an avid reader, having lost count of all the books he has read after 3,000.

The greatest joy in his life is his daughter, Heather. Affectionately they call each other "BUBBY."

Contact Information:

Those wishing to write to Mr. Musser may do so at dalemusser1944@yahoo.com. Although he attempts to answer all correspondence, heavy emails may prevent him from responding to everyone.

www.ingramcontent.com/pod-product-compliance
Lightning Source LLC
Chambersburg PA
CBHW030016180626
46810CB00001B/61